J.T. ELLISON

the cold room

MIRA®

MIRA®

ISBN-13: 978-0-7783-2714-1

THE COLD ROOM

Copyright © 2010 by J.T. Ellison.

For questions and comments about the quality of this book please contact us at Customer_eCare@Harlequin.ca.

www.MIRABooks.com

Printed in U.S.A.

For Scott and Linda.
You took a chance, and I'll be forever grateful.

And, as always, for Randy.

Understanding does not cure evil,
but it is a definite help, inasmuch as
one can cope with a comprehensible darkness.
—Carl Jung

Wednesday

One

Gavin Adler jumped when a small chime sounded on his computer. He looked at the clock in surprise; it was already 6:00 p.m. During the winter months, darkness descended and reminded him to close up shop, but the daylight savings time change necessitated an alarm clock to let him know when it was time to leave. Otherwise, he'd get lost in his computer and never find his way home.

He rose from his chair, stretched, turned off the computer and reached for his messenger bag. What a day. What a long and glorious day.

He took his garbage with him; his lunch leavings. There was no reason to have leftover banana peels in his trash can overnight. He shut off the lights, locked the door, dropped the plastic Publix bag into the Dumpster, and began the two-block walk to his parking spot. His white Prius was one of the few cars left in the lot.

Gavin listened to his iPod on the way out of downtown. Traffic was testy, as always, so he waited patiently, crawling through West End, then took the exit for I-40 and headed, slowly, toward Memphis. The congestion cleared right past White Bridge, and he sailed the rest of the way.

The drive took twenty-two minutes, he clocked it. Not too bad.

He left the highway at McCrory Lane and went to his gym. The YMCA lot was full, as always. He checked in, changed clothes in the locker room, ran for forty-five minutes, worked on the elliptical for twenty, did one hundred inverted crunches and shadow boxed for ten minutes. Then he toweled himself off. He retrieved the messenger bag, left his sneakers in the locker, slipped his feet back into the fluorescent orange rubber Crocs he'd been wearing all day. He left his gym clothes on—they would go straight into the wash.

He went across the street to Publix, bought a single chicken cordon bleu and a package of instant mashed potatoes, a tube of hearty buttermilk biscuits, fresh bananas and cat food. He took his groceries, went to his car, and drove away into the night. He hadn't seen a soul. His mind was engaged with what waited for him at home.

Dark. Lonely. Empty.

Gavin pulled into the rambler-style house at 8:30 p.m. His cat, a Burmese gray named Art, met him at the door, loudly protesting his empty bowl. He spooned wet food into the cat's dish as a special treat before he did anything else. No reason for Art to be miserable. The cat ate with his tail high in the air, purring and growling softly.

He hit play on his stereo, and the strains of Dvořák spilled through his living room. He stood for a moment, letting the music wash over him, his right arm moving in concert with the bass. The music filled him, made him complete, and whole. Art came and stood beside him, winding his tail around Gavin's leg. He smiled at the interruption, bent and scratched the cat behind the ears. Art arched his back in pleasure.

Evening's ritual complete, Gavin turned on the oven,

sprinkled olive oil in a glass dish and put the chicken in to bake. It would take forty-five minutes to cook.

He showered, checked his work e-mail on his iPhone, then ate. He took his time; the chicken was especially good this evening. He sipped an icy Corona Light with a lime stuck in the neck.

He washed up. 10:00 p.m. now. He gave himself permission. He'd been a very good boy.

The padlock on the door to the basement was shiny with promise and lubricant. He inserted the key, twisting his wrist to keep it from jangling. He took the lock with him, holding it gingerly so he didn't get oil on his clothes. Oil was nearly impossible to get out. He made sure Art wasn't around; he didn't like the cat to get into the basement. He saw him sitting on the kitchen table, looking mournfully at the empty spot where Gavin's plate had rested.

Inside the door, the stairs led to blackness. He flipped a switch and light flooded the stairwell. He slipped the end of the lock in the inside latch, then clicked it home. No sense taking chances.

She was asleep. He was quiet, so he wouldn't wake her. He just wanted to look, anyway.

The Plexiglas cage was the shape of a coffin with a long clear divider down the length—creating two perfectly sized compartments—with small drainage holes in the bottom and air holes along the top. It stood on a reinforced platform he had built himself. The concrete floor had a drain; all he needed to do was sluice water across the opening and presto, clean. He ran the water for a few minutes, clearing out the debris, then looked back to his love.

Her lips were cracking, the hair shedding. She'd been without food and water for a week now, and she was spending more and more time asleep. Her lethargy was anticipated. He looked forward to the moment when her

agonies were at an end. He had no real desire to torture her.
He just needed her heart to stop. Then, he could have her.

He licked his lips and felt embarrassed by his erection.

He breathed in the scent of her, reveling in the musky
sweetness of her dying flesh, then went to the desk in the
corner of the basement. No spiders and dust and basement
rot for Gavin. The place was clean. Pristine.

The computer, a Mac Air he'd indulged in as a late
Christmas present to himself, sprang to life. A few taps
of the keyboard, the wireless system engaged and he was
online. Before he had a chance to scroll through his book-
marks, his iChat chimed. The user's screen name was
IlMorte69. He and Gavin were very good friends. Gavin
responded, his own screen name, hot4cold, popping up
in red ten-point Arial.

My dollhouse is nearly complete, Hot. Howz urs?

Hey, Morte. Mine's on its last legs as well. I'm here
checking. Your trip go well?

My friend, I can't tell you. Such a wonderful time.
But it's good to be home.

New dolls?

One. Luscious. Easy pickings. Like taking a rat
from a cellar.

Gavin cringed. Sometimes Morte got to be a little
much. But what could you do? It was hard for Gavin to
talk to people, the online world was his oyster, his outlet.
He had other friends who weren't quite as crude as Morte.

Speaking of which…he glanced at the listing of contacts and saw Necro90 was online as well. He sent him a quick hello, then went back to his chat with Morte.

When do you think you'll be ready?

Morte came back almost immediately.

Within two days. Did you do it like we discussed? You were more careful with the disposal than with the snatch, weren't you?

Gavin bristled a tiny bit, then relaxed. Morte was right to chide him. After all, he had made a mistake. He'd quickly learned that following Morte's every instruction was important. Very, very important.

Yes. It was perfect. I'll send you a photo.

He uploaded the shots, breath quickening in remembrance. So beautiful. Within moments, Morte responded.

My God. That is perfect. Lovely. You've become quite an artist.

Thank you.

Gavin blushed. Receiving compliments gracefully wasn't one of his strongest attributes. He glanced over his shoulder, knew he needed to wrap this up.

Morte, I've gotta run. Long day today.

I'll bet. You be good. Don't forget, two days and counting. I'll expect pictures!

Bye.

A picture flooded his screen—Morte had sent him a gift. Gavin studied the photo; his ears burned. Oh, Morte was amazingly good with a camera. So much better than he was.

Morte's doll had no animation, no movement. Her eyes were shut. Gavin turned his chair around so he could stare at his own dollhouse, his own doll, lying in the darkness. Alone. He'd need to find her another friend soon. If only Morte's girl was a sister. He didn't have a taste for white meat.

Another chime—this time it was Necro responding. He asked how Gavin was doing, if there'd been any news in the community. Gavin replied with a negative—he'd heard nothing. Of course, his ear wasn't to the floor like Morte— Morte was the architect of their online world. Gavin had found his friends deep in a sleepy sex message board, and was so thrilled to have them. They made his life bearable.

He chatted for a few minutes with Necro, read a rambling account of a perfect specimen Necro had sighted on some white-sand Caribbean beach, then logged out. He stared at the photo he'd downloaded from Morte. He was overwhelmingly turned on, and no longer able to contain himself. With a last glance at his doll, he went up the stairs, unlocked the door, locked the basement behind him and returned to his life. It was time for another shower, then bed. He had a very busy day ahead of him. A very busy few days. The plan was in motion.

He was proud of himself. He only checked the doll's breathing three times during the night.

Two

Taylor Jackson was happy to spy an empty parking spot halfway up Thirty-second Avenue. Luck was on her side tonight. Parking in Nashville was extremely hit-or-miss, especially in West End. The valet smiled hopefully as she turned in front of Tin Angel, but she couldn't leave a state vehicle with a kid who didn't look old enough to have a driver's license, not without getting into all kinds of trouble. She drove past him, paralleled smoothly and walked the slight hill back down to the restaurant's entrance. She was looking forward to the evening, a girls' night with her best friend Sam and colleague Paula Simari. No homicides. No crime scenes. Just a low-key meal, some wine, some chicken schnitzel. A night off.

She was early, her friends hadn't arrived yet. She followed the hostess to a table for four right by the bricked fireplace. The logs were stacked tightly and burning slow, putting out a pleasant low, smoky heat. Even though the weather was warming, it was still nippy in the early mornings and late evenings.

She ordered a bottle of Coppola Merlot, accepted a

menu, then lost herself in thought. The envelope she'd addressed before she left for dinner was burning a hole in her pocket. She took it out and stared at the lettering, wishing she didn't recognize the handwriting. Wishing she didn't have to address letters to federal penitentiaries, even if they were the chinos and golf-shirt variety.

Winthrop Jackson, IV
FCI MORGANTOWN
FEDERAL CORRECTIONAL INSTITUTION
P.O. BOX 1000
MORGANTOWN, WV 26507

The edges of the envelope were getting frayed. She needed to decide if she was going to mail this letter or not.

She traced the outline of the address, her mind still screaming against the reality. Her father, in prison. And she'd been the one who put him there. Glancing to make sure no one was looking, she slid the single handwritten page from its nest.

Dear Win,

I am sorry. I know you understand I was just doing my job. I had no choice. I would appreciate it if you would stop trying to contact me. I find our relationship impossible to handle, and I want to get on with my life. Mom is still in Europe, but she has her cell phone. She can send you the money you need.

For what it's worth, I do forgive you. I know you couldn't help yourself. You never have.

Taylor

"Whatcha reading? You look upset."

Taylor started. Sam took the seat across from her, dropped her Birkin bag on the floor under the table and stretched her fingers, the joints popping slightly. She grimaced.

"Holding a scalpel all day does that to you. What's that?"

Taylor shook the page lightly. "A letter to Win."

"Really? I thought you'd sworn off dear old dad. Did you order some wine?"

"I did. It should be here any minute. Where's Paula?"

"She got called to a case. Sends her apologies. She'll catch us next week. It's just us chickens tonight."

Sam settled back into the chair, the firelight glinted red off her dark hair. Taylor still wasn't used to the blunt-cut bangs that swooped across Sam's forehead. She'd cropped her tresses into a sophisticated bob, what she called her mom do. Taylor thought she looked less like a mom and more like Betty Page with that cut, but who was she to comment?

"What are you staring at?"

"Sorry. The hair. It's so different. Takes me a minute."

"You have no idea how easy it is. Though I do miss long hair. Simon does too."

"I thought about cutting mine. When I mentioned it, Baldwin had a fit."

The wine arrived and they placed their orders. They clinked their glasses together, and Sam said, "Up to it, down to it."

Taylor laughed. They'd started that toast in eighth grade. *Up to it, down to it, damn the man who can't do it....* The rest of the toast was a crude allusion to their future lovers' skill, though they had no idea what it meant at the time. In high school Taylor had embarrassed herself at one of her parents' many dinner parties by leading a toast with it. When the men roared and the women blushed, her mother, Kitty, had taken her aside and explained why that wasn't an appropriate thing for a young lady of breeding to say. She wouldn't tell her why, though, and Taylor and Sam puzzled over it for days. Now, as a woman, she understood, and always laughed at the memory of her disgrace.

She thought of Win then, and sobered.

"I'm trying to shut Win down, Sam. He keeps mailing, keeps calling. I don't want anything to do with him. He's poison, and I need to get him out of my life. What if Baldwin and I have children one day? Can you imagine ole jailbird gramps telling stories at Christmas dinner? He'll either corrupt them or embarrass them."

"You're thinking of having kids?"

"Focus, woman. We're talking about my dad."

"You'd make a great mother."

Taylor stared hard at her best friend. "Why do you say that?"

"Please. You're totally the nurturing type. You just don't know it yet. You'll be like a bear with its cub, or a tiger. Nothing, and no one, will harm a hair on your kid's head. Trust me, you'll take to it like a seal to water. When might this magnificent event take place, anyway?"

"You mean my immaculate conception?"

Sam laughed. "Baldwin's still in Quantico, I take it."

"Yes. He gets back tonight. That's why I wanted to meet downtown. I'm going to head to the airport from dinner."

"You miss him when he's gone, don't you?" Sam smiled at her, a grin of understanding. Taylor had never needed a man to feel complete, but when she'd gotten involved with John Baldwin, she suddenly felt every moment without him keenly. She'd never felt that way about a man before. When she shared her feelings, Sam had patiently explained that was what love was about.

Taylor's cell phone rang, a discreet buzz in her front right pocket. She pulled it out and glanced at the screen.

"Crap."

"Dispatch?"

"Yeah. Give me a sec." So much for a quiet dinner with friends before a loving reunion with Baldwin. She glanced at her watch. His plane would be landing soon. No help for it. Dispatch calling her cell meant only one thing. Someone was dead. She put the phone to her ear.

"Detective Jackson, this is Dispatch. We need you at 1400 Love Circle. We have a 10-64, homicide, at 1400 Love Circle. Be advised, possible 10-51, repeat, 10-51. They're waiting for you. Thank you."

"I'm not on today, Dispatch. Give it to someone else."

"Apologies, Detective, but they're asking for you specifically."

Taylor sighed. *I'm your beck-and-call girl.*

"10-4, Dispatch. On my way."

A dead body, a possible stabbing. A lovely way to cap off her day.

"You have to go?" Sam asked.

"Yep. Aren't you coming? I'm sure you'll be getting the call, too."

Sam raised her glass. "Unlike you, my dear, I am still captain of my own ship. I'm off duty tonight. The medical examiner's office can live without me on this one. Give my love to the valet on the way out, he's adorable."

Only Sam could get away with teasing her about her demotion. Only Sam.

"Jeez, thanks," Taylor said, but she smiled. Getting busted back to Detective had been frustrating and embarrassing, the sidelong glances and whispers disconcerting.

But she was determined to make the best of it. Karma was a bitch, and the ones who'd wronged her would get their comeuppance in the end. Especially if she won the lawsuit her union rep had filed.

The food arrived just as Taylor stood to leave. She looked wistfully at the perfectly breaded chicken. Sam saw her eyeing it.

"I'll have it made into a to-go package and drop it in your fridge on my way home."

Taylor bent to kiss Sam on the cheek. "You're the best. Thanks."

"Yeah, yeah. Just remember you owe me an uninterrupted dinner. Now, go on with you. You're practically quivering."

Taylor retrieved her car, made all the lights through West End and finally got caught by a yellow in front of Maggiano's. The next intersection was her turnoff, and it flashed to red just as she rolled onto the white line.

To her left, Love Circle wound sinuously around the top of a windy hill in the middle of West End. It held too many memories for her.

She slipped her sunglasses off; she didn't need them. She'd gotten in the habit of putting them on the second she was out of doors lately, especially walking to and from her office. It allowed her to avoid meeting the pitying gazes she'd been receiving.

She fingered the bump at the top of her nose, just underneath where the bridge of her sunglasses sat. She'd broken her nose for the first time on Love Hill when she was fourteen, playing football with some boys who'd come to the isolated park at the top of the hill to smoke and shoot the breeze. Her mother had cringed when she saw the break the following morning at breakfast, dragged her to a plastic-surgeon friend immediately. He'd realigned the cartilage, clucking all the while, and bandaged her nose in a stupid white brace that she'd discarded the moment her mother left her alone. The hairline fracture never healed properly, giving her the tiny bump that made her profile imperfect.

The second time, it had been broken for her. Damn David Martin, her dead ex-partner, had roughed her up after breaking into her house. She'd been forced into violence that night, had shot him during the attack.

The car behind her beeped, and Taylor realized she'd been sitting at the left-turn arrow through a full cycle of lights. It was green again. Good grief. Lost in thought. That's what the hill did to her.

She turned left on Orleans, took a quick right on Acklen, then an immediate left onto Love Circle. It was a steep, narrow road, difficult to traverse. The architecture was eclectic, ranging from bungalows from the 1920s to contemporary villas built as recently as five years ago. Many of the houses had no drives; the owners usually left their cars on the street. She wound her way up, surprised by the changes. A huge, postmodern glass house perched at the top of the hill, lit up like Christmas. She remembered there was some flak about it; built by a country-music star, something about a landing pad on the roof. She drove past, admiring the architecture.

At the top of the rise, she stopped for a moment, glanced out the window to the vivid skyline. The sky was deeply dark to the east, with no moon to light the road. The dazzling lights of Nashville beckoned. No wonder the isolated park at the peak was still a favorite teen hangout. There was something about the name, of course. It *was* rather romantic to head up the hill at sunset to watch the lights of Nashville blink on, one by one, a fiery mass of luminosity cascading through the city.

Being reared in the protected Nashville enclaves of Forest Hills and Belle Meade, Taylor sometimes needed to move outside her parents' carefully executed social construct to find a little fun. Her honey-blond hair and mismatched gray eyes always drew attention, whether she wanted it or not. Coupled with her height, already nearly six feet tall at thirteen, she'd commanded the attention of her peers, friends and foes alike. It wasn't a stretch that she'd get into a little mischief here and there.

She'd been a regular on the hill for a summer; with Sam Owens—now Dr. Sam Loughley, Nashville's lead medical examiner—at her side. They'd gotten into the genteel trouble that was expected from well-bred teenagers: smoking stolen Gauloises, sipping nasty-tasting cheap whiskey, hanging out with boys who shaved their hair into Mohawks and talked big about anarchy and guitar riffs. It didn't last. Their constant posturing quickly bored her.

It made Taylor sad to think back to her youth; the things they called "trouble" back then were increasingly tame by today's standards. Here she was, newly turned thirty-six, and already feeling old when faced with teenagers.

She'd abandoned the Circle when she was fifteen, didn't return until her eighteenth birthday. A nostalgic drive with her first real lover, the professor. He'd driven her up there in his Jeep and parked, hands roaming across her body. They'd nearly driven over the edge when her knee knocked the gearshift into Second. He'd taken her to his place that night for the very first time, deflowered her with skill and care.

She smiled, as she normally did when a memory of James Morley first crossed her mind. The thought led to her father, a close friend of Morley's, and the smile fled.

She needed to mail the letter. Win Jackson was only eight hours away, and he'd be out in a matter of months, having cut several deals to assure him an early release. His missives came with alarming regularity, each begging for forgiveness. His dealings with a shadowy crime boss in New York were behind him. He was going to be on the straight and narrow path from here on out.

She wondered how many times she'd heard that before. Money laundering wasn't the worst he could have been charged with, but it was the charge that stuck. Well, there was time before she'd have to deal with Win in person. Not as much as she'd like, but enough.

She passed the apex of the hill and the crime scene beckoned to her. Blue-and-white lights flashed, guiding her in. Four patrol cars stood at attention next to a chain-link fence. The K-9 unit was parked at an angle. Taylor recognized Officer Paula Simari's German shepherd, Max, straining against the cracked window, searching for his master. Ah, so this was the crime scene that had kept her from dinner. It must be a doozy if they were calling in off-duty officers and detectives.

Taylor put her window down, cooed softly at the dog. "You're okay, baby. She'll be back in a minute." Max stopped fretting and sat, tongue lolling out the side of his mouth.

She drove another twenty yards, down the back edge of the hill. All of the attention was focused on a two-story house set back fifty feet from the street. The house was an original Craftsman, built sometime in the 1930s, if she had to guess. The thick, pyramid-shaped columns and slanting roof were well-kept. The exterior was awash in false light; the shake shingles looked to be painted a soft, mossy green, the details slightly darker. The whole house blended perfectly into the surrounding woods. Four joint dormer windows across the second story were square and forward, watching.

She was surprised to see the lawn and porch littered with milling people—a level of disorganization rarely in evidence at a Nashville crime scene. The crime-scene techs were setting up to take photos, video, collect evidence; two patrol officers were standing to one side, conversing in low tones. The command table had been set up on the porch. Uniforms and plainclothes techs were walking around the outside of the house. Neighbors had gathered, silently scrutinizing.

She parked next to a crime-scene van. The side door was open, the contents spilling out as if the tech was in a hurry to get moving on the scene. Paula Simari was twenty feet away. She caught Taylor's eye, angled her head with a jerk. Meet me inside, the look said. Taylor got out of the car, intrigued.

"Detective!"

A young man signaled her to join him on the lawn of the house. It was deep emerald in the false light, freshly mown; the tang of green onion and cut grass felt so familiar, so right. Normal and unthreatening, just another suburban evening.

But it wasn't. She shut the door to her car, trying to assimilate the scene. The man continued waving, gesticulating wildly as if she hadn't seen him already.

Her new partner. Renn McKenzie. Nice enough guy, but she wasn't willing to get to know him. It was too damn soon. She was still in mourning, recovering from the demise of her team, her career. Her future.

He galloped up to her, breathless. She nodded at him, willing some zen calm into him. "McKenzie."

"Just call me Renn, Taylor."

"Jackson is fine, McKenzie."

"I wish you'd just call me Renn."

Just Renn. "I'm not on today. I assume you had me called for a reason. Could you fill me in?"

She saw the blush rise on his cheeks. Just Renn had been transferred in from the South sector. He and Marcus Wade, one of her former teammates, had essentially traded places. Captain Delores Norris, head of the Office of Professional Accountability, was the architect of the restructuring.

She would kill to have Marcus by her side right now. Or her former sergeant, Pete Fitzgerald, or Lincoln Ross. But her entire team had been disassembled, and she felt the loss sorely. She was sure Just Renn was a fine detective, but he had his own rhythms, his own demeanor, an eagerness that belied the streaks of gray at his blond temples that was hard to get used to. He was gangly, all sharp edges, no real refinement to his walk or manners. Brown eyes, thin lips, three days of fuzzy golden razor stubble. A decent-looking man, if you liked the enthusiastic type. But he'd only been in plainclothes for about a month, which frightened her. Inexperience could blow an investigation; she was used to working with seasoned pros. Pros she had trained to work her way.

To be truthful, a small part of her liked keeping him off balance. It gave her the sense that maybe this wasn't forever.

"Sure, yeah. *Jackson.* Such a harsh name. I assume you're related?" He looked at her, his face turning blue, then white, then blue.

"Related to...?"

"Andrew Jackson, of course."

This boy obviously didn't know his Southern history. There were no direct descendants of Old Hickory—though he'd raised eleven children, none were his own.

There was a family connection though, through Jackson's wife Rachel's son…. She bit her lip, resisted the urge to scream. None of this had any bearing on her job.

"McKenzie?"

"Yeah?"

"Who's dead?"

"Yeah. Sorry. We don't know." He didn't make a move toward the house, just stood there.

"Could we possibly go see the body?"

"Oh, yeah, sure. Let's go. She's in the living room, or the great room, or whatever you call that big open space in the middle of the house. You can't see her from the front door, the best view is from the kitchen. Not a lot of walls in the downstairs, it's all open except for a few columns. She's, well, I'll let you see for yourself."

Now we're talking.

They reached the front steps. Taylor took them two at a time. Just Renn was right on her tail. It wasn't her imagination; the command center had been set up on the porch of the house.

"McKenzie? Why don't you suggest they move the command back a bit? We usually don't have all this activity so close to the scene. There's a chance of contamination. Crime Scene 101, buddy."

He looked down at the deck of the porch, chastised. She felt bad for snapping at him, mentally promised herself to be more careful. He was just a kid, learning the ropes. She'd been there once.

"It's okay. We all make mistakes," she said. It wasn't okay, but the damage was already done. She'd sort it out later.

Even with all the people worrying the scene, the interior of the house felt spacious. Teak floors, exposed beams, whitewashed walls, architectural and designer accoutrements. Elegant abstract paintings pranced along their neutral background to an exposed brick-and-stone fireplace.

The mood of the scene bothered her. The lack of concern about the exterior scene, the milling about, the simple fact that she'd been called in all bespoke the worst. Something was happening, something more than a typical murder. She felt a lump form in her throat.

Under the drone of voices, she heard music. Faint strains of a classical composition…what was that? She felt a buzz of recognition, reached into her mind for the name— Dvořák. That was it. *Symphony #9.* In E minor. Years of training, even more as a minor aficionado, and it had still taken her a moment. Funny how the mind worked. Her fingers unconsciously curled in on themselves, moving lightly in time with the notes. She'd played clarinet growing up, thrilled with her budding expertise when she was a child, mortified by the time she was a teenager looking for some fun up on Love Circle.

Looking back, she was sorry she'd given it up. Playing in a symphony had been one of her childhood desires, supplanted by the allure of law enforcement after a brief brush with the law when she was a teenager. Now she could see how that would have been quite satisfying. It was a game she rarely played—if you weren't a cop, what would you be? She'd never been in a position to have to think about *not* being a cop. Now that she felt the jeopardy slipping in like cat's feet on a fog, she'd started wondering again.

Taylor concentrated on the music. The last strains of the *allegro con fuoco* were fading away, then the opening movement started. A loop of the *New World Symphony,* as the piece was more commonly referred to. Bold and aggressive, lyrical and stunning. She'd always liked it.

She looked for the stereo, didn't see one. The music was all around her; it must be on a house-wide speaker system. It was hard to drag her attention away. She caught the eye of one of the techs she knew, Tim Davis. At least he was on the scene—she could count on him to preserve as much evidence as possible.

"Tim, can you cut the music?"

He nodded. "Yeah. It's on a built-in CD player. The controls are in the kitchen. I was waiting for you to hear it. The loop is driving us all mad. You know who it is?"

"Dvořák. *Symphony #9*. Keep that quiet, will you? I want to be sure that detail isn't leaked to the press. They'll seize on it and start giving this guy a name."

She hadn't even seen the body, and she was already assuming the worst. Not surprising; the whole tenor of the crime scene screamed "unusual."

"Where are they, anyway?"

Tim glanced out the window. "Channel Five just pulled up. The others can't be far behind."

She nodded to him and looked for Paula. She was standing in the open living room, looking toward the back door. The great room of the house was separated from the eat-in kitchen by three columns, which mimicked the pyramid-shaped support columns out front. There was a small knot of people surrounding the center column, a surreal grouping of cops and techs waiting on her. Three things hit her: she couldn't see a body, the faces glancing her way were visibly disturbed, and there was a fetid whiff of decomposition in the air.

She stepped lightly toward the group, making sure she didn't tread in anything important. As she passed the column, Paula pointed toward it with her eyebrow raised. Taylor turned and sucked in her breath.

The victim was young, no more than twenty, black,

naked, bones jutting out as if she hadn't eaten in a while, with dull, brittle bobbed hair. She hung on the center column.

To be more precise, she'd been tacked to the column with a large hunting knife. A big blade, with a polished wood-and-pearl handle that was buried to the hilt square in her chest. She was thin enough that the blade, which looked to be at least eight inches, had passed through her body into the wood. Her arms were pulled up tight over her head, the hands together as if in prayer, but inside out. Her feet were crossed at the ankle, demure, innocent.

Pinned. At least, that was the illusion. At first glance, it looked like the knife was all that held her in that position. Taylor shook her head; it had taken strength, or potent hatred, to shove the knife through the girl's breastbone into the wood behind.

Taylor ran her Maglite up and down the column, the concentrated beam reflecting off the nearly invisible wires that ran around the girl's body to hold her suspended in midair. Clever. Some sort of fishing line held the body rigid against the wooden post. It cut into her flesh; the victim had been up on the post long enough that the grooves were deepening as the body's early decomposition began.

The girl's shoulders were obviously dislocated. Her skin was ashen and flaky, her lips cracked. She was stripped of dignity, yet the pose felt almost…loving. Sorrow on her face, her mouth open in a scream, her eyes closed. Small mercies. Taylor hated when they stared.

She'd read the scene right. It was going to be a very long night.

Paula came to her side, fiddling with a small reporter's notebook. "Sorry I had to miss dinner. And sorry to ruin your night, too, but I knew you needed to see this. There's no ID. I can't find a purse or anything. This place is clean. The neighbors say the owner is out of town."

"This isn't her home?" Taylor asked, gesturing to the body.

"No. One of the neighbors, Carol Parker, is house-sitting, feeding the cat, taking in the paper. Owner's supposed to be gone all week. Parker came in, bustled around getting the cat fed and watered, then turned to leave and saw the body. She ran, of course. Called us. Swears up and down that she's never seen the girl around. There's a circle of glass cut out of the back door, the lock was turned. It's been dusted, there were no usable prints. The blinds were closed, that's why the neighbor didn't see anything amiss. The alarm was disengaged too; the neighbor can't remember if she turned it on yesterday or not. That cute M.E., Dr. Fox? He was here earlier and declared her. He said to bring her in; either he or Sam will post her first thing."

"Okay. I'd like to talk to the neighbor. Do you have her stashed close by?"

"She's at her place next door with a new patrol. God, they get younger every day. This one can't be more than eighteen. We took the cat over there so it wouldn't interrupt the scene. Last I saw the patrol was talking to it like it was a baby. Not far enough removed from his own childhood coddling, it seems."

Taylor smiled absently at Paula, then stepped back a few feet, taking in the full tableau. It was impressive, she'd give the killer that. Spiking the girl to the column like she was a butterfly trapped on a piece of cork was flashy, meant to shock. Meant to humiliate the victim.

Taylor longed for the good old days, when getting called out to a homicide was straightforward—some kid had deuced another on a crack buy and gotten knifed, or a pimp had beaten one of his girls upside the head and cracked her skull. As pointless as those deaths seemed, they were driven by the basics, things she readily understood—greed, lust, drugs. Ever since Dr. John Baldwin, FBI profiler extraordinaire, entered her life, the kills had gotten more gruesome, more meaningful. More serial. Like the loonies had followed him to Nashville. And that thought scared her to death. She already had one killer who'd gotten away, a man calling himself the Pretender, who killed in her name. What was happening to her city?

She pulled her phone from her pocket. There was no signal, so she stepped out onto the porch. Three bars, enough to make a call. She started to dial, felt McKenzie beside her. She hoped he wasn't going to lurk at her elbow at every crime scene. Maybe he just needed some instruction. She closed the phone and turned to him.

"Hey, man, do me a favor. Get them—"

McKenzie shook his head, lips compressed, eyes darting over her shoulder and back to hers with a kind of wild frenzy. She read the signs. Someone was behind her.

She turned and bumped into a small man with brown hair parted smartly on the right. It was thick and almost bushy, stood out from his head at the base of his neck and around his ears. Her first thought was *toupee*. He was older, easily in his sixties. She didn't recognize him, which wasn't too much of a surprise. Since the house-cleaning brought about by Captain Norris and the chief, there were plenty of new and unfamiliar faces at crime scenes, in the hallways, the cafeteria. The crime-scene techs were all the same, but there'd been some serious shaking up done among the detective ranks.

The little man looked up at her. She saw his mouth start to drop open, then he closed it, the back teeth snapping together.

"You are?" he demanded.

"Detective Taylor Jackson, Metro Homicide. And you?"

"You have a problem with my setup, *Detective?*"

My setup? Who *was* this guy?

"I must have missed your name," she said.

"Lieutenant Mortimer T. Elm. You may call me Lieutenant Elm. I'm with the New Orleans police."

"What are the New Orleans police doing at a Nashville crime scene?"

He looked confused for a moment, then said, "Who said anything about New Orleans? I'm with Metro Nashville."

Taylor stared at him for a second, then shrugged. "Lieutenant Elm. It's nice to meet you. Yes, there's a standard protocol when dealing with static crime scenes. We usually try to station the command post away from the primary scene in order to avoid contaminating the evidence that might be procured from the immediate vicinity." She realized she sounded completely textbook and hated herself for a moment. But that's what the demotion had done to her—forced her back into the realm of "there's only one way to do things." Great.

His wave was dismissive. He had pudgy fingers, the nails bitten to the quick. Her stomach flopped. A man's hands were the window to his soul. Lieutenant Elm's looked tortured.

"This is going to be just fine. The crime obviously took place inside the house, not outside. This makes it more convenient for everyone. There is a threat of rain. If we move quickly, the crime scene can be wrapped in an hour."

Taylor almost laughed aloud. Wrapping up a homicide in an hour. This guy was from Mars. Or Lilliput.

When she didn't immediately respond, he took a step

back. He stared at her, his eyes slightly bulged, his jaw thrust forward. She was reminded of a frog. She spoke quietly.

"I beg to differ, Lieutenant Elm. The external scene is just as important as the internal. We need to establish a point of entry, need to be looking for footprints, material the suspect may have discarded. It's anything but okay to be on top of the crime like this."

"This is the way I want it!" he said, anger bubbling up in his eyes.

She heard a hissing in her ear, felt a tug at her elbow.

"He's the new homicide lieutenant, Taylor. Our boss." McKenzie's whisper was frantic.

Taylor had to put a hand over her mouth to keep from bursting out laughing. This, this, *toad* was her new boss? Elm was the new homicide lieutenant? Oh, this was going to be priceless.

Elm's tone changed, sharpened. "You'll find that this setup is perfectly acceptable. I must deal with another matter. I trust you can handle this scene. I will deal with your insubordination in the morning." Elm was smug, obviously thinking he'd defeated her. Well, she'd been bullied just about enough over the past month.

"Insubordination? All I did was point out the obvious," she said. The porch twittered, the officers who'd overheard amused at the expense of the new lieutenant, who was vibrating in his displeasure.

Elm pointed a finger at her. "Do your job, *Detective*. I know how to do mine." He stepped off the porch, walked off toward the gathering media. McKenzie appeared at her elbow again.

"I tried to warn you."

Taylor caught the melodrama in his voice. A rabbit, scared and spooked, that's what Just Renn was. She smiled at the younger man.

"That, my friend, is a man who got up on the wrong side of the lily pad. Forget about it. I've had worse. Let's run this puppy."

Speaking of which…she flipped her cell back open and speed-dialed Baldwin.

He answered with a happy, "Hey, gorgeous. My plane just landed. You on your way?"

"Unfortunately, no. I'm on a call, and I think you'll want to see this."

He groaned. "Where are you?"

"Tell the driver 1400 Love Circle. You won't be able to miss it. And hey, stay away from a short man with a bad rug."

"Do I even want to know?"

"No. I'll see you shortly."

She hung up, went back into the house. The victim was calling her, the scene, the case. She'd been drawn in, already fascinated. Dead girl pinned to a post, in someone else's house. Classical music playing in the background. A message was being sent. By whom, and to whom? Taylor felt the intrigue slip in and grab her. She was going to be too busy to worry about all the changes, and that was a good thing.

Back in the living room, she circled the body again, looked closer at the filament that held the girl's arms, legs, torso and head in position. It was tied in little knots on the backside of the column. The killer had taken the time to staple the translucent fishing line into the wood to give it extra holding power. This was well thought out, planned in advance. It had taken time to get the girl up on the post. Which meant whoever committed this murder knew that the house was going to be empty, that he'd have a fertile, undisturbed playground. Either that, or they had another body to find, one belonging to the owner.

Taylor stepped three feet back from the post, taking in

the rest of the setting. The columns bisected the two rooms; there were crime-scene techs moving around, disturbing her view.

"Hey, can everyone hold up for a minute? I'd like to get some shots here."

Long accustomed to Taylor being in charge, people moved out of her way.

She fished her digital camera out of her jacket pocket, took a couple of pictures. Something felt strange, and she couldn't put her finger on it. Maybe later, once she'd had time for her mind to process the scene, she'd be able to see what was out of place. Or Baldwin would.

She turned the camera off. McKenzie appeared at her side, appropriately silenced by the gruesome visage in front of them. Paula took her flanking position and the three of them stood in a moment of peace, watching, reverent. The victim's nudity was embarrassing McKenzie. Taylor could see him shifting his feet like a little boy out of the corner of her eye.

She ignored him, stared again at the knife pinning the girl to the column. Tim Davis joined them.

"We're going to have a pissed-off home owner. I'm going to have to cut the post down, I think," he said.

"Why?" McKenzie asked, puzzled.

"Because there's no way to get that knife out of her without disturbing the wound tract." Tim stepped closer to the body, put his thumb on the flat end of the knife handle, exerting pressure experimentally. It didn't budge, didn't shift slightly. "See, this thing is jammed all the way into the wood. We've gotta cut her down, take a whole section of column with us to the M.E.'s office. No other way to do it."

"Oh. Yeah, absolutely. Gotta cut it." McKenzie was nodding like he'd thought of that himself.

Taylor cracked her knuckles and circled the column again. "This thing must be ten feet tall. Think it's load-bearing?" she asked Tim.

He shook his head. "No. See the line at the top? It's just decorative, glued then nailed into place. If it were one of the other two," he gestured to each side of the body, "we'd be in trouble. This one is detached, for the most part. Won't be too bad to replace."

"Okay, Tim, do what you need to do. Try to delay a few minutes for me, though. Baldwin is on his way. I'd like him to see this intact."

He nodded at her. "I'll go get the saw."

Taylor stepped back and considered the victim again. She couldn't shake the feeling that she'd seen this before. In addition to that, one very obvious incongruity screamed out at her.

She turned to the patrol officer on her left. "I have a question for you, Paula."

"Shoot," Paula said.

Taylor pointed at the dead girl. "Where's the blood?"

Three

John Baldwin decamped from the taxi ten minutes later. Perfect timing.

Taylor glanced around but didn't see Elm anywhere. She'd have to introduce him to Baldwin, and based on their brief exchange, she had no idea how he would feel about the FBI being at their scene. When she was the lieutenant, it was her call, and she was always willing to have a fresh set of eyes. Elm struck her as the type of cop who would get territorial. Well, she'd cross that bridge when she got to it.

Taylor watched Baldwin walk up the drive, vivid green eyes taking in everything until they settled on hers. She wondered what he saw there, sometimes. He was a veteran of crime scenes, had been the lead profiler on hundreds of cases. He knew the score. Knew what kind of monsters lurked in her head. They lurked in his, too.

Her mind was drawn away from the crime. She forgot how big he was when he was away. As tall as she was, she still had to look up at him. She loved that. In the dark, his black hair looked like midnight, his angled cheekbones highlighting his mouth with shadows. As he got closer, she could see he hadn't shaved, the soft stubble growing back at an alarming rate. Hmm.

He didn't kiss her, though she wanted him to. It wasn't professional—she knew that—but she hadn't seen him in two weeks and she missed the feeling of him next to her. He did caress her arm, just above her wrist, and it burned as she walked him to the sign-in sheet, then into the house.

"Make it quick," she said quietly. "We need to get her body down so the techs can finish up in here. And the new lieutenant is around somewhere. He might kick up a fuss that you've come."

Baldwin nodded. He still hadn't spoken, was simply processing. That's what she liked about him. There was no extraneous bullshit, no posturing. Just an incessant curiosity about what made people do bad things. That was something they shared, a core desire to figure out the why behind the crimes.

She escorted him over to the body, then stepped away and let him assess the scene.

His lips were set in a tight, thin line, and she could see the dark circles under his eyes. He was exhausted. Working a case always did that to him. His job as the head of the Behavioral Analysis Unit, BAU Two, was to guide the various profilers who worked for him, and to give the various law enforcement entities requesting help a thorough rundown of what they were dealing with. Taylor knew that it went deeper for him. He wanted to do more than look at crime-scene photos and pump out a report. He liked to get in the field, to smell the scene, see the crime in situ. Well, she was giving him his heart's desire with this one.

Baldwin broke his verbal fast. "Where's the blood?" he asked.

Taylor smiled. "I said the same thing. There's something else totally bizarre. There was a classical piece from Dvořák playing on the house's intercom system."

"Really? Hmm."

"The owner of the house is allegedly out of town. There was a piece of glass cut out of the back door so our suspect could turn the lock. The next-door neighbor is caring for the cat—she came over and found the body. She couldn't say if the music was on or off when she arrived—she wasn't paying attention. We included the CD in the evidence gathering. The lack of blood, the music, the position of the body—I can't help but think this is a ritual. That's why I wanted you to see it."

He ignored her for a moment, moving back and forth between the wall and the column. He spoke absently. "The suspect could have been playing the music to cover any noise he might have been making. Taylor, step over here with me a second. Look at the wide view."

She went as far back as the house allowed, to the bay window on the west side of the kitchen. He went with her, standing quietly while she looked. She had taken a picture earlier from this angle, a wide shot of the room face-on to the body.

"Okay. What am I missing?"

"Look at the painting on the wall by the door, in the left upper quadrant, line-of-sight to the column."

That was it. The strange sense that something wasn't right, the feeling that she was missing something. It was there in front of her the whole time.

"Son of a bitch. She's posed just like the painting. Who is that, Picasso?"

"Yes. *Demoiselles d'Avignon*. The victim's arms are up over her head, a perfect imitation of the center of the painting. And this was Picasso's most famous piece from his African Period. Your victim is black. He's accurately mirrored the painting. There's no blood. But the race…"

He drifted off.

"What is it?" she asked.

"Taylor, you don't want to hear what I have to say. I'm having a hard time believing it myself."

"It's too early to surmise that we might have a serial on our hands."

"It's not that. Actually, it's much worse."

"What then?"

"I think you may have *my* serial on your hands."

Four

Baldwin waited for Taylor's mind to register what he'd told her. Hell, he needed it to register in *his* mind.

"What are you talking about?" she asked.

He spoke quietly. "How much do you remember about a killer named Il Macellaio?"

"I don't. Not that much. Only what you've told me. He's a serial killer in Florence, Italy, has been working for a number of years. Doesn't the name translate to 'the Butcher'?"

"Yes. Il Macellaio has been around since 2000 or so. He's ruthless, and he's very, very good at what he does. He poses his victims to emulate famous paintings, leaves a postcard of the painting behind so we know exactly who he's imitating. Of course, that's after he tortures them. He keeps them alive as playthings for a while before he kills them. His earliest victims' cause of death was actually starvation, though his latest were starved and strangled, like he got tired of waiting. He has sex with the bodies, a final farewell, before he stages the scenes. Until now, we've not had a lot of physical evidence to go by. Did you get a cause of death on your victim?"

"Ugh. Necrophilia?"

"Worse, much, much worse. Necrosadism. Il Macellaio's pathology developed to the point where his fantasies about having sex with corpses wasn't enough. He was driven to actually capture and kill women to act out his fantasies with. Very, very rare. Starvation is a cruel way to die. It's somewhat passive-aggressive, actually, which is fascinating, considering he's being driven by his desires to kill. I'm not entirely sure why he does it, though I've got some ideas. And looking at this girl, she's certainly gone without nourishment for a while."

"Lovely. I'll make sure Sam is aware of the background. The COD isn't apparent but you're right, she's ridiculously skinny. Bones sticking out everywhere. Did you notice the knife went all the way through her chest and into the post?"

"I did. You'll have to—"

"Cut it down. I know," she interrupted, signaling to her crime-scene tech. The young man with solemn eyes Baldwin knew as Tim Davis nodded grimly and went to work with his hacksaw.

Taylor was pacing in short bursts. Baldwin led her a few feet away so they could talk privately.

"Baldwin, is it possible that Il Macellaio has come here from Italy? And why? Nashville isn't exactly on the beaten path of most world travelers. New York, Los Angeles, I can see. But us?"

He scrubbed his hands through his hair to help him think, not caring that it would be standing on end. "Part of what I've been dealing with in Quantico is a report from London. The Metropolitan Police at New Scotland Yard have three murders that bear an eerie resemblance to the Florence cases. If I'm right, and Il Macellaio went to London, it's within the realm of possibility that he could come here."

"What would take a serial killer from Florence to London, and then to Nashville?"

"You ask an excellent question. We had a break in the Florence case last week. Finally got some DNA. We're waiting for it to clear the Interpol databases, see if they have a match, and it's running through CODIS. I expect we'll have the results back sometime tomorrow. You know how things shake out. We might get a name, we might be off on another wild-goose chase. If we get a name, I'll probably have to head back up there."

CODIS. The wundertool. The combined DNA index system could match killings and killers. Baldwin sent a brief prayer of thanks out to Sir Alec Jeffreys for finding the DNA fingerprint that led them to this point. One day, there would be DNA on file for every criminal in every country, and there would be instantaneous matches.

Taylor was appropriately intrigued. "That's awesome, babe. How'd you get DNA after all these years?"

"Long story or short?"

She waved at the scene in front of them, Tim sawing away at the post, cursing in G-rated, first-class Southern style—*dagnabit, almost had you, dadgumit, get back here*—and he had to fight back a smile. She met his eyes and he could see the mirth bubbling in their stormy depths. She liked that Tim kid.

"I've got time," she said. "Tell me about your murders."

"That's got to be one of the most romantic things I've heard you say."

"I knew there was a reason why you love me," she whispered.

"I do love you. Desperately," he whispered back.

He felt a hand on his arm. A short man, bristling with indignation, stared up at him.

"Who is this, Detective?" the man snipped.

Taylor made eyes at Baldwin for a second, then did the introductions.

"Lieutenant Elm, this is Supervisory Special Agent John Baldwin, Unit Chief of the Behavioral Analysis Unit at Quantico."

"And what, pray tell, is the FBI doing at my crime scene?" Elm's face was turning red, a pot ready to boil over. Baldwin stuck out his hand to shake.

"I was in the neighborhood and Detective Jackson suggested I take a look. This isn't exactly a run-of-the-mill murder."

"I don't remember inviting you, Mr. Baldwin."

"It's Doctor, actually, sir. My apologies for the intrusion. But I must tell you that this looks like the work of an organized killer, and I wouldn't be surprised to see him strike again. I would be more than willing to sit down with you and give a profile."

"Profiling," Elm spat. "Voodoo, mind-reading crap, if you ask me. I think we'll be just fine without your help, Doctor. That is all."

Elm marched away from them. Baldwin glanced at Taylor. Her face was suffused with blood and she was biting her lip. He'd seen that look before; she was torn between laughing and cursing.

"That's your new lieutenant?"

She nodded.

"Well, this is going to be fun. At least he didn't try to bodily remove me."

"That happens?" she asked.

"You'd be surprised," he said lightly. "Where were we?"

"Florence, where I'd rather be right now."

He smiled at her. "Don't try to distract me. It won't work. Right. Three bodies ago, back in Florence in 2004, the carabinieri's very sharp crime-scene technician found a hair with an intact skin tag in a puddle of water in the kitchen where the victim was found. It didn't match her DNA. They put it in the system and kept it flagged, just in case. Last week, we got the call from the Met. They had a series of murders that they determined were serial, and asked for a consultation. When I looked at the crime-scene photos, I saw the signature of our Italian boy. But the beautiful thing is, the techs at the Met found an intact hair, too, this time curled in the back of their second victim's throat."

"Ugh."

"Yes. There were enough similarities between the cases that I insisted we test the two hairs' DNA immediately. Two hairs in five years. We're crossing our fingers that there's a match between the two. If he's committed any other crimes and is in the database, we might get a lead. Who knows? If the DNA matches, then at least I can confirm that he's on the road. That's what I'm waiting for."

"But how long does it take to starve a woman to death? It seems like the time frame is too short for this to be a part of the series."

"If you subscribe to the rules of three…three minutes without air, three days without water, three weeks without food. That's not a perfect formula, but close enough. Deprived of water and food, a small woman could easily die within two weeks. Maybe less. The last London murder scene was over a month ago. He could have made it to the States, taken your victim, starved her, then posed her. It's feasible. Any postcards around?"

"Not that I've seen."

Taylor was quiet. He could feel her thinking. After a moment, she spoke again.

"See, there's something else odd about this scene. I need to go do a ViCAP search. It wasn't my case, wasn't even in Nashville. It was south of us, in Manchester. But I remember reading something in the Law Enforcement Bulletin about an unsolved murder three years or so ago where classical music was playing when they arrived at the scene. Tonight, the CD player in the kitchen had that Dvořák piece playing on a continuous loop. Do you have any of that in your cases?"

"No, we don't."

"The owner of the house might have left it on accidentally. We pulled a palm print off of the casing, so we'll see. I'm relatively certain that the body was transported from another scene. The lack of blood on the girl's body and on the floor…she was killed elsewhere."

"Probably. There wouldn't be a lot of blood in a starvation case anyway."

"There could have been two people involved, one to hold the body against the post and one to tie the fishing line around her body. It might be hard to control alone, but a strong man, starting at the victim's feet, could have managed easily. The girl's toes were two feet off the floor. He could have had her in a fireman's carry, slumped over his shoulder, while he tied the line around her ankles."

"Or he might have looped the line around the bottom and tied it loosely, then inserted the dead girl's legs into the loop. Tighten it down, and voilà, there's a base to start with. He could have slowly worked his way up the body."

"Yeah, you're right," she said. "That's how I would do it if it were just me."

Elm was in the kitchen now, imperiously bossing around the videographer, Keri McGee. Taylor cringed at the sound of his voice. Baldwin knew how hard this was for her—the past few weeks had taken their toll on both of them. Maybe a big, juicy case would be a welcome diversion, even if they were being overseen by Napoleon.

He tried to draw her attention back to the victim. "Slamming the knife through the victim's body with enough force to embed it that deeply into the wood was overkill. She'd been dead long before she had been placed on the post. There's rigor leaving her jaw and some decent lividity on the edges of her legs."

Taylor's focus returned immediately. "So she lay on her back at some point soon after death," she said.

"Did you notice the fishing line eating into her skin?"

"Of course. There was also some petechial hemorrhaging in her eyes, but not so much that I'd automatically assume she'd been strangled. Hopefully Sam will have her in the morning for the autopsy. She'll get to the bottom of it."

Baldwin took the hint gracefully. There was more work to be done, things that he wasn't needed for. "Why don't I go make some calls? Is there someplace…?"

She handed him the keys to her pool car. "It's the one right by Tim's van. I'll be with you as quickly as I can. Thank you for coming out."

He longed to kiss her, but simply nodded and left. The post was coming down as he walked past, the girl riding the wood, still solidly attached by the fishing line and the knife sunk deep into her chest. It looked like half a crucifixion. Nothing he'd forget for a long while.

Taylor rubbed her eyes, forcing the itch of sleep away. It was two in the morning; the crime scene was winding down. Elm's prediction that it would only take an hour was six hours off.

Tim had successfully removed the body of the victim, still attached to a nearly seven-foot-long column of wood by the fishing line and the knife. It was a wild scene. Getting the dead girl in an appropriate horizontal plane so she could go into the body bag had been tricky, and they couldn't close the bag all the way. Despite the victim's low weight, the column was heavy. People on both ends of the post heaved and strained not to drop her, to preserve the evidence.

After that, the rest of the evening had gone smoothly.

Elm had vacated the house about an hour earlier, which was fine by her. She'd seen him talking to one of *The Tennessean* reporters who'd made an appearance, prayed he'd shown a modicum of discretion. Dan Franklin, the department's spokesperson, had shown up and handled the media after that. Some of the news folks were still hanging around; nothing else had captured their attention. A quiet crime night in Nashville, which guaranteed this murder would make the morning news.

Taylor had been avoiding the media all night, refusing to give a statement, leaving that to Franklin. She hadn't forgiven them for their role in her demotion, for running with the allusions and innuendoes planted by a man out for revenge against her. For showing videos of her having sex with her old partner; tapes that were made without her knowledge or permission. Every time she thought about the humiliation she'd endured, having to watch herself on television…

Stop it, Taylor. What's done is done. They are the media. You were newsworthy. Leave it at that. It wasn't personal. You'd investigate each and every one of them six ways to Sunday if you thought they'd done something illegal. Why should they be any different? Everyone needs to feed the family. *Focus.*

She went back to her mental wrap-up of the crime scene. Footprints had been found in the woods behind the house, and cigarette butts, but they were far enough removed from the actual scene that Taylor was skeptical

that they'd come from the killer. Every bit had been pro-
cessed, of course, the techs putting together the molds,
spraying the ground with Dust & Dirt Hardener, making
impression casts of at least four different shoe prints. If
they found a suspect, they could look for a match to test
against the shoe impressions.

There was still the issue of transport. The killer had
gotten the body to the house somehow, but so far the
canvas of the neighborhood had turned up nothing of use.
No one had seen a car or van around the area that didn't
belong. Of course, considering how many people tooled
around Love Circle for fun, she suspected the residents
were inured to the sight of strange cars.

There were tons of kids that roamed this area at night.
They were usually harmless, looking for a quiet place to
smoke some dope and drink, neck, and ponder the questions of the world. Not surprisingly, the regulars scattered when the police had driven up the hill, melting away
into the night. They'd be back. Taylor would wait them
out, talk to them another night. Maybe a stranger had
noticed something.

The odds that one of them was her suspect…well, she
never assumed. She would wait for the results of the investigation, let the evidence be her guide.

She'd talked to the neighbor, Carol Parker, had gone
at her hard to make sure nothing was missed. The woman
sat on her couch, hefty thighs encased in brown knit
firmly pressed together, feet flat on the floor, her round
face white. She held the Siamese cat from next door,
stroking the fur obsessively as she relayed her actions
during the past few days house-sitting. No, she hadn't
noticed any cars today, she'd been at work. No, she didn't
realize anything was amiss until after she'd fed the cat and
turned to leave. No, she couldn't remember if she'd heard

music, but the owner usually left some sort of noise playing, a television or a radio, for the cat, so she wouldn't have thought it strange. She thought she'd turned the alarm on when she left the previous day, but might have forgotten. No, she didn't remember touching anything but the front door and the cat's dish; she'd seen the body and run.

Taylor went through her every move, then gave up after twenty minutes. The woman didn't have anything that would be of use to them tonight. Maybe in the morning, when the shock of the evening wore off, she'd be able to recall anything that seemed out of place. She had given Taylor the name and cell phone number of the house's owner. His name was Hugh Bangor, and Taylor left him a voice mail asking him to call her as soon as he received the message. Parker said he was in Los Angeles, but didn't know where. If that were the case, it would certainly be tomorrow before he'd be able to come home.

He was in for quite a reception—Taylor planned to interrogate him extensively. Though the neighbor was adamant that Bangor was a great, stand-up guy, it's not every day that a dead body was arranged so artfully in your living room while you were conveniently out of town. He was certainly a suspect.

Taylor wandered through the house one last time, assimilating the scene. A fine black film covered all available surfaces. The house had been dusted for prints and many exemplars had been taken, including the magnificent palm print on the CD player. She'd love to get lucky, to get the prints into the system and get a match tomorrow. The victim had been printed as well, and her exemplars would be inputted into the statewide iAFIS database to look for a match. The integrated automatic fingerprint identification system was strong and quick, and could give them an answer within minutes if a match was located.

Taylor walked to the glass coffee table. Nothing unusual—coasters, an oversize art book on Spain and a *catalogue raisonné* of Picasso's life work. She used the tip of her pen to spin the book around toward her. Baldwin had mentioned that postcards had been left at the Macellaio crime scenes, postcards of the painting the killer was imitating. Well, this monograph of Picasso's work wasn't a postcard, but it might be a good substitute. She bagged the book, just in case.

Despite the confusion when she first arrived, Taylor was comfortable that the scene had been managed, that they hadn't missed anything. She stopped in front of the now-ruined column, which looked like a freshly sawed mangrove root. She turned in a circle, then went to the door, closed it behind her, and sealed the scene.

Taylor walked out onto the porch. Simari had just left, Max sleeping peacefully in the back of the cruiser. Just Renn had packed it in, too, as had the rest of the crime-scene techs. All that was left was the occupied car of the patrol officer who would assure the scene wouldn't be disturbed overnight by kids or vandals, and a Channel Four press van. Taylor was annoyed at their presence. Couldn't they edit their package back at their little castle on Knob Hill? As if they'd heard her thoughts, the engine revved and the van slid away into the night.

And Baldwin, of course, sleeping peacefully in the front seat of the unmarked. Poor guy, he was tired enough to crash in her car. She needed to get him home.

It was a pleasant night. Morning. Whatever you called those dim predawn hours, the deepest part of the night. The woods were alive, crickets and cicadas competing for air time, the blackness of the night almost sultry. A calm had settled over Love Circle. The chaos had been replaced by nature's serenity.

Taylor took a deep breath, felt some tranquility slink into her shoulders. It was the evidence they hadn't found that disturbed her. A knife through the heart should be a bloody mess. Taylor had talked briefly to Sam, who promised to handle the autopsy personally in the morning. Taylor wanted to witness, and wanted McKenzie to accompany her. He'd paled when she told him, but nodded stoically and promised to be there. This would be their first postmortem together, and Taylor wasn't sure what to expect from him.

Either way, it was time to go home. She stifled a yawn, waved to the patrol, and got into the car. Baldwin woke, smiled sleepily at her.

"Sorry it took so long," she whispered, then leaned over and kissed him. He kissed her back, hungry, and it took all of her control not to throw her arms around him and slide into the backseat. She disengaged herself, laughing. It had been too long.

"Let's go home."

"I think that sounds wonderful." When he reached over and took her hand, she was struck by the full circle she'd come tonight. First love to true love on Love Hill. Not a bad life's work.

She drove down the hill one-handed, listening to the dispatch crackle—"10-83, shots fired, repeat, 10-83, 490 Second Avenue, Club Twilight. Officers please respond."

Shots fired on Second Avenue had practically become a daily standard. Let someone else worry about that. The B-shift homicide team was responsible for these overnight calls. She just needed to make it home. She was tired, no doubt, but her mind was whirling. The same word kept winding through like the loop of the Dvořák piece.

Another. Another. Another.

Five

The house looked barren when she pulled into the driveway. She'd neglected to leave the front lights on—of course, she'd expected to be home hours ago. Baldwin had fallen asleep again on the drive; she hated to wake him, but didn't have any choice. She shook him lightly and he opened his eyes with a yawn.

"Sorry, babe. We're going to have to go in through the front, I don't have the garage door opener. I left it in my truck. I hate bringing the unmarked home."

"Okay. Yeah," he murmured.

They got themselves inside the house. She'd forgotten to turn the alarm on again, and Baldwin gave her a chastising look after he armed it.

It was past 3:00 a.m. Though Baldwin could sleep in, Taylor would have to be up in a few hours to start a fresh day. Her newly demoted status meant she had much less freedom in setting her own hours, the biggest chafe of all. She was expected to be in the office at 8:00 a.m. and work through to 3:00 p.m., but so far, she'd never had an actual 8:00–3:00 day.

Setting hours for a homicide detective was a moot

point. You catch a murder at 2:45 p.m., you're on until you've cleared the scene and the paperwork is done. As a lieutenant, she had the luxury of letting other people do the work and report their findings to her. That part of her career was temporarily on hold.

Baldwin wavered against her shoulder; he was asleep on his feet. She brushed a kiss against his lips and sent him up to bed.

Elm. How in the world had Mortimer managed to make lieutenant? He was going to be a difficult man to deal with, she could see that as plain as day. Cranky, nasty, like an ill-tempered yappy little dog. Insubordination. Yes, she probably should have bit back that last comment, but really, how big an idiot could you be? The officers on the metro police force received endless training. Hell, even the most amateur forensic enthusiast with a working knowledge of crime television and fiction would know not to make such freshman mistakes.

She dropped her weapon and badge on the counter, pulled her ponytail holder out, letting her hair cascade down her back. She opened the wine fridge, took out a bottle of Masciarelli Montepulciano d'Abruzzo. She poured a glass, put the bottle on the counter, grabbed a handful of grapes from the fruit bowl, nibbled a few and chased them with a healthy gulp of wine. The message light was flashing on the answering machine, four new messages. She hit play, then stood in front of it, left arm draped against the wall, her forehead on her forearm, the wineglass by her side, listening.

A political pollster. Delete.

A reminder that she had a dentist appointment next week. She left that one, just in case she forgot.

Baldwin, his deep voice filling the room. Just letting

her know he was in early, that he loved her, and planned to ravish her as soon as they got home. Fat chance of that.

She replayed it twice, a smile on her lips. She took a sip of wine and waited for the next one.

There was silence, then static. A chill moved up her spine, she stood straighter. Then a high-pitched voice, almost childlike. "Not. Me."

The click that followed made her jump. Her heart began to race.

She set her wine down on the counter. The caller ID showed the last number who'd called as Unknown Name, Unknown Number. She hit star sixty-nine for an automatic redial, but a quick beeping told her that it wasn't going to work without the correct area code.

Damn. She played it back three times, each time feeling a fresh wave of chills whip through her body. Part of her wanted to blow it off, assume that it was just a wrong number. But her instincts were on fire. She'd never heard the voice before, but she knew exactly who that was, and what the message meant.

He called himself the Pretender. He'd been a disciple of a serial killer in Nashville known as Snow White. Snow White had been dealt with, but the Pretender had slipped through the net. Every once in a while, he reached out to her. As recently as last month he'd made his presence known in Nashville, taking care of a pesky threat to her security. In a decidedly gruesome fashion, at that. He'd left what Baldwin termed a "love note" anchored to the dead man's chest.

What a chance to take, calling her at home. The Pretender wasn't careless, that much she knew. There had been a trap on their line for the past couple of months, but it would take more than a three-second call to trace.

The message freaked her out on two levels. One, the

simple fact that he was still watching her made her toes curl. He was close enough to know about the murder scene tonight, and that was exceptionally unsettling.

Two, her instincts about this evening's murder were right on. The ritualistic posing, the secondary crime scene, all pointed to an organized offender who had done this before. And would most likely try to do it again.

Baldwin needed to know. After her run-in last month with the assassin the Pretender had so unceremoniously murdered, she didn't hesitate. She ran up the stairs and flung herself on the bed. He jumped up with a snort.

"I'm not entirely dead to the world, woman. I thought you'd never come to bed. Come here and let me—"

"He called."

Baldwin stopped, his hand frozen on Taylor's thigh. "Huh?"

"Our boy. He called the house and let me know to-night's crime scene wasn't his."

She didn't have to explain further. Baldwin knew that the Pretender was out there, waiting to strike, waiting for the perfect moment to catch them off guard. Every murder they worked, they were forced to stop and think about him. He preyed on their minds.

Baldwin's rage eliminated all traces of sleepiness, palpable and deadly. The more controlled his voice, the angrier he was. This was as tight as she'd ever heard him. "He called the house."

She didn't know which scared her more, the constantly evolving relationship with a mass murderer, or the rigid fury in Baldwin's voice.

"Yes. At least, I assume it's him. He left a message. It said, 'Not me.'"

She heard Baldwin breathe deeply, mastering his emotions. "Son of a bitch. Let me hear it."

They made their way downstairs. "I wouldn't worry too much," she said. "It wasn't what I'd term threatening. I imagine when he's ready to strike, he's going to have a blast setting the stage."

"That's exactly what I'm afraid of. And you let me judge for myself. You need to stop downplaying this. He's dangerous."

He sounded so possessive, so intense, that it felt like he had stopped her on the stairs and slipped his arms around her body. Amazing how even his voice made her feel protected. Not that she needed protecting, of course, but it was nice knowing she had a fallback position.

In the kitchen, Baldwin replayed the message several times, then made a call, to Quantico, she figured, to see what the trap showed. She took the wine and went into the living room, booted up the laptop, retrieved the cord for the camera, and uploaded the pictures from the Love Hill crime scene. Busy work. Something to take her mind off that voice, the crawling terror that pervaded her senses. Despite what Baldwin thought, she did take the Pretender seriously. She dreamt about him. She caught herself looking over her shoulder, wondering if he was watching her. She'd made some changes to her routine to try and throw him off, but if he was mailing her letters and calling her at home, none of that mattered. He knew where she was, all the time. He knew where she slept, where she was most vulnerable. She had the brief urge to suggest that they move, but it wouldn't matter. The Pretender was far too clever for his own good.

"Damn," she whispered. She took a drink of the Masciarelli and willed her stomach to stay put. She needed a distraction, and the computer was ready. Baldwin had installed an e-mail program directly into her photo well. She selected the twenty or so pictures she'd taken and sent them to her work e-mail address so they'd be there fresh for the picking in the morning.

When the files finished uploading, she opened the slide show and scrolled through them, slowly, recreating the sense of the scene in her mind. The music. Fishing line. The Picasso book. A very posed corpse.

Not. Me.

She shook it off, forced the voice from her head. The crime-scene pictures were in vivid color, but they didn't capture the intensity she'd felt at the scene. This murderer was sending them a very clear message. If she could only decipher it before he felt compelled to tell them again.

Baldwin came and sat next to her, rubbing her leg through her jeans, then inserting his hand into the opening and running his warm fingers delicately up the back of her calf. It made her shiver.

"Now that you're awake…you mentioned the postcards left at the Macellaio crime scenes? I bagged a Picasso monograph that was on the coffee table. I'll ask the owner if it's his—it might have been left by the suspect."

"That's a great thought." He grew silent. "I'm sorry," he said.

"For what?" she asked.

"I can't keep you safe from him."

She sighed. "You do that every time you look at me, Baldwin. And don't you forget it." She kissed him, and her heart pounded in a much more enticing way. He tugged at the button on her jeans, slipped her arms out of her shirt. She wrapped herself around him. It didn't take long. It had been a while for them, and they were both anxious to make the connection. There would be plenty of time for candles and music; right now, all she wanted was to feel Baldwin inside her, to remind her that she was alive. His beard made the insides of her thighs feel red and burned, and she got carried away and raked his back with her nails. The depths of her passion for him never ceased to surprise her. She'd never felt so totally and completely in lust and in love at the same time.

Breath ragged, they clung together on the couch. Baldwin fell asleep in her arms, and she smiled into his dark hair. God, it was good to have him home.

She reached out a hand and managed to get her wine. Debated slipping upstairs into the pool room and having a game, think through the night's work. She'd have to get up in a few hours anyway. Almost reluctantly, she set the wine on the table and closed her eyes, let her breathing deepen and match Baldwin's. There would be plenty of time to deal with monsters in the morning.

Thursday

Six

With a whopping three hours of sleep under her belt, Taylor rose at seven so she could get a run in before she had to go to work. Baldwin had bought a treadmill for their bonus room so he could run off his excess stress, and she'd found it helped her, too. She was dreading today. She could only pray that the troll she'd met last night wasn't really going to be her new lieutenant.

After a quick three miles, she showered, put her wet hair in a ponytail, dressed in a new pair of dark denim jeans and a black cashmere T-shirt, then jammed her feet into her favorite pair of Tony Lama cowboy boots. Elm would probably be one of those sticklers for the dress code, but damn if she was going to wear slacks and pumps to work. She figured as long as her badge and weapon were visible, it was quite apparent that she was dressed for the job.

Downstairs, she grabbed a Diet Coke and shrugged into a black leather car coat. Summer was nearly here, but it was still getting chilly in the mornings. Weird weather. She backed out of the driveway, debating. Should she go to the office to face the music with Elm, or should she go to Gass Street, to Sam, and witness the autopsy of their victim from last night?

Her cell phone rang. Speak of the devil. Punching the talk button, she smiled as she greeted her best friend.

"Howza," Sam said, and Taylor burst out laughing. It was code from their high school days at Father Ryan. *Howza* was one of their ways of letting the other know they'd gotten in trouble with the nuns. Neither one could remember where and how it started, but it stuck.

"Who are you in trouble with?" Taylor asked.

"Me, in trouble? I hear it's you who's in hot water."

Taylor groaned. "What did you hear?"

"That you told off the new guy."

"And where, pray tell, did you hear that?"

"Your new dick is in my lobby."

"Just Renn?"

This time Sam laughed. "Just so. He's here to witness the post. He was worried that you were getting reamed by the new guy, and that's why you're late."

"I'm not late."

"No, you're not. He's early. He was waiting for me when I got here, and *I* was early. You need to give him some saltpeter or something, get him calmed down."

"Doesn't that affect his Johnson?"

"Probably wouldn't hurt that either. I think he's got the hots for you."

Taylor rolled her eyes. "Great. Thanks for the warning. I'll head into the office before I come to you."

"By the way, you may want to avoid the paper. It seems your new boss gave the reporter a lot of detail from the scene. You may want to talk to him."

"I tried that last night. He wasn't listening."

"Try harder. See you in a bit."

Sam hung up before Taylor could reply. Damn. It was face-the-music time.

Traffic was unbearably light. Just her luck. She was downtown, pulling into the parking lot of the Criminal Justice Center before the clock turned 8:30 a.m.

The CJC was one of those never-changing entities in her life. In one way, shape or form, she'd been here at least five times a week for the past four years. And for the previous nine, she'd been filtering in and out, bringing suspects in for booking or questioning, meeting with superiors, taking exams…. Thirteen years of her life, this had been her home base. Stocky gray cement with a red-and-brown brick facade, the close smell of the Cumberland River, the back stairs with an industrial ashtray littered with cigarette butts, all served to make her feel a familiar sense of calm.

It was the inside of the building that had undergone the dramatic transformation.

The new chief had systematically decimated everything the Metro Nashville Police Department stood for, accomplished, and created during the thirteen years she'd been a cop.

The changes had begun subtly—a command shift here, a group moved there, and Taylor hadn't worried about it too much. A new chief would certainly have new plans. And then he started replacing the upper levels of management with his own people.

He followed with a Machiavellian administrative swoop, moving many of the criminal investigative detectives into the six separate city precincts. By splitting up seasoned teams and bringing in new people, the homicide close rate of eighty-six percent dropped to a measly forty-one. Decentralization of the homicide teams had been only one of the huge shifts in the past few years. Buyouts and early retirements cut a swath through the experienced ranks of the detective division—all of the Criminal Investigative Division groups had been affected.

Despite the vociferous complaints by the rank and file, the realignments went on. The new chief publicly claimed that the crime rates were dropping dramatically, when in actuality there was simply some creative accounting going on. One of the new guidelines that upset Taylor was the new definitions for rape. An assault could no longer be called a rape unless there was penile penetration. Taylor knew a few women who'd gotten away by the skin of their teeth, had been forced to fellate an attacker, had been beaten and terrorized, but it was only categorized as a sexual assault.

It burned her to no end, these little petty political plays. Her force was being dismantled, slowly, but surely.

Her own world had suffered the most dramatically of all. Taylor's team was known as the murder squad. They worked out of the old offices, handled high-profile cases. To be on the murder squad, you had to be the cream of the crop. As the homicide lieutenant, Taylor had run it for three years. The loyalties of her men and women were unassailable, and they'd managed to get past the decentralization and keep on solving crimes, which was the only purpose they had.

But Captain Delores Norris was the new head of the Office of Professional Accountability, and hated Taylor with a passion. They'd gone head-to-head, and for now, Taylor had lost, and big. Her team had been split apart, reassigned to other sectors and her boss, Mitchell Price, fired. Price was fighting tooth and nail to get his job back, and the Fraternal Order of Police was backing him to the hilt. They just needed time to make the case and take Metro to court.

By breaking her away from Lincoln Ross and Marcus

Wade, trying to force her sergeant, Pete Fitzgerald, into early retirement, Delores Norris guaranteed herself a spot on Taylor's shit list. But getting Taylor demoted two spots, back to detective… Well, Taylor was fighting that with her union rep strong at her side. Totalitarianism had no place in this police force, and it would, eventually, be eradicated. All it would take would be a massive mistake on the chief's part, or a mayor with the balls and fore-sight to concede his city was being torn apart.

But for the meantime, if Taylor wanted to keep her job, she had to show up in her old office and play nice. And that's exactly what she planned to do.

She was about to swipe her pass card when the door swung open. A group of young Academy cadets clattered out and down the stairs, happy and joking. One solemnly stopped and held the door for her. Once the path was cleared, she smiled at the young man and entered the CJC.

She followed the blue arrows embedded in the linoleum floor to the Homicide offices. The halls were relatively quiet and she was inside the small room within moments.

Lieutenant Elm stood in the door to her—no, his—office. His arms were crossed, his bushy brown hair smoothed into place. He greeted her with a smile, which completely caught her off guard. She almost saw his third molars as the smile widened, a pink tongue nestled deep inside.

"Good morning, Detective," he said. Pleasant, non-threatening, disarming. Taylor wasn't falling for it. Her senses went on immediate alert.

"Good morning," she said, stopping in front of him, arms behind her back, spine straight. She waited for the dressing-down, but it didn't come.

"Come into my office, if you will. I'd like to cover some ground with you." He pivoted, and entered the tiny little space that used to be her office. She followed him,

sat in the chair next to the door. There was just enough
room for her to stretch her legs out; the tip of her right
boot touched the corner of the door. Elm sat behind the
desk. The scarred wood was free of paper, the normal
detritus that built up—pens, pencils, Post-it notes, referral
sheets, call sheets—was all neatly stowed away.

Something drew her eyes to the ceiling. For as long as
she could remember, by the window, there had been a
ceiling panel with a large brown water stain on the corner.
She'd asked the facilities manager to have it replaced
countless times, and the requests had fallen on deaf ears.
But this morning, the stain was gone, the panel replaced.
She didn't know if that was a coincidence or whether Elm
had actually managed in one brief morning to do what
she'd struggled to accomplish for years. Coincidence,
she decided. No other decent explanation.

"So, Detective. We didn't get off on the right foot yesterday. And that's a shame, because I see that you have
an exemplary record and certainly are capable of taking
orders from a superior." He paused, looked around the
room like he was speaking to an audience. His gaze
finally settled back on her. "Such a shame that you've had
so much trouble lately. I assume there aren't any more,
ahem, *surprises,* in your closet?"

Taylor stared at him. "*Excuse* me?"

Elm waved her umbrage away. "You might have mentioned that the FBI agent who crashed my crime scene
last night was your fiancé."

"That has no bearing on my job. Dr. Baldwin is the
leading expert in the field of criminal profiling, and has
worked cases with Metro in the past. With great success,
I might add."

"Yes, I heard that. Don't get so defensive with me. I'm
willing to let him help with this one, so long as he doesn't

get in my way. So let's just put last night behind us and start fresh, shall we?"

He stuck a hand out across the desk.

"Morty Elm. I'm from New Orleans, I worked with the chief down there and was very happy to come onboard when this unfortunate situation warranted your, well, let's just call it disciplining, shall we?"

Before she had a chance to speak, he continued.

"I'd like to establish a few ground rules. I like to be kept informed of everything my detectives are doing, so you'll report in regularly. I prefer to read your updates, so if you'd be kind enough to turn in a detailed sheet every evening of your day's accomplishments, that will make my life grand. I'd also like a full rundown of where you stand with each of your cases, and your plans for solving them.

"I run a tight ship, so I expect you to be at your desk by eight, and to adhere to the dress code. Jeans are not suitable for my detectives. You will sign in and sign out every time you leave the office. In addition, you will find a listing of what is appropriate and what is not on your desk. I spoke with Detective McKenzie this morning, he seems like a fine young man. You have considerably more experience than he, so I trust you'll be comfortable mentoring the detective, teaching him the ropes."

"Of course."

"Then we understand each other. No more surprises at crime scenes, Detective. That's all I have for you right now. I'll expect that status report by five. You may go."

She struggled to reconcile the man with his words. Smiling and friendly this morning, making reasonable statements, yet still lobbing comments full of allusion. The shot across the bow regarding the videotapes was uncalled for. She could just imagine Elm and Delores

Norris in the Oompa's office, lights off, watching Taylor in all her glory with her dead ex-lover. She didn't know who to be more furious at—Norris, Elm, or David Martin, for putting her in the situation in the first place. If he weren't already dead, she'd like to strangle him.

Last month, after videotapes of Martin and Taylor having sex surfaced on a pay-as-you-go Web site that featured amateur, unwillingly taped pornography, she'd broken a few rules to solve the case. She was being summarily disciplined for her actions defending herself.

Elm's dictates were ridiculous. Written plans for solving her cases? It would take two weeks to write out her assumptions and thoughts on the forty or so open cases she'd caught over the past few weeks. And establishing the ground rules was one thing, but dismissing her without an update on the most current case? Sloppy. Just like she suspected, Elm wasn't there to be a cop. He was going to be an administrator. At least he wasn't fighting her about Baldwin.

She gathered herself. "You don't want—"

Elm shook his head vehemently.

"I *said* you may go. I have other duties to accomplish this morning." He gave her a brief, feral smile and nodded at the door.

She stood, biting her lip, holding back the invectives she'd prefer to spew.

"Close the door on your way out, please," he said.

She pulled the door shut a little harder than necessary and walked to her desk. There was a sheet on it, color coded, with starred items. The appropriateness list, she assumed. She balled it into a wad and tossed it into the trash unread.

She sat down hard, yanked her ponytail holder out, ran her hands through her hair, stopping for a moment to massage her temples. Elm was certifiable. One thing at a time, she told herself. Focus. Focus on the case.

If she wanted her old job back, solving this case and showing his incompetence was paramount.

She put her hair back up, took a deep breath, then pulled out a reporter's notebook and started making herself a list. There were several items that needed to be accomplished today, and she wasn't going to let King Toad get in her way.

The list was straightforward. Need to talk to neighbor again, need to talk to home owner, need to revisit the case in Manchester, file the ViCAP updates, check iAFIS for a fingerprint match and check on that palm print, gather crime-scene reports from all of the patrol officers, create the murder book, report in to Page. As she wrote, her mind slowly shifted away from Elm and onto their un-identified victim.

"You're lost in thought."

Taylor jumped. A.D.A. Page was standing by her left elbow. She hadn't heard the woman slip in.

"*Lost* is the operative word in that sentence. How are you, Julia?"

"Curious why you didn't call me the second you woke up this morning. The Love Hill case? You know I love a good serial killing in the morning."

"Jesus, don't say that. Speaking it aloud might make it come true." Taylor showed her the list she'd been drawing up. "I was just making some notes on what I'm doing on the case today. You're practically at the top of my list. See?"

"Goodie. So fill me in now instead of later."

"I don't have much to go on just yet. We've got some little bits of trace evidence, lifted some prints, but until the post is done, I won't know more."

"The press is claiming it's the beginning of a serial. They're calling him the Conductor. I want your honest assessment. Do you think this is someone who might do this again?"

Taylor noticed that Page's right eye had a blue fleck deep in the brown. She'd known the A.D.A. for years, how had she missed that? She was avoiding the answer. Page crossed her arms, preparing herself as if she already knew what Taylor was about to say.

"Yes," Taylor answered.

Page's chestnut curls bounced as she leaned against Taylor's desk. She was a small woman—leaning, she was eye level with Taylor sitting. She always made Taylor feel huge.

"Seriously?"

"Seriously. I'm going to run a ViCAP search here after the post, see if we can't find something similar out there. This was pretty sophisticated. Either he's trying to get media attention or he wants us to see how brilliant he is. But the Conductor. Where did they get the name from?"

Page gestured over her shoulder at Elm's office. "The new guy told them there was a CD playing classical music."

Taylor shook her head, pinched her fingers across the bridge of her nose. Damn it. She wanted that detail kept quiet. "You have to be kidding," she mumbled.

"Nope." She leaned a little closer to Taylor. "Are you doing okay? I know this is hard."

Taylor sat back in the chair and sighed deeply. "You're sweet to ask. I'm fine. This is just a hiccup. Besides, I like getting my hands dirty. I spent a long time on this side of the desk, it's a bit like coming home. I always did love the investigative side of the job, it was the administrative crap that was no fun. So this is the best of all possible worlds right now—I get to follow leads, do the legwork, and hopefully solve this case quickly. It's why I became a cop in the first place, you know? Right the wrongs, and all that."

Page stared at her for a moment, then patted Taylor's shoulder. "You're a gracious woman, Taylor. I'll see you later, I've got to get to court."

"Put away the bad guys, Julia. We're all counting on you."

"Bah," Page said, but grinned.

As she left, Taylor glanced at her watch—it was 9:30 a.m. Perfect timing. It would take her fifteen minutes to get to Forensic Medical. She closed the notebook, stuck it in her back pocket, and started from the room. She wasn't lying to Page; she did have a sense of nostalgia and adventure about all this. Even when she was the lieutenant, she liked to be in the trenches with her team, guiding and directing from the field, instead of from her office.

And truth be told, she'd been a stellar detective, which was a bane and a curse. Do the job too well and you get promoted, with all the attendant headaches. She couldn't deny that she missed having command of the murder squad, but she'd live. She was still a cop, with a job to do.

She negotiated the rabbit warren to the door, saw the new sign-out whiteboard nailed to the wall to the left of the door frame. She balked for a moment, then moved her magnet to "Out of Office," wrote "Forensic Medical" in the column next to her neatly printed name and walked out the door. She'd learned one thing during her thirteen years on the force. Sometimes, you pick your battles.

Seven

Gavin had a new voice mail when he returned to his studio this beautiful sunny morning. He listened to it before he shed the messenger bag slung around his shoulders. It was from the primary on his latest job. Her name was Wilhelmina, and she paid well for his services.

"Gavin, the new photos are in. Would you look at them and see what fits the Frist exhibit catalog requirements? The deadline is Tuesday, and we certainly don't want to be late. Oh, and thank you."

The thank-you was an afterthought. Wasn't that always the way?

He set his breakfast—a whole-grain bagel with organic peanut butter and a ripe banana—on his desk and started his computer. The messenger bag went on the chair next to his desk, the one covered in industrial orange-and-brown tweed. All he could afford at the time he bought it, he was pleasantly surprised to see it was more handsome than it looked online. His desk was made of solid oak, a plank, thick and sturdy, across two sawhorses. His chair—sleek, ergonomic black leather—was his prize. He could drop the arms when he needed to work at the drafting table in the corner, under the plate-glass window that over-looked the brick of the building next door.

The computer took exactly three minutes to boot up. He took the time to nibble on the banana and look at the stains of pigeon shit on the exterior ledge above his window. Amazing how they landed in such interesting shapes. It was the velocity from their flight, he knew, but still. He wondered if Jackson Pollock had been inspired by something so simple, so organic. But even an artist of his caliber couldn't reproduce that randomness.

A chime let him know his computer was booted and ready. He quickly located the e-mail from the Strozzi Palace museum in Florence. He read the brief message, the English broken but passable.

Enclosed please find pictures requested by you for the exhibit to start 11 June.

Grazie mille.

He clicked Download All and waited, watching his screen fill with shot after shot of gorgeous pictures. The Strozzi was a beautiful building, a former palace, home to the noble Strozzi family—sworn enemies of the Medicis. It was a geographical square block of stone and columns and open courtyard. He dreamed of going there one day. To see Italy, walk among the history, the beauty, gaze for hours upon the priceless artwork…

He couldn't help himself. He gazed at the Strozzi pictures, strolling through time, reveling in the detail, living through the luscious artistry of the photographer. The short angles, the presentation, the perfect balance of light to show off the art were masterful. The paintings breathed colors into his screen; the sculptures so visceral that it seemed the edge of a bicep or the length of a thigh could be stroked, the flesh alive under the finger.

The photographer on this shoot was truly superb. Gavin couldn't have done better himself. He played a game with himself. There were only three museum collection photographers he knew who were this talented.

If he were to guess… Gavin went through the photos again slowly, deliberately ignoring the line at the very bottom of the page that would give him the answer. The edging was unique, the angles for the light dramatic. It had to be the work of Tommaso.

That was his only name. Tommaso was reputed to be a difficult man to work with, but one of the most brilliant still photographers in the industry. A rock star in the art world.

Gavin snuck a look. He was right. The pictures *were* by Tommaso. A bloom of happiness spread throughout his stomach. He knew his stuff, that was for sure.

He shot a message back to Wilhelmina, acknowledging he'd received the photos and would have the catalog press-ready by the deadline. Then he started the laborious process of designing.

Gavin enjoyed his job. He was a freelance graphic designer by trade, and often did work for the printers in downtown Nashville. He did contract work for ad agencies, for sports teams, for all of the cultural corporations of Nashville. But the art photos were his true love.

His studio was off Broadway, way off Broadway, in a small storefront that butted up against the alley for a Thai restaurant. The scent of cumin and rotting cabbage was just bearable. As was the price of the shop. He couldn't work for someone directly. It was better this way.

His desired vocation was photography, but he'd found it difficult to make a living with his camera. He had skills, but his eye was no match for someone like Tommaso. So he'd started his pre-press business, typesetting catalogs and developing Web sites. His work was sought after, and he quickly rose to prominence. He was known as the quirky designer who wouldn't talk to clients, only took orders online, didn't return phone calls but sent plenty of e-mails and never, ever missed a deadline. He didn't like to talk to people if he could avoid it. There was no point. He just didn't have that much to say. He couldn't relate. To be honest, there was very little that couldn't be expressed in an e-mail.

He was good at his job, and people recognized his talents. In a few short years, he had developed a wonderful niche that made him money and allowed him to revel in art. He typeset museum catalogs. He had started small and worked his way in through a side job designing museum Web sites. Once he was established, he did exhibition catalogs and permanent collection catalogs from all over the country. A couple of years ago, he'd gotten big enough to branch into *catalogue raisonnés,* the monographs detailing the life's work of a particular artist. He'd done a lovely job with a Picasso monograph last year, and was bidding to do several more.

That reminded him, he needed to look at the status for the Millais. He scanned his e-mail, but there was nothing from the Tate Britain Gallery in London. Damn. John Everett Millais was one of his favorites, he wanted to win that job.

Nothing to worry about. His current job for Wilhelmina was a dream come true. At the moment, the Frist Center had arranged for a once-in-a-lifetime exhibit. A number of paintings from one of the art capitals of the world, Florence, Italy, were going to come to Nashville, and Gavin had been hired to do the catalogs. Which meant

oodles of stunningly beautiful pictures from three of the
most famous art galleries in the world, the Uffizi Gallery,
the Pitti Palace and the Strozzi.

He forced his attention back to the Strozzi pictures,
and started in. It didn't take long to see that one of the
photographs hadn't downloaded properly. Gavin felt it
was divine intervention. He could send an e-mail to Wilhelmina, ask her to contact the photograper and ask for
him to resend the shot. Or… Gavin felt his heart beat just
a bit harder. Why not? He'd always been an admirer of
Tommaso, there was no reason why he couldn't contact
him directly. Was there? Granted, the man was exceed-
ingly private—to the point where he refused any interview that wanted a photograph of him. Gavin wondered
if he were disfigured in some way. He could understand
the desire to let your work speak for you.

Never one to make a move without thinking it through
thoroughly first, Gavin sat back in his chair. If he con-
tacted Tommaso, there would be the slightest chance of
mentioning his own work. It might open a few more
doors; God knew the Italian worked everywhere. Tommaso's reputation was well-known all over the world. It
might give Gavin a chance to explore past Nashville.
They could become friends.

He came back down to earth with a sigh. Like that
would ever happen. His friends were all dungeon masters.

But before he lost his nerve, he filled out the contact
information on the e-mail and sent a quick note to
Tommaso's address.

Dear Tommaso,

I'm a great admirer of your work.

The catalog photographs from the Strozzi collection are utterly superb. Unfortunately, JPEG 10334 did not come through properly. Would you please resend the original shot?

Thank you so much.

G. Adler

Gavin hit send and sat back, breathing deeply. Should he have said *Ciao?* Or would that have been stupid? What had come over him? Was it too late? Could he undo the e-mail? What was he thinking?

He ran his hands across his scalp, vaguely noting that his hair was growing back. He'd have to shave again soon. No, there was nothing to be done about the e-mail now. As his mother always said, "Don't do something you might regret, Gavin." He didn't really regret it. Chances were someone as big as Tommaso had an assistant who looked at the e-mail, and the message hadn't come from him directly, anyway.

He forced the action from his mind, vowing to think about it no more. The rest of the photos were fine, he could work around the missing image for now.

He worked quietly, humming under his breath on occasion, placing photos here and there, getting the most pleasing backgrounds, choosing a variety of accent colors and washes, until he felt comfortable that his settings would showcase the photographs perfectly. This was another nice thing about working for yourself—you could spend an afternoon in contemplation of what shades really did show off the Strozzi paintings, keeping in mind the art that might be coming in from the Pitti and the

Uffizi. It was a delicate balance. He was always struck by the fragility of the ancient art pieces. Combined with the robust options the computer provided—Old World Masters and cutting-edge technologies made beautiful bedfellows.

All the information for each painting had to correspond and fit onto the pages of the catalogs: its history, dates and provenance, the artist's background, the artist's influences, who donated the cash to allow the loan to take place, every conceivable trivia tidbit was sandwiched into the pages. Small public relations kits needed to be made, and special upgraded catalogs designed for the "Friends of the Frist" to take home from the private opening. And then the catalogs would be reproduced for the Web sites and the gallery showings.

There was plenty of work to be done. Plenty to keep his mind occupied, away from the joy that awaited him at home. That was Gavin's greatest talent. He could focus. Put away one facet of his being to explore another. He'd been compartmentalizing for years.

Eight

Being a member of the Behavioral Analysis Unit meant being on call 24/7, so when Baldwin was working an actual case, there were few breaks and many sleepless nights. Part of it was the nature of the job, but it was also his fault. He couldn't turn it off. Couldn't walk away. And that was dangerous. He thought he'd been successful in pulling away a bit over the past year, setting up a home and life in Nashville, only consulting on the biggest of cases. But lately, he found himself being dragged back in, bit by bit.

The problem was, he loved it. He hated the means that brought him the cases, despised what the men and women he hunted did, was constantly amazed at the depths of human cruelty. But as a student of psychology, finding out why some sociopaths choose to become serial killers had become his vocation. His art.

The call he'd been waiting for came at 9:10 a.m. He received the news, said thank you, and set the phone back in its cradle.

The phone call confirmed it. They had a match. The same man had killed in Florence and London. He paced the house, thinking. His mind was in overdrive. Il Macellaio, the Italian serial killer who'd been operating for ten years, had finally made a huge tactical mistake.

Baldwin was tired. So very tired, and so very jazzed. Now they had the confirmation that Il Macellaio had moved his hunting grounds to London three months prior. He'd claimed three victims, all slightly out of his usual victim profile. These were working girls. In Florence, he preyed on students, and he was careful to choose girls who would go unnoticed for a time if they disappeared. Mousy, shy girls who didn't have a lot of friends.

At the beginning Baldwin assumed he flattered them, seduced them, got them to leave their lives and go home with him. He would hold them for weeks, slowly starving them, until they were so sluggish that fighting him wasn't an option. Once they died, he had sex with their bodies, then washed them and left them posed, with a print of the painting he was mocking nearby.

Necrosadism wasn't something he came across every day, though it did happen. The very act of murdering a woman to have sex with her corpse was an extreme variation of necrophilia, which many times was characterized more by fantasies of having sex with dead women than actually going through with it.

But there was something out there for every killer to devolve into, and Il Macellaio was a true necrosadist. He'd started by starving the girls, but quickly moved on to strangulation. Even then, in his later cases, the girls were given zero nourishment, no water at all, so they were weakened, couldn't put up a fight.

Il Macellaio's desire was playing havoc with his self-control. In his early days, he wasn't rushed, was able to sate his needs with a kill a year. Now, he'd gotten a taste for dead flesh, and he hastened the deaths of his victims along so he could have more time with their bodies. It was good news, in a way. When a serial killer's self-control slipped, you had a chance to catch him.

Baldwin turned back to the files on the table in front of him. The new murders in London, with the prostitutes as victims, shook him. Geographically, serial killers tend to stay in certain areas. To jump countries, well, that was a huge step.

If he had actually crossed to America as well, they'd catch him. Baldwin flipped through the pictures from the Nashville crime scene. So very familiar. The posing, the emaciated body. The one huge difference between the London and Florence killings and this possible American murder was the race of the victim.

All the overseas victims were white. This one was black. And that was enough to give Baldwin serious pause. For a sophisticated, organized serial, a well-defined signature can evolve over time, getting more specific, more exact. Killing methods are perfected, the suspect learns from each crime scene. He figures out what works and what doesn't, what turns him on and what doesn't, and adapts. Just like any predator.

But killers didn't usually start with one race then switch to another. If he'd been equal opportunity from the beginning...but Il Macellaio hadn't. He'd exclusively killed white women. At least that they knew of.

Baldwin sighed deeply. He sent an e-mail to the Macellaio task force, asking them to pull any unsolved murders of young black women in Florence or London over the past fifteen years. The carabinieri kept meticulous records; the search shouldn't take too long. The Metropolitan Police at New Scotland Yard were fully automated. They could have their answers by end of day tomorrow.

He was afraid of what those answers might be.

His phone rang, the caller ID showing a London exchange. They'd been faster than he expected.

"This is John Baldwin," he answered.

A British voice, cultured and aristocratic, said, "Dr. Baldwin? Detective Inspector James Highsmythe, Metropolitan Police. Have you seen the results of the tests you ordered?"

"I have. Nice to meet you, Highsmythe. I've heard good things."

"As have I, Dr. Baldwin. We have submitted a formal request for the FBI's help in this matter. I trust you've seen it?"

"I have."

"Then you will appreciate the nature of the request. My superiors are sending me to Quantico to give you a full briefing."

"Detective Highsmythe—"

"Do call me Memphis."

"Memphis. I'm in Nashville now, attending to a murder that looks eerily similar to Il Macellaio. Perhaps you'd like to join me here, then we can head to Quantico to meet the rest of the team?"

"Nashville?" The man sounded surprised for a moment. "He's struck in the United States as well?"

"It seems there is a possibility, yes."

"I'll see what I can do about rearranging the travel arrangements. Barring unforeseen complications, I should be there tomorrow."

"Good. I'll get you a place to stay, don't worry about that. Least I can do for dragging you down here. It will be worth your while, I think."

"I appreciate the offer. Tomorrow, then."

Nine

Before she left the house, Taylor had downloaded the Dvořák piece to her iPod. Baldwin had been converting all of her CDs over to the computer, and had installed a plug in her truck's radio so she could stick the nano in the slot and hear all of her music. It was a wide-ranging and eclectic mix, gathered over two decades. It reflected her alternative tastes, but there was a great deal of classical as well, leftover vestiges of her early days in the orchestra. She didn't play anymore, but she still loved the music.

She climbed into an unmarked pool car, wishing for her truck's speakers. She put in the earbuds, hit play and left downtown for the fifteen-minute drive to Forensic Medical. The flow of the Dvořák was calming. She liked the scherzo, forwarded to that spot. The opening was the brand music for something, she couldn't remember what. Some financial institution, something that had quick television spots that needed the grabbiness as their theme.

She forwarded again to the Allegro. The score for *Jaws* must have been based on this piece. The two-note heartbeat, the quickening pace—John Williams was obviously a Dvořák fan. It was grand, in-your-face music. She wondered what the killer was thinking when *he* chose it, then admonished herself. She didn't know for sure that he had chosen it. She pulled her to-do list out of her pocket and added a note, driving with one hand, writing on her knee. *Check with owner about CD.*

She arrived at Sam's office well before the piece ended. She sat in the car for a few minutes, letting it play out. Assuming it *was* the killer's music, why had he chosen the *New World Symphony?* Perhaps that was a message, too. If this was the same man who had committed the murders in Italy and England, why was he here in Tennessee? Did he think of it as the new world? It was such a leap, a serial killer crossing the Atlantic to start killing in her backyard with a slightly different M.O. That seemed so highly unlikely, yet Baldwin was struck by the pictures of the scene. The similarities were unmistakable. She groaned aloud when the next thought crossed her mind. Was it a copycat?

Like she needed another one of those.

ViCAP, ViCAP, ViCAP. That was the first thing she'd do when she left the postmortem. She couldn't shake the feeling that there was something more to come. Damn Julia Page and her prescient comments.

Abandoning the nano and her thoughts, Taylor entered the building on Gass Street. She couldn't help but sigh. The scents were so familiar she sometimes didn't smell them, but today she felt like she'd walked into her high school biology lab. The pervasive, artificial smell of formalin, the reek of death. It was too much to bear. She wondered how Sam did it sometimes, how she could cross the threshold of this place, day after day, and work. She left the twins at home with a nanny and became another person for ten hours a day.

Taylor wished she could do that as well. Just morph, become someone else, someone who didn't have to think about death all the time. She knew that would never happen. She wouldn't trade the idea of working with the police for anything. It was important to her to actually be who she said she was, to be the person she'd set out to be in the beginning. Four deaths on her conscience, cold-blooded murders, yet all justified. She was a cop. It was her job. These were the things that she had to do to survive, and to make the people around her, the strangers she loved, safe.

The desk was manned by Kris, a smiley girl with butter-yellow hair and too-big implants. She'd gotten them recently and they hadn't dropped yet; they stood out on her chest like overfull water balloons. She waved at Taylor and the breasts bobbled joyfully. Taylor waved back and moved to the door that led to the biovestibule that separated the administrative offices from the gut work. She swiped her card and the lock disengaged.

The locker room was empty. She covered her clothes with surgical scrubs, slipped on blue plastic clogs, then went through the smaller air lock into the autopsy suite. Renn McKenzie was sitting on a stool, gazing anywhere but at the action. Sunlight from the skylights shone down on his hair, making the blond strands at his temples glint silver.

Sam was washing the body of a teenager. She was reverent and slow; Taylor could feel her intensity, aching with the need to make it right for this young man. It was heartbreaking, watching her brush the hair back from his forehead, a thick shock of brunette shot through with lighter streaks of caramel, like he'd been in the sun for days on end. Closer inspection showed Taylor that his head was lying flat against the plastic tray. No, that wasn't right. It was just his face, straight on the table. There was nothing to the back of his head, he was practically two-dimensional.

"What happened to him?"

Sam started, looked at Taylor guiltily. Caught in the act of caring for her subject. When she realized it was just Taylor, she relaxed and went back to stroking the boy's hair. Only then did Taylor see she was actually using a fine-tooth comb to gather particles.

"Do you remember Alex, from sophomore year? My French tutor?" Sam asked.

Taylor remembered. How could she ever forget? "Yes, I do."

"Our boy here took a shotgun, put it in his mouth, and pulled the trigger. He did this to himself. The dummy. Just like Alex did."

Sam's voice was thick with emotion. Alex had been a bit more than her tutor. Sam had nursed a horrid crush on him for ages. Alex hadn't ever reciprocated her puppy love. He was a sad boy. Dark black hair and matching eyes, hidden scars inside the irises.

When they were in tenth grade, Alex could stand the torture of life no longer. He wrote a long note, explaining his actions, loaded his father's shotgun, slipped it between his lips, and shot himself. He had pulled the trigger with his toes.

It was inconceivable to them, at the time. They sat around in friends' houses, numb, drinking beer and smoking cigarettes, pondering. What could have been so bad in a fifteen-year-old's life? How had Alex's world been destroyed to the point he felt the need to take his own life? His note explained his rationale, his father's coldness, the inability to please. Taylor always suspected it was more than that, but never had the proof.

Sadness overwhelmed her. She looked at the young man on the table, wondered what drove him to despair.

"Do you know why?" Taylor asked. "What might have pushed him to this? Was there a note?"

"No, there wasn't. But there was a lot of anal tearing. It was pretty apparent that he was being abused, for a prolonged period of time. I'm not sure exactly what his story is, but he doesn't have biological parents in the state. He was a part of the foster system."

Taylor felt the fury bubble up from within her soul. "So we have foster kids being raped who kill themselves with shotguns now. Jesus, Sam."

McKenzie spun on his stool and faced them. "I had a friend kill herself. It was awful." He spun away and Taylor met Sam's eyes. That sentiment they understood all too well.

Sam signaled to one of her assistants. "Could you finish this for me? I'll be back to post him next."

She walked two tables over to the prepped body of the victim from last night, stripped off her gloves and replaced them with a fresh set.

McKenzie followed them reluctantly. "The prints are back. Her name's Allegra Johnson."

Taylor looked at the girl, so insubstantial. The steel table dwarfed her, like it would a child. The wound tract from the knife that had been buried in the girl's chest glared under the lights, an angry slit.

"She was in the system?"

"Yeah. Solicitation. *Shocking*. Skinny girl like this— drugs and prostitution were my first guess," he answered.

Sam and Taylor's eyes met again. Taylor took a deep breath. "McKenzie, kill the sarcasm. You can never assume, or guess, when it comes to a victim. You end up planting ideas in your head about them, and then you try to make the crime fit your preconceived notion of what makes sense to you. There could be other explanations for her physical appearance. She could very well be ill, or homeless, unable to feed herself. This could have been a crime of opportunity. We don't know yet why she was chosen. We won't know until we do a thorough victimology, okay?"

McKenzie's brows furrowed for a moment while he thought it out. What she said must have made sense, because his forehead smoothed and he nodded. "Okay," he said. Maybe training him wasn't going to be as hard as she expected.

Sam cleared her throat, and another tech, a quiet man named Stuart Charisse with incongruously lighthearted curly hair, appeared to help her. He started taking pictures while Sam turned on the microphone attached to her face shield, and started the case rundown. Taylor listened with half an ear as Sam gave the details—date, time, who was present, all the minutiae that was necessary to the formal autopsy process. McKenzie stood next to her, bopping his head up and down in an internal rhythm to Sam's dispassionate recitation.

Allegra's body was a mass of wretchedness. Every bone was clearly defined; Taylor could count each rib individually. The girl looked like she'd literally wasted away.

Sam started her assessment. "The body is that of a malnourished twenty-one-year-old female African-American who looks younger than her recorded age. The body was received to the medical examiner's office naked, attached by fine filament to a post measuring six feet, three-quarter inches long by ten inches square. The filament was wrapped around the forehead, wrists, torso, waist, hips, thighs and feet of the victim's body." Sam turned off the mike.

"It was a bitch and a half getting her off that post. The knife was buried two inches into the wood. We documented the whole thing, video and stills. This will be a good teaching case. I don't think I've ever seen something as bizarre."

Taylor nodded. "Good. That's the kind of stuff A.D.A. Page loves. Helps for when we catch this guy and try his ass. Was the filament holding her up fishing line?"

"I think so. Trace will tell us exactly what kind. If we're lucky, maybe he's some kind of famous bass aficionado and we'll be able to track the line to his tackle box."

"Wouldn't that be nice?"

Sam turned her mike back on and bent over her work. "The body is five foot one inches tall and weighs sixty-nine pounds. Body Mass Index is thirteen point four. The body is cachetic, with temporal wasting, prominent bone protrusions, concave abdomen. Pale oral mucosa, pale conjunctivae with some minor petechial hemorrhage. A vitreous fluid level is taken."

Taylor glanced at McKenzie, expecting him to freak, but he stood his ground and watched. Good. He was toughening up.

Sam took the victim's hand, pinched a fold of skin between her gloved thumb and forefinger and pulled gently. The skin tented and stayed that way. The silent attendant took a picture. She moved to Allegra's abdomen and repeated the action. The results were the same.

"Skin is ashy and has exceptionally poor turgor. No one can say this girl was just plain skinny. I'm seeing severe dehydration, for starters," Sam said.

Taylor nodded. "About that. Baldwin mentioned something last night. He's been dealing with a serial case in Italy."

McKenzie brightened. "Il Macellaio or Il Mostro?"

"How do you know about them?" Taylor asked.

"Oh, I follow serial-killer cases. I find them fascinating."

Ha. McKenzie didn't have a clue what it would be like to really follow a serial killer. He wouldn't be nearly as enthusiastic.

"Il Macellaio. Tell me what you know," she said.

"Well," McKenzie began, suddenly blushing at being the center of attention.

She needed to train him away from that, and fast. The minute A.D.A. Page, who was cute as a button and fierce as a shark, got him on the stand, started asking him questions and he blushed, the jury would assume he was lying.

"Relax," she said. "I'm just curious, okay?"

He continued to redden, though he nodded his head yes. "Il Macellaio likes to have sex with dead girls," he managed.

"Ugh," Sam said, but Taylor nodded her approval.

"It's actually a bit more complicated than that, McKenzie, but you're right. He's a necrosadist, a killer that murders in order to have sex with the dead victim. Very rare. And he poses his victims like famous paintings after he's through with their bodies. Which is where I was going. Baldwin said several of the earlier cases' COD was starvation, but Il Macellaio moved on to strangulation. I guess he got tired of waiting for them to die."

Sam had moved on to the next phase of her exam, had the victim in stirrups and was between her legs taking samples. "Yo, we've got lubricant here. Starvation and necrophilia, huh? Sounds like a nice guy. If that's the case for Ms. Johnson, and I can't say one way or the other until I finish the post, he'd probably need some lube to get things in the right place, if you know what I mean."

"Why?" McKenzie asked.

Sam kept working, but spoke over her shoulder to him. "When you're severely dehydrated, all your fluids dry up. All of them. Your blood thickens, your blood pressure drops dramatically, you'd feel sluggish and unable to move around. With no nourishment at all, it wouldn't take long to be dry as a chip. That's why her skin is tenting, there's no fluid in the body to help the skin return to its normal state. It would be a rough way to go. But here's our pièce de résistance. Stuart, could you help me roll her? Gently, now."

It didn't take much to get the girl over onto her face. Taylor saw the pattern on the girl's back and sucked in her breath.

Sam traced her finger along the girl's back. "Yeah. Pretty wild, huh?"

McKenzie cocked his head to the side. "Is this lividity?"

Sam shook her head. "There's a little bit of lividity, but this is more like prolonged exposure to whatever caused the pattern."

"Burns, maybe?" Taylor asked.

"Nope. I think it was something she was on. For a while. It created massive indentations in the skin, and once she died, the lividity settled in. That's the only reason we can still see it. She's been dead for a few days, you see the level of decomp. Lividity would have passed by now."

Taylor looked at McKenzie. "What time did the neighbor call it in?"

He consulted his notebook. "5:30 in the evening. Said there was no body when she came over in the morning."

The lab tech documented the scene, and Taylor moved closer to get a good look. Postmortem lividity was one of the most significant clues a cop had to determine whether a body had been moved or not. The girl's entire back, including her arms and legs, was a dusky black, much darker than her skin, with perfectly round, equally spaced cocoa-colored circles every few inches along her body. The circles were only an inch or two in diameter, and were equidistant from one another. It wasn't readily apparent at the scene, but her left arm had what looked like a seam down the outer edge, as if it were wedged against something sharp. This was past lividity, this was almost scarring.

Taylor had never seen anything like it. "It's like she has polka dots. What in the world would cause that?" she asked.

"That's something you'll need to figure out. She was certainly on her back for an extended period of time when she was still alive, lying on something that had these holes." Sam nodded to the tech and they rolled the girl over onto her back.

"Why not on the back of her arms?" McKenzie asked.

"Good question. She was shoved up against something, that's what caused that line down her arm. Maybe they were crossed on her chest? I don't know."

Taylor took a lap around the table, looking closer. The fishing line had cut into the girl's flesh and the marks were clearly visible, concentric circles around her body. "So the knife to the chest was just massive overkill? That didn't cause her death? What about the lack of blood?"

"The knife acted like an anchor. It helped hold the body up. There wasn't any blood to spill at that point; it was coagulated and her heart wasn't pumping."

Taylor nodded. "Okay. I'm comfortable with the working theory that Love Circle was the secondary crime scene. There's no way the neighbor would miss the body if it was already in the house. She seems like the type to open a few cabinets and drawers, if you know what I mean. So Allegra was killed elsewhere, then strung up on the post. But why would you do that in someone else's house? I need to talk to the home owner. That's just fishy as hell."

Sam moved toward the scalpel on the tray by her right hand. She used the blunt end to part the knife wound, pointing her finger at the meager layer of yellow just below the dermis. "This chick has zero subcutaneous fat. I mean it's less than an eighth of an inch. Starvation would certainly do that. What else did Baldwin say about this Mach guy?"

McKenzie perked up again. "Il Macellaio. The Butcher. You say it like this—eel *matcha* lie o, emphasis on the *matcha*. Though why they call him that is lost on me. He doesn't cut them up or anything."

Taylor gave the kid some points for getting the pronunciation correct.

Sam was moving along. She opened the torso and McKenzie stared in fascination at the dead girl's desiccated organs. "Are they supposed to be so gray?" he asked.

"Honestly, no. And they've atrophied, which is why they look so shrunken." Sam moved through her work, dissecting, observing, taking samples and making notes. She talked to McKenzie the whole time, explaining how starvation worked, that your system breaks down proteins, carbohydrates and fat in different sequences, that the carbs are burned first, then the fat, then the proteins. When the body starts feeding itself on the protein, or muscle mass, death occurs. In someone so small, like Allegra, death would come quicker than a full-grown, nourished, healthy woman. Without water and sustenance, death could occur in as little as a week.

Sam moved to the girl's head and Taylor turned away, purposefully letting her mind wander as the Stryker saw buzzed to life. She went back to the crime scene. Why choose a house that isn't your own? To send a message. To frame someone. To obscure your true meaning.

"Brain is unremarkable," Sam called out.

"Wouldn't the brain shrink up like the rest of the organs?" McKenzie asked.

"You'd think so, but no. Our histology slides should look relatively normal, comparatively."

"What's it like to starve to death?" McKenzie looked sad, and Taylor knew they had him. She'd been wondering what kind of detective he was going to be—blustery and sarcastic, deflecting the daily horror with sharp words, or compassionate and caring. A good detective needed to find the balance between reality and compassion. Overly involved and you burn out. Too cynical and you can't relate to the victims and can't find their killers. Finding the middle ground was something that couldn't be taught, but the look on McKenzie's face said everything. He was going to do just fine.

Sam began wrapping up. "I need to get all the tox screens back, and look at the electrolytes and the other readings. But if she did starve, it wouldn't have been pleasant. Hunger pains are one thing, but without water, she'd lose blood volume, and her blood pressure would drop. Headaches, rapid heartbeat, constant fatigue. Toward the end, muscle spasms and delirium. She would have been exceptionally sluggish, and dizzy. She wouldn't be in much of a position to fight back. T, I'll run everything, see if I can find any biologicals to test, but the body is pretty clean. Like she'd been washed, clean. Who knows, we might get lucky."

Sam nodded at McKenzie and went to wash up. Taylor tapped him on the arm and said, "Let's get out of here. You did good. I need you to track down her particulars, find out an address, see if there's anyone to do a notification to. Then call the chaplain, we have to have him with us. Let's grab something to eat and get our ducks in a row. Meet me at Rippy's?"

"Okay. I'll see you there." McKenzie left the autopsy suite dutifully, lost in thought. Taylor wondered what he was thinking.

Sam called out, "Hey, I'll get the lube tested first thing and call you later."

Taylor waved at her. "Thanks. Maybe that will tell us something about who this killer really is."

Ten

"Oh, fack off and die, why don't you?"

Detective Inspector James Highsmythe threw the phone down onto his desk. Another person who wasn't all that thrilled to hear from him, and another dead end. He'd been chasing down the murders of three of London's finer professional citizens, and was getting exactly nowhere. Calling up the known clientele of a lady of the night didn't exactly endear him, letting them know he was calling from the Met meant an immediate diatribe of invectives, about him, his mother, his education and his dog, in that order.

Well, there was nothing to be done for it. The consultation with the chap from Quantico was scheduled for three o'clock tomorrow, which meant his sorry arse needed to be at Heathrow sharpish. He'd been laboring under the illusion that he could solve the case and avoid the transatlantic flight, but that wasn't meant to be.

Nashville. He'd been through there once, as a child. His mother was an Elvis fan, and on a summer holiday his parents had taken him to Memphis to see Graceland. They had stopped in Nashville for a night, visited the Bluebird Café to hear John Hiatt sing. When he performed "Riding with the King," Memphis remembered his dear mamma tearing up. He was too young to understand then, but he had an appreciation for the irony now. And of course, the visit had launched his nickname. He had fond memories of the state of Tennessee.

He wondered if the Bluebird was still open. Well, maybe he would find time to do a quick bit of sightseeing.

His door opened a crack, and a winning smile appeared in the darkness, a veritable Cheshire cat grin. Pen, his assigned DC on the case. She was a freshly minted detective constable, and he had high hopes for her. Adorable girl. Brown hair, soft as a wren's feather, firm body, compact and tight. Pert nose and a wicked tongue. Too bad she batted for the other team.

"Memphis, you need to leave. Now. Only a half-wit would try to get out of London during rush hour and it's already past five. There were no direct flights, but we found one that has a single stop. You'll be in before midnight. I've alerted the Nashville Police that you'll be stepping on their patch."

"Wonderful. Be a darling and see if you can rustle me up some wheels, would you?"

Pen pushed her way into the office, the door swinging open and crashing into the wall behind. They both winced.

"Don't worry, I'll get maintenance to sort it out while you're gone. The car's been waiting downstairs for the last half an hour. Just promise me you'll come back? Don't get seduced by America. I don't think I have it in me to take on a replacement—not now I've got you so nicely house-trained."

"Penelope, I promise you. I'll be back. The deepest darkest corners of the earth couldn't keep me from your side for long."

"Jesus, Memphis. Do you have to call me that?" She

helped him into his coat, settling it on his shoulders. "My mum was bad enough."

"I beg your forgiveness. I just like to see you all wound up." He raised his eyebrows into what most women would interpret as an erotic leer, shed their clothes and present themselves to him. Pen simply shrugged.

"Oh, get off with you, then. Safe travels. Don't get pissed on the plane."

"And me the Queen's representative? You must be joking, darling." He grabbed his bag from the top of Pen's desk. "Cheerio."

The ride to Heathrow was blessed quiet. The driver was his favorite kind, silent, nodding his head in time to some invisible beat. He debated shuffling through his papers, decided against it. He knew the files back and forth already. Going through them again, looking at the crime-scene photos, the posing, the bones jutting out from the girl's bodies, the blackened bruises across their necks, well, those images lived in his brain already.

Security was its usual pain in the arse, the government paperwork in his bag only lessening the grief slightly. No honor among thieves anymore, what with the terror situation so wholly out of control. He made it through unscathed and settled in with a Glenfiddich at the first-class lounge. When his flight was called, he went to the gate and boarded with the first-class passengers. His seat was luxurious and the attendant handed him a glass of champagne with an inviting smile.

"Anything else I can do for you, sir?" she asked.

He met her eyes and saw the blatant invitation in them. He wondered for a moment exactly what she could do for him, then simply smiled and said, "No. Thanks."

She winked at him, then went back to the other seated passengers.

A mustachioed man in a black-and-white sailor shirt who looked suspiciously like an overweight gondolier shoved him a bit as he walked past down the aisle, and said, "Oi!" as if Memphis was at fault. Tamping down his annoyance, he distracted himself with the flight attendant, who was shooting smoldering glances over her shoulder at him. The mile-high club with a stranger, eh? The idea of it was probably much more exciting than the reality. Not like he'd really do that. Not now. Not after…well, that was no matter.

His mind was no longer there. It was lost in time, re-membering a sweet smile, blond hair tickling his chest, and the fragrant scent of citrus. Damn, he missed her.

Eleven

Back in the Caprice, Taylor accessed her voice mail. The department secretary had left her a message—Hugh Bangor, the owner of the house on Love Circle, was on his way back to Nashville on a red-eye from Los Angeles. He would be met at the plane and waiting back at the CJC within an hour. The message was left forty-five minutes earlier, which meant Bangor was already there, or close to it.

Damn. She was hungry. It was past noon. She speed-dialed McKenzie and told him to grab the sandwiches and bring them back to the homicide offices.

Flexibility. One of the most important components to being a cop. You needed to be willing to strike when the iron was hot. Self-deprivation was second nature.

She made it downtown in ten minutes flat. The super-charged engine had obligingly launched itself down the street; the drive left her feeling a little frisky. Despite the fact that Elm might be in the office, she felt good. It was always helpful to have information, to know what you were dealing with. She'd drawn a psycho, someone who'd most likely starved a woman to death, someone who may have a number of murders under his belt, but at least they had something to go on.

Allegra Johnson's presentation fascinated her. What could she have been lying on that made her back and legs look like a spotted cow? Taylor ran through some of the possibilities then discarded them immediately. Who knew? They'd have to find the primary crime scene, then they'd have a chance at figuring out that piece of the puzzle.

She made her way to the homicide offices and stopped at her desk. A Post-it was stuck to her phone—*Bangor, Inter. 1.* She grabbed the note and balled it up. Her desk phone rang, but she ignored it. Her mind was already getting into the interview with Bangor.

She stopped at the whiteboard, erased her earlier status and marked that she was in the conference room. This level of accountability was going to drive her mad.

The walk to the interrogation room was short. She stopped at the soda machine and grabbed two Diet Cokes. Her cell rang, and she juggled the cans trying to get it out of her pocket. She didn't recognize the caller ID, but answered anyway.

There was static, and then a loud clanging. The scream of a bird rent the air. She had just enough time to think *seagull* before the phone went dead.

Damn it. She leaned back against the wall, stared down at the tiny screen of the cell phone, chills skittering through her body. What, the Pretender had her cell phone number, too? She bit her lip. When was this going to end?

The phone rang again, and she jumped. When she answered, she didn't say anything, just listened. The same noises, loud clanging, followed by a deep voice cursing, one that she readily recognized. Not the Pretender. Oh, thank God.

"Fitz? Is that you?"

Pete Fitzgerald, her former number two, was yelling, the background noise nearly drowning out his deep baritone. He was off with his girlfriend, sailing around the Caribbean islands while he decided whether to take the enforced retirement Delores Norris had arranged, or join the lawsuit and get his old job back. Sailing, for God's sake. That's what love did to you. It took a perfectly normal cop and put him on a forty-two footer with a rum drink and a bikini-clad cohort. Taylor couldn't begin to imagine that scene. Honestly, she didn't want to.

"Taylor?"

"I'm here. Is everything okay?" She was yelling, too, as if that would help him hear her.

"Yeah, think so. Just saw something strange, thought I should tell you about it. How's the fed?"

"Baldwin's fine. Working in town for the moment. What did you see?"

There was more squawking, another series of shrill sounds from the gulls. Fitz's voice was breaking up, the connection getting worse. She plugged her left ear, dropping the Coke cans with a clatter.

"What was that? I couldn't hear you. Where the hell are you, anyway?"

"…Ados."

"Barbados? Nice work if you can get it. It's good to hear from you."

The signal cleared at last, and Fitz came through like a foghorn.

"Yeah. It's beautiful down here. Listen, just wanted to give you a heads up. There was a guy following us. Gave me the creeps. Tall, tan, super-short jarhead bristle cut. Sound familiar?"

"Quit yelling. Yes, it does. The Pretender looks like that."

"I know. I saw the composite you and Owens put together." Fitz was forever calling Sam Loughley by her maiden name. Fitz wasn't a big fan of change. "This guy was pretty much a dead ringer."

Taylor went back into the homicide office, leaving the cokes abandoned on the floor. A small frisson of panic started moving through her body. "Tell me everything. I can, well, I don't know what I can do, but…just tell me what you saw."

"That's it, little girl. Don't have any more for you. Susie and I are docked in port, waiting on a part. Last stop was St. Lucia, last week. Didn't see him there, so this might just be a coincidence."

Coincidence. Like she believed that.

"So he followed you around in port?"

"No. He followed Susie. She was looking for some sort of conch to make for dinner, was coming out of a shop. I was watching from the boat, through binoculars. He walked right up to her, bumped into her, apologized, helped her pick up her stuff. Then he looked right at me, and I swear to God the sumbitch smiled. I woulda shot his sorry ass, but he was too far away. Then he strolled around a corner and disappeared. I got Susie back on the boat, but we've got a broken raw water pump, are waitin' for a new impeller, which means we're stuck here until the damn thing clears customs. Had to ship it down from Fort Lauderdale."

"Huh? Fitz, you know I'm not a boat person."

"We got no juice 'cause we can't cool the engine. We can't sail until it's fixed—we got no GPS, no depth finder, none of that. We're anchored in the harbor, so we're safe enough, and I'm watching for him. No one can get to us without pulling up next to the boat. I left word with the local constabulary, but they can't do anything. We're safe, no worries. He's probably already long gone. But I just wanted you to know."

Safe. Like that word could ever be applied to the same sentence as the Pretender.

"You need to check in with me, let me know what's happening. Now you have me worried, old man. When are you due back?"

"Next week. I'll let you know if I see anything else. I gotta go, the connection's for shit on this crappy cell phone. And it's costing me four bucks a minute. Be good. And don'tcha worry. I can take care of myself." There was a loud click, and her ear filled with static. She turned her phone off, slapped the cover shut.

Friend, mentor, father figure, Fitz was all these things and more to Taylor. Hitting him would be as close a blow as hitting Baldwin. The Pretender knew that. He was stalking her through her friends.

Rage bubbled into her mind, blackening the edges. One more instance of her life catapulting out of her control.

How had he known where Fitz was going to be? He was obviously keeping tabs on more than just Taylor. And how could he be cognizant of a murder in Nashville while in Barbados?

An itinerary. She went back to her desk, took out her directory. Bob Parks was one of her favorite patrol officers, and a good friend of Fitz's. She called his cell, and he answered with what she could tell was his trademark grin.

"Loot! How the hell are ya?"

"Wishing I was still a Loot, Parks. I need a favor."

She gave him the instructions, thanked him and hung up. Parks could hit Fitz's house, see if anything had been disturbed, while she did her interview with Bangor.

She stared out the window for a long minute, then made two more calls. She got voice mail for both

Lincoln Ross and Marcus Wade, left messages asking them to meet her after work. If the Pretender wanted to start playing games, they needed to be wary as well. She called Baldwin too, left him a voice mail. Jesus, where was everyone? She had a brief, horrifying moment imagining that they were all gone, disappeared, then shook it off. That was silly. She didn't have to worry about them.

McKenzie appeared in the doorway to the homicide offices.

"Um, Jackson? Are you coming? I've got food in the conference room, and Bangor is getting antsy. I've talked to the chaplain, he can meet us after 3:00 to do a notification. I'm still tracking down the vic's address."

She looked at McKenzie, wondered how much warning she should give him. Later, she decided.

Food. Suspect. Food. Suspect. She sighed.

"I'm coming," she said, abandoning her troubles at her desk.

Hugh Bangor wasn't anything like Taylor was expecting. And here she'd been telling McKenzie not to make assumptions.

His presence filled the interrogation room with energy. He was in his early to mid-forties, small, dapper and prematurely gray. He jumped to his feet and greeted her with a warm handshake. She was immediately at ease with the man, a dangerous sign. Complacence could get her in serious trouble. But his smile was friendly, his face affable, and she'd spent her whole life reading people. Nothing set off her alarm bells, so she returned the handshake cordially and gestured to the chair for him to sit.

She rattled off the date and time, stated that she and Detective Renn McKenzie were in the room, and what they were there for so the session would be duly documented. She felt a bit like Sam at one of her autopsies.

"Mr. Bangor, I'm Detective Taylor Jackson," she started.

Bangor interrupted. "I know. I've lived in Nashville all my life. We've never met, but I've always been a fan."

She bristled, went on the defensive, looked for the hidden innuendo behind his words. Was he joking with her? Had he seen the tapes? Seen her in flagrante delicto all over the evening news?

Bangor sat a little straighter in his chair. "This is being taped, correct? Let me just say, for the *record,* that I think your treatment has been deplorable, and the chief of police should be indicted for his incredible mismanagement of our police force. You don't deserve to be back at detective. I thought your demotion was petty and ridiculous."

Oh, she liked this guy. Immensely.

But she restrained her smile. "Thank you. That's very kind."

Bangor settled back in his chair with a satisfied nod. "Just so you know where I stand, ma'am."

"Can you tell me a bit about yourself, Mr. Bangor?"

"I'm a screenwriter. Actually, I've become more of a script doctor these days."

"What's a script doctor?" McKenzie asked.

"Just what it sounds like, Detective. I take scripts that have potential but aren't ready to shoot and make them sing. Not to brag on myself, but there it is."

"What took you to California? A script?"

"Yes. I've been working on a piece for a friend, needed to give it a walk-through with the writers. I left last Monday, wasn't planning to return until this Friday. What exactly happened at my house, if you don't mind me asking?"

"What have you heard?" Taylor asked.

He raised an eyebrow. "Miss Carol, my neighbor, told me that a young girl was murdered in my home. I'm just sick about it. I don't know who did it, and I assure you, I can't imagine why someone would break into my house and leave a dead girl behind."

"Where were you last night? I don't mean to be rude, Mr. Bangor, but can people corroborate your whereabouts?"

He gestured to a black leather briefcase that sat at his feet. "May I?"

"By all means."

Bangor rooted in the briefcase for a moment, then brought out a green folder. "This is my travel folder, where I keep all of my receipts. I've been on my friend's dime, and I get a nice per diem, which means I need to keep track of the records for my income tax. I keep everything."

He handed the folder to Taylor. She opened it and flipped through, speaking aloud to catalog the contents for the record. Bangor wasn't kidding; he was perfectly covered.

"Restaurant receipts, coded by date, people attending the meal, valet stubs, car-service receipts, all dated for the period in which Mr. Bangor states he was away from home. Wish I could be this organized." She set the folder on the table. "I'm sure you understand that we'll still have to check these items out."

"Of course. I've alerted my business manager, and my lawyer, that you'll be contacting them. I've included their phone numbers in that folder. You can keep it, I've got copies. Anal-retentive, that's me." He laughed, and she fought the urge to laugh with him. Disarming, and charming as Mr. Bangor was, he was still a suspect.

"Thank you for making it easy for us, Mr. Bangor. Tell me, how does a Hollywood screen doctor find himself living in Nashville instead of Hollywood?"

"Who could leave? I'm a native. Born and bred. I've

been in and out of the house on Love Hill since I was a baby. It was my grandparents', they built it when they moved to Nashville. My parents moved in after my grandparents passed, and they left it to me when they retired ten years ago to Florida. I renovated and made it my own."

"And the Picasso reproduction? Did you inherit that too?"

Bangor's eyebrows went higher, and Taylor noticed the fine shape of them, arching above his brown eyes. His nails were cleaned and buffed, his skin firm and tanned. The haircut was expensive, the clothes very fine. He was a well-kept man. Either the parents had been well-off, or he was good at his doctoring.

"*Desmoiselles D'Avignon?* Did the…person who invaded my home take it?"

"Not exactly," Taylor said. "It is a beautifully done piece."

"It is at that. You have a good eye. There's a great story behind it. The painting was done by a starving art student who made a great deal of money copying the works of the masters for a very well-heeled New York clientele. People who want the world to think they hold the original. This particular painting was part of a collection owned by the late George Wilson."

"The philanthropist? I thought he left everything to his dogs."

Bangor smiled. "Everything but the art collection. He had some beautiful genuine pieces, a Chagall I coveted but couldn't afford, and some wonderful copies, including the Picasso. They auctioned off the collection, and I bought the Picasso. That was fifteen years ago. I adore art, as I'm sure you noticed. I started collecting when I was in my twenties, bought a small line drawing with my very first screenplay paycheck. Granted, it wasn't much, but my interests grew from there. I have some originals of my own now. But the Picasso is my finest reproduction piece."

"How much would you pay for an imitation?" Taylor asked.

"I paid $10,000 for my *Desmoiselles.*"

"Ten grand for a fake? Wow."

"It's a lot of money, I know, but considering the quality and the backstory, I felt it was worth more. This is more common than you know. It's not black market, but it comes close. There are a number of pieces that make it all the way to auction, provenance intact, that are fakes. It takes a true master to know the difference. That's why Sotheby's and Christie's are who they are."

McKenzie was scratching notes in his reporter's notebook. "So where's the original?"

Bangor smiled at him. "The Museum of Modern Art in New York. It toured through here in an exhibit a while back, but it's a part of their permanent collection."

"Who would know about the Picasso, Mr. Bangor?" Taylor asked.

"That it's a reproduction? Anyone with any knowledge of art would know that, it's a terribly famous painting."

"I meant that you have it in the first place."

"Oh, I see. Well, any guest in my home for the past fifteen years, I suppose. It's not exactly a secret. Detective, why the interest in the Picasso, may I ask? I heard that there was some damage done to the house, but I haven't gotten the details. Was the painting desecrated?"

"In a way," Taylor said, and Bangor sucked in his breath.

McKenzie jumped into the fray. "The painting is fine. The victim was posed like the women in the painting." McKenzie started to speak again, but Taylor glared at him and he stopped. Jeez, give it all away, why don't you?

"Posed?" Bangor asked.

Taylor waved his question away. "Right now, Mr. Bangor, we'd like to take you back to the house so you can show us if anything is missing or otherwise disturbed. We can go into the details there."

Bangor sat forward in his chair and stroked his chin. "You know, about a year ago, I was broken into. The thieves were after cash, they trashed the house but didn't give the art a second glance. Pity, really. Our criminals are so uneducated these days."

"You reported it?"

"I surely did. There's a report on file. I wonder if this might be the same people? Though a year later? Probably not. That was a silly thought."

"No thoughts are silly, Mr. Bangor. Detective McKenzie will check that out. You never know. If you'd be so kind as to wait for me for a few moments, I have a few things to take care of, then we can run out to the house. Okay?"

"Certainly. Do what you need to do. Could I possibly have a drink while I wait? I'm a bit dehydrated from the plane."

Shit, the cokes. She'd forgotten them in the hallway. "I'll have something for you in a jiff. Coffee? Water? Coke?"

"A coke would be great. Diet, if you have it."

Taylor nodded, then stood. "Detective Taylor Jackson, terminating interview number 2009-1397 with Mr. Hugh Bangor," she said, then used the remote control to turn off the tape. She stepped out of the room, let McKenzie come out and shut the door before she addressed him.

"Be sure you give him the can, and save it. I want to print him, and get a DNA sample. Chances are he's going to cooperate with that, but just in case. When you're done, get moving on the family of the Johnson girl. And Mc-

Kenzie? Don't ever offer up details of a crime to a suspect without my okay again, okay?"

"Yes," he mumbled. "I won't do it again. I'll just go get his coke."

She watched him walk off, shoulders hunched, and sighed. She didn't think Bangor had anything to do with this, and knew McKenzie had followed her cues when he misspoke. No real harm done.

Too many things to do. Before she went any further, she needed to load a search into the ViCAP system. It was moments like this that she missed Lincoln Ross. He would have already taken the initiative, plugged in the information, added in parameters that Taylor herself wouldn't think of, and have the results to her *before* she'd gone to autopsy.

McKenzie was green, and while she was technically his superior, he was just another detective, like her. It wasn't like she could give him orders and leave him behind to work on things. He was her partner, needed to be coached and coddled, brought along on everything. Elm's orders. Damn it.

She stepped into the conference room and retrieved her now-cold barbecue sandwich. She tossed the beans—they'd be gross unheated and she didn't want to waste time getting to the microwave in their tiny, utilitarian office kitchen—but the pulled pork would be fine.

She took it with her and ate it in the hallway, leaning against the glass case that held the departmental bulletins. When she finished, she wiped her lips with the back of her hand and stared at a Missing poster of a thirteen-year-old girl and her baby. The poster had a NOTES section at the bottom stating the girl's arms were scarred from repetitive cutting. No kidding. Thirteen, with a two-month-old baby? Yeah, there was a good chance that child was completely screwed up, would do anything to get some positive attention. At least her family had filed an MP report; so many families didn't. Which led her back to Allegra Johnson. Who was missing her?

She jotted down the thought in her notebook's to-do list: Look through the missing-persons reports for the past two months.

The computer room was housed three doors down from interrogation room one. She unlocked the door, turned on the light, and took the computer out of sleep mode. They all had their personal computers on the desk, but fingerprint searches in iAFIS and requests to the FBI's Violent Criminal Apprehension Program had to run through a separate system that was tied to the state and federal databases. Antiquated systems out here in the field, but at least Lincoln had set these computers to go as quickly as was humanly allowed.

Within twenty minutes, she hit Send. The questionnaire was forty pages long, but she didn't have a lot to go on, would update the file as more information came in. She filled out the forms as completely as she could, using her notes when necessary. She included the photos she'd forwarded to her work address. Having the crime-scene pictures would help with the analysis.

She asked for three separate searches. One, for art thefts in the metro Nashville area. Two, for any murders that might have an artistic component to them, with music or paintings or sculpture. And third, for murders in which the victims were starved to death. They'd process while she and McKenzie took Bangor back to his house.

That was the trick with ViCAP. You needed to give it parameters to search within, but keep them focused enough that it wouldn't be a wild-goose chase. She wished it would spit back answers, but instead it looked at trends, which she'd need to interpret.

But just in case something fantastically close to their murder popped out… She left a note for Rowena Wright, the department administrator, that she was expecting the results back on a ViCAP search. Rowena was a jovial black woman who'd been a cop before Taylor was born, blazing a trail that Taylor was honored to follow. Rowena had started in admin, then became a patrol officer, a training officer, passed the sergeant's exam and nearly made detective before a mild heart attack forced her to step out of the field. There weren't a lot of people that Taylor trusted around headquarters these days, but Rowena was one of them.

When she made it back to the interrogation room, McKenzie was passing Hugh Bangor a hand wipe. He turned to greet Taylor with a big smile.

"Mr. Bangor was happy to give us his fingerprints and a DNA swab for comparison."

"That's good. Excuse us for a moment?"

Bangor smiled. He knew the score. She stepped out in the hall with McKenzie. "What did you find on Allegra Johnson?"

"Nothing much. There's an address listed on one of her arrests, down in one of the projects. I cross-checked it, and it's also listed as the address for three other people with arrest records. Either she was in with a bad crowd, or they're using the address as a fake."

"Okay. We'll do this thing with Bangor, then head down there. Father Victor is available to go, just in case?"

"Yes. He said to call him whenever you were ready, he'd meet us there. He seems like a nice guy."

"He is. You haven't met him yet?"

"No. Never had cause."

"You've never done a notification?" she asked, incredulous.

"No. Everyone always sends me off to do something while they handle the family. So if she has any, this will be my first."

"How old are you, exactly, McKenzie?"

"I'll be twenty-seven here in another month."

Twenty-six, and already a detective. She'd thought he was older. They'd moved him along quickly. She wondered why.

"Okay. Let's do this."

They retrieved Bangor from the interrogation room.

As they walked to the car, Bangor tried to make conversation. "Detective McKenzie here was just telling me he used to have a girlfriend who was quite a fine artist."

"Um, yes, sir. I did." He looked at Taylor apologetically, as if he'd been caught doing something very bad.

"What kind of artist was she, McKenzie?" Taylor asked, openly forgiving him so he'd relax. No harm done letting the man see a little compassion from her this morning.

"Oils, mostly, and some pastels. She was very good."

They walked out into the parking lot, and Taylor realized she hadn't signed out. *Tough beans, Elm.*

"*Was* very good?" Bangor asked, gently. Taylor had missed something. McKenzie looked like he might cry.

"Um, she's dead. She killed herself. Today's actually the anniversary."

Oh. That was the same girl he was talking about this morning at the autopsy, Taylor figured. Poor kid. Never good to lose someone you loved.

Bangor obviously felt the same. He clapped McKenzie on the shoulder in sympathy.

"I lost my partner five years ago." Bangor hesitated for a moment, then said, "AIDS."

McKenzie just nodded, didn't say anything. Taylor looked at Bangor again. She hadn't picked up that he was gay. Polished, certainly, but he had no affectation, no femininity about him. That made life a little less complicated. This crime screamed hetero, man on woman violence. Bangor was most likely not their suspect. Taylor had already gotten that sense, but the biographical details helped solidify her conclusions.

The drive out West End to Love Hill was quick, with Bangor regaling them with stories of famous actors who were in fact gay despite all appearances.

When Taylor made the left onto Love Circle and wound her way up the hill, she was shocked. Last night, in the dark, it still held that romantic feel. In the harsh light of day, she could see how run-down the Hill had actually become. Trash littered the grassy banks of the park, some graffiti on the electric transformer box had been inexpertly painted over. A ragged chain-link fence was sagging in spots, bearing the kick marks of some drunken youth. It wasn't the Hill she remembered, and she remarked on that to Bangor.

"Yes, it's been hard to keep the vagrants out of the park at night. It's so quiet, and there aren't a lot of patrols through here. We force them out, they reappear. The kids who come up here aren't the nicest element. Between them and the break-in, I'm glad for my security system."

"We didn't get any alarms from your system last night. Is it possible that you left it off when you left town?"

"No. I'm religious about setting the alarm. But it's entirely possible that Miss Carol failed to turn it back on. She was taking care of Sebastian for me, and sometimes she forgets. It's happened before."

Taylor glanced at McKenzie. That matched the neighbor's statement, at least. Convenient that the alarm was turned off. She wondered if the killer knew there would be a good chance of that, or if he'd come prepared to disengage the system. That would speak to an even higher level of intelligence than she'd previously thought. And a more personal connection to Hugh Bangor.

In the daylight, Bangor's home was a sharp contrast to the surrounding grime. The lawn was neat and well-cared for, though trampled a bit by the multitudes of law enforcement who'd been tromping through it all night.

The crime-scene tape fluttered around the porch. Taylor unwound it from the support columns and let Bangor and McKenzie pass. Once inside, Bangor immediately tensed. Taylor watched his reaction with interest, wondered briefly whether they were going to have an issue. But Bangor merely shook his head, and turned to her with his eyebrow raised.

"I'm missing something rather dramatic, aren't I? What happened to my post?"

Taylor looked at McKenzie. "Go ahead," she said.

"The victim was pinned to the post with a knife. We had to take it with us to preserve the integrity of the wound tract."

"My God. Who could do such a thing? You'll replace it, won't you?" Bangor asked.

Taylor nodded. "I'm sure we'll be able to figure something out. Destruction of private property isn't in our purview. We didn't have a choice last night."

"Fair enough."

They moved to the back door, where Taylor showed him the cutout piece of glass.

Bangor tsked. "This is just so violating."

Taylor touched his arm. "I know it's hard. Just bear with us a little longer."

They drifted toward the kitchen as they talked.

"Are you a fan of Dvořák?" she asked.

He cocked his head to the side. "Actually, not so much. I'm more of an Outlaws type—good old country music.

Did you know that John Rich built that house down the street? He's a very nice man. I'm not a big fan of his music, there's a bit too much ego in it, but he's been a good neighbor. Raised the property values, at least."

"That always helps. Do you have any Dvořák CDs?"

"No." Bangor sat heavily at his kitchen table. "Why?"

"There was a Dvořák CD in your wall system here, playing on a loop last night."

"Now that's one I know I had nothing to do with. I left it on Lightning 100. Sebastian likes alternative rock, I usually leave it on for him while I'm away. Maybe it's his?"

"The cat?" McKenzie looked serious all of a sudden, but Taylor laughed.

"Now there's a scenario I haven't encountered in a murder investigation. The cat did it."

McKenzie got the joke and joined the laughter, a little too strongly.

"Maybe the cat will solve it. Do you know where Sebastian is?" Bangor asked.

"Your neighbor took him to her house last night."

"Too bad I'm not a cat whisperer. That would make life easy. He could tell me what he saw." Bangor grew serious. "I'm sorry for that girl, whoever she is. Do you know her name?"

Taylor nodded at McKenzie, who replied, "It's Allegra Johnson."

Bangor shook his head. "I don't know anyone of that name, though it's beautiful. Maybe I'll put her in a piece one of these days, as a memorial. My God. Did she die right here?"

He was staring at the invisible column as if he could imagine the scene from the previous night. Taylor was glad that he couldn't; it wasn't one she'd soon forget.

"No, sir. I don't believe she did. Do me a favor and take

a quick look around. If you don't see anything else out of place, we're going to get out of your hair."

Bangor searched the house for five minutes, then returned to the kitchen shaking his head. "Nothing. It's all here except for the book from my coffee table. Do you think I'm in any danger?"

Taylor shook her head. "We took the Picasso monograph for examination. I don't think you're in danger, but I can't say one way or another. I'm reluctant to jump to the conclusion that someone was sending you a message, but that may be the case. I'd appreciate it if you did some sleuthing of your own, look into your e-mails and correspondence for the past few days, see if anyone made threatening gestures. Maybe someone involved in your screenwriting didn't like what you had to say about their work?"

Bangor smiled. "I'm actually to the point where young screenwriters fight to have me play with their words. They are usually more sycophantic rather than threatened. But I'll give it some thought."

"Okay, then. I appreciate your cooperation. And I'd appreciate you keeping the information I gave you to yourself."

"Can I go back to the coast?"

"Stick around for another day or so, while we check some things. We'll be in touch."

Bangor walked them out. "I'm going to go get Sebastian, bring him home. Thank you for being so cautious. I appreciate how difficult this must be."

They shook hands. Taylor and McKenzie got into the vehicle. She watched Bangor knock on Carol Parker's door and go inside, heard the loud meowing of the cat in the background. A happy homecoming for one member of the family, at least.

"He didn't have anything to do with it, did he? He seems like a really nice guy." McKenzie was fiddling with the crease in his slacks, running his thumb obsessively over the edge.

"Probably not, but that doesn't mean someone wasn't sending him a very clear message."

"Made him an offer he couldn't refuse?"

"Why McKenzie, I never pegged you for a *Godfather* fan."

She put the car in gear and drove. Someone was sending Hugh Bangor a message. And she needed to find out who it was before he tried again.

Twelve

The J. C. Napier Homes were one of Nashville's nastiest projects. Many of the city's homicides happened there; Napier and its fellow, the Tony Sedekum Homes, accounted for half of the arrests in all the housing projects in Davidson County. Poverty begat deeper levels of poverty. Guns were rampant. Some murders and assaults were fueled by drugs, most others by desperation. Whatever the cause, the effect was that the Napier projects saw nearly thirty percent of all the murders in Nashville in a given year.

The patrols in these projects were on bikes— the streets were few and far apart, running lengthways. There was little to no access between the buildings and courtyards. On bikes, they had a chance. But it was dangerous work. The residents didn't have much hope, anyway. Taking potshots at cops was a favorite pastime.

Taylor's window was down; she heard the usual catcalls. She smelled burning garbage: another boredom-killer on warm summer days, setting fire to the Dumpsters. In these projects, men, women and children roamed the streets aimlessly at all hours of the day and night, talking, watching, being. The typical crowd gathered around her Caprice; McKenzie grew pale under his already light complexion.

"Ignore them. They're just playing." But she put the window up.

"It's not that. How can people live like this?"

Taylor glanced at him. "Do you think they have another choice?"

"Yes. They could try. They could get a job instead of having babies so they can collect more food stamps for beer. Have you ever been inside one of their apartments? They've got better electronics than most yuppies. Where's the money coming from? Certainly nothing legal. And if they have enough to trick out their homes, why in the world would they choose to live here? I've never understood it."

That was quite a speech.

"To use a terrible cliché, McKenzie, it's not that black and white. I want all of them to get jobs, as well, to stop running crack and heroin, to clean this shit place up and try to make a better life. You give them driveways and pretty houses, the crime rates dwindle. Look at what HUD did with the Hope IV grants—John Henry Hale, Preston Taylor, Vine Hill are all clean, safe places. It's amazing the difference architecture and bright colors can make. But down here, they're still in the land time forgot. The power of a few overrides the desires of the many. They're scared. They've been brainwashed not to trust anyone who wants to help them. The dealers and pimps threaten the women, rape them, force them into this life. They terrorize the children, conscript them into the game by making them run the drugs from the buy to the sale. I agree, they should want out, and I applaud the ones who try. It's sad, but it's out of our hands. All we can do is enforce the law to the best of our abilities."

Father Victor's Chevy Lumina slid in behind Taylor's Caprice. She and McKenzie got out of the car and met him by the trunk. It was department policy that a clergy member attend all death notifications. It was a welcome policy; having a spiritual guide along certainly helped.

"Ready?" she asked the chaplain.

"As I'll ever be. Detective McKenzie? I'm Father Victor." The two men shook hands. The chaplain's blue eyes were sad, and Taylor realized that he'd started to go gray. His predecessor, Father Ross, had been stolen away by a diocese in Maine just two weeks earlier. Father Victor had been the backup chaplain. But Taylor knew the Father from around town. He'd been a fixture in the archdiocese for years, was a priest at the Cathedral. She knew he was in his late forties, but didn't know his exact age.

"It's good to meet you, sir," McKenzie replied. Taylor glanced at him sharply. He seemed deferential to the priest. Catholic, maybe? With a name like McKenzie, it was a good chance.

They turned to the building that hopefully housed some answers about Allegra Johnson.

Taylor ignored the rude gestures, the propositions and threats. She walked through the manufactured similitude of the run-down buildings to the front door. The screen was cut. The wooden door stood open. The homes had been renovated just a few years earlier; they were already falling in on themselves again. No one cared enough to worry about upkeep.

They knocked. A cracked voice yelled, "Come in."

Taylor rested her hand lightly on her weapon, just force of habit entering a strange building. They entered the cramped ground-floor apartment. The walls were paneled with dark walnut. Lace curtains, yellowed with cigarette smoke, hung limply over the window. Taylor could see a bullet hole in one pane. The carpet was a dirty orange shag, about a million years old, that didn't quite reach the four corners of the room. Fetid despair hung from every corner like deserted cobwebs.

Wrinkling her nose, Taylor took the four steps that led her into the kitchen. Small things scuttled away from her feet—mice, roaches, silverfish? Taylor didn't know, didn't want to know. She immediately realized why the home was such a mess—there was an old woman sitting at the tiny, unstable kitchen table. Her eyes were milky white, made more opaque by the contrast with her blue-black skin. She was old, very, very old. Her blind eyes searching for her guests. Taylor bit back a curse. The woman should be in a home with people to take care of her, not living on her own.

There was something akin to recognition behind the woman's blank eyes. For a moment, it seemed they were alone, just the two of them in the putrid little kitchen. She looked right into Taylor's soul. Taylor got goose bumps, rubbed her hands up and down her arms to shake off the creepy feeing. She stopped a foot away and didn't stretch out her hand to shake.

"Ma'am? I'm Detective Jackson with Metro Homicide. This is Detective McKenzie, and our chaplain, Father Victor. Do you know a young woman by the name of Allegra Johnson?"

"She dead?" the woman asked.

"Ma'am, are you related to Miss Johnson?"

"She my grandbaby. She dead?" she asked again.

"What's your full name, ma'am?" Father Victor asked softly.

"Ethel Johnson. My girl's dead," she said with finality, then started to cry, silent and haunting, tears slipping unchecked down her mahogany cheeks.

Taylor recognized the tone in the old woman's voice. Despair, tinged with irony. With the knowledge that there would be no other reason for a police officer to be in her home other than to inform with bad news. Her shoulders slumped a little, and Taylor moved closer. She hated that she had to bring a lonely old woman so much pain, but she had to press on, needed to get as much information as she could.

"Yes, ma'am. We found Allegra's body late yesterday. We matched her fingerprints to prints in the system this morning." Taylor had brought a picture to do the notification, a morgue shot, but that was a moot point. "Is there any way we could do a formal identification? A picture of Allegra, perhaps? We want to be absolutely sure we're talking about the same girl."

"Gots a picture in her bedroom down the hall. That should do it for you. That Tyrone finally beat her to death, huh?"

"Who is Tyrone, ma'am? Her boyfriend?"

"Haw," the woman spit out. "Boyfriend. Girl, child like that, she got herself a pimp. A sugar daddy. Tyrone Hill been whoring her out, give her the drugs. Allegra been acting a fool for a while now. I told her it would come to no good. I told her that man would kill her, one way or the other. She don't listen to her Gran, though."

"Do her parents live close by?"

"Her daddy's in Riverbend. Three strikes. Her momma done died when she was ten. I been raisin' her since. Best I can, leastways. The good Lord don't always give us the right tools to do His bidding." She waved a hand toward her face. Prophetic blindness, it seemed.

A young woman, probably in her late teens, came through the front door into the kitchen with a baby on her hip. Curiosity was obviously getting the better of the neighborhood.

She stopped in the doorway to the kitchen. "Miss Ethel, what's dis about? Why da police here?"

The grandmother just snorted. Taylor reintroduced herself.

"May I ask your name, miss?" Taylor said.

The woman regarded her suspiciously for a few moments, then said, "D'Andra. I'm her cousin. Allegra be dead?"

"Yes," Taylor answered.

"She hurt bad?"

Taylor glanced at the grandmother, who was leaning forward a bit. She had no intention of going into detail, but she still hated this part.

"Allegra was very, very thin. We don't have all the answers, but it seems she starved to death. Did she ever have any issues with anorexia?"

D'Andra just looked at her like she was an idiot. The baby started to squirm, and she set it down on the filthy floor. It scooted under the table on all fours. Jesus.

"Let's back up. When was the last time you saw Allegra?"

"She been gone for ages," D'Andra said.

"How long is ages? Weeks? Months?"

"'Bout three weeks."

"And you didn't report her missing?" McKenzie asked.

This time both women laughed joylessly. D'Andra spoke first. "Why would we go and do something like dat? Din't know if she were off with her man, or what. Like you'd ever even give a shit to look for her? Come on, brother. I weren't born yestaday."

Taylor looked into the woman's eyes. The whites were yellowed and bloodshot, the brown coagulated. Track marks cruised up and down her arms. Lacking hope, so many of these women sought refuge in drugs.

It usually became so bad that they'd do just about anything to get their fix.

"I would have looked for her, if I'd known," Taylor said.

"Yaw, sure. I believe that. Where Allegra be now?"

"At the medical examiner's." Taylor turned back to Allegra's grandmother. "Once we're finished, she can be released to you, ma'am."

She looked confused. "To me? What would I do wit her?"

"Bury her, perhaps. Give her some peace. She deserves that much," the chaplain said.

They both shook their heads. D'Andra spoke quietly. "Ah, hell, preacher man, we don't have money for dat. You folks get her in the ground. She be your problem now."

Taylor watched as she scooped up the baby, who was gnawing on its dirty fist, and walked out into the sparse backyard. Shoulders slumped, head down. Another generation oppressed by drugs and poverty. God, it was depressing out here in the projects.

McKenzie was busy scribbling in his notepad, actively avoiding the situation. Father Victor sat at the table, took one of the old woman's hands in his. She grasped onto him like he was a tiny bit of flotsam in a wide ocean. Starved for a touch of kindness.

"Is there anyone we can call to come be with you?" Father Victor asked.

"No. There's just me. I take care of myself. The girls come round, D'Andra and her momma, look after me some. One of the neighbors takes me to church and gets my groceries."

"Do you mind if we look at Allegra's room?" Taylor asked.

The old woman waved toward the hall off the kitchen. The apartment was a two-bedroom with a single bath at the end of the hall. Maybe eight hundred square feet, if they counted inside the cabinets and closets.

The tiny room to the right was the grandmother's; it smelled of urine and sandalwood and dark things. The one on the left was smaller, but less fragrant. A black cloth, draped half on and half off the window, let little bits of sunlight stream into the room. A single, unmade bed was pushed into a corner; the pink-and-white striped sheets looked like they needed a wash. A wooden cross hung over the bed, and a yellowed photograph of a smiling young girl, maybe eight, with her arms wrapped around an older version of herself. The picture was definitely of the same woman at the medical examiner's office. Taylor stared at it without removing it from the wall. The older woman must have been Allegra's mother. They had the same nose, the same tilt to their eyes.

The picture and the cross were the only adornments on the gray walls. There was nothing superfluous in the cheap decor—a bed, a small wooden dresser with a scratched top, clothes on the floor. They moved systematically through the room, looking in drawers, under the bed, sifting through the small pile of clothes in the corner. Taylor found what might have started as a diary but had turned into a doodle pad. She set the journal on the desk.

"We need a crime-scene tech to go through here. See if there are any foreign prints or DNA that we can trace to her abductor," Taylor said.

"I'll make the call."

The bathroom had the usual female accoutrements, cold cream and lotion, makeup, mascara, a crumpled box of yeast-infection treatment, all the things that would signal a young woman used it. There were two syringes in the makeup kit, a little spoon, and a crack pipe. Allegra's tox screen would be interesting. She was definitely into narcotics. And she hadn't taken them with her, which was a surprise. It told Taylor that Allegra wasn't planning to be away from home for very long.

So how does a girl from the projects end up hung on a column in a house on Love Hill?

"Damn shame," McKenzie whispered.

"No kidding," Taylor said. "Get the crime lab on this and let's get back to them."

She walked down the short hallway into the kitchen. Father Victor was saying a prayer of solace over Mrs. Johnson.

"May Christ support us all the day long, till the shadows lengthen, and the evening comes, and the busy world is hushed, and the fever of life is over and our work is done. Then in His mercy may He give us a safe lodging, and holy rest and peace at the last. Amen."

Taylor watched until he made the sign of the cross and stood before she addressed the woman again. She was almost afraid to speak. She didn't want to invalidate the prayer, chase away whatever goodness might be hovering around the woman, if only for an instant. Then the old woman coughed—hard, sharp, barking catches—and the moment was gone.

She asked gently, "Ma'am, do you have any contact information for Tyrone?"

"He hangs out at the minimart on the corner of Claiborne and Lafayette. Should be there now, lest someones around here already done tipped him off. That girl just through here, she work for him, too. Best be quick if you want to see to him. She's got a mouth on her like a motorboat."

The woman made the guttural noise again. Taylor understood it was a mirthless laugh. She got quiet, then seemed to shrink in on herself, drawing into the collar of her stained dressing gown like a turtle.

Taylor nodded to Father Victor, then thanked Mrs. Johnson. McKenzie was standing by the front door, phone to his ear. She gestured to him to follow her, left the dank space and went into the fresh air. The breeze was tinged with the cloyingly sweet scent of marijuana smoke. She didn't care at the moment. She just wanted to get out. She felt dirty.

She got in the Caprice, McKenzie slid in beside her. She keyed the radio, asked dispatch to put her through to Gerald Sayers, head of the Specialized Investigative Unit. Gerald's people handled the drugs and prostitution in Nashville, plus all the other vice-related activities. He was a good man, not afraid to do whatever it took to get the job done. She trusted him.

Within five minutes, Sayers was back to her. He called on her cell. She put it on speaker so McKenzie could hear.

"Gerald. How are you?"

"Good to hear from you, Taylor. You holding up?" The show of support she was getting from her fellow officers was so heartening. No one agreed with the actions taken against her.

"I am. Listen, my new partner's here, too, Renn McKenzie. We've got a question for you. You know a pimp named Tyrone Hill, out of the J. C. Napier homes?"

"Oh, yeah. Dealer, pimp. Informant if the price is right. Got his greasy paws in a few different pies. Took over some of Terrence Norton's territory after Lincoln popped him last month. Word is Terrence is calling the shots from the inside. Why do you ask about Tyrone? What's he done now? I hope it's a jailable offense."

"One of his girls ended up dead yesterday."

"OD or hit?"

"Neither. Looks like she was held for a while, starved, then left in a stranger's house, nailed to a column."

"Oh, the Love Hill murder. Heard that one was pretty weird. It doesn't sound like Tyrone. He'd be more likely to smack her upside the head a few times. I don't think he's graduated to rub-outs yet. I can have one of my undercovers snoop a bit, see if he's out there braggin' he did it. These idiots love to take credit for their work."

"That would be great. My vic's name is Allegra Johnson. We just did the notification to her grandmother. She said Tyrone hangs at the corner of Claiborne and Lafayette."

"Yeah, that's his little fiefdom. I'll send one of my boys over there, see what's shakin'. Call you later?"

"That'd be great, Gerald. Thank you."

He clicked off. McKenzie looked at her.

"This is breaking, you think?"

"I don't know. Have you met Captain Sayers yet?"

McKenzie shook his head.

"When you meet him, you'll see. Gerald knows his clientele. We need to go run down a few other leads."

"Of course."

Father Victor tapped on her window. She put it down.

"We're taking care of Miss Ethel. I've got social services setting up a call schedule, and I'll make sure that we get some folks to come in and get her straightened out. It's unconscionable to let an old woman like that live on her own."

"Thanks, Father. I knew you'd find a way to help. I appreciate you coming with us today."

He nodded, murmured a prayer over her, then went back to his car and drove off, slowly. Taylor could see him looking left and right, saddened by the area. She felt the same way.

She turned the car engine over, slid away from the curve, following the chaplain's path.

"So talk to me, McKenzie. Tell me what you think's happening here."

"Honestly? I don't think a pimp who hangs out at a

minimart has the wherewithal to transport a body across town, tie her to a post and stick a knife through her chest, if that's what you're asking."

He slipped on a pair of aviator sunglasses. He looked so much like a cop that she wondered if it was purposeful, whether he practiced the move in the mirror before work.

"Better be careful, we might start calling you Miami Vice."

"Why? I transferred in from Orlando."

She bit back a laugh, refocused on his words. "Never mind. Before your time. I agree with you about Tyrone. But I'd rather hear from Gerald before I make that decision. What else?"

"I think Allegra Johnson was an easy target. Someone relatively transient, with a sketchy background and a difficult life. Someone no one would miss if she was gone for a few weeks. I think whoever killed her watched her, knew about her, knew she would be easy pickings."

"Not bad. Lure her with drugs, or a sex act for money. Tyrone might know who she went off with, if he's really her pimp." She sighed. "I did a ViCAP search earlier trying to see if this case matches one from Manchester a few years back. If my hunch is right, we'll need to take a trip down there tomorrow. Will you join me?"

"Absolutely. What else do you want me to do?"

"If you were running the case, what would you do next?"

McKenzie was quiet. They were almost back to the CJC. She glided into the side lot and put the Caprice in Park. She shifted in the seat so she could face him. He was playing with his hands, practically wringing them in frustration.

"This may sound crazy, but I think I'd like to know more about Mr. Bangor. He might be a target. He's a homosexual, perhaps this was aimed at him, a hate crime."

There was something odd in McKenzie's voice, a tone she wasn't familiar with. She looked at him sideways. Fury. His fists were balled, his brow creased. Those little actions set off her alarm bells. Was McKenzie closeted? Not that it mattered to her, but he'd mentioned a girl-friend. She tucked that away to be dealt with later.

"A message? I've thought about that, too. It seems a bit extreme, but he was broken into last year. He might be into something that we don't know about. Have you run him yet?"

"Yes. Nothing. Clean as a whistle. He's a law-abiding citizen, pays his parking tickets. His prints weren't in the system."

"He could be clean, he could be good at hiding things. We'll see."

Her cell rang. She recognized the caller ID, an internal number to the Criminal Justice Center. She answered it, hoping it was Gerald. It was. She put it on speaker.

"We talked to your boy."

"That was quick."

"Well, these runners are predictable, at least. Lets us monitor them easier, get them into the fold as confiden-tial informants. My guy had a chat with him, said it was pretty apparent the news upset him. He might have actually cared about the girl."

"That would be a first. How can you make someone you care about have sex with strangers for drug money?"

"Your guess is as good as mine. I'll never pretend to understand these fools." Gerald laughed. "Anyway, Tyrone said, and I quote, 'Shorty was a fine-looking girl, ya know what I mean? Why would I be offin' her ass? She makes me money. Now I'm sad.' He seemed genuinely surprised to hear she was dead. My guy asked when he saw her last. He claims she split about three weeks ago."

"That fits with the witnesses at her house. He didn't have any ideas where she split to?"

"Naw. He was more angry than anything. Thought maybe another pimp hooked her up. Here's the other thing. You say the murder was yesterday?"

"Thereabouts. Allegra was placed in the house between 9:00 a.m. and 5:00 p.m."

"My UC was with Tyrone most of the day yesterday. They were over at the minimart, doing a deal with some Mexicans who came through town. My interdiction boys and girls picked up the Mexis on their way out. So the timing might have been close."

"Okay, Gerald. I'll strike him from my immediate list. Thanks so much for your help. You guys are miracle workers. Stay safe." She hung up.

"So, McKenzie, we move Tyrone to the back burner for the moment. Let's go see what awaits us inside."

Thirteen

It was past 5:00 p.m. Taylor sent McKenzie home, promised to call him if anything new broke. She was filling out her forms when a soft voice caught her attention.

"Miss Taylor? ViCAP results are back."

Rowena Wright stood over Taylor, her bulk creating a shadow on the desk. Her gray hair was curled into a riot of miniature corkscrews. Taylor was reminded of a Gorgon, though Rowena was one of the most even-tempered creatures Taylor had ever come across. She was happy to do her work, go home to her family at the end of the day. She never complained, never called in sick. She'd received departmental awards for her attendance. Taylor thought the world of her.

"Thank you, Rowena. How's your husband?"

"He's just wonderful, Miss Taylor, thank you for asking. How's that fine man of yours? You ever going to marry that boy?"

Taylor fiddled with her engagement ring, the Asscher-cut channel-set diamonds nestled flat into their platinum home. "We're getting there, Rowena. I practically feel like we're married already."

"He's a good man, Miss Taylor. Don't you go letting him slip away cause you've got the cold feet." Rowena started to leave, but paused, like she had something more to say.

Taylor squeezed her shoulder. "Thank you for getting these for me. I appreciate it."

Rowena just smiled and left the offices. She was tucked into a space next door—she handled all the Criminal Investigative Divisions administrative details. She literally knew where the bodies were buried, and knew when to look the other way.

Funny, people were always warning Taylor not to let Baldwin slip away. She found it curious—did they think she'd never find another man as good as him? Or that she'd never find another man, period? He was a good man, and she had no intention of trading him in.

She turned her attention to the ViCAP pages.

The first search string had showed up several art thefts in Davidson, Williamson and Wilson counties, but nothing that seemed linked with their case. She discarded that report for the moment and moved on to the next.

The second search yielded some promising results. She'd set the parameters to gather anything that might be remotely related to art, sculpture and classical music, and the case she remembered from Manchester, Tennessee was on the list, as well as three others. Her heart skipped a beat. There might be a pattern here. She set the pages aside and went to the third search, the one with cause of death as starvation.

There were several cases that matched this description—mostly attributed to elder-abuse cases from various long-term care facilities. But on the fourth entry, she felt the excitement begin to build. It was a case from Chattanooga, one year earlier. She laid the two ViCAP searches side by side. The Chattanooga case had several elements that were comparable to the Manchester case—music playing at the scene and the victim profile, a thin black female. The Chattanooga COD was starvation, while the Manchester victim was drowned, but there was enough there for Taylor to feel they may be related.

Now she had three cases with exceptional similarities. One in Nashville, one in Chattanooga and one in Manchester. Jesus.

She kept going through the files, looking for anything of note, something out of place. In the end, she had a total of six cases that she thought were worth looking into, all scattered across the state of Tennessee. She knew in her gut several of them wouldn't pan out, but the facts made chills run down her spine. Three were most likely linked. And the related cases would wreak havoc on Baldwin's theory that Il Macellaio had just come to the United States. Unless he was flying back and forth...oh, this was crazy. She decided to approach the cases with no preconceived notions. Let the evidence and the investigation tell her where to head.

She called the case officers for the six cases she'd pulled and requested their files. She was met with polite enthusiasm—free assistance was always wanted, especially if it would clear a case. Two were solved; she put those aside. The Manchester case was being run by the Coffee County Sheriff's office.

Sheriff Steve Simmons was more than happy to have her help, even suggested she take a trip down to look at the case materials in person. She told him she was hoping he'd say that, she'd be happy to come, would be bringing McKenzie along. It would only take an hour to drive down to Manchester. She scheduled an appointment with him for the morning. He confirmed some of the details before he signed off—yes, the victim was black, yes, there was classical music playing at the scene, no, there were no suspects. Taylor felt the excitement rise in her chest. Leads were all good things.

Tim Davis entered the homicide offices, stuck his head around the wall that led to her desk. She waved him in.

"Hey, Tim. What do you have for me?"

He sat in a rolling chair to the left of her, at the desk of one of the B-shift detectives. "The palm print matches the exemplars from the home owner. But we got a hit off one of the prints we lifted from the Picasso monograph— to a sex offender we've got locked up."

"Locked up?" she asked.

"Yep. He's in Riverbend, doing three to five for child rape."

"Hmm. How long has he been in?"

"A little over eight months."

"So no chance the print was left last night."

"Nope."

"Bangor mentioned a break-in a year ago."

"That's within the realm of possibility. It was a little smudged, I had to fume it because it was so old, but there were enough points to match easily."

"So we have what could be a year-old fingerprint. What's the guy's name?"

"Arnold Fay."

"Looks like we need to have another chat with Mr. Bangor. See if he knows this Arnold Fay character. What else?"

"There's a lot of random DNA, but that's more than likely the home owner's. It'll take a while to sort out. The knife was clean, so was the fishing line. Thirty-test, manufactured by Berkley, a brand called FireLine Crystal. I've requested all records of orders for the past three months, but it's sold in every sporting shop in Middle

Tennessee, so that probably won't help us. We plastered four different shoe impressions. The ones closest to the house are from an Asics-brand running shoe and a pair of Timberland climbing boots. Find me a suspect, I'll be able to able to match his shoes, at least."

Taylor thought about that for a minute. How many footprints might have been disturbed by the team responding to the murder? She pushed that away. What was done was done.

Tim was playing with a piece of paper. "There was something else. The Picasso monograph? There was a page missing from the back of the book."

"Missing. What do you mean?"

"I brought it, I'd like to show you. It may have nothing to do with this at all, but it seemed strange." He put the large book on her desk, then slit the seal on the evidence bag. Taylor could see the smudged fingerprint that he'd been talking about. Tim flipped the book open.

"See this, right here? It looks to me like a page was cut out of the back."

Taylor ran her finger along the sharp edge of the thick, glossy paper. It *had* been cut, close to the spine. If they hadn't collected the book, if Tim wasn't as careful and meticulous, they'd easily have missed it.

"What was here?" she asked. "What was on this page?"

"I don't know."

Taylor fingered the edge of the paper again. She flipped through the book to see if she could tell what the mysterious missing page might hold, but couldn't come to any conclusions. Tim sat quietly at her side, letting her think.

Bangor's house was loaded with books, the built-in bookshelves crawling with tomes on every conceivable subject. And he had more coffee-table books. Was this an anomaly specific to this book, or something he did to all of his titles? Or was it something their killer had done? She smiled at Tim.

"Great catch, man."

"Thanks. I don't know what it means, but it struck me as odd."

"Might be nothing, might be everything. I'll tell you what. The scene has a ton more books just like it. What do you think about going back out there and pawing through a few of them, see if you can find any torn pages?"

"I'm already on my way. I've called the home owner, a Mr. Bangor? He seems very nice, said for me to come on. He said he'd start looking, too. Maybe we'll find something."

"Tim, you're the greatest. Call me as soon as you know, okay?"

He left a packet of information for her and took off.

She retrieved her voice mail—Lincoln and Marcus would meet her at Rumba at 6:00 p.m. She glanced at her watch. She could just make it. Baldwin would be joining them by 7:00 p.m. He was finishing a project.

She called Sam and left her a message about the evidence found so far. She told her about Tyrone Hill and Allegra Johnson's business relationship, and about the fingerprint match to Arnold Fay, just in case that would be relevant later on. Nothing to get excited over yet, but each piece would play an important role. Besides, Sam was a spitfire about the details. She wanted to be kept in the loop about everything, no matter how minute, because you never knew how it related to the autopsy. Taylor understood that desire. She felt the same way.

Elm's door was open, but no one was inside. Good. She'd typed up two brief lines to sum up her day— *Autopsy & Notification on Love Circle victim, Allegra*

Johnson; Interview with home owner, Love Circle, Hugh Bangor—and left them on his desk.

That would just have to do.

The drive up West End was quick. She pulled into Rumba, a fusion satay grill, dreaming about a caipirinha. It was one of her favorite restaurants in town—Cuban, South American, African, Caribbean, Malaysian and Indian influences all met, mixed and got a little tipsy on the world-class rums. She valeted the truck, went into the cool, dark restaurant.

The boys were already there. She felt the grin spread across her face. Man, she missed them. It had only been five weeks since their dislocation, but it felt like much more.

Marcus Wade nearly knocked her off her feet with his hug. His brown hair was too long, kept falling in his eyes. When he released her, Lincoln Ross did the same, openly wrinkling his Versace suit. He was still sporting the shaved head and close black goatee. If you didn't know him, you'd think he looked dangerous. Just seeing his gap-toothed grin made her happy. She stepped back from them, a bemused smile on her face.

"That was quite a reception. You two look great."

Lincoln shook his head. "You have no idea how much we miss working with you. It sucks out here in the precincts."

Marcus nodded. "South isn't exactly where I thought my career was going, you know? *Estoy aprendiendo hablar español.*"

"And butchering it. Good grief, Wade, where the hell did you get that accent? Speedy Gonzales? You're learning some *bueno* Spanish there, my friend." Lincoln jostled Marcus, who just shook his head.

"Whatever. You come down and try it, wiseass."

Smack in the heart of the South district was little Mexico.

Crimes there often went unsolved because the residents were afraid to talk to the police. Most of them were illegals, though with Nashville's lax stance on deportation, getting caught didn't necessarily mean getting sent home.

The hostess, a pretty co-ed with a lip ring and spiky blond hair, held up three fingers, questioning.

Taylor said, "Four of us. One's still coming." The girl led them to a table in the back of the restaurant. The table was at an angle, so none of them had their backs to the entrance. It was one of the reasons they chose to eat here.

They slid into place, Taylor alone on one side, Lincoln and Marcus on the other. They placed their drink orders and asked for cheese-stuffed naan and flatbreads, then waited for the waiter to leave. He deposited waters for them, then gracefully disappeared.

"So how's your new boss?" Lincoln asked.

"Terrible," Taylor answered quietly. "He's a mess. Administrative, all the way. A total jerk, too. He leaked one of the details we were trying to hold back about the murder last night. With any luck, he'll blow himself up without any help from me. Either of you talk to Price lately?"

They shook their heads.

"Me, neither. All I know is the case for our reinstatement is coming along. Not to skip the niceties, boys, but here's why I wanted to meet. Fitz called me this afternoon."

"How is he? Ever coming back?" Lincoln sounded melancholy. She knew her boys weren't at all happy with the way things had shaken out. They'd been working as a cohesive unit for three years, each relying on the other's strengths. They were a team. To think about that symbiotic relationship in the past tense hurt everyone.

Taylor patted Lincoln's hand. "He says he is. But he's in Barbados now, stuck in the water without some sort of pump thingie. He thinks he saw the Pretender on shore.

Said he ran into Susie—literally, knocked her down—then took off."

They both raised eyebrows. Lincoln asked, "What the hell would the Pretender be doing in Barbados? Is he following Fitz?"

"That I don't know. I can't understand the point of that. And it's not definite. It could be just a fluke, someone who just looks like him."

Marcus looked her straight in the eye. "You don't believe that, do you?"

She weighed her words carefully. "He reached out to me, too, left me a message on my home voice mail. Let me know he wasn't to blame for the murder I caught last night."

They both went on alert. "He called you?" Lincoln asked, incredulous.

"Yeah. Baldwin's already chasing it down."

"Do you have a unit on you?"

"No. And I want to keep it that way. I can take care of myself. It's y'all I'm worried about."

"I'd like to see him try," Marcus said. "We could have some real fun. The Love Hill thing? Vic was Allegra Johnson, right?"

"That's her. You know her?"

"Busted her a few times when I was coming up in patrol. Pro, solicitation and drugs, mostly."

"Well, some creep got her, and good. I've been partnered with a new detective—"

"Renn McKenzie," Lincoln said. "He's okay, once you get past the shyness."

"No kidding. Boy blushes constantly. You think he's sound?"

"Yeah. Just shy. He's smart once you get him past the preliminaries. He knows some about computers, too."

"I wish I'd known that, I'd have made him do the ViCAP search for me."

Their appetizers arrived and they placed a dinner order. Taylor glanced at her watch—6:45. She ordered a plate of combination satays and jasmine rice for Baldwin; he'd be there by the time the food came out.

Marcus brought them back on topic. "So you think the Pretender is keeping tabs on us?"

"It sure looks that way. Unless it was just a coincidence that he and Fitz were on the same island at the same time. He may be testing the waters to see how many of us know what he looks like. But I'd really like to know what he's up to. Parks took a ride out to Fitz's house, said nothing looked out of place. I was wondering if the Pretender had broken in and gotten the itinerary. I guess that's still possible, but it seems like one hell of a lot of effort to go to."

Lincoln sat straighter. "I think he's just trying to intimidate us. I *want* him to come after me. I'll fuck the boy up."

Baldwin walked through the door. Taylor caught his eye and he joined the table, kissing her lightly as he sat.

"Gentlemen," he said, shaking hands with both of them across the table.

Taylor filled him in on her day, told him about Fitz. He was concerned; she could see the grooves between his eyebrows deepen, even while he smiled. They spent the rest of the meal catching up, skipping the shop talk in favor of gossip and rumors.

Taylor declined a second caipirinha. She knew from experience that one was her limit—the Cachaça rum was too potent. She was tired. It was good to see the boys, even better to have a civilized meal with Baldwin, but she'd had an exceptionally long day.

They finally split at 9:00 p.m., with plans to meet again for lunch in the next few days and promises to watch each other's backs. The valet brought Taylor's truck and a black Suburban that Baldwin was driving.

"You didn't bring your Beemer?" she asked him, stifling a yawn.

"Well, no. I've got to pick up the lead on the Il Macellaio case from the London Met, a Detective Inspector Highsmythe, at the airport. His flight arrives late tonight. He requested an emergency consultation, and since I'm not in Quantico I suggested he come here. Besides, I'd like him to have a look at this case, if you wouldn't mind."

"I don't mind. You still have to go back to Quantico?"

"Yes. Now that we've got the DNA and know the London and Florence killings were done by the same man, we need to coordinate. I've got to help him out. We'll take this case with us and I'll have my team plug it into our system, see what shakes out. I'm still struck by change in M.O.s, but it's eerily similar to his earlier crimes. What kind of forensics do you have?"

"Not nearly enough. Lubricant. Fishing line. A fingerprint that matches a sex offender we've already got locked up, and a missing page from the Picasso monograph. Some shoe prints. Nothing definitive, I'm still running it all down. Tim's at Bangor's right now, looking for more information."

"You want to head up there, see if he's got anything?"

It was tempting. "No, I probably shouldn't. I had a drink at dinner. The last thing I need is for someone to tattle to my new boss that they smelled liquor on my breath. 'Alkie detective horns in on case, news at ten.' No, that's okay. Tim will call if he finds anything."

Baldwin was tossing the keys from hand to hand.

"What?" she asked.

Baldwin reached into his pocket and pulled out a pack of spearmint Trident. "Here, have some gum. Let's go up there. I'd like to take another look around. I'll follow you, okay?"

"All right. If you say so."

Taylor popped a piece in her mouth and climbed in her truck. Damn, but this day was never going to end.

Fourteen

It only took them a few minutes to reach Bangor's house. Taylor parked the truck on the street, Baldwin pulled the Suburban in close behind her. They walked hand-in-hand to the porch. The door swung open just as they hit the first step.

Hugh Bangor's smile was welcoming. He was holding a lowball with about two fingers of amber liquid.

"Detectives. What can we do for you? Mr. Davis is already combing through my bookshelves. Come in, come in. Can I get you something to drink? Wine, tea, coffee? Maybe a little of Tennessee's finest?" He shook his glass, the ice cubes tinkling softly against each other. Gentleman Jack. The smell reminded her of her grandfather. If Bangor only had a pipe….

Taylor shook Bangor's hand and introduced Baldwin. "Mr. Bangor, this is Supervisory Special Agent Dr. John Baldwin, with the FBI. He's the Unit Chief in charge of the Behavioral Analysis Unit."

Bangor's eyes lit up when he looked at Baldwin. The two men shook hands. "My goodness. You should be an actor. You're stunning."

Baldwin shook his head a little bit, confused, then realized that Bangor was actually admiring him sexually. He blushed deeply, and Taylor fell for him just a little bit more. As much as she enjoyed seeing his discomfiture, she threw him a rescue line.

"No whiskey for us tonight, Mr. Bangor. We'd like to take a look at some of your books, too, see if we can't help Tim out. You've got such an extensive collection, it will probably go faster with more eyes."

"But of course. I've just made a pot of chai tea for the officer. If whiskey isn't on the menu, can I get some for you?"

They accepted the offer. Bangor's manner was so pleasant; as they chatted, Taylor realized he was someone she'd like to have as a friend. Too bad they had to meet under these circumstances.

The chai was creamy and spicy, perfectly warmed. She sat on the couch in the great room and complimented him.

"It's Starbucks. I buy the boxes at Publix and make it myself with fresh organic milk. I'd go broke if I bought them every time I had the urge. So, what's happening with the case?"

"Nothing much yet, sir. We're only a day in. But we have some things we want to look at."

"God, don't call me sir. It makes me feel old."

"Okay. Listen, we need to talk to you about something we've found. Do you know a man named Arnold Fay?"

Bangor paled. "Why do you ask?" he choked out.

"So you do know him," she said.

Bangor nodded and wrapped his hand around his throat. "Arnold and I haven't spoken in a very long time."

There was something in his voice, his gestures, which made her immediately suspicious.

"Are you sure?"

Bangor took a long drink of his whiskey, emptying the glass, then went to his bar and refilled the lowball from a crystal decanter. He came back to the living room and sat on the couch, a decisive look on his face.

"Yes. I'm sure we haven't spoken for at least five years."

"We found his fingerprint on the Picasso monograph that was on the table."

Bangor visibly deflated.

"I haven't told you the whole truth."

Taylor crossed her arms, waiting.

"The break-in I mentioned? I know who it was."

"Arnold Fay, I presume?" she asked.

"Yes. He stole as much money as he could, but left the Picasso monograph as a…present."

"Why would he do that?"

Bangor sighed deeply. "Arnold was my partner. The one I told Detective McKenzie died of AIDS. I wish that were the case. He's dead to me in my heart, anyway. It's just much easier to tell people he died than admit the truth. That he…I can't even bring myself to say it."

"Molested your neighbor's boy," she finished for him.

"Christopher. Yes. We'd already ended our relationship when he started up with Chris. I just didn't have the heart to kick him out. I wasn't here half the time, anyway. But when all this happened—he claimed they were having an affair. Like a thirteen-year-old boy is capable of making a decision that momentous. I knew in my heart there was no way it was consensual. Honestly, it's a period I'd rather forget. He left the book to say he was sorry for taking the money. I didn't have the heart to throw it away."

"I've found something," Baldwin said. He brought a book to her, another Picasso monograph.

Bangor smiled. "Picasso is my favorite," he said, simply.

She set the cup down, pulled a latex glove out of her

pocket, slipped it on her right hand, and turned the Picasso *catalogue raisonné* to face her. Tim had joined them now—all three men watched her expectantly as she flipped the book over and opened the back cover.

Another missing page. Just a few millimeters of hard-edged paper nestled deep within the book's binding. The cut was barely perceptible. It must have been done with a razor, maybe an X-Acto knife. The edge was neat and clean. Unless you were looking for it, you'd never guess that a page was missing.

"It's a better calling card than a postcard, I'll tell you that," Baldwin said.

"Do you think that the killer might have removed the pages from these two books? Why?"

"That's an excellent question, Mr. Bangor. Do you have any more of these?"

"I do." He went to the bookshelf, pulled down two more large books. "I have four Picasso monographs in my collection. These are early ones that I bought years ago. The one you're holding, Detective, I bought in New York two years ago. It was the *catalogue raisonné* for the latest Picasso exhibit at the Museum of Modern Art. The one my friend left me is the fourth, and it's also relatively new."

She flipped through the books. Every page was intact.

"So two of your four Picasso books have been defaced. We need to figure out what was so important on those two pages."

She went to the bookshelf, took down another monograph, this time of Whistler. She brought it to the table, turned to the back. This book was intact, and she saw what was probably missing from the Picasso book. A copyright page—with the names of the designers, the printing, where it was printed. All things she could use to move the investigation forward. The mood in the room changed from curiosity to intensity in a fraction of a second.

Was this the work of their killer? And what was he trying to say?

"This is a different signature than what I've seen before," Baldwin said.

"It's a mistake," Tim said, a rare smile lighting up his normally somber features.

Baldwin nodded in agreement. "If it *is* the killer, it's a miscalculation. There's something he wants to obscure on those pages. Something vitally important that he didn't want us to see."

Taylor sat back on the sofa, stripped off the glove. Tim took the second monograph into evidence. She took a sip of the chai, then asked Bangor, "No chance you have another copy stashed away, is there?"

"Nope. Sorry. I only brought the one home from New York."

"We're going to have to take it with us, test it for trace. See if we can't find some prints or something."

"What do you think might be so significant on the copyright page, Detective?"

Taylor smiled at Baldwin, they shared a moment of hope. She turned to Bangor.

"Copyright pages have names. Maybe our boy's is on it."

Fifteen

Taylor couldn't help feeling excited. Breaks were always a good thing.

"Mr. Bangor, do you have a phone book?"

"Of course. Let me get it."

"Calling the bookstores?" Baldwin asked.

"Oh, yeah. They should still be open, it's only 9:30 p.m. With any luck, one of the downtown stores will have it in stock. Fingers crossed."

She took out her notepad and transcribed the title of the book. Bangor brought her the yellow pages, and she flipped open to the *B*s.

"Bookstores, bookstores…okay. Borders on West End and Davis-Kidd in Green Hills are the closest. Mr. Bangor, would you like to take the first pick?"

"Call Davis-Kidd. They have a great art section. And please, call me Hugh."

"Okay, Hugh. Davis-Kidd it is."

She dialed the number, got a recording. She hung up and dialed it again. This time, a gruff voice greeted her.

She told him what she was looking for. He put her on

hold for a few minutes, then came back and said yes, they did have one copy. Would she like him to reserve it?

She said yes, gave him her name and hung up.

"Shall we?" she said to Baldwin.

Bangor saw them to the door.

"Detective, may I ask a favor?" he said.

"You can ask anything. Whether I can grant it is another story."

"Do you have to tell Detective McKenzie about Arnold?"

"I'm afraid I'll have to, yes. Why?"

Bangor's face fell. "Oh. That's too bad. I didn't want to tarnish my image with him. He seems like a very nice young man."

It was almost 10:00 p.m. before they got to Davis-Kidd. They got stopped at all the red lights; the signals on Hillsboro Road weren't sequenced properly, an issue Metro Public Works was continually revamping. Taylor was half a second from pulling out her flasher when the light at Woodmont finally turned green. They entered the Green Hills Mall, found parking spots in the first row, right in front of Davis-Kidd. At this time of night, most of the patrons of the mall had gone home. It was pleasantly deserted.

They hustled to the door just as an employee started to throw the bolt. He shook his head, so she badged him, resting her shield against the glass. That got his attention. He opened the door and allowed them in.

"I'm Detective Jackson. I called about a couple of Picasso monographs? *The Complete Works of Pablo Picasso and Picasso, the Early Years.*"

"Oh, yeah. Sure. Follow me. I've got the *Complete Works* at the desk. Didn't think you were going to make it."

He stepped around the counter. Taylor and Baldwin waited. And waited. The clerk finally popped his head back up and handed over a thick book. Taylor took it greedily, and felt her excitement fade just as quickly.

"Damn. This isn't the same one. Same title, but not the same book."

"Oh," the clerk said. "Sorry. That's the only one we've got. Do you know the publisher of the one you're looking for? I can try to order it for you."

"I only know what it looks like. There is a second title, too." She handed him her notebook. "Can you pull up anything that has these titles and let us look at the covers?"

The boy glanced at his watch. "Yeah. We need to be quick, though. I need to close up and go get my daughter from the sitter. Wife's out of town on business. You understand."

He motioned them behind the counter, plugged the title into the store's database.

Amazing. There were at least twenty *catalogue raisonnés* with matching titles. But halfway down the page, she saw the right ones.

"There," Baldwin said just as she pointed to the screen.

The clerk clicked on the cover. "Oh. Bad news. They're both out of print. Have been for about a year."

Taylor bit back the surge of frustration. "Any idea where we can get either of them? We need a page from it. Like, yesterday."

He read for a minute. "Says here the publisher is a specialty art press in New York. Pretty well-known and well-respected outfit. I bet they did the *catalogues* as a part of an exhibit. You might try contacting them directly, or calling the museums up there." He glanced at his watch again. They took the hint.

Taylor wrote down the name and address of the publisher. Bangor had bought one of the monographs in New York, so that fit. Unfortunately, it was just after 11:00

p.m. Eastern time. There was no chance of anyone answering the phones. And it was past 10:00 p.m. local time, which meant Borders, and all the rest of the Nashville bookstores, were now closed. Choices. Rouse managers and comb through their stock for a book long out of print in the off chance that they had it? Or get some much-needed rest and start fresh in the morning? Rest won, though she couldn't contain her disappointment.

"This isn't defeat," Baldwin said, sensing her mood. It was a rare talent of his, divining her thoughts. She wished she was as adept at reading his emotions. That would come, in time.

She leaned against her truck. "I thought we had it. So damn close."

"Well, there's no rush. A subject like this isn't going to pop off with another body so soon. He takes his time. Plans. Executes. Nothing rushed. Unfortunately, it takes time to get his victims to the perfect tipping point. And he thinks he's not making any mistakes. It was pure damn luck that we found the page cut out of the book like that. You should give Tim Davis a raise."

"No kidding. Something that subtle, we might have taken weeks, months to uncover. Good thing Bangor was involved with a criminal, we might not have connected things so quickly. This was quite fortuitous. Go get this Detective Highsmythe and drop him at his hotel. I'll head home and do a search, see where else the book might be."

He kissed her lightly. "Okay then. I'll meet you back at the house."

Baldwin scanned the scraggly line of passengers feeding their way out of the bowels of the airport until he saw the only option—the one who looked like a cop. The man was shorter than him, blond, solid and tight, and carried himself well. He stepped forward to greet him.

"You must be Highsmythe."

He looked tired, and didn't smile. "That I am. You're John Baldwin?"

"Yes."

"Good to meet you, John."

"Call me Baldwin. Everybody does."

"Righto, Baldwin it is. Do call me Memphis."

"Do you have bags?"

Highsmythe pointed to his carry-on. "This is all I have."

"Great." Baldwin started walking toward the exit, Highsmythe followed. "I've got a reservation for you at the Loews Vanderbilt. I think you'll find it meets your needs. I know you must be tired, so I'll drop you off and we can start fresh in the morning."

They chatted a bit as Baldwin drove them into downtown, then pulled up to the entrance of the hotel. He escorted Highsmythe in to make sure all was well. As it turned out, the hotel had made a mistake on the itinerary. Because it was after midnight, the room was booked for the next day, not for this evening. They were hosting a convention and had no extra rooms, even when Baldwin flashed his FBI badge. The manager came over and offered to walk them to another hotel, upgrading on their dime, but Baldwin could tell Highsmythe was dead on his feet.

"How about I put you up at my place, and we'll get you checked in tomorrow morning?"

Highsmythe nodded gratefully. "That's fine with me. Thank you."

They went back to the turnaround and climbed into the Suburban. Highsmythe leaned his head against the window and closed his eyes. Baldwin dialed Taylor's cell but she didn't answer.

He clicked off and drove them into the night, through West End and into the sleepy suburbs. He hoped Taylor was still awake so he could warn her they had a guest.

Sixteen

Gavin was beside himself with excitement. He'd arrived
home to find the best possible news.

It was time.

He was trembling, though the fire was lit in the potbellied stove that he kept in the basement for heating
emergencies and seductions. The room was bathed in an
orangey glow, the flickering flames dancing in the
shadows. A small table was set with white linen and fine
bone china. Candles in polished silver holders glistened,
their light casting pools of yellow on the table. He'd
opened a bottle of Silvio Nardi Brunello, poured it into
a flat-bottomed crystal decanter to breathe. There was a
box of chocolates on the table, divinely rich truffles he
had imported especially for this evening. He had one of
his favorite operas playing, *Turandot*.

Gavin unsnapped the locks on the Plexiglas box. His
love lay still. He was overcome for a moment, then
gathered himself and lifted her body, setting her gently
in the chair closest to the fire. The chair was high-backed;
a quick loop of thirty-test line and she was upright. He
set her hand on the chocolate, arranged her face in a

smile. There, that was better. In the flickering light, the hollows of her cheekbones were like gorges, her mouth appropriately slack. Her eyes, deepest chocolate, like the truffles, watched him wherever he went in the room.

He settled across from her and poured the wine. Raised his glass in a respectful toast, took a sip. He cleared his throat, and began singing an aria from *Turandot,* softly, under his breath. "Nessun Dorma," Puccini's fateful words about a lonely princess, silent in her cold room, waiting for the love of a worthy man. He was that worthy man. He had no ear for the tune, knew he couldn't do it justice, but he whispered the phrases, and they flowed around her body, soft as a lover's caress. He hoped she could hear him, wherever she was, hear him making love to her with sweet words.

"...Ed il mio bacio scioglierà il silenzio che ti fa mia! Il nome suo nessun saprà e noi dovrem, ahime, morir."

He dropped to one knee and followed the words in English, whispering still, knowing she'd never fully comprehend in Italian. "On your mouth I will tell it when the light shines. And my kiss will dissolve the silence that makes you mine."

He untied her. She leaned on his shoulder in a deathly embrace, her hands dangling down his back, touching him, holding him, and he wept with joy. Scooping her up with both arms, he crossed to the fire. A soft feather mattress with silken sheets was warmed by the flames. He laid her carefully on the bed, arranged her hair to spill over the fluffy pillow. She gazed into his eyes. When he kissed her, and her mouth parted, he nearly lost his mind. So sweet.

He took his time, making love to her gently, not wanting to hurt her. She accepted his embrace, never fighting, always willing. He took her again, and again, and again.

The night passed much too quickly. At the dawn, light

creeping in through the cracks under the doors, Gavin extricated himself from between her legs, leaned up to give her a kiss. She wasn't as stunning in the light.

"It's time to bathe, my love. Oh, why did you have to leave me so soon?"

Friday

Seventeen

Taylor woke with the sun. She'd actually slept, at least six hours straight. Usually in the middle of a case she was up all hours, playing pool to try to calm her nerves. But when she'd gotten home last night, after twenty minutes on the computer confirming that no one in town had the Picasso books available, she climbed into the bed. Baldwin had joined her an hour later, mumbling something about the Met detective that she wasn't awake enough to hear. She'd fallen back to sleep tangled around him like a piece of yarn.

She gave an indolent stretch, then slipped out, trying not to jostle him. No sense in waking him just yet; he'd been out terribly late.

She slipped down the stairs, turned off the alarm, went out the front door for the paper, then headed into the kitchen to start some coffee for Baldwin, tea for her. She flipped the paper over as she went, looked at the glaring headline.

No Clues in the Hunt for the Conductor

Great. Just what she needed; the media getting in the middle of her case, starting a panic among the citizens of Nashville. At least nothing about the posing or the link to Italy had gotten to the media yet. It would, but with any luck she could contain and control the information.

"Good morning," a deep voice called out.

She screamed in surprise, the newspaper scattering all over the kitchen floor. There was a man sitting at her kitchen table, a strange man. She fumbled for her weapon but quickly realized she'd been caught at a disadvantage—she was wearing a tank top and a pair of Baldwin's boxer shorts, the waistband folded down three times to fit. The man stood and took a step toward her. She calculated the distance to the block of knives sitting out on the granite countertop. He grinned and held out his hands.

"Whoa, there. Name's Highsmythe. Your chap didn't warn you that he'd brought me along last night?"

Taylor stopped short just as Baldwin came clattering down the stairs.

"Is everything okay? I thought I heard a scream."

She turned to him, hoping her voice didn't break when she spoke. Jesus. "It's fine. I wasn't aware that we had a guest."

"Sorry about that. You were conked out when I came in. Loews messed up his reservation, offered to walk him, but it was late, so I just brought him here. Taylor Jackson, meet James Highsmythe."

The man raised an eyebrow and looked her up and down before meeting her eyes.

Taylor was acutely aware of several sensations at once, mortification crowding out the faint zing she felt when their eyes met. The white tank top she'd slept in was thin and she wasn't wearing a bra. She suddenly felt ice-cold, and knew her body was betraying that. She crossed her arms in front of her chest and said, "I'll just go get something on," then scooted out of the kitchen.

She heard Baldwin murmur something, and the Brit had the audacity to laugh.

Damn men. They could wander around barely clothed among strangers and never feel a moment's shame.

By the time she'd managed to get herself together and back downstairs, dressed in yoga pants and a black T-shirt, Baldwin had taken care of brewing her tea and was making breakfast. She accepted a cup gratefully and sat at the table, across from the British cop.

"Memphis was just telling me about life in the Met. Sounds a lot like Metro to me." He set a plate of eggs in front of her, another in front of Highsmythe.

"Oh?" she said. She saw that Highsmythe had gone pale, wondered if he wasn't feeling well. Probably just tired. Time to fix her earlier inelegance. She handed him the salt and pepper, then shook his hand.

"It's good to meet you. I'm Taylor Jackson. You must be Baldwin's contact from Scotland Yard."

"Please, do call me Memphis," he said, a warm smile playing on his lips. He looked down at his cup of tea, and Taylor could have sworn she saw the briefest moment of pain cross his features.

"Are you all right?" she asked.

He started, then glanced at her briefly. "Yes. Yes, of course. Jet lag, you know."

"It's a killer," Baldwin said. "Sorry for the confusion last night. We'll get you squared away after breakfast."

"Much appreciated." Highsmythe picked up his fork with his left hand and delicately placed a bit of egg in his mouth. Exemplary manners, Taylor noticed. The color had returned to his face. She decided he was fine.

A good-looking man, if you liked blonds. She didn't. But she could see how another woman might find him attractive. He looked...beautifully menacing. His fingers on the teacup seemed ridiculous—perfectly manicured yet thick enough to snap the handle from the china with a flick. He was wearing a gray button-down with a black cashmere sweater over it, tight enough to show both the shirt's excellent tailoring and his muscled chest. His whole countenance was like granite, a block of tension and strength. Intractable, physically and emotionally. Though why she touched on his emotions escaped her.

He was different from Baldwin, whose tall, lean body made her want to reach out and stroke the length of him, to nestle in and not let go. No, Highsmythe was a bundle of violence hiding behind a sculpted facade. She made a mental note to make sure she wasn't alone with him. He unsettled her, and there was no sense in anyone getting the wrong impression.

She finished her eggs, then excused herself. She had things to do before she left for the day. The Brit stood when she did and nodded at her. Well, at least he'd fit in just fine with the rest of the Southern men, who knew just how to treat a lady.

She took her tea and went upstairs, sat down at her desk, pushing all thoughts of strange men in her kitchen away. The first order of business was tracking down the art books.

She hit pay dirt with her first try. The publisher, Taschen Books, had a New York branch. A knowledgeable staffer took down the information, then put her on hold. She came back and told Taylor they didn't have actual copies of the books—the print runs had been small and they were well and truly out of print—but they did have access to the corporate entities who held the electronic files the books were printed from. She'd put in a request first thing, would get back to Taylor with the information. Hopefully this morning. Taylor gave her cell number and a fax number at the office, so they could print off the two pages in question and get them to her as quickly as possible.

She'd arranged to meet McKenzie at a truck stop at I-65 and Old Hickory at 8:30 a.m. She took a quick shower and was putting her wet hair in a bun when Baldwin appeared in the bathroom doorway.

"You look good wet, you know that?"

She laughed. "You're nuts."

"I'm not," he said, reaching for her. "I wish we were alone."

She wrapped her arms around his neck. "Me, too. What are you going to do today?"

"Depends on what this guy from the Met has to say. I'm going to plug in everything we have down here, too. Something about these cases...well, you know. It feels so similar, but something is wrong. Will you call me when you finish in Manchester, tell me what you have from there? If these cases *are* linked, then the killer has been at this awhile and we might have something to go on. I'll use the new information to flesh out the profile, present it, and hopefully, we'll catch this son of a bitch."

"Oh, speaking of which, remind me to fax you the ViCAP reports. I found another real possibility down in Chattanooga. I'm going to follow up on that today, too."

He looked worried. "You didn't tell me you had a third."

"I don't know if it's linked for sure. Just a gut feeling, you know? I'll get you all the details."

"Okay. Nice work, by the way. You'd make one hell of an agent." He kissed her, so deeply it made her dizzy, then gave her a wicked grin. "Don't forget to fax me the ViCAP report."

"Smart-ass," she said, but smiled back. "I've got to go. Will you be going to Quantico tonight?"

"Tomorrow. Need to get Highsmythe in front of the rest of the team." He released her, and she felt that sense of disappointment she always had when they stopped touching. He made her feel alive, and when they were disconnected, she missed the electricity.

She gave him another little kiss, then finished dressing. Baldwin slipped into the shower. She stood in the doorway and watched him this time, his lithe body, the water rushing over his broad shoulders, the way he turned his face into the water like it could wash away the bad things he was forced to see. She felt a tug, deep in her stomach, and sighed. He was just so beautiful. So intelligent, so giving. She was lucky to have him.

She glanced at her watch. If she lingered any longer, she would be late for McKenzie. She opened the door to the shower and motioned for him to come closer. She kissed him this time, and saw the effect it had. Grinning, she tweaked him, then turned to leave.

"You tease," he called out, and she laughed.

"Sorry, babe. I'm gonna be late. Have a good day."

She could hear him growling as she walked down the stairs. It tickled her, how she could get him going so easily.

Highsmythe was still in the kitchen, staring sadly into his cup of tea.

"What's wrong?" she asked.

"It's empty," he said, then grinned at her. She smiled back at him. Crazy Brits.

"Enjoy your day," she said. "See some of Nashville while you're here."

"I'll do that. Thank you."

She looked at him a moment longer, wondering if he was being sincere, then grabbed her keys. He was charming, she'd give him that.

"Goodbye, Mr. Highsmythe."

* * *

"Goodbye, Miss Jackson," he said, but the door was already closed. He sat back in his chair, realized he didn't have any breath. He felt like he'd been holding it from the moment she'd sauntered into the kitchen in that tight white top, those incredibly long legs bringing her closer and closer. She was possibly the most gorgeous woman he'd ever seen.

He felt a twinge deep in his heart. There were photographs of her and the FBI agent in the living room, taken on a vacation, all smiles and gooey eyes. In the photograph the woman looked a lot like his Evan; he'd been expecting someone who had a similar bone structure, but in person, the dynamic of her was…overwhelming. Tall, lissome, curved in all the proper places, hair the exact same shade of natural honey-blond that Evan had worked so hard to replicate. They didn't smell the same—Evan's shampoo made her hair smell faintly of citrus.

Memphis poured a fresh cup of tea and took a deep swallow. He was mightily impressed. Baldwin had made him the tea—china pot, loose-leaf Earl Grey. The real thing, not those tepid bags with a string hanging over the edge of a plastic cup. He didn't think Americans had any idea how to brew a real cup.

He replayed the morning, moment by glorious moment.

"I'm Taylor Jackson," she'd said. "You must be Baldwin's contact from Scotland Yard."

He resisted the urge to correct her—New Scotland Yard, actually, we haven't been Scotland Yard since the 1890s—but bit back the retort.

"Please, do call me Memphis," he'd managed, then gave her a most winning smile. She'd responded, he felt the grip of her hand tighten just for an instant, and her previously polite smile reached all the way into those loch gray depths. His heart, quite literally, skipped a beat.

"Are you all right?" she'd asked.

God, no. He would never be all right again.

The remembered scent of lemongrass and gun oil forced its way back into his senses, and he looked up, face to face with the woman again. Jesus, at least she didn't smell like Evan. That would have been too much to bear.

"Forgot my phone. Sorry for the interruption."

He stumbled to his feet, his chair scootching back with a screech, but she'd already turned and was walking back to the garage door. There was something odd about Taylor Jackson's eyes, a clear gray, with the right slightly darker than the left, like a storm was moving in and hadn't reached all the way across her face. She was a true beauty, far from perfect, which gave her even more allure. Good Lord, and she was armed. He was bewitched. He felt himself harden, turned back to the table, busying himself with the plate in front of him. Good grief. He was sporting a stalk like a spotty youth.

What the hell was wrong with him? He took stock of the situation, broke it into pieces, just like the police shrink would want him to. The woman was beautiful, yes. She looked like his dead wife, yes. She was alive, and near, and smiled so very nicely at him, oh, yes. She belonged to the agent he was working with on one of the biggest cases he'd touched on in years, yes again.

He struggled to push the woman from his mind, to get his head back to his job. There were three girls whose deaths needed solving, that's why he was here.

It worked for a few minutes. He poured himself the last of the tea, sat back at the table. He couldn't help himself; his mind drifted back to Taylor Jackson.

There were two huge differences between Taylor's voice and Evan's—while Evan's was almost high-pitched, and her British upper-class diction perfect, Taylor's voice was deep and smoky, like she'd been up all night, tinged with the slightest of drawls. It did terrible things to his insides.

Evan's eyes were different, too, the color of the warm summer sky. Like his.

For a moment, he and Taylor had been exactly eye to eye. He could have sworn he saw some sort of recognition there, an understanding. But he was tired, and she was too familiar.

He heard the garage door close, she was officially gone. He laughed mirthlessly. Get it together, man. The mental admonishment sounded exactly like his tutor at Oxford, who was also the coach of his house's rowing crew. "Get it together, man. Get your head in the race." He was relentless on the river—they'd called him the Terror of Balliol College behind his back.

There was a voice by his shoulder. "Hey, Earth calling Memphis! Where did you go?"

Whoops.

He turned and saw Baldwin staring at him. He realized he must look daft, his teacup dangling in his hand, eyes locked on the closed door.

"Sorry. Sorry. Got distracted for a moment."

"I'll say. You looked lost in thought. Let's get you downtown, then we can go over the case."

As if he was going to be able to focus on his job.

Eighteen

Taylor revisited the events of the morning, blushing deeply when she thought about the look on the Brit's face when she'd walked into the kitchen. Like Paris seeing Helen for the first time. How embarrassing. She tried to put the whole event out of her mind. She needed to focus. There was a lot to do today.

The bucolic drive up Old Hickory was pleasant; the green pastures of the Steeplechase on her left, the woods where she'd chased and caught the Rainman to her right. No matter where she looked in Nashville, there were reminders of her past cases, her successes and her failures. The Rainman, a serial rapist named Norville Turner who'd terrorized Nashville for ten long years, was due for trial soon. She'd have to check with A.D.A. Page to see what the exact dates were, but she knew she'd be testifying. The bastard had clocked her in the face during his attempt to flee, and she remembered the satisfaction she felt when she punched him back. She'd knocked him out; her black eye had lasted a full week. It had been a perfect ending to a bitter and difficult case.

She crossed Hillsboro and wended her way into Brentwood. Traffic was heavy, but within ten minutes the gas station appeared on her right. McKenzie stood by a department-issued Caprice, dressed in a gray suit and light blue tie that made his eyes look dark hazel, holding two cups of coffee. She pulled up next to him, hopped out of the truck, and relieved him of one of the drinks.

"You like lattes, right?" McKenzie said.

"I do. Thanks." Taylor was trying to cut back on the Diet Cokes, using lattes for the caffeine rush.

"You want to drive?" he asked.

"Sure," she said. They climbed in and got situated. In addition to getting the coffee, McKenzie had brought donuts from Krispy Kreme. They were still warm. Taylor selected a plain glazed and savored it. She finished it, licked her fingers, then turned the engine over.

"That was sweet of you. Thanks."

"No problem. The hot light was on. Figured we could use some sustenance, it being this early and all."

"That was a kind thought. By the way, we tracked down a piece of evidence last night. Remember the Picasso monograph on Hugh Bangor's coffee table?"

"No. What was it?"

"A *catalogue raisonné*, a book representing the pictures and background of the artist's life work. There was one of Picasso on Bangor's coffee table. Tim Davis found a print that matched a sex offender named Arnold Fay. We had a long talk with Bangor. Turns out he and Fay used to be an item; Fay was the one who broke into Bangor's house. He left the monograph as a present, and that's how we got the print. But Tim found a page missing from the back, so we went up there last night and had another look around. We found a second monograph, this one a catalog from an event at the Museum of Modern Art, and it was missing the back page, too. Someone cut those pages out.

I've got a call into the publishing house to see what was on the sheet. They're supposed to fax us a copy."

"Hey, that's great news. You should have called me, I would have helped. You were at Hugh, I mean, Mr. Bangor's place?"

"Yes, but it was pretty late. We stopped on a hunch."

"Oh. Okay." He sounded disappointed. Taylor was starting to think that the attraction Bangor had for McKenzie might just be mutual.

He sighed. "I sort of already know about Fay. I was doing some research on Bangor, looking at his background and all that yesterday. Remember when he said his partner died of AIDS five years ago? He wasn't telling the truth. I found his name, and looked him up, too. It was the Fay guy."

Taylor glanced over at McKenzie. "Bangor told us all about it last night. It sounds like a bad situation. Did you find anything else?"

"Not yet. I've had the file pulled from the archives. But I asked Mr. Bangor about it last night. It must have been after you left. The boy was thirteen when Bangor's partner was twenty-one. He came out to his parents and introduced Fay and they freaked. They pressed charges and Fay went down for statutory. The boy was so upset by his parents' reaction that he recanted his affair, said it was a rape, let Fay get convicted. At least, that's what Hugh said."

"What's the kid's name? Did you run his record, too?"

"I did. Christopher Gallagher. He's in Texas now, clean. I'll keep following up, see if he's got an alibi. It would be a solid motive. Though coming from Texas to commit a murder seems like a lot of effort."

"Well, think about coming from Italy. I'm not willing to disregard anything just yet." She decided to take a chance.

"McKenzie, be careful with Hugh Bangor. We don't know why he was targeted, and we haven't completely determined his role in this murder. He could be an innocent, he could be implicated. Whatever you do, if you decide to get involved, wait until the case is done, okay? We don't need any more bad press."

"You know?" he said. He sounded miserable.

"I suspected. And it's not a problem, okay? Just promise me that you'll watch your p's and q's with Hugh."

He was quiet for a minute. "You know my girlfriend, the one who killed herself?"

"You've mentioned her."

"It was because of me. We were engaged and I called off the wedding. I just couldn't do it. I'd been in a relationship with a man from college for a couple of years, on and off. I kept thinking that if I just got married, I could lead a normal life. But in the end, I couldn't go through with it. She didn't handle the news well. It was horrible. Took me two years to stop carrying around the guilt. You won't tell anyone, will you?"

"Of course not. That's your business."

"I appreciate that. I moved up here from Orlando to get away from it all. I couldn't take living in the same city as her parents. We'd run into each other at the grocery store. It was awful."

"I can imagine. Okay then. It's our little secret. Now. When the information comes in from the publishing house, I'll need you to go through that page, run down every single detail you can. Who, what, where, when, why and how, okay? There's something there that can help us, I feel it in my gut. You know Lincoln Ross?"

"Sure. He's a great guy."

"Lincoln said you're handy with the computer. Show me what you've got with this, okay?"

Once she hit I-24, she drove fast, in the left lane, buzzing around slower cars and flashing her lights at the eighteen-wheelers who strayed into the left lane from time to time. She passed the 840 loop, headed into Murfreesboro. Not long now.

McKenzie kept looking over at her, like he wanted to say something else. She waited for him, watched him out of the corner of her eye. He was staring at her, trying to be subtle about it. She finally got impatient.

"You're staring. What is it? Do I have donut on my face?"

He blushed when he realized she'd been aware that he was looking.

"Seriously, man, what is it? You're giving me a complex."

"Can I ask you something?"

"Of course."

"Your scar. Is it true, the story? About how you got it?"

Taylor subconsciously ran her right hand across her neck. She rarely thought about the scar anymore, though it was there, in sharp bas-relief across her neck, the souvenir of a crazy, desperate man. Four inches of desecrated flesh. Another millimeter and she wouldn't be here today.

"What story? Guy got desperate. Never get in close with a suspect with a knife, McKenzie. You'll end up getting stuck."

"I meant that you killed him."

Ah.

"I've only killed when I had no other choice, McKenzie." She was amazed at the coldness in her voice. Calm, dead, frigid. The air in the car was charged. McKenzie squirmed, realized he'd crossed some invisible line. She was just about to apologize when the car radio buzzed.

"Detective Jackson? This is Dispatch. Be advised, 10-64, possible 10-89, drowning, code two, Radnor Lake. Please respond."

Taylor groaned and muttered a few choice expletives. She nodded at McKenzie, took the last Murfreesboro exit.

McKenzie keyed the mike. "10-4, Dispatch. We're on our way. We're just south of Murfreesboro, it will take a bit for us to get there. Out."

Taylor dug her notebook out of her pocket and handed it to McKenzie. "Call the Coffee County Sheriff, his name is Simmons. Tell him we got pulled back to town. Tell him I'm sorry and I'll get in touch with him later."

Taylor was already back on the highway heading north. She put the flasher on and took advantage of the rest of the drivers scurrying out of her path to exceed the speed limit. Another murder. At the lake, the 10-89 was logical, but the code two meant there was something urgent about the call. She had to assume it was a murder. It never failed—they tended to pile up on one another. Though Radnor Lake—they didn't get called there too often. She wondered what was going on, then contented herself with putting her foot on the gas.

At least this got them off the topic of her scar. She still wasn't comfortable enough with McKenzie to talk about the terror she'd felt when she saw her own blood spilling down her chest. That insane moment of clarity between the cut and the pain. She knew she was dead. She should have been dead. She was damn lucky Baldwin had been there. His medical training saved her life. Always handy to be hanging out with a doctor during a chase.

She forced it from her mind. No sense going there.

They made it back up to Davidson County in twenty minutes, took the Bell Road exit, blew up Old Hickory to Granny White. Within minutes they'd plowed through the tony neighborhood surrounding the lake and turned right on Otter Creek. The entrance to the park was a half a mile up the road. Leafy green oak trees overhung the street, three red posts halted traffic into the preserve. There was a parking lot to her left. She pulled into it, joining the rest of the responding officers.

Several police cruisers were in the lot, lights off, which was strange. Tim Davis's crime-scene van was parked by the entrance to the trailhead.

Taylor and McKenzie exited their vehicle. Taylor was struck by the verdant beauty of the surroundings, the quiet. All this ten miles from downtown Nashville.

Paula Simari was standing by her cruiser with a blond, white-faced park ranger. Max was in the backseat, straining against the window.

The ranger's name tag read R. Kilkowski. A pair of oval-shaped brown plastic glasses rested on her impossibly small nose. When Taylor shook her hand, she noticed it was trembling.

"Simari. Ma'am. What's happening? Why no flashers?"

"It disturbs the wildlife," the ranger said. "We've had three bald eagles, two adults and a juvenile, in the park in the last week. We've canceled everything in the hopes that they might nest here. Officer Simari was kind enough to agree to try to limit the commotion."

Taylor raised an eyebrow but didn't say a word. She knew how deadly serious the conservation efforts were at Radnor Lake. It was one of the only protected wildlife sanctuaries—a real biological ecosystem—near a major metropolitan city in the country. Radnor Lake consisted of twelve hundred acres of pristine lake, wildlife and walking trails. No biking or picnics were allowed—the fragile ecosystem was dependent on clean, quiet and calm. This was sure to rattle everyone's, and everything's, cages.

The "Friends" of Radnor Lake were a veritable who's who of Nashville's elite, and they threw some serious cash behind the conservation efforts. The lake had started in 1913, as a water-filling depot and hunting area for the L&N Railroad Company and had morphed into a privately held, privately funded nature reserve. Taylor knew that a dead body wouldn't be high on the board's wish list.

Simari shook McKenzie's hand, tapped Taylor on the shoulder. "Glad you got here so quickly. You've got to see this. Thought you might find some similarities to your Love Hill victim. Body is female, black, skinny as hell."

Taylor felt the first bits of adrenaline crash through her system. She'd assumed this was a run-of-the-mill homicide. As if there was such a thing.

"Drowned?"

"I don't know. You just need to see it, I don't want to influence you." Simari nodded to the ranger. "Lead the way."

"Do I have to go back there?" Kilkowski asked, voice tremulous. Her eyes were wet behind the glasses.

Taylor reassured her. "Don't worry, you don't have to look. Just take us down the right path." The girl nodded, started walking up the hill from the parking lot, stiff as a board. The three of them followed her.

Simari looked back to Taylor. "It's damn quiet out here. I'm surprised this doesn't happen more. No one around at night, the park's closed."

"Video?" McKenzie asked.

"Yes. They're making us a copy. But their guards never saw anything suspicious, on the feed or on their foot patrol. We'll have to go over the tapes minute by minute. There are no cameras pointing at this spot. Either he was smart or lucky."

"Or knows the park," McKenzie said.

They walked about fifty yards up the hill which Taylor knew led to the dam. They disturbed a murder of crows, who flew noisily into the air, then redistributed themselves among the branches to the side of the trail, cawing their displeasure. They watched as Taylor and her crew walked by. She wasn't fond of crows; it was almost as if they knew her thoughts and were on guard against her.

They heard a distinct crashing sound and everyone jumped, then laughed nervously. There was a flash of white; Taylor assumed it was a deer. It took her heartbeat a moment to get back to its normal rhythm. She was on edge, just waiting for something unexpected to leap out at her.

There was a creek running under the stretch of road they were walking on. It was full, the water moving peacefully. The recent rainfalls had increased the water tables tremendously. Taylor looked down the lip and saw a snake gliding off into the water, its head high. Water moccasin, probably. As they moved through the woods, the crows' echoing calls were quickly replaced by the pervasive silence. The lake was quiet, the stillness terrifically loud, filled with living creatures' call signs.

Taylor remembered this stretch of the path. She'd been a part of the search for Perry March's wife, Janet, the frantic days looking for her body stretching into weeks, months and eventually years. As a cadet, she'd been a lead on one of the search teams, had been on foot for days on end looking under brush and in the woods.

Janet's body had never been found, but Perry March, after several years in Mexico claiming his innocence, had been extradited and stood trial. He'd been convicted after his father gave a confession that he helped get rid of Janet's body. Taylor hoped he would rot in jail!—he'd been the cause of heartache for half of Nashville for years. She'd always known he'd done it, too; his smug arrogance in thinking he'd gotten away with it was his downfall. It usually was for men like that.

The sun slipped behind a passel of clouds. A storm was

brewing. Taylor started worrying about preserving evidence. They rounded a curve in the trail and the lake spilled out in front of them, rippling in the soft breeze. It was a stunning sight, beauty and horror commingled. Twenty feet to her right, Taylor could see Tim Davis picking his way down the opposite side of the path, a camera in his hand.

"The body isn't in the lake?"

The ranger's voice quivered. "No. She's in Otter Creek itself."

Taylor looked into the flowing creek. She could clearly see the object of Tim's attentions—a body floated in the shallow water. A few people stood around watching, taking notes.

Ranger Kilkowski made a small mewling noise, handed them off to a handsome man with silver hair, a great tan, and crinkly blue eyes.

He scrambled up the bank, hand outstretched. Where Kilkowski was shy, this guy was a bundle of energy.

"Hey, I'm Dick Harkins. Park manager. Glad to meet you, though I'm sorry about the circumstances." He waved to the scene below them.

Taylor did the introductions. "You found her?"

"I did. I was taking a walk around, just checking on things. Saw something out of place, a flash of color. I thought it might have been a piece of cloth, something someone discarded. Instead…"

A weeping willow hung over the water, and a fallen branch was sticking up out of the rocky shoal. The combination created a tunnel of shade. Taylor could see easily despite the shadows. She sucked in her breath, started down the bank.

A small woman bobbed gently, moving with the creek's slight ebb and flow. She was on her back, mouth and eyes open, arms stretched out by her side. In her right hand, she clutched a bouquet of flowers, some red, some blue, some yellow. Her neck was ringed with purple flowers, violets, by the look of them. She was dressed in a long, flowing gown which stuck to her legs, outlining them in white cotton. The skirt had gotten snagged on the dead branch. That must be how she ended up here. Taylor instinctively felt the girl was supposed to be adrift.

"Tim, tell me you've documented the hell out of this."

Tim carefully joined her. "I have."

"I need to get Baldwin out here. Immediately."

"What's up with this? It looks so staged."

"It is staged. Completely. This time I know what he's trying to say. This has to be the same killer."

Nineteen

Baldwin was in the lobby of the Loews Vanderbilt, finishing a call with Quantico and waiting for Memphis to get himself situated, when his other line rang. He saw it was Taylor but sent the call to voice mail—he needed to finish this meeting. He wrapped it up in five minutes and saw the message light blinking. He checked his voice mail, played the message. Felt the disbelief and excitement rise in his chest.

Il Macellaio had struck again.

"Son of a bitch," he said. Highsmythe, who'd appeared wearing jeans and a well-cut brown blazer, looked at him strangely.

"Sorry, not you," Baldwin said.

"Bad news?" Highsmythe asked.

"In a way. In a way, good news. It looks like our boy has left us another victim. Hang on while I get the details. Have a seat, get a drink. I'll be right with you."

Highsmythe nodded and walked over to the restaurant, where he took a chair at the table and busied himself with his briefcase. Baldwin dialed Taylor's number; she answered on the first ring.

"I'm at Radnor Lake. I've got another body," she said. He could hear the exhilaration in her voice, knew something major had happened. "You need to get out here. Bring the Brit, he may be a help. I think I know what he's doing this time, but I want you to see it. Tell me what you think."

"Same guy?"

"Absolutely."

"Okay. We'll be right there."

He ended the call and put the BlackBerry back in his pocket. He ran his fingers through his hair, scrubbing it to make his mind work better. Why had Il Macellaio come to the United States? Why had his victims suddenly switched races? To throw them off the trail? Maybe he thought that no one in Nashville, Tennessee, would be bright enough to piece his earlier killings together with the new one. Well, he had another think coming. Baldwin was onto him.

Memphis was just about to go looking for the FBI agent when he spotted him on the way back to the table with a worried frown.

"Highsmythe, we have a conundrum. Il Macellaio may have struck again. Why does this killer move from Italy to England and on to the United States? And why does he switch races when he crosses the pond?"

"Good questions, all."

The waiter appeared, apologizing for the wait.

"Coffee, tea, water, soda, gents. What's your poison?"

"I'm sorry, but we have to leave." Baldwin tossed a five on the table.

"Certainly, sir," the waiter said, pocketing the money.

Memphis stood and yawned widely, felt his ears crack. That was better. He hated to fly. He followed Baldwin's swift steps out of the restaurant. "We're going to the crime scene?"

"Yes. I'm sorry, but Taylor felt we both needed to see this."

"It's not a problem."

They walked through the lobby and retrieved the Suburban from the valet. Memphis didn't know where they were headed. West, it seemed. He flipped the Suburban's sun visor down and glanced in the mirror. Despite having a couple of hours of sleep and a chance to clean up, he was still looking rough. His blue eyes were bloodshot, his blond hair mussed, his cheeks and jaw covered in two days of golden stubble. He looked hard-ridden and put away wet. International travel did it to him every time. He slapped the visor back into place.

"Tired?" Baldwin asked.

"A bit. This case, you know. Been keeping me up all hours for weeks. Your bit of skirt is quite the woman, isn't she?" Memphis asked.

Baldwin looked up in surprise, then smiled.

"Oh, Taylor? Yes, my *fiancée,* not my bit of skirt."

"Must be awfully hard to work so far away. Woman like that, I'd want to keep my eye on. So tell me, is she a wine-and-roses kind of a girl, or is she a bit of a tigress between the sheets?"

"I live in Nashville full-time," Baldwin said flatly. "And my personal life is none of your business."

"Oh. Just so. My wife was the wine-and-roses type." He took the hint. Mr. FBI didn't like to talk about his private life. That was fine.

"Back to the case. Let's talk about this development," Baldwin was saying.

"Why do you live in Nashville and work in Virginia?" Memphis asked. He was needling, he knew it, but he couldn't help himself. He'd known plenty of men like this. Reserved to the point of being standoffish, but

Memphis could pry them open like an oyster with a few well-placed questions. The woman was off topic, but he'd yet to meet a man who didn't like to talk about himself.

Baldwin looked over at him. "Why do you care?"

Hmm. That was a good question. Why was he fishing for information? *Because you want to hear more about his woman, you fool. Get yourself together, get back in the case.*

"Just getting to know you," Memphis said. "Tell me about the developments."

"I'm putting the finishing touches on the profile, but if this murder is connected we need to rethink a few things. The victim's race has changed, which is an anomaly. And I didn't expect him to strike again so soon."

"Anomaly. Excellent. Something like that will help us run him to ground, right?"

"Perhaps."

Memphis thought about it for a few minutes. "You said his new victims are Afro-Caribbean. Why would he change midstream?"

"That's the question. A stressor, an event that's driven him over the edge. Maybe a girlfriend broke up with him and now he's transferring, which isn't something he's done in the past. I don't know. He's altered his methods as well, the murders in the States are much more like Florence. Showy. Planned. London feels more opportunistic. Couple that with the fact that he's been killing black girls in the States for possibly four years, and we've found two kills that match his M.O. so far…there's more to be understood. Remember, my profile won't tell you *who* he is. It is just a guide for the type of person you need to be looking for."

Ah, that was the way to get in with Dr. Baldwin. Shoptalk. He didn't feel comfortable with the man. Not enough to share that he'd been offered a position with the

FBI. Pen was going to kill him when she found out. And Memphis got the distinct impression that news wouldn't go over so well here, either. He stuck to the case at hand.

"Maybe he's a bit of both," he said.

Baldwin's forehead creased. "A bit of both. You mean organized and disorganized?"

"No. He's killed black women and white women. He likes them both. Perhaps he's a bit of white and a bit of black himself."

That captured the tall man's attention. He glanced over in appreciation, then said, "Nicely deduced. That's one of the adjustments I've included in the new profile. I'm assuming he's biracial. It explains how he could fit in with both types of women. We have no record of their disappearances being against their will. I think he charms them."

"Or hires them. Some of the street girls we know will take money for just about anything. They allow themselves to be hurt."

"Yes. That, too."

"Glad to be of assistance," Memphis said.

"We'll have a look at this crime scene, see if we think it's another Il Macellaio victim. I'm planning on presenting the entire profile tomorrow in Quantico. Listen, we've got another ten minutes before we'll be at the lake. Why don't you fill me in on your side of things, and I can include my impressions. We can talk this through, see if you think it could be the same man. If your schedule permits, we'll head up to Quantico first thing tomorrow morning instead of this afternoon—I'd like to stick around for a bit and see more about Taylor's new case. Are you okay with that?"

Hmm. More chances to tête-a-tête with the blond goddess?

"Sounds lovely."

He launched into a breakdown of the cases he'd been working.

He forced Evan's doppelganger from his mind. Most of the way.

Twenty

The sun disappeared, replaced by inky gray fog. The forest muffled the sounds of the storm; the drizzle created an insulating barrier cutting them off from the rest of the world. Taylor stuffed her hands into the front pockets of her jeans and sighed. Outdoor crime scenes were a complete pain in the ass. You never knew what would be relevant, had to document and collect even the tiniest shred of disturbed grass. Tim had a massive pile of brown paper bags in the back of his van. The crime lab had a long evening ahead of them.

There was activity on the trail. Good, Baldwin was here.

He and the Brit came around the curve and hurried to her side.

She introduced Highsmythe around. She hurried; she could tell Baldwin was fidgety, anxious to get moving.

"Where's the body?" Baldwin asked.

She pointed to the creek. "Down there. We're about ready to get her out of here. Come on, I'll take you."

They scrambled down the bank, Taylor in the lead. She stopped five feet from the body.

Both men spoke at the same time. "Ophelia."

Taylor nodded at them.

Memphis bent down, edged a bit closer. "'There is a willow grows askant the brook, that shows the hoar leaves in the glassy stream, therewith fantastic garlands did she make, of crow-flowers, nettles, daisies and long purples that liberal shepherds give a grosser name, but our cold maids do dead men's fingers call them.'"

He looked back over his shoulder at Taylor.

"You're quoting *Hamlet?*" she asked.

He blushed. "I wasn't good enough to play Hamlet. I was quoting the queen, actually. It's Gertrude's soliloquy to Laertes upon finding Ophelia drowned." He smiled at her, and she couldn't help but smile back.

"You know your Shakespeare," she said.

"Oh, it's nothing. I played Laertes a few times, dramatic society and what not. Those were my cast-about years."

"Still, I'm impressed that you remember. I can't ever recall like that. You and Baldwin must be having a blast together."

His eyes shot over to Baldwin, who stepped closer and put a hand lightly on Taylor's back.

"Not to interrupt, but back to the victim?"

"Oh, of course. I told you this looked like the drowning of Ophelia. There must be a hundred versions of this out there."

"It is many renaissance painter's favorite subject, no doubt. I thought you were going to Manchester."

"We were. We got called back around Murfreesboro."

Baldwin was tapping his fingers against the small of her back.

"I was wrong. I didn't think he'd strike again so soon. Damn it."

"It happens," Memphis said. "We've gone off on many a wild-goose chase with Il Macellaio."

Baldwin shot him a look. "Still, two women in two days. He's escalating. We need to stop him now."

They made their way back up the bank. Highsmythe excused himself to wander for a bit. When he was twenty feet away, he stopped and stared off into the lake. She and Baldwin watched him for a moment.

"I recognize that look," Taylor said, gesturing to him. "He's going to come up with something brilliant."

"Recognize his looks already, do you darling?"

"Baldwin, don't tease."

He cupped her chin in his hand and looked deep into her eyes.

"Just remember something."

"What's that?"

"In the school play? I was Hamlet."

They had the body out of the water, ready for transport to Forensic Medical and Sam when the rain started to fall in earnest. The only noise was the spatter of raindrops on the leaves, the wet slap against the water's edge and discreet cursing as the doors to the medical examiner's van slammed shut.

Baldwin and Highsmythe had taken photos, then scattered back to Baldwin's office to get the profile adjusted.

Taylor and McKenzie stood with the anxious rangers, who were worried for their safety. Kilkowski was still shuddering. Harkins was trying, and failing, to comfort her.

"Should we keep the park closed?" he asked.

"I think it will be fine to reopen, but block off this part of the trail so you don't have any lookiloos disturbing the crime scene."

"Okay. Robin, let's get you something warm to drink. A nice cup of tea should help," the park manager said. He shook Taylor and McKenzie's hands. She could tell that wasn't enough reassuring, but it would have to do.

McKenzie watched them go. "They'll have the security tapes ready in a minute. Hopefully we can get a timeline on the intruder. Harkins explained their security measures, but they're more designed to discourage poaching than something like this."

"Did they give you an idea of the currents? Where she might have gone in the water?"

"I think he put her in that exact spot. You said it's just like a painting you'd seen, right? I bet he wouldn't have chanced it."

Taylor did a three-sixty. McKenzie was right. They were close enough to the west parking lot that the killer could have walked in with the body slung over his shoulder. The tapes would help, if he'd been stupid enough to be caught on them. Taylor somehow doubted this guy would be that careless.

Two bodies in three days. Their boy was getting antsy. She tried doing the calculations—Allegra Johnson had been missing for three weeks. She had no idea who this new victim was, or how long she'd been gone. But with the bodies being dropped in such close proximity, she wondered if he'd had them both, at the same time. Jesus.

No way to tell until Sam got a look at her.

As they walked back to the car, a Newschannel Five van pulled into the parking lot.

"Shit. Stall them," she said to McKenzie. She slipped into the car and called Rowena to check on the fax from New York. Nothing yet. She asked if Elm was in the office. Rowena just snorted and said hold on. A click later, the phone rang. Elm answered.

"Lieutenant, this is Jackson. I'm at Radnor Lake, attending—"

"Where are you?"

"Radnor Lake. It's—"

"Not what I meant, Detective. Why haven't you checked in yet today?"

"Um, sir, Detective McKenzie and I were heading to Manchester to look at an open murder case down there when we got called to this crime scene."

"It is simply not appropriate for you to start your day anywhere but in this office. Do you understand?"

Taylor swallowed the reply telling Elm where to go. She said, "Yes," instead.

"That is all," Elm said, then hung up.

Taylor looked at her phone as if it could give her the answers she sought, then closed it and shoved it in her pocket. She needed to do something about Elm, and fast. This administrative bullshit was going to end up getting someone killed. Probably Elm. By her.

Channel Four had joined Channel Five, and the Channel Seventeen van was pulling in now too. The respective reporters tumbled out of their vans like puppies, pulling on rain gear and opening golf umbrellas. She needed to nip this in the bud, fast. Taylor knew how the Nashville press could work a story. She decided to get ahead of it.

She got out of the car. McKenzie leaned against the trunk ignoring the rain streaming down, stone-faced, not answering the multitude of questions being asked him. Good. The kid was learning. She opened an umbrella and went to him. He nodded in appreciation. The news teams were still setting up shop. The cameras weren't rolling yet. Perfect.

The reporters saw that she was going to talk to them and started scrambling. She really shouldn't enjoy that, but she did. Oh, well. She was probably going to hell anyway.

"Hi, Scott, Cindy. Hey, Cynthia. Listen, I don't have a prepared statement. Here's what I can give you. An unidentified black female, no apparent wounds, found floating in Otter Creek, just off the lake. We have no determination of homicide or suicide. We don't know who she is, and we don't have a cause of death. I'll make sure Dan Franklin gets with you as soon as we have more. Okay?"

The three reporters started peppering her with questions. The one that mattered came from Fox's Cindy Carter. "Is this related to the Love Circle crime scene? We've got two dead girls in two days, both black. Is there a serial killer on the loose?"

"No comment. Seriously, I have absolutely nothing to indicate that the crimes are related."

"What's your gut say? Is this the work of the Conductor?" Scott asked.

"I learned not to discuss my gut with you long ago, my friend. Nice try, though." She spied Cynthia Williams edging away; her cameraman had one of the park rangers in his sights. She'd given them enough. They could conjecture the rest.

She ignored the rest of the questions and left them. They wouldn't be allowed inside the crime-scene tape while Tim was still collecting evidence, and the angle they had wouldn't give them anything concrete. It was time to move on.

She and McKenzie shook themselves off and got in the car. They needed to get to Manchester. She really wanted to see those files now.

By the time they reached I-24, the rain had stopped.

They started south again and she asked McKenzie a question.

"Talk to me about the differences in the two scenes, so we're fresh and clear when we look at the Manchester case."

"Okay. There was no music playing at Radnor Lake, for one. The victim was clothed, not naked like Allegra. No obvious signs of trauma on the lake girl, but who knows what's under that dress."

"And the similarities?"

"Black, bone-thin, staged scenes. Cause of death would be helpful, if she *was* starved we have something to go on. She's holding those flowers…with the ring of violets around her neck, too, there's something about the flowers that have meaning for him. It seems gentler than the Love Circle murder, more serene. But this definitely feels like the same killer, don't you think?"

"Yes, I do. Why do you think he's changed his M.O.?"

"Thinks he's smarter than us, maybe? Wants to be seen as a criminal mastermind." He was quiet for a moment. "So you think he's talking to us?"

"Absolutely. He wants the glory, wants to be seen as clever and important. He's playing with us. The first crime scene he posed Allegra like the Picasso painting. This one looks like a variation on the drowning of Ophelia, but narrowing it down to one artist will be difficult. Many, many painters interpreted Shakespeare."

They continued comparing notes until the Manchester exit. Taylor turned right and entered the small town. Maybe there would be a solid clue here.

Coffee County was named after a confederate general named John Coffee, a good friend of Andrew Jackson's and a hero of the War of 1812. Down here, there was still pride about the role Tennessee played in the forming of the nation. They called the Civil War the "Late Unpleasantness," and confederate flags flew high. Most were just country folk; honest, hardworking people who recognized their heritage for what it was. History can't be undone, regardless of who it might have hurt.

The Coffee County Sheriff's office was on Hillsboro, only about five minutes from the highway. Taylor hadn't been down here in years, not since a school field trip to see an air show in neighboring Tullahoma. Now, Manchester was world famous for hosting the hippie jam Bonnaroo, a yearly pseudo-Woodstock.

It wasn't a rich area, by any means. But it was clean, and safe. For the most part.

The sheriff's office was quiet and cool. A receptionist called back to Sheriff Simmons, who came out to the front with a big smile and a heavy handshake. He nearly broke Taylor's arm from her shoulder. He was a bear of a man, wide through the shoulders and gut. A former defensive lineman, she guessed. He was built like a house. And young, too, no more than her age. Probably a little less.

"Detective Jackson, Detective McKenzie! Thanks so much for coming down. I've got us all set up in my office. You had another murder in Nashville this morning?"

"Yes," Taylor said, following him back a short hallway. "Another black female, very thin and posed. I'm doubly anxious to go through your records now."

He got them seated, asked if they needed a drink. They both declined. Simmons went around to his side of the desk, sat heavily in a gargantuan leather chair. The springs squeaked in protest.

"So here's the deal. I've got the files for you." He waved his hand at the desk, where three file folders were stacked on each other. "But there's not a lot there. I read through them all again. I don't know what help it's going to be."

"We appreciate you putting this together for us." She picked up the first file. "Were you involved in the investigation?"

"I sure was. It was my last case as a deputy, I got promoted right after. But I'll never forget it. The victim, LaTara Bender, was a girl in my younger brother's class at Central. I knew she'd gotten into some bad stuff, but you never think things are going to go that far south. The scene was straightforward. The girl was found in the bathtub by her mother. Her death looked like it could have been a suicide or an accidental drowning. You know, maybe the girl got high, passed out, slipped below the water. Her mother kept insisting that LaTara was clean, that she'd been murdered. Once we got the autopsy done, seems like she was right. Medical examiner, right nice lady who I'm sure you know, Dr. Loughley up there at Forensic Medical, found a skull fracture. We investigated her death as a homicide, and it's still unsolved."

"So was she drowned?"

"Looks like. Knocked on the head first, right on top of the noggin, too. Not an injury she could have easily given herself."

"Did your brother know her well enough to talk to us?"

"I'm sure he did. It's not a huge school, you know. Want me to give him a ring? He's a deputy now, too, and he's on shift."

"Please. That would be great."

He picked up the phone, asked for Shay Simmons to call in. Within a few minutes, the phone rang.

"Shay, it's Steve. Can you swing in my office for a minute? Got a coupla detectives from Nashville want to talk to you about LaTara Bender. Okay, thanks." He hung up.

"He'll be here in five."

"Fabulous. Thank you. So, while we're waiting, what kind of stuff had LaTara been getting into?"

"You know how it is in these small towns, Detective. Some of them want to break free, some are mired in worlds of their own making. LaTara was one of the latter. If you want my opinion, that girl never had a chance. I wasn't surprised to find her dead. For a while we thought it was just a sad accident, like I said. When we found out she'd been murdered, well…it's hard for these girls. They get themselves into drugs and spiral out of control."

"And there was classical music playing at the scene when you arrived?"

Simmons looked at her, a frown creasing his forehead. "Yes, there was. We didn't think much of it at the time. It was another bone of contention with the family— LaTara's mother said they didn't have any classical music, wasn't her kind of thing. There was a CD playing on the stereo in LaTara's bedroom."

"Do you know what it was?"

"It's in the files, I'm sure. Can't say I recall off the top of my head."

A soft knock made them all turn and look at the door. A younger version of Simmons filled the doorway. Taylor laughed to herself. These corn-fed farm boys were huge.

"Shay, come on in," Simmons said. The younger man entered the office and gave his brother a handshake. Taylor could tell they were close.

"Shay, this is Detective Taylor Jackson and Detective Renn McKenzie. They're investigating a series of murders in Nashville, want to hear about LaTara. Can you tell them what you remember?"

The younger Simmons' face colored. "Poor LaTara. That girl…such a sad case. She got into drugs, started staying out all night. Stopped going to church, stopped coming to school. By the time we graduated, she was turning tricks. She had a hard life—her uncle raped her when she was seven or eight, and she had to testify against him. It was all done by video, but still, it was a horrible situation. She used to talk about it, how scared she was sitting in the judge's office. She never really got over it."

"It sounds like you knew her well."

"Not that so much as I tried to help her. She was a scared mouse in school, you know the kind. Jumping at shadows. But she got into drugs, and once that happened, there was nothing I could do for her. Mostly prescription stuff in school, some pot and meth, too, though I'm sure she moved on to the harder drugs once she dropped out."

The sheriff spoke. "We found a prescription for methadone at the scene. Seems she was trying to turn over a new leaf. She hadn't entirely cleaned herself up, her tox screen showed opiates. It was consistent with what we knew about her lifestyle. It was just such a damn shame, seeing a sweet girl go down that road."

"Deputy Simmons, is there anything else you know about her? Who she was hanging around with? A boyfriend? Did she have a pimp, a dealer that you remember? Was she close to anyone? Have any enemies?"

He thought for a minute. "There wasn't anything like that. I can't recall her having a boyfriend. There was one guy who hung around her, this skinny kid. Oh, what was his name? I can't remember, I'll have to go look through the yearbook. Otherwise, it was just on the sly. Her momma was strict, I do know that. But it broke her when LaTara died."

"Is her mother still around?"

"Sure. Lives in the same house where LaTara passed. Bless her heart." He looked at his brother. "Listen, I've got to go, I need to get back out on the road. Bubba's covering for me, he's ready for lunch."

The sheriff got to his feet, signaled to his brother. "Get on out of here. I'll see you at dinner. Judy's making pot roast. Thanks for coming in." They slapped each other on the back briefly.

The sheriff gestured to the files on his desk, caught Taylor's eye. "Besides, we're waxing poetic here. Y'all need to go through the files. We're going to step out, let you get up to speed, then I'll answer any more questions you might have. Got a good old boy in the drunk tank that needs springing. Just shout down to Debbie if you need me."

"I appreciate it, Sheriff. Deputy Simmons." They all shook hands again, then the two men sauntered off down the hall, one of them whistling.

Taylor settled into the chair, pulled the top file toward her, pushed the second in the stack at McKenzie. "Let's get started."

It only took half an hour to get through the meager files. According to the reports, LaTara was discovered by her mother, Marie Bender, who allegedly dragged her daughter's body out of the tub, then called 911. The scene had been disturbed, no doubt about it. A CD of Vivaldi's *Four Seasons* was in the stereo, the repeat button pressed so "Winter" played over and over. No one knew what the significance was, so they'd printed it, gotten nothing off it, and placed it into evidence. Taylor wasn't entirely sure what the significance was either, but the simple fact that it was there, so out of place in the Bender household, stood out starkly. That, and it matched the tentative M.O. they had from the Love Circle crime scene.

McKenzie traded files with her silently.

After a few moments, Taylor said, "There's only one big thing that's leaping out at me."

"What's that? The head injury?"

"No, that's not it. LaTara had been bludgeoned, causing the skull fracture, then drowned in the bathtub. There were signs that she'd had sex recently, but no trace of semen had been found. Granted, she was lying in a tub of bathwater. I can't imagine they did a rape kit and looked for DNA. Why would they? It didn't look like a sexual assault, plus the victim was known to be engaged in illegal activities. This was a small town's investigation—autopsy done in Nashville, evidence passed along to the TBI for analysis—for the most part, obvious answers fit the crime. Standard forensic work had been done. The case was handled just fine, only without a final resolution."

"So what's jumping out at you?"

"According to the crime-scene reports, there was a large area of damp carpet outside the bathroom door."

She gave McKenzie a moment to process. She saw the lightbulb go off a few moments later. She bit back a smile.

"You think he killed her, then took her out of the tub and had sex with her."

"It's a possibility. Assuming we're dealing with the same killer, it fits. I don't know if that's the case. We need to find out if the mother dragged the girl's body into the bedroom, or if that event was confined to the bath. If it was, we've got something to go on."

She made a note to ask the sheriff about it. All kinds of ideas were running through her head. Was it the mother, or an EMT, who splashed water on the carpet? Or was it something more nefarious? Because knowing the M.O. of her killer, the postmortem sex scenario made perfect sense.

Simmons popped his head back into his office. "Need anything?" he asked.

Taylor grabbed the sheet she'd been reading from. "Actually, yes. Perfect timing. Do you remember the wet carpet outside the bathroom door?"

"Let me see." She handed him the report. He looked it over, then got a faraway look in his eye and rubbed his meaty chin, like it would help him remember.

"You know, I do. Seems her mama pulled her from the tub. That bathroom's not so big, I'd assume it was splash from the tub's water. At least, we did at the time. It was about two feet from the bathroom door, just to the right of LaTara's bed. Why do you ask? It mean something to you?"

"I hate to even be thinking it, but if this is the same killer, we need to look at all the possibilities. You never tested LaTara for semen, correct?"

"Yeah. It wasn't an assault, leastways it didn't look like it at the time. You think we missed something?" His voice had taken on a wary tone, slightly defensive. Taylor needed to keep him on her side.

"We suspect our killer is a necrosadist, someone who kills women to have sex with their bodies. If this is our same guy, it's possible that he killed LaTara, took her wet body into the bedroom, had sex with her, then put her back in the tub. He washed one of his victims that we know of, and the one from this morning was set adrift in a creek."

"I'm starting to think he has a water fetish," McKenzie added.

Simmons was looking at them with pure disgust on his face. "He has sex with dead bodies? What's this guy, like a Ted Bundy?"

"It's possible. Bundy used to dig up his girls and have sex with them for weeks. Right now, it looks like our guy discards them within a few days. The FBI is investigating a series of crimes overseas that match the M.O. We're concerned that perhaps the same killer is working this territory. We need more to work with, though. We're trying to trace him, to see if and when he started killing in Tennessee. There was another murder similar to this in Chattanooga, last year. Black girl, skinny, found in her bedroom, classical music playing. I'm waiting to hear back from their homicide office to see what matches."

Simmons still looked freaked out. She tried to get him back into the game.

"Listen, your brother said LaTara's mother still lives in the same house. Any chance we could go talk to her, see what she remembers? If she took the body into the bedroom, this is a dead end. If she didn't, and there's a chance our killer might have moved her around..."

"You think you can find something now, three years later?"

"It's worth a shot," McKenzie said.

"Then let's get you out there," Simmons said. "Miss Marie's place is a five-minute drive."

Twenty-One

Taylor stood in the front yard of a run-down, ramshackle single-story house on the outskirts of Manchester proper. Another mile into town and all of this would have been under the Manchester Police's purview; since it was outside the city limits, the Coffee County Sheriff had handled the investigation. It was getting late; they needed to wrap this up so she and McKenzie could get back to Nashville. Sam had called to say she'd be doing the post on the Radnor Lake victim last thing this afternoon. Taylor wanted to witness, had asked her to hold off for another hour or so. She'd really like to wrap Manchester in a tidy bow.

Simmons knocked, and LaTara's mother came to the door. She was tall and elegant, skin like the deepest espresso, eyes liquid and expressionless. She stared at the contingent of cops standing on her front porch, sighed, and stepped back to allow them entry. Taylor noticed that one of her arms was drastically shorter than the other.

The inside of the house was better kept than the outside. Though the furnishings were worn, they were clean, kept with pride. A sewing machine and bolts of fabric stood unobtrusively in a corner of the wide living room. Drapes, Taylor thought. She spied a card on the sideboard that confirmed it; Marie Bender was a seamstress.

The four of them settled in the kitchen, glasses of homemade lemonade in front of them. Taylor listened while the sheriff explained why they were there, saw the pain flit across the woman's eyes.

"You have a suspect in my girl's murder?" she asked.

"No, ma'am. Well, possibly. I don't want to get your hopes up. I'm just trying to flesh out a few details. Is it okay if we talk about that day?"

"Yes. I want the person who did this to LaTara to be brought to justice. There's not much I can do for her 'cept fight for that. I watched her slip away from me, into drugs, whoring around. I would like to see some closure for her. She was so unhappy. Nothing I ever did could make up for the...incident."

"Her uncle?" McKenzie asked gently.

Mrs. Bender's eyes grew hard. "Yes, damn his soul to hell. He stole the light out of my little girl. She couldn't ever put it behind her. But she was trying so hard to change. She'd started at a clinic, was trying to get off the heroin. It was just so easy for her to use it to forget. I can't say I blamed her. It's not right, and she had to pay too big a price. Her daddy was gone, Eddie was the male figure in her life. When he betrayed her, she was lost."

Taylor turned to the sheriff, who read her mind. "No chance Eddie Bender's involved, he got himself killed in jail. They don't take kindly to child rapists, you know." Taylor nodded, then turned back to Mrs. Bender.

"Ma'am, when you found LaTara, the report says you took her body out of the tub, held her while you waited for the paramedics to come."

Sadness crowded the woman's eyes. "I did. She was

gone, any fool could see that. I just wanted a few more minutes with my baby. I shouldn't have touched her, the sheriff here done told me that, but I couldn't help it."

"Where, exactly, did you take her?"

"Where? What do you mean?"

"When you had her in your arms, where were you in the room? Were you in the bedroom, or still in the bathroom?"

"I was still in the bathroom." She started to cry. "I only had her a few feet from the tub, on the tiles. I remember how cold she was, how cold the floor was."

"You're sure you didn't take her into the bedroom?"

She gathered herself, dabbed the tears from her eyes. "Positive."

"Did you spill water in the bedroom, something that would get the carpet wet?"

"No. No one knew how that water got there."

Taylor felt the excitement building. "Ma'am, have you had your carpets cleaned lately?"

"Detective, I ain't got no money for that kind of thing. It's all I can do to keep the chores done around here and keep my business afloat." She gestured to her deformed arm. "LaTara used to help with that. It's just not as easy to keep things up with one arm, though I do my best."

Taylor smiled. "I completely understand. Ma'am, would you excuse us for a moment?"

Mrs. Bender nodded and stood, leaving them at the table.

Taylor spoke quietly. No sense upsetting the woman more than she had to. "Sheriff, would you mind if our crime-scene tech came down, took a sample of that carpet? It's probably a long shot, especially after all this time, but if there's a chance that we can lift some DNA, I'd sure like to take it."

"We've got a pretty sophisticated forensic setup. Why don't you let us handle the evidence collection? We can get it done before your man drives down here, get you on your way sooner."

"That would be fine with me, if you don't mind."

"I don't mind if Miss Marie doesn't. I'll go talk to her."

He came back with Mrs. Bender. She had distrust smeared across her face.

"You gonna replace it?" she asked.

Bangor had said exactly the same thing about his post.

Taylor nodded. "We'll do our best to get things back to normal for you as quickly as possible. You have my word."

"Well, then, if it will help catch who did this to LaTara, do what you need to do."

Simmons flipped open his cell phone. "I'll go call my crime-scene techs, see who's free. Give us ten minutes or so, we'll get things moving."

Mrs. Bender sat back down at the table. Taylor took a drink of her lemonade. It was exceptional. She told Mrs. Bender that, which brought a warm and rueful smile to the woman's face.

"LaTara used to go on and on about my lemonade. Damn that girl, I miss her so much." She took a moment to gather herself. "Why now, Detective? Why, after all this time, are you looking into my girl's death?"

Taylor decided to tell the woman the truth. She looked like she could handle it. "Well, ma'am, I hope that I'm wrong, but I think she might be connected to a series of murders in Nashville this week. Do you remember the music that was playing in LaTara's bedroom the day she died?"

"Of course. I don't have anything like that. It's just not the kind of music I like. And LaTara, well, she was into all that rap. I know that wasn't one of our CDs."

"Did LaTara have any girlfriends, people she might have confided in?"

"When she was younger, yes. But as she got older, got deeper in the drugs, I'm afraid I don't know who she was hanging around with. She stopped coming to services, stopped listening to me. I hate to say it, but I kicked her out. It wasn't very Christian of me, and I regret it now. But I don't truck with drugs, can't abide that kind of behavior under my roof. When she got her head back on straight, tried to clean up, I welcomed her back with open arms. She was trying so hard."

"So no boyfriends?"

"Not that I know of. None that I saw sniffing around. She was a pretty girl, my LaTara. Boys always noticed her. But once she got deep into the drugs, she din't look too good. She was getting back to herself when she passed."

The sheriff walked back into the kitchen, followed by a young woman with a brunette pixie haircut and ridiculously high cheekbones. A no-nonsense kind of girl. Though she looked young, she oozed smarts. He introduced her as Deputy Ann Clift. The woman nodded and shook Taylor's and McKenzie's hands.

"Let's get started," she said. "Show me the bedroom."

The five of them trooped dutifully down the hall. Taylor signaled to McKenzie to hang back. The sheriff and Deputy Clift walked into the room, Marie Bender followed reluctantly. Taylor couldn't imagine how hard this must be for her.

Though three years had passed, the room was still decorated as LaTara left it, in the style of a little girl, pink and floral and lace. Posters adorned the walls, a single bed with a flowered eyelet coverlet stood against the wall. Taylor was struck by the similarities and glaring differences between LaTara's room—warm, inviting and safe—and the room that belonged to Allegra Johnson—dank and dark, with no frills or unnecessary items. These were two girls who were alike, but miles and miles apart. It wasn't just their physical non-proximity that made them different. It was rather amazing that they'd ended up the same, into drugs and prostitution, dead much too young, possibly at the hands of the same killer. Was there something about Allegra Johnson that reminded the killer of LaTara Bender?

The sheriff didn't waste any time, had a diagram from the original crime scene out and was measuring the area to the right of the bathroom door. After a few minutes of consultation, Deputy Clift drew a wide rectangle with an orange marker, then got on her knees and carefully swabbed the entire area, working in quadrants. She sealed each individual swab, labeled it, and moved on to the next section. After she'd collected over fifty samples, she cut the area of the rug out. It measured about four feet by three feet, and rolled easily into a conveniently placed paper bag. It was labeled and sealed, and they were done.

They bid Mrs. Bender farewell; Taylor gave her a card and asked her to call if anything else came to mind. They left her standing in the doorway to the bedroom, lost in the nightmares and sorrow she had been living with since her only child's death.

Twenty-Two

The basement was so empty.

Gavin sat at his corner desk, staring unseeing at his computer screen. The vast black space behind him seemed to grow and breathe, the shadows lengthening ominously. He didn't like to be alone in the basement.

So lonely.

He woke from his reverie when his IM chimed. He glanced at the screen. Morte had opened a private chat with him.

Hey, Morte. Good timing. I was just sitting here by myself. I'm alone again. They're both gone.

The response came immediately.

WHAT IN THE NAME OF GOD DO YOU THINK YOU'RE PLAYING AT?

Morte was furious, Gavin could read that clearly. But why? The last time Morte had gotten angry with him was about the car. No, it wasn't smart of him, but he was still learning. What else could have set Morte off? Oh, the music. He shouldn't have told him about the music. Morte had been very clear in his instructions, in how the scene should look. But Gavin was an artist, and the music was so lovely, so necessary. He needed to hear the flowing, building crescendos as he worked. He couldn't help himself. He decided to play dumb.

What are you talking about?

You know exactly what I'm talking about. How dare you contact me in the real world?

Gavin's brow furrowed. Contact Morte in the real world? What?

Morte, I don't know what you're talking about. I haven't been in contact with anyone.

As he typed the period, a moment of insanity passed through him. He had been in touch with someone. Someone very far away. Someone unattainable. A slow burn began in his chest. He started to type, stopped himself. No. That was crazy. There was no way.

Another message flashed into the chat room.

Listen to me, little Gavin. You have absolutely no right to cross the line. NO RIGHT! Haven't I given you everything you've always dreamed of? Friends, a home for your basest desires, a family, the benefit of my vast knowledge?

Oh, my God. He couldn't lose Morte. He just couldn't. He typed frantically.

Of course you have. I appreciate everything that you've done for me, Morte. But I don't understand. What have I done?

There was nothing for a moment. The online equivalent of dead silence. It took Gavin a second to realize Morte had called him by his real name, not his screen name. How would Morte know his real name? Then the words came, flowing onto the screen in quick succession.

You really don't know who I am? You're saying the e-mail was a coincidence? I don't believe in coincidences, Gavin. I'm afraid our relationship has come to an end.

NO!

Gavin felt the despair showering through his system. He couldn't give Morte up. He was one of the only people in the world who understood him. Who cared for him. But it was too late. Morte had left the chat room. Gavin was alone again. He began to cry, typing desperately through his tears.

Please, Morte, please don't go. I swear I didn't know. I still don't know.

Gavin stayed logged in for an hour, waiting, but there was no answer. Morte was gone. He sat there crying, feeling a loss so deep that he could barely breathe, like half of his soul had been sheared away. He was again incomplete.

Twenty-Three

Taylor and McKenzie bid the Manchester contingent goodbye. They declined the invitation for a late lunch at the Jiffy Burger, the best burger in the South, because they needed to get back to Nashville for the post of their Radnor Lake victim.

Sheriff Simmons wasn't going to take no for an answer. He convinced them to stop and take a bag of food to go, his treat. He called ahead, had an order of burgers and fries ready to be picked up as they drove out of town. The Jiffy Burger was right next to the library, and obviously packed; the only open parking spaces were in the library lot. Taylor double parked behind a Ford F-350 and let McKenzie run in for their order. He returned in three minutes with their food and an open invitation from the mayor's daughter to come back anytime.

On the highway north, Taylor drove with one hand and bit into the juicy, cheesy burger. It was heaven.

"Simmons was right, this burger is pretty good," McKenzie said through a wad of bun.

"That's an understatement." Her cell rang. "Hey, get that for me, wouldja? Put it on speaker."

McKenzie answered her phone in a mock Scottish accent. "Detective Taylor Jackson's phone. Please hold for Detective Jackson."

She laughed. Who knew McKenzie had a sense of humor? It was getting easier to be around him—she had the feeling he might just make a good detective one of these days.

She swallowed her mouthful of burger and answered. "This is Detective Jackson."

"This is Clyde Stone, from Chattanooga homicide. Got your message about an open murder case you're requesting information on. What can I do to help?"

"Fabulous, thanks. I had a ViCAP match from your jurisdiction, a victim named Sharonda Guilmet. Remember the case? What can you tell me about the investigation?"

"Ah, Sharonda. That was a weird one. She was killed a year ago. She was a pro, turning tricks for crack. You know how that goes. She disappeared for a while, then showed up dead back in her apartment, skin and bones, with some kind of classical music playing on her stereo."

Too much of a coincidence, Taylor thought. "What was the music?" She could hear him shuffling papers, looking for the information.

"Here it is. Something called *Requiem Mass,* by Mozart. Creepy-ass shit, lots of chanting and stuff."

Taylor bit back a laugh. Chanting wasn't exactly the term she'd use to describe it.

"Fitting that he'd choose a requiem mass. Was her cause of death starvation?"

"Yeah. She'd been gone for a couple of weeks, no one knew an exact date. She shows up back in her own bed, bones sticking out everywhere. It was weird."

"No staging, no arrangement of the body?"

"Nope. She was in the bed with the covers drawn up. You got a suspect for me?"

"No, not yet. But I think we're getting close. This is the third murder that I've found that has the music, the second confirmed COD of starvation. I've got another victim that we found today floating in a lake being autopsied this evening. That could make four in Tennessee alone. Did you collect any physical evidence?"

"Sure, the usual. Rape kit was positive for semen, we've got it in CODIS, but never had a match. She was a whore, remember. Lots of Johns could have left it."

"Whoa! You've got DNA?"

"Sure do."

"Clyde, you just made my day. Can you fax me the results, and send me the CODIS information? I'll get it to Quantico, they're investigating a string of similar murders in Italy and the UK. Seems our boy has been kind of busy. And is there any way you could courier the case files to me? I'd love to come down, but I won't be able to get there until tomorrow afternoon at the earliest. If you'd be willing to share what you have, I might be able to help you clear the case."

"Sure. Why not. I'll have them to you in a few hours."

"You are my new best friend. Thank you so much."

She gave him the information he needed, then clicked off.

"Well, McKenzie, things are looking up. Let's go see how our lady of the lake is faring with the M.E."

Getting close. Getting very close.

Twenty-Four

Baldwin and Memphis had been hammering away at the details of the profile for two hours when Baldwin's phone rang. He saw it was Taylor calling and excused himself.

"Hi, babe. What's up?"

"I've got great news for you. I've been connecting the dots, looking at possible earlier crimes. I think we have two more definite kills, and we may have DNA for you."

"Seriously? That's excellent."

"Yes, it is. And I just got a call from Taschen Books in New York. They've tracked down the copyright pages from the Picasso monographs, I'm still waiting for their fax. We're getting close, I can just feel it. How are things with you?"

"Highsmythe and I have been running through our cases in Italy and England. I'm making alterations to my profile based on some of his theories. When will you have the DNA?"

"It's already in CODIS. Your forensics analyst can access it. Victim's name is Sharonda Guilmet. I'm heading to the autopsy of my Radnor Lake victim right now, I'll get you what I have as soon as I get it. I'm waiting on a courier to bring me the case files and relevant information from Chattanooga."

"Babe, this is incredibly great news. Keep me posted, okay? You remember Pietra Dunmore, right?"

"Of course. She's the one who came down to Nashville on the Snow White case, with Charlotte."

"She's working this for me. She'll run the forensics as soon as we have all the pieces. If there's a match to be found, Pietra will find it."

"Okay. I'll call you after the autopsy. I should have everything ready for you then."

"Would you mind if we joined you?"

"At the post? Not at all."

"Good. I appreciate it."

He hung up and gave Memphis the thumbs-up sign. "We're in. Let's go."

Twenty-Five

Forensic Medical's parking lot was nearly empty—only Sam's BMW 330ci convertible was parked in its arranged spot. The sun was setting, the post-storm sky fired with billowing pink-and-red clouds. Taylor and McKenzie made their way to the front doors.

McKenzie was riffing. "Our second autopsy in two days. I was hoping that homicide had a few less homicides in it and more assaults."

"McKenzie, I think there might be hope for you yet." She swiped her passcard and the door unlocked. "It's not always like this. Homicide is usually quiet, boring and staid, loads of paperwork and trial follow-ups. These kinds of spree killings are rare."

They entered the lobby, dark and quiet. It was rather sinister with the lights off, the ghosts of sentient beings flowing around in the gloom.

"When you were lieutenant, didn't you handle some of that? Didn't the murder rates drop while you were running things?"

That was the first time he'd openly alluded to her demotion.

"Yes, I did. Before we were decentralized, when we had the Murder Squad, our close rate was eighty-three, eighty-four percent. Now, with all this infighting and backstabbing, the chief not being at all in touch with the troops, things are deteriorating. I think the bad guys know we aren't as stable as we used to be. They can get away with more, and the chief calling on the communities to police themselves is a joke. Ah, well. What can you do, McKenzie?"

"I heard a rumor that you're fighting to be reinstated as lieutenant."

They were at the doors to the autopsy suite. She stopped, turned to him. She weighed her answer carefully. She didn't trust McKenzie, not completely. Even after today's revelations. She wasn't entirely sure that he wasn't a plant, someone Delores Norris, Elm and the chief hadn't assigned to keep tabs on her, looking for more ammunition. He seemed like a regular guy, another young homicide detective eager to learn, to move up in the ranks. But she'd been burned before. Hell, look at the David Martin situation. And she'd *slept* with him.

"McKenzie, I can't discuss the situation with you. No offense, but my lawyer and my union rep want me to keep my mouth shut."

"You think I'm just a tool for the chief, don't you?"

His face fell, a sad, puppy-dog look crowding his features. She felt bad for him, but she couldn't take the chance. The kid could be a damn good actor. She made a mental note to check when she'd gotten so cynical, then said, "McKenzie, seriously, I don't know what to make of you. You seem like a decent, willing cop. I'd like to think that you and I can foster a solid working relationship. But right now, all I can afford to do is cover my ass. Surely you understand that."

He straightened, his lips thinning more as he appraised

her. "I do. But know this. I've learned more from you in two days than I have in five years on the force. I think you're amazing. You know I don't mean that in a sexual way. I mean that as the highest compliment I can give. You are being railroaded, and I'd like to do everything I can to help you get your command back. Because I tell you, Jackson, I'd work for you any day."

The speech floored her. She took the compliment gracefully, nodded her thanks. She didn't trust her voice. She was overwhelmed with emotion, but tried her best to turn it off. She wanted her command back, too, damn it. The sheer unfairness of how her superiors were treating her could easily boil into a black rage if she wasn't careful.

Sam was wrong. McKenzie didn't have the hots for her. He respected her. She liked that much better.

They split up, went to the separate locker rooms to put scrubs over their street clothes, then met in the antechamber to the autopsy suite.

"Ready?" she asked.

McKenzie nodded. She swung open the door to Forensic Medical's inner sanctum.

Sam stood over the body of an incredibly skinny black girl, a scalpel in hand. She was well into the autopsy. She looked up, saw Taylor and McKenzie and spoke quickly, with no preamble.

"Finally. I'm almost done here. Sorry I couldn't wait, but you didn't need to see the preliminaries anyway."

"Sorry. We've had a long day. Baldwin and the inspector from the Met are on their way."

"The more the merrier. You think you've had a long day? Tell me about it. Do I have to wait?"

"No, go ahead," Baldwin said. He and Memphis entered the room, and Taylor felt odd. Seeing them together, so intent on the case, and on her—both men were smiling at her. She ignored Memphis, went to Baldwin. Grazed his lips with hers. He squeezed her arm, glanced at Memphis. Mine, it said. She's mine, mate. Lay off. Taylor couldn't help but smile. She liked the jealous side of him. It was cute.

Sam was tapping her scalpel against her palm. "Ready? Okay, cause of death was starvation, she was dead before she went into the lake. No signs of water in her lungs. She's got those funky spots on her back, too. One big difference. Her eyes were glued open, probably with some sort of cyanoacrylate adhesive. I'm running exactly what kind through the LCMS, could be Super Glue, or Vetbond. I've documented everything we've done so far, it's on the table over there."

"So she couldn't look away," Taylor said softly.

"And he could watch her die," Memphis added.

Taylor let the horror of that sink in for a minute, then let the emotion turn itself to anger. Man, she wanted to catch this bastard.

"How long was she in the water?" Baldwin asked.

"Not too long. Less than five hours. She was never submerged, I think she got caught on a branch or something and it kept her afloat. She does have track marks, mostly up her left arm."

Taylor thought about that for a minute. "Is she a habitual user?"

"The injection sites are relatively new. She doesn't have any scarring between her toes, the webbing of her fingers, inside her thighs, all places I'd expect to see them if she'd been at it for a while. And the trajectory of the needle is off, too. She's new to it."

"Was she injecting herself?" Memphis asked. Sam gave him a harried look. Four investigators crowding the autopsy suite, peppering her with questions was starting to get on her nerves.

"Possibly. Probably. But let me finish this rundown, because I have good news for you. We might be able to get DNA. I found skin under her nails. Just a tiny bit, but it might be enough to run a DNA profile. I can nail the bastard if he's in the system or you have another sample to compare it to."

"We've got samples to compare galore. Speaking of which…" Taylor filled her in on the story from Manchester and Chattanooga.

McKenzie held up the evidence bags from Marie Bender's house. "We've got more DNA for you guys. Will you handle this, or should we call Tim?"

Sam shook her head. "Better call Tim. I'm the only one left here today and I have to go get the twins. I'm getting ready to slide her in the fridge, then skedaddle. Tim's got some stuff for you anyway. I think he was trying to run everything down before he touched base."

McKenzie nodded, and Taylor forced her focus back to the body. "Sam, I also need to get into the records for an autopsy you did three years ago."

"That would be archived. Kris can pull it tomorrow. Why, did I do something wrong?"

"As if. No, the case relates to ours here. Manchester, a drowning. Young black girl, music playing at the scene. It's eerily familiar, and we've got samples to run now."

"You say I did the post?"

"That's what the sheriff said. Simmons, Coffee County. Nice guy. Seems like he knows what he's doing."

"I don't remember it offhand, but if I read the report it would probably come back to me. You know how many of these I do in a year."

"Too many."

"You said it, sister. Back to our lake girl. We identified the flowers she was holding—"

"Daisies, poppies and pansies." Memphis was a few feet away, fingering the posy in its stainless-steel resting place.

"Yes, that's right. She had a necklace of violets, too, just like the painting."

"What painting?" Taylor asked.

"It's Millais," Memphis said. He turned to Taylor with a big grin on his face.

Sam smiled through her face shield. "That's right. It's John Everett Millais's *Ophelia*. I had one of my techs do a little research."

"How did you know that?" Taylor asked Memphis.

"Oh, the Tate Britain in London has the original. I live not far away, in Chelsea."

"That's convenient," Baldwin said. Taylor heard the note of surprise in his voice. She started to wonder exactly what the rivalry was between the two men—was it desire for her, or an intellectual duel to solve the cases? Now that was an interesting thought. She was definitely getting a vibe from Memphis. And she had to admit he was growing on her. He wasn't at all what she expected after their awkward meeting this morning. He seemed quite competent, and no doubt he was charming.

She realized she'd been watching him and abruptly turned away.

Sam started straightening her tray. "You haven't talked to Tim this afternoon at all, have you?"

Taylor shook her head. "No. We've been in Manchester digging up old dirt all afternoon."

"He found a postcard of the painting in the grass near the bank of the lake. It was a dead ringer for the scene."

"A postcard of the painting? Oh, wow." She looked at Baldwin.

"That's Il Macellaio's signature. Well, at least we have that out of the way. Looks like this *is* the same guy. Jesus. A trans-Atlantic serial killer." He shook his head, then excused himself. Taylor saw him flip open his cell phone. She assumed he was calling his team at Quantico to warn them.

Taylor turned to McKenzie. "Would you mind calling Tim and setting up a meeting? See if he's available now? And make a note to follow up with Kris tomorrow to pull the autopsy record for LaTara Bender."

"Sure. I'll be right back."

Sam had abandoned her scalpel and was suturing the Y-incision on the victim's chest.

"Show us her back," Taylor said.

Baldwin and Memphis stepped closer. Sam clipped the thread on a knot, then rolled the girl's body toward her, exposing the naked skin of the victim's back. There it was, evenly spaced circles, all along her shoulders, the lower part of her back, her buttocks and her legs. There was one spot just above her tailbone that didn't have the marks. Taylor looked at it for a moment, thought about the physics of someone lying on their back.

"Someone this thin, there would be a gap above her butt, below her lower back, where the body wouldn't come in contact with whatever she'd been lying on. That's why there's a space in the circles."

"Look at her arm," Sam said.

A long dark seam ran up the length of her right arm. The left was clear.

"Just the opposite of Allegra. That is too bizarre," Taylor said. She looked at it closer, mentally conjuring Allegra's similar lividity. "Same storage area, perhaps?"

Sam shrugged. "Maybe."

"Makes sense," Memphis said. "But none of my victims had anything like this."

"Nor mine," Baldwin added. "This is unique to the American crimes. Taylor, was there anything in the previous two murders that had a description of these marks?"

"No. It's only been the two most recent murders."

"So he's changed up how he's storing them," Memphis said.

"You're pretty good at this, aren't you?" Taylor said, smiling at him in admiration.

"I've had some…practice," he replied.

McKenzie joined them at the table, pointed at the victim. "Good news. We have an identification at least. Leslie Horne. Twenty-two. Tim found prints in the system, she's been busted for prostitution. He said to meet him back at the CJC, he'll take the evidence from Manchester into custody and enter everything into the system."

The five of them stood silently, bearing witness to the girl who now had an identity, a name, a life lost.

"I think she knew Allegra Johnson," McKenzie said.

"Why do you say that?" Taylor asked.

"Because her address in the system? It's the same as Allegra's."

As they were filing out, Sam stopped Taylor.

"Hey, stick around for a minute."

Taylor stopped, said, "Y'all go on. I'll catch up with you in a second."

When the room was empty, Taylor asked, "What's up?"

Sam was fiddling with a scalpel. Taylor saw something unexpected in her eyes. Anger.

"What the hell are you doing?" Sam asked, her tone heated.

"What do you mean? I'm working the case. We've had a lot of new information today and I—"

"I meant with the Brit. What are you doing?"

Taylor frowned. "What are you talking about, Sam?"

"You were flirting with him."

Taylor glared at her best friend. "I was not."

Sam tossed her scalpel onto the tray with a clatter.

"You most certainly were. In front of your fiancé and your newest detective, I might add."

"Oh, please. That's not true, and you know it."

Sam came around the autopsy table, stood eye to eye with Taylor.

"Do I? I've seen that look on your face before, Taylor. You're interested in him."

Her chest felt tight, and she measured her words carefully. "See, that's where you're wrong. He's *interesting,* but I'm not *interested.* See the difference?"

Sam shook her head.

"You need to be careful, Taylor. He's obviously interested in *you.* He can barely take his eyes off of you. And you were practically preening."

"Watch yourself, Sam. You don't know what you're talking about."

"Don't I? You forget who you're talking to, Taylor. I know every look you have. I've nursed you through every crush since we were little girls. You find Memphis attractive, and he feels the same about you."

"You're hardly being fair. I just met the man. I don't know the first thing about him."

"Ah, but you'd like to."

"Sam!" She'd only raised her voice to Sam a handful of times in the time they'd known each other. She felt her temper stealing away from her control, and bit her lip hard to contain it. They stared each other down for a few moments, then Sam shrugged.

"You're a big girl, Taylor. Just remember what happened the last time you found someone you worked with attractive."

Sam turned away, and Taylor stared at the back of her best friend's head. A moment later, she whirled away and stomped from the autopsy suite. She couldn't believe Sam would lob such an insult. This was nothing like the situation with David Martin.

McKenzie was waiting for her in the vestibule after she dumped her scrubs.

"Everything okay?" he asked.

"Fine," she said, curt and dismissive. "Let's go."

It was nearly 8:30 p.m. when Taylor and McKenzie finished with Tim. Baldwin and Memphis had gone back to the hotel to play with the profile. She couldn't help herself; she was glad they were both gone. She had replayed the afternoon at least fifty times, and still didn't see that she'd done anything wrong. She most certainly had not been flirting with Memphis, and she was utterly annoyed with Sam for insinuating that she was.

She shook it off and focused on the information she was gathering. There'd be plenty of time to deal with this later.

While they were at the autopsy, the files had arrived from Chattanooga. The perfect distraction. Taylor went through them laboriously then handed them over to McKenzie for processing. Tim had inputted the DNA signature from Leslie Horne's autopsy into their system and taken all the samples from Manchester, put them in the system as well. If there was a match to be had, he'd find it. He copied Pietra Dunmore at Quantico on everything he was doing.

Taylor was torn. Even she didn't relish the idea of

going back into the Napier Homes after dark––anything and everyone was fair game to be shot. Without a full contingent of cops at her side, she wasn't exactly thrilled at the thought of rolling up into the hood to question them about Leslie Horne.

So she did one better. She called Gerald Sayers at home, asked him if he could get a few of his folks to rouse Tyrone Hill.

Gerald cursed a few times for good measure, but agreed to have Tyrone brought into the CJC to have a quick chat. He'd be there in an hour. 9:00 p.m., and that would be perfect. She'd like to wrap as much of this up today as she could.

She didn't relish the idea of running into Elm in the Homicide offices either, but she had to take the chance. She needed to get some of this stuff written out.

The burgers from Manchester seemed like ages ago. She called for Thai, ordered enough for the three of them to nosh before they dealt with Tyrone.

McKenzie was still working with Tim on finalizing the Manchester data, seemingly fascinated by the legwork. Tim was enjoying himself, too, explaining his techniques and the data collection methodology. She'd almost forgotten that this was McKenzie's first real homicide investigation—he'd certainly come a long way in two days.

The impact hit her. They'd only been on this case for forty-eight hours. They were making spectacular progress. Momentum meant everything in a homicide investigation, and she could feel how close they were.

The food arrived and they inhaled it. When they were finished, Tim adjusted a few files, then announced that he was done, so they cut him loose and walked from the lab across the street to the CJC. There were dark shadows shifting in the parking lot, which made her remember

Fitz's call. The worry welled up inside her, then the quiet. She'd been so wrapped up in the case that she hadn't tried calling. She did now, finding the return number in her cell phone history. There was no answer, so she left a message. She tried to sound upbeat, told Fitz they were working on a great case and for him to come back soon and help her out.

She clicked off and stowed the phone. She didn't like the feeling she was having. Something was up, something wrong. She didn't believe in coincidences. A man who looked just like the Pretender showing up where Fitz was stuck vacationing was too convenient by half—oh, God. She hadn't thought about that. Fitz had said a part had broken on the boat. Could they have been sabotaged?

Just in case, she tried again. The phone rang and rang. There was no answer, and no voice mail. Nothing.

She swallowed back her worry. She had to trust that Fitz would be able to take care of himself. Maybe this was all a mistake. Or maybe the Pretender was sending her a message.

Which brought her back to the here and now. They still had too many unanswered questions. Why had Hugh Bangor been chosen? Why was his house defiled? Why had Il Macellaio chosen him? A connection to his old lover? She needed to talk to Arnold Fay just in case. But there was another route she could explore, too.

She had a momentary qualm, then pushed it away. McKenzie was a big boy. He could take care of himself.

She entered the building and found McKenzie in the hall, grabbing them sodas.

"They're ready for us," he said.

"Great." She accepted a Diet Coke. "Listen, I want you to do something for me. Spend a little time with Bangor. See if you can't find out why he was targeted. It seems like a big chance to take, breaking into the man's house. See if you can piece together what message Il Macellaio was sending us."

"You know, I was just thinking about that. There must be some connection between them, even if Bangor doesn't realize it. I'm happy to talk to him some more. He seems like a good guy." He looked away and she knew where this was going. McKenzie had caught Bangor's eye, and the feeling was mutual. She decided to caution him again, and not just to assuage her own conscience.

"Listen, Bangor likes you. Just be aware that he may not be telling you the whole truth."

"I'll be on my guard. I'm pretty good at reading people."

"Okay then. That's your job for tonight. See what you can find out. Now, let's go meet Mr. Hill."

Gerald was in the homicide offices with a very unhappy-looking black man. He was a big boy, at least six foot three, heavily muscled, with creeping tattoos parading up his neck and down his arms. His shaved head was covered in a black silk doo-rag. He wore a dingy white wife beater tucked into a pair of low-slung Sean Jean black denim jeans, a massive crystal dollar-sign belt buckle holding the jeans in place, and white leather sneakers with no laces. He was nervous, sweating. Taylor raised an eyebrow at Gerald in question.

The vice commander just smiled.

"My boy here was carrying. He's already done a stint in Riverbend, he's on parole and knows better. I made it clear that if he tells you what you need to know, I might be persuaded to forget he was in violation. Just for tonight. He knows I catch his ass again and in he goes. Ain't that right, Tyrone?"

The man mumbled something, and Gerald yanked at his arm.

"Yessir," the man said again, clearer this time. Hell,

Taylor didn't even think *man* was right; he looked like a teenager. He was obviously intimidated. Good. That would do nothing but help them.

"Let's go in the conference room. We'll have more space." And it would set Tyrone's mind at ease a bit; she could tell he was jumpy as a cat on a hot roof. The threat of jail wasn't always enough to get a confidential informant to speak.

Once the four of them were settled, Taylor sat back in her chair, trying to put him at ease. She adopted her most conciliatory tone.

"Tyrone, I do appreciate your being here. We want to capture the man who hurt Allegra. You might be able to help us. But first, can you tell me about a woman named Leslie Horne?"

Tyrone looked desperately uncomfortable and started to sputter. Before he said anything, Elm stormed in the room, shouting. They all jumped at the sudden intrusion.

"What are you doing? You can't interrogate a murderer in here. He needs to be in chains!" He made a beeline for Tyrone.

Taylor stood, putting herself between her lieutenant and her informant.

"Lieutenant, this isn't a murderer. This is a confidential informant working with the Specialized Investigations unit."

"Don't try to bullshit me, young lady. I know Dominick Allen when I see him. He's been wanted by the New Orleans police for ages. We must put him in chains! We can't let him escape again."

Taylor looked at Gerald, who was shaking his head. This was the second time Elm had spouted off about New Orleans. What the hell was going on? Elm was quivering with his need to get his handcuffs on Tyrone, kept lurching around her trying to get to him.

"Sir, this man isn't from New Orleans. He's from Nashville. He's a confidential informant named Tyrone Hill. He's not Dominick Allen."

Elm stood for a moment, staring through his bulgy eyes at them, then a frown creased his forehead. He calmed, staring at Tyrone. He still looked suspicious, but nodded and left the room. Taylor didn't know what to make of the interruption. Elm was looking more crackerjacks by the minute.

She turned back to Tyrone, who was staring at the floor. She settled back into her chair.

"I apologize for that. Tyrone, listen. You obviously know Leslie Horne. Talk to me about her. Tell me who her family is so I can talk to them."

"That man crazy. I ain't never been to New Orleans."

"I know, Tyrone. Don't worry about him. Tell me about Leslie."

"I'm her family. She ain't got no one else."

"What about Allegra? Were they friends?"

He hesitated, chewing a large dry spot on his chapped lower lip. "Yes and no. They fought like bitches in the wild sometimes, those two, then braided each other's hair and went shoe-shopping at Payless. Never could figure out what set them off, other than the usual competition."

"So Leslie was one of your girls, too, is that it?"

"Mebbe." He looked genuinely upset, so Taylor softened her tone.

"When was the last time you saw Leslie, Tyrone?"

She could tell he was calculating the answer. "Just tell me the truth, okay? I'd like to find out who killed them."

"Ha. Like you'd actually worry about some brother who killed a coupla black girls."

Taylor slapped her hand on the table. "Actually, I do care. I don't give a crap what color you are, and that kind of bullshit is going to get you absolutely nowhere with me. A crime is a crime, and it's high time for you to tell me what I need to know. Now that we have that clear, when was the last time you saw Leslie?"

Tyrone looked impressed. She imagined he was thinking how much he could charge for her. But he quit the posturing, answered the question.

"Three weeks."

"And you didn't report her missing?"

"She were with Allegra."

Taylor resisted the urge to smack herself on the forehead. Of course Leslie was with Allegra. That's how the timing was so perfect. He took two at once, dumped them one day apart. Who had died first? No way to know that until Sam determined the time of death through her tests, but they'd obviously died near the same time.

"They had a trick together?"

"Yeah. Some dude in one of them Pious cars pulled up to the curb asking for a date. He don't look crazy or nothin', so I let them go with him. Dat's the last time I saw them."

"What did he look like?" Taylor asked.

"Hell, I hardly noticed him. Meek. Brother, but a mutt. Medium build, light skin. That's all I noticed. All I'm concerned about is the green, if you know what I mean."

"Could you identify him if you saw him again?"

"Naw. Hell, he just drove up, flashed a wad of cash, asked for two. I didn't pay him no attention. Though if he a killer and dat's his car, not one he stole, he be one dumb bunny."

Taylor laughed. "Tyrone, that's something you and I can readily agree on. What do you mean when you call him a mutt?"

"Cross-breed. He were an Oreo. Dat's the only think I really noticed about him."

"Biracial?"

"Dat's what you folks say. More po-litically correct dat way."

Taylor's mind was whirling. Il Macellaio was attacking both white and black girls. Was it because he was both white and black?

"When you say a Pious car, what do you mean?"

"Ah, you know. One of dem stupid gas savers. Pious. Toyota."

"A Prius?"

Tyrone laughed at her. "Dat's what you white folks call dem."

Great. Sarcasm always helped.

"Okay, so he was a light-skinned black man driving a Prius. What color was it?"

"White. And I wouldn't be callin' him a black man. He had too much honky in him for dat. Gotta have some pride in your roots, ya know?" He thumped his closed fist, knuckles in, against his heart three times.

Pride. Pride drove this man to be a pimp and drug dealer, to base desire and abuse. And he called an attempt to save gas pious. The irony was not lost on her.

"Anything else you can remember? Any bumper stickers, or maybe you wrote down the license plate so you could keep track of the girls?"

"Naw. No reason to keep track of them before now. They didn't have anywhere to run off to. I give them everything they need."

Except for safety. He'd given them everything they needed to be preyed upon by a serial killer. Given them to the killer himself. She didn't feel the need to point that out to him.

"Okay, Tyrone, that's a help. I appreciate your cooperation. Gerald, I'm done with him. Thanks for all your help."

She shook Gerald's hand, left him to deal with his informant's weapons issue.

She turned to McKenzie. "Time for you to split. Go talk to Bangor. I'll wrap things up here. We'll start fresh in the morning."

"Sure you don't need me?"

"I'm sure."

"See you then. Don't stay too late. We're on the right track. We'll find him."

Taylor watched him go, hoping sending him like a lamb to the slaughter was the right thing to do, then went back to the homicide offices. Elm was standing in the door to his office, staring at her.

"Evelyn?" he said.

Taylor was thrust back in time, to a vision of her grandfather looking blankly at her mother, Kitty, calling her by her grandmother's name. All of the pieces slammed into place.

She went to Elm. "No, sir, I'm Taylor Jackson."

He shook his head for a moment as if to clear the cobwebs, then said, "Of course you are. No need to reintroduce yourself every time we see each other. Don't forget to leave me a summary of your day. That is all."

He went in the office and closed the door. Taylor sighed heavily. She went to her desk and called her union rep, a fantastically nice guy named Percy Jennings. She left him a message to call her on the cell. This needed to be dealt with, and fast.

Percy called her back almost immediately.

"What's up, Goddess? Your case is going great, we should have you reinstated in no time. Just need to get the Oompa out of there."

"Cool. That's good news. We have a different problem. Hold on a sec while I get somewhere more private."

She stepped out into the hall, past the conference room to the Ladies' bathroom. She opened the door, and the motion sensor lights flickered on, illuminating the tiled darkness. Good, no one here. She locked it behind her just in case.

"Okay, Percy, sorry about that. We have a situation with Lieutenant Elm."

"Tell me about it. He's a nitpicker, you have no idea the complaints we're getting about him. Totally inconsistent, forgetting people's names. The guy's completely erratic."

"I think I know why. He just called me Evelyn, then snapped back to reality. Half an hour ago he charged into an interrogation insisting we were talking to a murderer from New Orleans. I've seen this behavior before. My grandfather had Alzheimer's, an absolutely wicked, nasty case. I think Elm's got it, too. It explains why he's so bad in the evenings, too. A lot of Alzheimer's patients get worse as the day goes on. Elm's much easier to deal with in the morning. Nearly pleasant, comparatively. That's how my granddaddy was, lucid in the morning, growing more and more confused in the late afternoon and evening."

"Jeez, that sucks. He still alive?"

"No, he passed a while ago. Elm isn't young, but he's got some good years left in him. His mind will go, but his body will take a much slower trip."

"Okay. I'll go talk to the people in charge, let them know."

"Keep it quiet, Percy. It's a humiliating disease. He may think something's wrong, but I doubt he's been diagnosed yet. It's going to be a touchy situation, at best."

"All right, Taylor, will do. Thanks for letting me know. Go catch some bad guys."

They clicked off. She went to the mirror, splashed

some cold water on her face. Remembering her grandfather was always hard. He'd suffered, and there was nothing anyone could do to ease his mind. She'd never known him well; Kitty hadn't been close to her parents. Strange, she never realized that she and her mother had that in common.

She forced thoughts of family from her mind. She couldn't afford to be sidetracked, not now.

When she went back into the offices, Elm's door was open and his light off. He'd gone for the day. Taylor breathed a sigh of relief. Now that she suspected the truth, she wouldn't be able to look at him without pity, and a man like that would sense her emotions, even if he didn't understand them. Better that he was gone.

On her desk was a piece of paper with Rowena's spidery handwriting. "Fax is in your top drawer," it said.

She'd nearly forgotten. The information she'd been waiting for all day.

She opened her desk drawer greedily. It was a two-page fax—a cover sheet from Taschen Books Manhattan, then a copyright page. Editor, Designer, Production Manager, Library of Congress information. Okay. One of the three names had to be what she was looking for.

She wrote them all down, then called Baldwin.

"We have some names," she said. "The puzzle is starting to come together."

"Excellent. Would you like to meet Memphis and me for a drink before we leave? We're at Ruth's Chris."

"Sure, why not. I'll be there shortly."

She shut down her computer, then drove up West End to the restaurant. A valet greeted her and took her keys. She fluffed her hair in the reflective glass entrance, then entered the steak house.

Baldwin spotted her first and hailed her with a wave.

She joined the men at the table, asked for a glass of Seghesio Zinfandel, one of her and Baldwin's newest discoveries.

Memphis was drinking scotch, she could smell the peaty, musty scent. She'd always hated whiskies of all sorts; they tasted like wood chips. Baldwin was drinking a draft Sam Adams.

"We've got a plane at ten. I decided to go back to Quantico tonight, get moving on this new information right away. I want to get everything plugged into the profile so I can get it to you tomorrow," Baldwin said. "As a matter of fact, I need to call and confirm our reservation. Did you eat?"

"I did. We ordered in Thai."

"Okay then. By the way, Memphis made the astute observation earlier that he thinks we're dealing with someone who's biracial."

She smiled at him, then checked herself. "Damn. Here you are, beating me to the punch. I interviewed a pimp tonight who said both of my current victims got in a white Prius, together, mind you, with what he termed an *Oreo*."

"That's a rather derogatory term for it."

"Well, he wasn't a very nice guy. So that fits."

"So the wit confirms that he took two at once?" Baldwin asked.

"Looks that way."

"Anything else new?" Memphis asked.

"No, that's it. I wish I had more."

"But it's progress, my dear. Progress. I'll be back in a minute. You and Memphis play nice."

She narrowed her eyes at him. Why did it feel like everyone was ganging up on her today?

Baldwin slid out of the booth. Memphis immediately shifted to the left so he could look Taylor straight on.

"So. Come here often?" he asked.

"Highsmythe—"

"Oh, do call me Memphis. Please. I'm just kidding. I like to needle."

"I noticed." She relaxed fractionally. She knew Sam was wrong, she hadn't been flirting. If she had been, there'd be no mistaking it. She smiled at him again, this time without worrying about who might think what.

"Fine. Memphis. I hope you're finding Nashville to your liking. I'm sorry it's been so crazy, but with any luck, today's murder will bring us all a step closer to catching this man."

"That's a lovely speech. Maybe we should get you in one of Shakespeare's creations. Let's see…we'd need a strong woman, one who doesn't like to be pushed around or told what to do. Viola, maybe. No, I have it. Portia. Without a doubt."

She rolled her eyes and took a sip of the wine. It was perfect, spicy and bold.

He leaned closer. "Tell me, why did you become a copper? Did you lose your baby brother? A little abuse in your background?" He smiled a wicked, lazy grin at her and she bit her lip trying not to smile back. "You can tell me. I can keep a secret." He licked his lips, slow and suggestive. Jesus, if Baldwin saw that he'd be off his head.

"Highsmythe, you've got to knock this off."

"What?" he asked, all kinds of innocent. Baldwin came back to the table, and Taylor swore she felt a hand on her knee before Memphis slid back into the seat, crossing his arms on his chest.

"All set," Baldwin said. "What's happening here? Did you guys go over the names?"

"No. Memphis would like to know why I became a cop."

"Oh. That's easy. Her dad."

"Baldwin."

He looked at her in surprise. "What? It is, isn't it?" He leaned over toward Memphis conspiratorially. "Taylor's dad isn't the most upright character, if you know what I mean."

"Baldwin!"

"Is that where you got the scar?" Memphis asked.

Taylor's hand went to her throat. "My God, no. My father may be a crook, but he never laid a hand on me. This was courtesy of a suspect. Baldwin saved my life. It was our first case together."

Memphis leaned back in his chair. "Isn't that romantic? Well, then, you shouldn't be so fussed about it. My father used to say, 'The average man bristles if you say his father was dishonest, but he brags a little if his great-grandfather was a pirate.' Time will remember your father fondly, I'm sure."

Taylor shot him a look. "Is this some sort of British quote, like the upper-class secret handshake?"

"There's a secret handshake? I didn't know. Must be why I'm in the Met instead of loafing around the family estates." He grinned at her, his blue eyes twinkling with delight. He enjoyed annoying her, she could see that as plain as day. Sam was wrong, so very, very wrong. She wasn't flirting with Memphis, but he was most definitely and without reservation flirting with her. But all the fun had gone out of it since Baldwin had brought up her father; sharing her personal embarrassment with a total stranger snapped her back to the real world.

Memphis toyed with his fork. "I don't know who said it, I just remember the quote. Surely not my father, it was something he read somewhere, I suppose. But it's fitting, don't you think?"

"What, now you're giving me advice?"

"Memphis's father is an earl, Taylor. You're getting

advice on the family dynamic from the Viscount Dulsie, so I'd listen if I were you." Baldwin gave her a quirky, teasing smile. She sniffed.

"I see. Somewhere down the road, one of my invisible offspring will look back and think what Win has done is romantic, somehow? That stealing and lying and cheating and cavorting with serial killers is a good thing? I hardly think that will be the case. You don't know my father, Memphis. He is not a good man."

"There must be something good about him. He produced a child who knows right from wrong."

She looked down at her wineglass. It was something she'd always wondered—was her moral code, her ability to shut down her feelings of family and remorse for the way things could have been a direct cause of Win's actions? How could a man who had no regard for the law produce a child who lived by it?

She finished her wine. "Oh, look at the time. You boys are going to miss your plane if we don't hop to it. Detective Highsmythe, do you need to stop off before we go?"

"Back to proper names already, are we? As you like, Miss Jackson. Yes, I need to grab my bag from the concierge."

He stood and gave her a mocking little bow. Without saying goodbye, he strode out of the restaurant into the darkened lobby of the hotel.

Baldwin peeled off some cash and left it on the table. They followed Memphis, then turned and exited onto the street. When Baldwin reached for her hand, she pulled it away.

"What's wrong?" Baldwin asked.

She stopped and stared him in the eye, vaguely noticing that the ambient light from the downtown illumination made them smolder. She was too upset to care about that right now. She spoke low, so no one would overhear.

"What are you guys, best friends now? Why did you tell him about my dad? You know how I feel about that. It's…personal. Private. Our private business."

Baldwin recognized how distressed she was at last, apologized profusely. "I didn't think you'd care. You've never taken issue with it before."

"This is different. He's a stranger. There's no reason to go telling him sordid details about my personal life." Her family life was an embarrassment to her, no doubt, but most of Nashville was familiar with the more torrid stories. She knew she was overreacting, and didn't know why.

"Taylor, don't get huffy. I said I was sorry. No one holds you accountable for your dad's actions. Besides, Memphis is one of the good guys." He stepped to the valet desk, handed over the ticket.

She pulled her hair up into a ponytail. *That's what you think.* Memphis was starting to get to her. She had no idea why she cared about him seeing her in the best possible light. Maybe Sam was right, maybe she was showing off for him. Add in that look of longing tucked deep into the recesses of his eyes… She sighed. Just when things were going so well, she suddenly had to contend with the advances of this posh boy.

And posh was just the word for him. Floppy blond hair, falling into his cornflower-blue eyes. Strong jaw, straight nose, decent teeth. That ridiculous accent, every word strung out from his tongue, pronounced. Good thing she didn't go for light-haired men—for the briefest of moments, she'd felt a ridiculous pull of attraction to his clean good looks. Baldwin had the Black Irish in him, that deep silky hair the color of night and those clear green eyes. Cat eyes. Baldwin was the better looking of the two, bigger and taller as well. Memphis looked more like a very well-kept greyhound.

What in the name of hell are you doing, Taylor?

Baldwin came back to her. He looked at her strangely, like he could read her mind. He could, sometimes. She prayed he hadn't glimpsed too deeply in that thought process.

"Where's Memphis?" he asked.

"I'm not his babysitter. How should I know?" Taylor said.

"Hey. Are you okay?"

"Of course. Why wouldn't I be?"

He was watching her curiously, and she felt like she'd been caught doing something wrong. That was crazy. She took a deep breath and blew it out, hard.

"Seriously, I'm fine. I'm just not all that hip to discussing my personal life with him. He's…it's nothing. I just don't like thinking about Win, that's all."

"Okay. I promise not to bring him up again in public." He leaned down and kissed her gently. She accepted the kiss, squeezed his hand in forgiveness.

Memphis appeared through the hotel doors, looking excited.

Baldwin looked at his watch, tapped the face. "Time to go."

Memphis held up a hand. "My apologies. My DC called with some news. She thinks she's found a witness to one of the Macellaio dumps."

"That's great news," Baldwin said. "I asked the valet to grab us a cab, we can talk about it on the plane."

"Where's your car?" Taylor asked.

"At home. We've had a driver tonight."

"Yes, quite fancy," Memphis said.

The valet pulled up with Taylor's 4Runner. "Oh. Well, do you want a ride? I need to go back to the office for a bit anyway."

"You don't mind?" Baldwin asked.

"Of course not. Hop in."

It was cool downtown. A few cars traveled up and down West End, and a group of drunk Vanderbilt students huddled together on the corner, ready to cross the street onto campus and head back to their dorms. What she wouldn't give to have their innocence, their naïveté. They couldn't know what a mean world they lived in, unless they'd been personally touched by violence.

They talked about the hopeful ramifications of a possible witness as Taylor drove them to John C. Tune airport, trying to stifle the horrible memories it brought her. She'd been spirited out of town from that airport, unconscious, at the whim of a killer who manipulated her entire family. She forced herself to breathe, to move the tension out of her jaw and shoulders. She felt a hand along the back of her neck, deft fingers digging deep into the cords. She looked over to Baldwin with a smile of thanks, saw him working his BlackBerry. With both hands.

She bucked upright, jerked the brakes a bit and the hand disappeared.

"What's wrong?" Baldwin asked.

"Nothing," she said. Memphis's eyes met hers in the rearview mirror. He was smiling. "Nothing at all."

Twenty-Six

Gavin didn't usually stray into Williamson County. Though he lived on its northwestern edge, he rarely had cause to cross the county line. But today he had no choice. The printer in his office was out of its special ink, and there was only one place in town that carried what he needed. The store was in Franklin, twenty minutes south of Nashville. It was a private enterprise, run by a quiet man who didn't feel the need to talk very much, either. Gavin liked working with him—it was a simple "I need this, it will be ready Friday" kind of relationship.

His, well, *friend* would be much too strong a term, wasn't even in the shop, but had left the package on the counter with Gavin's name printed in block letters. Gavin left one hundred and ninety dollars in cash in a drawer under the counter. It would be safe. This was a good neighborhood.

Leaving the house had been especially hard today. He should be in mourning for his dearly departed doll. He just wanted to be home, to smell the fragrant air surrounding her resting place, to look at the pictures he took. Maybe even talk with Morte. Morte always understood

Gavin's upset after a doll was finished. But Morte wasn't speaking to him.

He could reach out to Necro, but that wouldn't be much help. Necro was still role-playing. Paying women to have sleepy sex with him. Of course, he thought Gavin was doing the same. Morte was the only one who knew that Gavin's dolls were truly his for the taking.

He got back into the Prius, took the circle through downtown Franklin, turned left at the McDonald's, then crossed back onto 96 West. The sun was low in the sky, bright in his eyes. He flipped down his visor and put on sunglasses. The suburbs of Franklin quickly gave way to verdant farmland, dotted with gated drives, large houses and an abundance of cows.

He thought of his doll, and cried a little. He hated to see them go. It took so much out of him. He'd stopped collecting for quite a while, because the loss was too much to bear. He'd never been caught, but that was probably pure luck. To keep safe, he used the Internet to satisfy his desires for a long time. Then he'd met Morte and Necro. Morte pushed him right back over the edge, and the urges overwhelmed him again. Morte gave him new power, new desires. Permission. Encouragement. He wanted to show Morte he was just as good as him. What was he going to do without him? He had to find a way back into Morte's good graces.

The massive concrete double-arched bridge that carried the Natchez Trace Parkway over Highway 96 appeared in front of him. He marveled at its size, the beauty of the lines, the grace of the curves echoing the breasts of a woman. He was nearly to the bridge when he saw a car on the side of the road. A car, and a woman.

His pulse quickened, he reflexively slowed his Prius. She was waving at him. Gesturing. He couldn't believe what he was seeing. She was stunning: tiny waist, delicate features, her hair long and braided. He stopped behind her car, heart in his throat. She walked to him, thin hips swinging. Her skin was the color of mocha cream. Dear God, was this a sign? He was frozen.

She tapped on his window. When he met her eye, he knew.

He pushed the power button, the window slid down with a whisper.

"Thank God you stopped. I've been out here for twenty minutes and haven't seen a soul!" She smiled at him, friendly, open. He didn't quite know what to say. She took care of that for him.

"Can you give me a lift? My car's out of gas and the battery is dead on my cell phone. My dad keeps telling me not to forget to charge it, but I did. Hey, cool Prius!"

The girl walked around to the other side of the car. Gavin just watched, knowing his eyes were wide and he must look like an idiot. He quickly redid his features into a semblance of friendliness, and unlocked the passenger-side door.

The girl yanked open the door, slid in and tossed her backpack on the floor in front of her. "So, like, what kind of music do you have in here?"

She reached for his iPod. Gavin held himself back. He didn't like people touching his things, but this was a gift. This was a sign. This was his *chance.* He swallowed, and managed to grind out the words.

"All sorts. Where do you need to go?"

The girl cocked her head to the side like a spaniel. "Bellevue. I was on my way to the Y. I'm a lifeguard up there, and I am totally late for my shift. They'll probably fire me. Hey, don't I know you? I've seen you there before, right?"

Oh, dear God. How to answer? Should he admit it?

What if… He nearly laughed out loud with glee. He could tell her anything. He could lie. He could tell her a multitude of lies and she'd never know the difference. She would never know.

He put the car in gear. "The Y. Sure. Yeah. I think I recognize you, too," he said. He'd never seen the girl in his life. Yet here she was, practically gift-wrapped. Sweat broke out on his forehead. Was this a test? Or the most beautiful of opportunities?

The girl was nannering on about his playlist on the iPod. Why didn't he have anything cool and hip? Didn't he have some Ashanti, or maybe some old-school Run DMC?

"I like classical," he replied.

"That's dumb," she said, pouting. He nearly burst out laughing, then realized he hadn't laughed in a very, very long time. It must be fate. This girl, his present, his doll, had made him smile.

"What's your name?" he asked.

"Kendra. Kendra Kelley. What's yours?"

He'd already made the decision by then, though he wouldn't realize it until much, much later. "Gavin Adler."

"Gavin. Cool name. Oh, hey, you just missed the turn. You need to go back that way."

He ignored her. Within two miles, he could have her home. He finally took a second and listened to the nagging little voice in the back of his mind. *That wouldn't be smart. Not smart at all. You haven't prepared. You know nothing about her. She might be missed. Don't do it.*

The anger at Morte's harsh treatment burned in his skin. He didn't do it on purpose. He'd had no idea Tommaso was Morte. That Tommaso was like him. It was purely a fluke that he'd uncovered the connection. He heard Morte, Tommaso's voice in his head, the lines scrolling on an invisible computer screen.

Don't even think about it, Gavin. She's delectable, and would be a perfect doll, but you haven't prepared. No preparation, no doll. Those are the rules. You know the rules.

But what if I succeed? What if she isn't missed? I've missed the opportunity of a lifetime.

Don't do it.

But I'm lonely.

Gavin thought about the dollhouse, lying quietly in the dark, empty. Waiting. Abandoned. So lonely. He was so good at his vocation. He could make her disappear. He could have a new doll. She'd practically asked for it. Stupid, stupid girl.

"Ga-vin," Kendra singsonged. "You're going the wrong wa-ay." She smiled at him, her lips full, teeth straight, those braids clicking, and he thought he would burst. She would make such an exquisite doll! He could already see the bones of her collarbone sticking out; she was a tiny thing. It would be quick.

"This way is faster. It's a shortcut," he said. He sped up, taking the curves on Highway 100 at speed. Half a mile now, a quarter, Kendra next to him, chattering about something. He tuned her out. He tuned out his conscience. He tuned out Morte's scrolling language, his anger. He would show him. He didn't need Morte's instructions. He started alone. He could stay alone from now on. Morte was the only reason he'd gotten flashy lately, gotten into the performance art. He was acting out the paintings, taking things a step further than Morte. Their competition was the driving force, and Gavin was winning. He was still the better artist—had more fully realized his settings. He'd acted his out, for God's sake. Morte only imitated. Gavin was a conductor, Morte was first violin.

The Conductor. Oh, how he liked that.

His driveway was just ahead. He slowed, then turned. The drive was gravel; he needed to go carefully. He'd always meant to pave it, but never got around to it.

"I really think you're going the wrong way," Kendra said, with the tiniest tremor in her voice, guileless, clear chocolate eyes turned on him in doubt.

He pulled in front of the rambler and stopped. She glanced at him, at the house, and the first signs of panic started to cross her face.

"Didn't your daddy tell you not to get into cars with strange men?" Gavin asked, and this time, he did smile. Kendra's eyes flared white. She grabbed the handle of the door. Gavin was faster. With the refrain banging in his mind—*don't do it don't do it don't do it*—he clobbered her over the head with the heavy printer cartridge. It slowed her down enough that he was able to take another shot. That one knocked her out. She slumped against the door, blood trickling down her face.

Gavin was breathing hard. *See!* he told his invisible voice triumphantly. *I am the Conductor!*

This was glorious! He needed to move. He launched himself out the driver's-side door, rushed around the side of the car, slipping and going down on one knee at his right rear bumper. He righted himself, then opened the passenger door. Kendra fell out into his arms.

She was light; he carried her to the front door. He unlocked the door, then realized that maybe he should have gone in through the garage. He usually brought the dolls in under cover of darkness; it was still evening and the sunset outlined him against the door frame.

He glanced around, the girl becoming heavy in his arms. No, this was fine. No one around for miles.

He locked the door behind him, went directly to the basement door. The cat meowed loudly, unsettled at seeing his master rushing around without paying the slightest bit of attention to him.

Down in the basement, he opened the case. He stripped the prize, wiped her face clean of blood, then maneuvered her body into the box. Her arms and legs flopped unceremoniously. His erection strained painfully against his zipper.

"In you go," he panted, out of breath. She fit perfectly. He closed the lid, locked the latches, and grabbed his chair. He sat heavily, staring. Unbelieving.

He had a brand-new doll.

And she had come to him.

Twenty-Seven

Taylor sat in her old office, away from the B-shift detectives, watching a replay of the late local news with disgust. She'd like to strangle all of the reporters, and a few people in Metro's ranks as well. They had a leak. She'd been playing with the stupid Brit and hadn't been on top of this. Served her right. She'd lost her focus.

Channel Four had scooped everyone, had gotten someone from the Radnor Lake crime scene to talk. One of the rangers, more than likely. But they would have had to confirm the information with an officer or technicians who'd been on the scene, and that's what had her so riled up. Her people knew better. At least, when they were her people they did.

She watched as Demetria Kalodimos read the copy against a cutaway shot of the entrance to Radnor Lake. She threw it to Cynthia Williams, who let all of Middle Tennessee, parts of Kentucky and the northern tip of Alabama know that a postcard of a famous painting had been found at the scene, and that the police felt the two murders were connected.

Oh, this was not good. She'd never be able to unring

this bell. They already had that damn name for him, the Conductor. Catchy and descriptive. Great. Just great. The crackpots would start coming out of the woodwork and lead them down false trails. The networks would get involved, and the national media platform would lead to the international news forums.

It all served to make her more determined. It was getting late and Taylor was tired, but she pushed that away. She needed to catch this suspect, now.

She shut off the television, went to her desk in the bullpen and turned on the computer. She started with the databases available to her, looking to match the names on the sheet to the DMV database. She wished the name would leap out at her, declare itself. *I am your killer.* Wouldn't that be nice? It would certainly save her a lot of time.

The names from the copyright pages weren't entirely unique either, which was going to be a problem. She'd have to run down every Gavin Adler, Al Hardy and Paul Theroux in town. The remaining names belonged to women, so Taylor triaged them. These crimes didn't have a feminine touch, that was for sure.

The first search turned up seven entries for the Theroux name alone. She worked quickly, running addresses and criminal records for each name, cross-referencing with the DMV database, looking through the tax rolls.

She ended up with forty-six possibles. Forty-six. Too many. She needed to keep looking.

She narrowed the search further to Prius drivers, and got it down to eight. Eight was more manageable. Two G. Adlers, three A. or Al Hardys, and three P. or Paul Therouxs. Still, she was amazed that so many names matched white Priuses. It might be a mistake in the system. She'd have to check each one out, just to be certain. The Prius and the Infiniti G35 had usurped the

BMW as Nashville's car of choice, so it did make a perverse kind of sense.

Tyrone Hill's interview popped into her head. He was right; the odds of a killer being foolish enough to use his personal vehicle in the commission of such a major crime would be slim. But it was a chance, and she took it, making a note to herself to look at rental agencies if this didn't pan out.

She started with the full names, just in case. Initials usually meant women.

She matched the addresses from the car registrations to the driver's license database, and had her jumping-off point. She ran arrest and probation histories, and narrowed the list down to four. Two Al Hardys and two Paul Therouxs. None of the Adlers had a history with the department. One of them, as a matter of fact, was so clean that she added it back into the mix. Their boy was careful, and it stood to reason that he might, just might, be completely off the radar.

That was a good enough start for her. Five possibles. Astounding, really, that so many of the names and cars matched and were in the system. She'd found a good groove. She'd had plenty of experience with the databases being a dead end.

She glanced at her watch—it was nearly midnight. She debated for the briefest of instances, then grabbed her keys. So she'd wake a few people up. Too bad. She was the one with the gun and the badge. She called Bob Parks to run the gauntlet with her; no way was she going to go knocking on doors at midnight alone. He'd recently been moved to the B-shift and was her overnight go-to guy. He was happy to join her; it was a quiet night for Nashville's criminals and he had nothing cooking.

They hit the four houses closest to town; no one answered. Two of them had garages that could easily house a matching car with a matching license plate, so Parks check-marked them as a yes. She'd send someone out again tomorrow, in the daylight.

Two of the houses looked completely deserted; the addresses were most likely defunct. The DMV databases weren't necessarily exact and current. They put a question mark next to those two names. The fifth and final address was out in her neck of the woods. They agreed to swing by this last address, and barring unforeseen issues, she would head home after and Parks would go back to prowling the streets.

She followed Parks down Highway 100, the moon lighting their path, careful to watch for deer. They loved to leap across this stretch of road. Close to the Davidson-Cheatham county line, this area was completely rural, quiet and dark.

They both missed the road where they needed to turn off, had to make a U-turn in the middle of nowhere. She pulled ahead of Parks and found the cross street on the second try. The house's address was stenciled in white on only one side of the black metal mailbox. This was it. She pulled into a long, gravel driveway slowly, then exited her vehicle. Parks rolled in behind her, the lights of his cruiser blinding her for a moment. She shut her eyes, let them re-adjust to the night.

Nothing was happening here either, it seemed. The house was pitch-black, no movement, no lights. No white Prius.

They approached the door anyway, knocked twice. Nothing. Frustrated, they went back to their respective cars, boots crunching in the gravel.

"You givin' up?" Parks asked.

She stretched, rubbing her fists in the small of her back. "Yeah. It's late. I'll send some patrols out here in the morning, try again."

"You heard from Fitz?"

"No. Nothing."

"I'm sure he's fine. Don't worry your pretty little head about it."

His radio crackled; Dispatch requesting his assistance in a drunk and disorderly arrest outside The Corner Pub. He rubbed his moustache wearily, gave her a mock salute, then climbed into his patrol car and edged backward out of the driveway.

Taylor waved at him, then stood at the door to her car for a few moments, staring back at the deserted house. Could be whoever was inside was just a heavy sleeper, or no one was home at all. She felt a chill creep up her spine. What if this was their guy, and he was out hunting right now?

Oh, come on, Taylor. You're making some serious leaps of logic now.

She climbed back in the car, yawning widely.

Time to call it a night.

There were noises. Cars in the gravel, doors slamming. Footsteps walking around the fountain. A shadow…my God, whoever it was just passed his basement window. He wasn't worried about anyone seeing in; he'd applied a film that allowed him to look out but appeared dark from the outside. But it unnerved him, knowing someone was out there.

He heard the knocking and froze. It was very, very late. He wasn't even sure it was knocking at first; maybe he'd fallen asleep, was dreaming all of this. He was in the basement, it might be Art, playing. But no, there it was again. All the lights were off. He didn't move.

The doll whimpered in her sleep. He stood and walked to her, looked into the glass dollhouse. He'd been fighting with himself all night. He wanted to talk to Morte, but he was still so upset at how he'd been treated.

The car doors slammed again, engines revved. Must have been a wrong address.

He kept telling himself that, holding his arms while he shook.

Twenty-Eight

It was late, past 2:00 in the morning, when Baldwin heard a knock on the door, looked up to see Memphis standing in his office. They'd arrived in Quantico at midnight, and Baldwin had arranged for a room for Memphis in one of the dorms.

"You should be sleeping," he said. "We have a long day ahead of us."

"I could say the same of you. I was sleeping, but my body clock thinks it's morning, so here I am. I don't suppose you have any real tea, by any chance? Maybe a drop of something stronger?"

Baldwin scrubbed his fingers through his hair. "Yes, I do. I'll go get it, and then I'll fill you in on what we've got."

Baldwin took the hallway down to the row of cubicles that housed his team. He was technically the unit chief, though he transitioned between the Nashville Field Office and the Behavioral Analysis Unit in Quantico. There were three Behavioral Analysis Units in the Behavioral Science Unit—Unit One—Terrorism and Threat Assessments, Unit Two—Crimes Against Adults and Unit Three— Crimes Against Children. He managed BAU Two—had been the unit chief for four years. He had his fingers in BAU One as well, though his involvement was tertiary and very, very quiet. Terrorism was the number-one priority of the Bureau, had been since the evolution of their purpose after 9/11. It played well for him—in his other persona, Baldwin profiled assassins for the CIA in a covert operation known as the Angelmakers. That part of his life had been thankfully lacking in necessary endeavors lately.

He had forewarned his BAU team that they'd be needed to help finalize the profile for the Metropolitan police. He'd chosen two excellent lead profilers for this assignment—Charlaine Shultz, a former Little Rock homicide detective with a boisterous laugh and a deadly acumen for murder, and Dr. Wills Appleby, a psychiatrist turned profiler Baldwin did his residency with. They'd met the first day of classes at Johns Hopkins, spent four years grinding through med school together, then a completely grueling psychiatric residency.

When they'd finished up, Baldwin had gone on to George Washington University to get his law degree, thinking he'd be a medical ethicist. Instead, he met Garrett Woods. Garrett recognized the potential in him immediately, potential Baldwin didn't know existed. He snatched him up for the FBI, and Baldwin hadn't looked back. He was a Supervisory Special Agent now, and Garrett was running all of the Behavioral Science Unit.

Baldwin recruited Wills in turn. Outside of a few people from Hampden-Sydney, where he did his undergrad, Wills was his oldest friend.

Not all his profilers had doctorates or medical degrees. He'd found early on that instinct can't be taught—some people have it, and some don't. Appleby was one of the few psychiatrists who were also profilers; most of his staff were former police officers. It was easier to teach the psychological components of profiling than it was to train instinct. Practical investigative experience, how to read a crime scene, that instinctive ability to assimilate a violent crime, none of those things could be taught. All of his recruits went through an extensive, intensive training program. Very few washed out—he'd gotten very good at picking who would mesh with this type of work.

Except for one. He'd made a massive, colossal blunder when he'd hired a woman named Charlotte Douglas.

He had unconsciously stopped at the office that used to belong to her. Charlotte had deceived them all. She'd passed every psychological test the FBI had, had risen to the position of Deputy Chief of BAU Two. And all the while, she'd been utilizing the tools available at the FBI—specifically CODIS and ViCAP—to track down killers she was interested in, for her.

Whispers had been circulating that Charlotte's computer contained material that could be used to blackmail certain agents into submission. The investigation was ongoing. Good riddance, Baldwin thought, then felt immediate sorrow, as he often did when Charlotte came to mind. She'd been dangerous to him on many, many levels.

He'd love to know what her little files held about him. Ex-lover, definitely, he was sure she'd probably documented every minute of his time with her, though it was a short-lived relationship. But what other secrets did Charlotte harbor? A brilliant woman, her encryption codes had proved nearly impossible to crack. They'd only tapped into a third of what she had stored on her computer. It was as if she was a codex from an earlier era, when codes were unbreakable because they were written in dead languages no one could possibly decipher. Charlotte's mind was an undiscovered country.

He shook himself, pulling out of the reverie, realized one of his teammates, Dr. Pietra Dunmore, was staring at him. He caught her eyes, silky brown and deep-set, and recognized that she'd known exactly what he was thinking about. She just nodded, too polite to call him out. She'd worked closely with Charlotte, too.

"You should be in bed."

"Ha," Pietra said. She gave him a rueful smile. "Boss, I got the DNA sample profiles from Taylor Jackson, checked in CODIS. The murder in Chattanooga was a match. I don't know why it didn't show up when we ran the search on the DNA from London and Florence—I've sent the issue to the database team for them to work out."

Baldwin sighed. "Might have been one Charlotte dug her fingers into, rerouted to her private database," he said.

"That's probably a pretty safe assumption. We'll get it figured out. But Il Macellaio is definitely responsible for at least one of the four Nashville murders. There's another DNA chain running, from the case yesterday, but I won't have that until tomorrow."

Baldwin was torn between groaning and throwing his fist in the air in glee. It was expected, but this definitely threw a monkey wrench into the profile. Memphis's assumption about Il Macellaio being biracial was quite prescient. It was the only decent explanation for why he was killing both black and white women.

"Starvation, strangulation and necrophilia. This one is a real piece of work." Pietra looked pissed off—Baldwin could understand why. She was the perfect physical type for the U.S. killings—petite and black.

Baldwin scrubbed his hands through his hair, then said, "Okay. Let me work this into the official profile. I've been operating with that theory all along, just in case. Won't take me but half an hour."

"I'm happy to help."

"That's okay. Tomorrow's going to be a long day. Go grab some sleep."

"Sure thing, boss." She disappeared down the hall, he continued on his path to Garrett's office, thinking.

The killer had changed M.O.s definitively, working back and forth across the Atlantic. The Florence killings and the two latest Nashville killings were by far the most sophisticated; the London murders seemed more like crimes of opportunity. Il Macellaio lived in Florence, then, where he knew the lay of the land. Which meant he must also have a place in Tennessee. Someplace private. A room of his own.

The London murders were an exercise in convenience. Something took him there—a job, a woman, vacation. Il Macellaio's urges had gotten so strong, his desire to kill was overwhelming him. Even away from his home base, outside his comfort zone, he couldn't wait until he got back to Florence. Three months, that's how long the murders had been going on. Okay then, so for three months he'd been living in or regularly visiting London. So what made him come to Tennessee?

Baldwin was dawdling. He went to the end of the hall, to his boss's office. Garrett was in D.C. at the moment, but Baldwin knew he kept a bottle stashed in his desk. The head of the Behavioral Science Unit was a scotch man, too. He usually kept it in the bottom left drawer; yes, there it was. Dewar's White Label. He shook the bottle; plenty left for a nightcap.

He started back to his office. This case was eating at him. Maybe he was losing his touch. Losing his focus. He'd been fighting the realization that with Taylor in his life, he cared more, and less, about his job than ever before. Every minute he spent away from her was too long. Perhaps his feelings were clouding his judgment. Perhaps he needed to reexamine his role at the BAU, his motivations, his goals. Assess whether he really wanted to stay in this job, or wanted to move back to Nashville full-time. Or try again to convince Taylor to join his team at Quantico, where he could keep an eye on her. The Pretender wasn't going to give up, or give in, until he saw them both destroyed. Could he live with himself if something were to happen to her? Of course not. It would be his final undoing.

He forced the thoughts aside. He'd revisit them once this case was over. Il Macellaio was haunting him. He was missing something. Something important, that would lay out all the answers.

But what?

Memphis was skulking around Baldwin's office when he noticed the framed photograph on Baldwin's desk. It was of Taylor, an utterly lovely picture highlighting her glowing skin, honey-blond hair, gray eyes, pillowy lips. She was smiling without showing her teeth, a dreamy expression on her face. She'd been utterly unaware of the camera, that much was evident.

God, she looked so much like Evan.

Yes, the eyes were the wrong color, but that mouth, the teasing look. He could read Evan in the shadows of Taylor's face.

He missed her already. He wasn't sure what drew him to Taylor Jackson, her face, her intelligence. The fact that she was alive and Evan was dead? "Bugger," he said softly.

Baldwin finally returned clutching a bottle of Dewar's and two cut-crystal lowballs. At least the man had good taste.

Baldwin put the glasses on his desk and poured them each three fingers.

"Drinking on the job?" Memphis asked.

"Might help us both sleep," Baldwin answered.

"Perhaps it will," he said, then clinked his glass against Baldwin's. "Perhaps it will."

Saturday

Twenty-Nine

The Tennessean headline made Taylor grit her teeth.

**2nd Body Found
Is a Serial Killer Stalking Nashville's Streets?**

She read the article, worried, but aside from the detail of the postcard at Radnor Lake, they didn't have the full story. No one had made the connection to the Italian murders yet.

She made a quick call to Dan Franklin, the department spokesman, and dumped the mess in his lap. For a brief instant, she was glad she was just the detective of record. Franklin and Elm would have to be out in front of the media getting lambasted—she could spend her time working the case.

She made a pot of tea, the morning sunlight streaming in her kitchen window. She felt good. She'd slept a couple of hours after her midnight drive through Nashville. She'd confirmed a few addresses, but really hadn't gotten anywhere. But today was a new day. There was a murderer to catch, and she intended to do it.

She needed to fill Baldwin in on the leak. He'd left a message at the house sometime in the wee hours while she was driving around, letting her know he'd gotten to Quantico. She felt bad for snapping at him last night. She'd been overreacting to Sam's warning and her own fool tendencies. She'd always been easily flattered. As soon as Baldwin delivered the profile, Memphis would go back to England and Baldwin would come back to Nashville, and they could catch this killer together. Without a third-party intrusion.

She held the phone between her ear and shoulder, the line ringing, once, twice, three times. Then Baldwin's gruff, sleep-strewn voice filled her. He sounded tense, but warmed immediately.

"Hi, babe. Did I wake you?"

"Hi back. No, I'm awake. Sort of." He yawned.

"Sounds like you were up as late as I was."

"You have no idea. Our consultation with the Met is in an hour. I'm ingesting coffee as quickly as humanly possible. How are you?"

"Tired, too. I was up half the night knocking on doors, trying to confirm addresses with the names from the Picasso monograph. I've been trying to track them down in Nashville, cross-referenced every match against drivers of white Priuses, but I was hoping you could take a look in your federal databases, as well."

"For the white Prius?"

"Against the names, yeah. My informant saw Allegra Johnson and Leslie Horne get into a Prius for a trick. That was the last time he saw them alive. Stands to reason."

"It's not that, I remember. I just find it highly unlikely that an organized offender would be dumb enough to use his own car. But I'll plug them into my system, too. Fax them up. I'll get Pietra on it."

"Must be nice having a staff."

"Things go south this morning?"

"Last night. Sorry, I didn't get a chance to tell you. If you can believe this, I think my replacement has Alzheimer's. And I'm not kidding. I talked to Percy yesterday, asked him to look into it. But I've got a bigger problem—the press has just enough detail to be dangerous. We need to catch this creep now before they put the whole story together and start an international crisis."

"We're getting close. I can feel it."

"I hate that we have to work apart on this. I feel like things are breaking, though. When are you coming back?"

"I'll be back in Nashville this afternoon. After the presentation, and after I get Lord James *call me Memphis* Highsmythe, the Viscount Dulsie, out of my hair."

"Oh, he's not that bad." She couldn't believe she'd just said that. He *was* that bad, and then some. Since when did she start defending him? "Besides, I thought you liked him."

"I don't dislike him. He's a good cop, smart, intuitive. He just gives new meaning to stiff upper lip. I hate to profile someone I'm working with, but he's in extreme pain. He overcompensates by trying to get under people's skin, make them as uncomfortable as he is. You saw that firsthand. He's a very capable investigator. I think he needs more work, that's all."

No kidding.

"Well, I'm glad you're coming back. I want this case solved. I miss you."

"In that order?" he teased.

"No, I miss you first and foremost. There, happy?"

"Very, love. I'll talk to you later."

"Good luck with the profile," she said. They hung up, and she sipped her tea. James Memphis Highsmythe. She knew exactly what Baldwin was talking about. The viscount had gotten a little too far under *her* skin, as well.

Tossing that thought away, she rinsed out her cup, snapped her Glock into its holster, put her badge on her belt and headed downtown.

McKenzie was already at his desk when she walked in, a steaming latte at his elbow. The smell made her stomach rumble.

He turned to her with a smile. "I got you one. It's on your desk."

"Thank you. That was sweet. How are you this morning?"

"You haven't heard?"

"Heard what?"

"Elm's gone. He's been placed on medical leave indefinitely. I didn't know he was sick."

"Oh." She sat at her desk, grabbed the Starbucks. "Listen, about that. I talked with my union rep about him last night."

"You filed a complaint?" McKenzie's eyebrows shot up in surprise.

"No, no, nothing like that. I figured out why he was so erratic, that's all."

"Why?"

She looked at him for a moment. He'd been pretty damn honest with her over the past few days. She decided to bring him in the loop. Her life would be much easier if she could start trusting him.

"Can you keep your mouth shut?" she asked.

"Of course."

"Alzheimer's."

McKenzie sat back in his chair. "Now that makes sense."

"You're familiar with it?"

"Yes. My dad. He's in a home right now. I couldn't

take care of him after my mom died." He said all of this without looking for sympathy, just reciting facts.

"Jeez, McKenzie, I'm sorry about that."

He smiled sadly, took a sip of his coffee. "Well, what are you going to do? I thought something might be wrong with Elm, but I didn't want to say anything."

"Why?"

"It wasn't polite."

Taylor decided right there and then that she liked Renn McKenzie.

"So have you heard anything else?"

"Like who they're replacing him with? No." But he smiled at her, and she relaxed. No sense getting herself worked up about management issues. She had a killer to catch, and a hot trail to follow. She brought McKenzie up to speed on her midnight travels.

He got visibly upset. "You should have called me before you went out prowling. I was just talking to Bangor. Something could have happened. I could have had your back."

"McKenzie, I'm a big girl. I can take care of myself. Besides, Parks went with me. We were fine."

"Be that as it may, you're my partner. Something goes down and I'm not there, I would feel bad. So next time, just call me, okay? I don't sleep much, anyway."

"Funny, me either. Okay, I promise. What did Bangor have to say? Did he divulge any good secrets?"

McKenzie blushed. She wondered what exactly she'd said to make him spook like that. He recovered quickly, answered her with feigned nonchalance.

"Oh, a little bit of this, a little bit of that. We talked movies, mostly. He's a fascinating guy. We didn't come up with any connections to the Johnson girl. One thing that did stand out was that he's a big supporter of the Frist Center.

He donates money all the time so they can get good exhibits. He's sponsoring part of a new exhibit that's coming from Italy, had a fund-raising party at the house about a month ago. So he's connected to the arts here in town." He smiled slyly, and Taylor saw where he was going.

"McKenzie. Did you get the guest list from the fund-raiser?"

He grinned. "Of course I did. Thought we could cross-reference the names against what we have so far, see if anything matches."

She clapped him on the shoulder. "Nice work, kiddo. That's just the kind of stuff we need. Great. Let's get to it. I think we should send some patrols out to the addresses I hit last night that looked deserted. You and I can tackle the ones that looked more promising. Let's go through the guest list, see if any names match the copyright page and match the DMV list of white Priuses."

Rowena Wright came into the offices. "Detective Jackson?" she said, getting Taylor's attention.

Taylor turned and smiled at Rowena, but just as quickly jumped out of her chair and went to the woman. Her face was gray, haggard. She looked like she'd aged twenty years overnight.

"Rowena, what's wrong?"

"My niece. Kendra. She didn't come home last night. Her father just called me, he found her car by the side of the road, off of Highway 96 down in Williamson County."

"Any sign of foul play?" McKenzie asked. Taylor shot him a look; it wasn't the most sensitive question to ask a distraught aunt.

Rowena shuddered. "No. Nothing. She hasn't answered her cell phone. That girl lives to text message, but none of her friends have heard from her. I've just filed a missing-persons report, but I wanted to talk to you. To ask you personally to look for her. She's a good girl. Head-strong, silly, but such a treat. She's…I just…I would hate to have something bad happen."

"I'll do everything I can, Rowena. What's her full name?"

"Kendra. Kendra Kelley."

"Do you have an extra picture? And can you get me on the phone with her father?"

"Yes. I can do that."

"Then let's go into Elm's office and start making some calls. McKenzie, you come with me."

Rowena pulled a photo out of her capacious handbag. She handed it to Taylor, who felt all the breath leave her lungs. Kendra was tiny, petite, with long black hair in braids.

A perfect candidate for Il Macellaio.

She looked at McKenzie. "Those addresses just became our number one priority."

Baldwin hung up with Taylor and grimaced. He shook three Tylenols into his hand, letting the water warm in the shower. He'd woken up with a wicked headache, which was getting worse by the second. Scotch always did that to him. He and Memphis had shot the shit, told some stories, finished the bottle and crawled off to their respective beds at four in the morning. He was too damn old to have a hangover, especially when he hadn't been drunk the night before.

None of that mattered. He needed to focus on Il Macellaio now.

He showered, shaved and left the apartment he kept for just these kinds of overnight visits. It took him five minutes to get onto the FBI campus, and by the time he swung through the gates his headache was gone. He was thinking about the profile.

The consultation had to look at the whole, rather than just the sum of all the parts. And for a case this big, he felt like he needed a full team—he'd pulled Wills and Charlaine in, then added a forensic expert and a computer analyst. Pietra was his forensics go-to girl. Kevin Salt was his most talented computer expert. He entered his offices and continued down the hall to Kevin's cube. He knocked on the bar across the top, a tinny echoing clang.

"Kevin, briefing on Il Macellaio in five. You ready?"

"I am, Chief. Got everything right here. I'll go get set up." He pointed to a laptop, then scooped it up and walked off down the hall. He was ridiculously tall, nearly six foot nine, whiter than a starched linen handkerchief, with flame-red hair. He'd been a point guard for UCLA but blew out a knee his last game senior year. He'd been good enough for the NBA, too; was being recruited by the Lakers and the Nuggets. A damn shame, but Baldwin saw his scores on the FBI entrance exams and had been grooming him ever since. Taylor had her Lincoln, but Baldwin could stake money on Kevin's ability to outdo him. It would be a close, tough fight between two very different and talented men.

He moved on to Pietra's cube. She looked tired but greeted him with a smile.

"Pietra, briefing in five."

"On my way," she said. "I'll grab Charlaine and Wills. The Brit's already in the conference room. He's much too chipper this morning."

"That's not fair. He was up all night, too. Thanks, Pietra. I'm just going to grab some coffee and I'll be right there."

He stepped into the break room, the luscious scent of fresh-brewed java making his head swim. He poured a cup and drank it down, then poured another. Caffeine buzzed through his veins and he felt more alert. It was time to finish this.

We're ready to get you, you son of a bitch.

Thirty

Gavin rose at seven, achy, tired. He'd spent most of the night in the basement, watching the doll, worrying about who had knocked at his door.

He went into the kitchen, yawning. Art was sitting at his dish, meowing mournfully at Gavin. Oh, damn it!

Gavin cursed his fragile memory—in the excitement of finding Kendra ripe for the picking on the side of the road, he'd neglected to stop for cat food. Art ate more than a cat his size had a right to, and Gavin was forever running out of food for him. He should join one of those clubs, buy it in bulk. He just never got around to it—it was simpler to grab Art's food when he bought his own.

No help for it, the cat had to eat. He made sure the house was secure, then drove the five miles to the Publix. He ran into the grocery store and bought several packages of Whiskas and a twenty-pound bag of dry food. That should keep them for a while.

At the self-checkout, he started thinking about yesterday, about his luck. His mood lightened. He got so excited he dropped his wallet on the floor. He needed to calm down; someone would notice. He paid for the cat food, exited with the food in his reusable bags, then climbed in the Prius. He couldn't wait to get home, to see if he'd just been dreaming, or if there really was a new doll waiting for him.

He was two miles from home when he passed a Metro police car sitting on the side of the road. The officer inside the vehicle had a radar gun trained on him. Gavin wasn't worried, he wasn't a speeder. No sense in drawing attention to yourself. But to his surprise, the officer moved the patrol car out into traffic, right onto Gavin's bumper. Then he hit his lights.

Panic bloomed in Gavin's chest. Surely not. How could that have happened so quickly? Had the doll managed to get out of the box, found a way to call for help? The knock in the night; had the person come back and somehow entered the house? Oh, Jesus, what was he going to do?

The blue-and-white lights were still flashing frantically behind him. He knew he had no chance to get away, so he pulled over. Bluff. He could bluff. Think what Morte would do if he were caught like this.

Swallowing hard, he put down the window, flashing back to the scene just hours before when the luscious Kendra appeared at his side. This time it wasn't a stunning young black girl, but a thick and burly sandy-blond police officer. A weightlifter. Gavin recognized the signs; he was a fan of the gym himself, though he was more streamlined than this behemoth. The officer approached the window slowly, left hand on his hip. With his right, he touched the back of the car, palm down. He wasn't smiling. He came to the window and glared at Gavin.

"License, registration and proof of insurance, please," the policeman said.

Gavin fumbled for the information. He managed to get the wallet out and his license in hand. Registration, where was his registration? Oh, that's right, the console. Paper-clipped to his insurance card. Tennessee required proof of insurance, there were serious fines and you could lose your license without it. Something Gavin would never risk.

He handed the material to the officer, still not speaking. Gavin was scared to death. The officer took his information and returned to his patrol car.

It was five minutes before the officer returned to Gavin's window.

"Do you know why I pulled you over?" he asked.

"N-no," Gavin stuttered. Stop blathering, Gavin. "No, sir." His voice was shaking. The officer noticed.

"Everything okay in there?" he asked.

"Yes. Yes, of course. I'm sorry, I haven't been pulled over before."

The cop got more conversational. "Ever?"

"Never." Gavin gave him a small smile.

"Well, you're not wearing your seat belt. That's a ticketable offense. I'm going to have to give you a citation. You can pay it online or appear in court on July 17. Since you're a first offender, traffic school will wipe your record clean. I'd just pay the ticket and do that if I were you. No points against your insurance."

Gavin didn't hear a word. The police officer was going to let him go. His seat belt! Gavin's hand went to his shoulder. No, he hadn't fastened it. What a lapse. He never forgot the seat belt. Scattered mind. He quickly clicked it into place.

"Yes, of course. I understand. Thank you so much. You're very kind." Maybe he was pouring it on too thick. "I mean, I'll pay it." Stop talking, Gavin.

The officer handed him the slip of hard white paper, then wished him a pleasant day. Gavin watched him get back into his patrol car and speak on his radio. Not quite sure if he should leave or not, Gavin waited a few moments, then carefully turned the engine over, flipped on his blinker, and slowly eased back onto the road. The cop didn't follow.

He debated driving past his driveway, but the cop already had his address. No sense in pretending he didn't live there.

He needed to get rid of the doll immediately. What a thoroughly depressing thought. He needed to talk to Morte. Morte would tell him what to do. But Morte wasn't speaking to him. There had been no contact since his blowup yesterday. Now Gavin was in trouble, and Necro was the only place he could turn.

He unlocked the basement, ran down the stairs. He booted up the computer, started a private chat with Necro. No answer. Oh, all of his friends were deserting him in his hour of need.

He had to try one last time with Morte. Beg, plead, whatever it took.

He typed the words, chewing on his lower lip. He didn't hear anything but the tapping of his fingers on the keyboard.

Morte, I'm in trouble. I need your help. I swear on my life that I never knew there was a connection between us professionally. I'm still trying to digest that. But please, for now just forgive me. Talk to me. I need you. Please.

He sat back, swung his chair around to face the doll. She was staring at him. He could see the fury in her eyes. A warmth began to spread through his chest. He snatched up his camera and started taking pictures. He was so absorbed that he almost missed the discreet chirp that

signaled a new message. The doll shut her eyes and the
spell was broken. He returned to his seat, delighted and
relieved to see the flashing icon.

Morte had returned to the chat room.

Tell me the truth, Gavin. Yesterday was an accident?

Gavin's heart leapt into his throat. His brain wasn't
working—his fingers typed the letters without mental
command.

You're talking about the e-mail I sent to Tommaso?
Yes. That was a fluke. Morte, tell me the truth. Are
you Tommaso?

A pause, then the three letters appeared on the page.

Yes.

Gavin felt his world shattering with possibility.
Tommaso was Morte. Tommaso. Was. Il Morte.
Tommaso, the man whose work he most admired, the
artist, the most incredible photographer in the world
was also the architect of his online world, his sanity,
the man who'd set Gavin free. The man who'd encour-
aged, loved him like a brother. Gave Gavin the only real
family he'd ever had—that hag who'd adopted him
didn't count.

He didn't know what to do.

Gavin, are you there?

Gavin fought tears as he typed.

I didn't know. I swear to you, I didn't know. Please don't be mad.

I believe you, Gavin. There's no real way for you to have tracked me down. I felt it had to be divine intervention. We were meant to be together this way. Through our words, and our actions. You have been an apt pupil.

Gavin started to breathe again. It was all going to be okay. Morte would fix things. He always did.

Now, tell me what's wrong.

Oh, Morte. I got a ticket.

A ticket? Like a speeding ticket?

No.

Gavin needed to tell him everything. The story spilled out, mistakes littering his words as he typed, careless and intense. When he finished, he sat back, panting.
Morte's answer came quickly.

Oh, you stupid, stupid boy. You knew better. You must get rid of the doll. You're on their radar now, whether they know it or not.

I can't get rid of her. It's not time yet.

Fool! Don't you understand? Think, for a moment, Gavin. You can't risk losing everything. Strangle the

bitch and be done with her. DO NOT PLAY WITH HER.
Dispose of the body someplace quiet, don't pose her
or leave a clue. Nothing that can be traced to you.

There was a pause, then another message appeared.

I think it's time we meet in person. Do you have
a passport?

Yes, I do.

Dump the girl, pack a bag. I'll send you instructions
and a plane ticket. Follow the instructions exactly,
Gavin. We can't have you getting caught.

Morte?

Yes.

You've been calling me Gavin. How did you know
my real name?

Gavin hated to say goodbye to his dolls.

The glow from the monitor bathed him in muted gray.
He flipped through the pictures he'd taken, one by one.
Slowly, so slowly. Light flashed across his face as the
gallery forwarded to the next shot. His finger grew wet
on the mouse, a droplet of sweat gathered on the cord. It
slid down the white worm and onto the floor, making a
dark spot on the concrete.

Click.

That was the one. That was his favorite. Oh, the fire,
the fury in those wide brown eyes. The blush rising from

her depths, her cheeks aflame. He could practically hear the beads in her hair clicking in protest. Even the smattering of freckles on her latte-colored skin looked angry.

Defiant was the best word for her. She refused to bend. Refused to acknowledge that her life was going to end. He could see it, forcing itself from behind the dilated pupils, some insane hope that he wouldn't kill her.

Click. He went past his favorite, but returned quickly to the earlier shot. The only noise was his labored breathing. He checked himself. Panting like a dog. How disgusting. He modulated his breath, then looked back at the screen.

There was that spark again, right there, the fourth shot. Oh, the power in those eyes. The slim jaw, the hollowed cheekbones, her clavicle sticking out like a sword from her shoulder. The hint of her breasts, just the slightest swelling. The memory of those dark ruby nipples.

Click.

The next shot wasn't as intoxicating. The spark faded to resignation. He'd captured the moment perfectly. He preferred the righteous indignation she'd showered into the lens, though there was something to be said for the moment of truth.

Click. Click.

Click, click. Click, click.

He really should listen to Tommaso's instructions and destroy his hard drive, erase everything. He couldn't travel with the computer anyway for fear of someone getting their hands on it or losing it. His finger lingered on the mouse. He couldn't do it. He couldn't destroy his whole world. He opened a spare thumb drive, copied all his photos onto it. Then he opened an administrative program, created a password protection system that would encrypt the files within. No one would guess this password. He spoke aloud as he did it, talking to the doll. So sweet. Once he was done, he shut it all off.

Despite Tommaso's instructions, Gavin felt it was crazy to destroy something that might not need destroying. He would be coming back.

He abandoned the computer, turned on the small desk lamp. The forty-watt incandescent bulb highlighted the doll, drawing her away from the shadows.

She had never truly surrendered.

He had loved her. He loved her still.

But it was time to get rid of her. He got out the syringe he kept in cases of emergency, just like this.

He had power now. A more important journey. A purpose.

He was going to join his brother.

Thirty-One

Baldwin listened to Highsmythe's summary of his three murder cases with half an ear. Unlike Baldwin, he didn't seem the least bit hungover. Considering he'd outpaced Baldwin to the bottom of the bottle, that was telling.

Memphis was a good speaker, his thoroughness with the cases showing. His investigation had been done right, by the book, methodical and patient, truly a virtue in police work.

Baldwin tuned back in. He'd already heard all of this yesterday. The London murders had started three months earlier. Three prostitutes, three strangulations. All three were staged, all three left with a postcard of a painting: the first was *Flaming June* by Frederic Lord Leighton, the second, *Venus, Satryr and Cupid* by Correggio, the third was *The Tepidarium* by Sir Lawrence Alma-Tadema. All the paintings were of women reclining. The Leighton was the only one who depicted a woman clothed, and that particular crime scene matched—the victim wasn't naked but dressed in a long, flowing nightgown.

Memphis had prepared a slide show, was going through each scene in detail. He'd show the actual crime scene, then the postcard, then the two superimposed together, then side by side. The resemblance of the dead victims to the paintings was uncanny.

All three women were strangled, all three were small and exceptionally skinny. It hadn't been determined whether they were starved like the Italian victims, or were skinny as more of an occupational hazard. All three women had been repeatedly sexually assaulted post-mortem. DNA found on victim number three was the key to the match between Italy and London.

Il Macellaio was evolving into a more efficient, opportunistic killer, and something had changed in his life. Something that made him alter his preferred method of killing. Anything could tip a psychotic over the edge. There were common denominators that Baldwin could draw on to explain this sudden shift. A death, for example, or a significant job loss. A momentous stressor.

Adding in the total shift in the States to women of African descent, they had another confounding piece of the puzzle. The carabinieri had faxed a report—none of the few murders with black female victims matched Il Macellaio's M.O.

Baldwin relayed this to Memphis, who just nodded and turned the floor over to Baldwin's team so they could formulate their plan of attack.

Baldwin listened to Pietra discussing the forensics with Memphis, writing himself notes on what type of man he thought this killer was. When he was done, his notepad looked like chicken scratch, but he was beginning to feel closer to the truth.

He looked around the table. Files, photographs, paper for all the cases were stacked neatly along the center. His team listening hard, heads cocked at angles, notes being taken. A whiteboard to his right was full of conjecture, the one to his left held facts. The left was meager in comparison. That would change after this.

Memphis tapped his finger on the edge of one of the Radnor Lake photos. "He's obviously escalating."

Baldwin nodded. "Well, two bodies in two days, yes, I'd agree."

"I mean escalating as an artist. His Nashville crime scenes were fully realized. The London scenes that I've worked weren't nearly as elegant. Even his Italian murders weren't this elaborate. This chap thinks he is an artist. The two crime scenes from Nashville are realizations of the paintings he's recreating, not just posed. It took time, and planning and effort. My London cases were slaughters, nothing more. The postcards almost felt like an afterthought. Either he's getting very, very good at this, or he's getting sloppy."

Baldwin nodded in agreement, then started his portion of the program. The profile was as complete as he could make it, and made for a chilling narrative. He was pleased with the results.

There were five sections to the profile. Charlaine had typed them up into proper presentation format, with a front page full of information and disclaimers. The first few pages of the profile were the summary, a breakdown of all fourteen cases on record, details of what was found at the individual crime scenes and evidentiary material relevant to the cases. Namely, the two matching DNA samples from the recovered hairs.

The next section dealt with the victimology. They had looked carefully at the apparent patterns—all of the European victims were white females, all were fine-boned and small in stature, between eighteen and twenty-six years of age. Their hair color ranged from dark blond to medium brown, their eye colors varied. He wasn't killing the same woman over and over, but he definitely had a type. All thirteen victims had been posed as a painting, all had a postcard of the painting they'd been used to recreate left at the scene.

Memphis's point was something that particularly fascinated Baldwin—Il Macellaio had fully realized the fantasy of the painting in the Love Hill crime scene, placing the victim not only in a staged environment, but with the painting itself nearby. He was evolving, setting the most elaborate of tableaux. It was more than just the kill, more than having sex with the bodies. He was staging differently, opening the door to more mistakes.

He turned it over to Charlaine, let her explain the differences, the exceptions that stood out starkly. In Italy, the early victims had starved, while the later victims had been strangled. All of the London victims had been strangled. The time frame in Italy was practically leisurely compared to London: ten women over ten years versus three women in three months. The victim type had changed as well. The Italian women were students—shy, mousy girls who didn't have a lot of friends and wouldn't be quickly missed. In London, as in Nashville, the victims were prostitutes, an inherently high-risk profession where they, too, might not be reported missing immediately.

The dump sites for the London victims were especially notable—all were found in public, rather than the Italian victims, who'd been left in the hills surrounding Florence à la Il Mostro, Florence's most infamous serial killer. The London women had been found much quicker than the Italians. The Nashville victims had been left in places they would be found that would increase the shock factor, yet another discrepancy.

Honestly, if they didn't have a DNA match, he'd think this was a copycat.

That started him down a whole different path. Yes, the Pretender had called, had let them know right from the beginning that he had nothing to do with the crime on Love Circle. But what if he was lying? He had to keep that in the back of his mind.

The Pretender could have planted the DNA in London. And if all the DNA in Tennessee matched, too…well, they knew he'd been there.

Though this didn't feel like the Pretender. All the murders he'd copied so far had one thing in common. Blood. He liked blood. None of these murders had any. No, this just didn't feel like him.

He forced himself back to the profile, back to what Charlaine was saying about the London murders. The profile stated Il Macellaio wasn't living in his own place in London—he had taken a temporary apartment or was staying in a hotel. Visiting. Which meant the profile must be disseminated to other countries so they could look at unsolved murders that may match. It wasn't so strange for a serial killer to be transient, but it was uncommon for him to be moving from country to country. If their killer was a traveler, he'd be in the system, somewhere.

They still needed to ascertain what took Il Macellaio from Italy to England and to the United States. Contract work fit that scenario.

The second set of criteria, the Abduction Environment, showed that all the London victims had been taken off the street, while the Italians were kidnapped from environments where they'd feel safe, namely their homes. The London victims' profession again stood out—being prostitutes, they'd be more likely to get in the car with a strange man.

The third part of the profile determined whether the killer was organized or disorganized, an easy one for

Baldwin's team. Il Macellaio was clearly an organized offender who brought his preferred weapon to the crime, planned every detail, hunted outside his immediate neighborhood, and was most likely a friendly, affable, pleasant man who had friends. The boy next door. Someone people would be shocked to find out was a killer. He could move among the masses easily.

The assessment was the meat of the profile. It covered more victim evaluations, whether the women were targeted or were representative victims. Baldwin felt that Il Macellaio was combining the two elements: targeting women who helped him live out a detailed fantasy, specifically, having sex with their dead bodies. He was certain Il Macellaio had been exposed to death during his youth.

The last section covered specific suggestions, who to look for, what type of behavior, the level of sophistication to expect, what the motivations were, everything that a law enforcement agency would need to capture, interrogate and try this particular killer.

In the end, they had an exceptionally clear picture of their killer. Evidence, instinct, and years of investigative experience told them what kind of man they were looking for.

They were ready to hunt the hunter.

Thirty-Two

Taylor and McKenzie were coordinating their plan of attack. Finding Kendra Kelley was paramount. Taylor had that awful feeling in the pit of her stomach that told her Il Macellaio was involved in the disappearance. She'd dealt with enough serial cases, knew when a killer was gearing up. She just prayed they could find Kendra in time.

Baldwin had faxed down a copy of the profile so she had all the tools she could have at her disposal. He would be back in a few hours, and that would help. He was fantastic in these situations, steady, levelheaded, always on target with his assessments.

She felt like she should be strapping on a cannon, get loaded for bear, but she settled for a few extra magazines. McKenzie had his service weapon and was carrying a department-issue Remington 870 shotgun. Absolutely nothing could strike fear in the heart of a suspect as well as the sound of a pump action shotgun jacking a shell— that deep steel *ca-CHUNG* snap as distinctive and scary as the growl of a rabid wolf. It was an effective tool, one she hoped they wouldn't have to use.

Thanks to McKenzie, they had a confirmation on the name. A name that appeared on both the guest list for Hugh Bangor's party and on the copyright page of the Picasso *catalogue raisonnés*. A name that matched the DMV listing of registered white Priuses.

Gavin Adler was their suspect. Taylor had absolutely no doubt that he was Il Macellaio.

And she had knocked on his goddamned door last night.

She'd assembled a coterie of officers to help them in the search. She gave directions, assignments, feeling strangely back in control.

She was upset with herself. She should have pushed harder. Something about the place on Highway 100 had given her the creeps last night. It was quiet, and rural and didn't have any close neighbors. It was a perfect setting for someone who needed to take his time. If Kendra was there, and she was dead, Taylor was going to have a very hard time forgiving herself.

Of course, now she cursed herself for her nocturnal foray. She'd probably scared the bastard off.

It was time. Everyone had their assignments, the BOLO, be on the lookout, had gone out on the Prius in case he was running. Taylor called Julia Page, laid out the particulars for the warrant. Julia agreed to shepherd it if she could come out to the scene with them. Taylor reminded her to be quiet about it. They were trying to fly below the radar, keep the media out of play until they knew for sure if Adler had killed another.

Poor Rowena was sitting woodenly at her desk, fingers moving through files, eyes unseeing. How she managed to sit with her back straight was unfathomable to Taylor. The woman had the strength of ten men. She was a cop. She knew the case. She knew the odds. Yet she still was participating, as best she could.

Taylor put an arm around her as they trooped out. "I'll find her, Rowena. I promise."

"Thank you, Miss Taylor. If anyone can, it will be you."

Taylor just nodded, then gathered McKenzie. They took a Caprice, drove through downtown quickly. It had only been thirty minutes since Rowena came into the office.

The sky was the deepest blue, humidity so low that it felt like fall. A perfect day.

As she drove, McKenzie read the full profile of their killer out loud.

"According to this Il Macellaio is a biracial male, between thirty and thirty-five, and was adopted or was a foster child. He's a loner, but has friends who think he's solid and dependable. He works in the arts, quite possibly as a painter or as a photographer. His job is international in scope, allowing him to travel without raising suspicion. He has his own homes in Nashville and Florence, but rents in London."

"That partially matches Adler. We know he was connected to Bangor through the monograph. There may be more, he could be a local artist or a patron."

Taylor's cell rang. Dispatch. Oh, no. She answered warily, hoping that she wasn't about to get bad news.

"Detective, I've got Officer Barry Armstrong on the line, from West Precinct. He needs to speak with you urgently."

"Put him through, Dispatch."

Armstrong greeted her, then said, "Listen, I don't want to beat around the bush. Heard you're looking for a white Prius. I pulled over a guy this morning out in Bellevue, fits the description of who you're looking for. I've got his particulars, you want them?"

"Yes, absolutely."

"Name is Gavin Adler. Lives off Highway 100. Squirrelly guy, really nervous. Jumpy. He wasn't wearing his safety belt, I cited him, and he seemed, I don't know, so relieved that it made me suspicious."

"Barry, that's the name of our suspect. We're on our way there right now. Are you on? You could meet us there."

"I'm on. Let me give my shift commander the heads-up. I can be there in five."

"Okay. Meet us at the base of the drive."

"You know it?"

"Yes, I was out there last night. Damn it." She hung up the phone. "Get in touch with Julia Page, see if the warrant is ready. We'll make an exigent-circumstance entry if we have to, because I doubt Julia will get there fast enough. I'd like this to be aboveboard. Thank God for Judge Bottelli."

"She's a hard one," McKenzie said, fingering the radio mike.

"But she's fair. We have a shot with her. Go, go, call."

Taylor gripped the steering wheel hard, put her foot on the gas.

The house looked less sinister in the daylight. A well-tended but minimalist garden in front, grass that was due for its weekly cut, a small, trickling fountain. Anyone could live here, anything. Was there a monster behind the walls?

Taylor had her vest on, was checking magazines and her Taser. All seemed to be in order. McKenzie stood next to her, shotgun at the ready, nostrils pinched. Officer Barry Armstrong was five feet away. There were three others there—Julia Page had shown up with the ink barely dry on the papers. Bottelli had agreed to a no-knock warrant on the basis of the evidence from the Bangor house, the name on the guest list, the missing pages from the Picasso monographs, and Armstrong's assertion that the man he pulled over this morning perfectly matched the physical description in the profile. Top that with the fact that a kid was involved, and they were good to go. They'd made entry with much less.

Tim Davis was ready with the video camera to document everything, Keri McGee was on her way to help him collect any evidence they might find.

Paula Simari was standing by with Max, ready in case the suspect bolted. Max could chase him down quicker and more effectively than any of the officers on the scene.

Taylor missed having Lincoln and Marcus along, but this crew would have to do.

They'd all get their asses handed to them if they were wrong, but Taylor felt it was solid. She could sense this was the right place. She could just feel it. Evil, hidden behind a pretty garden and a sweet little fountain.

They were set. Armstrong took the back, Taylor and McKenzie the front.

"You gonna knock?" McKenzie asked quietly.

"Nope. I'm not exactly in the mood to get shot. No knocking. Fast and hard." They counted off thirty seconds to let Barry get into place, then Taylor raised her right boot and slammed it into the door. She felt the reverberation in her hip, but the lock cracked under the pressure. It swung open, smashing back against the wall behind it, and they were in, McKenzie expertly drawing off to the right as she went left. The kid knew how to make an entry, she'd give him that.

The house was empty, she could feel that immediately. And it looked like whoever lived there left in a rush. The bedroom upstairs had clothes scattered around, drawers hanging open, the closet door ajar. A toothbrush was missing from the bathroom.

They cleared the rooms on the first floor. The living room had floor-to-ceiling bookshelves, crammed full of classical CDs. Around the corner, in the hallway, Taylor noticed the shiny new Master padlock on what must be the door to the basement. A gorgeous gray cat sat quietly at the door, watching them with sad yellow eyes.

McKenzie came in from the kitchen. "I cleared the garage. Car's gone," he said.

Armstrong joined them, looked at the lock on the basement door. "I've got bolt cutters in my trunk."

He went out the smashed front door, gave Taylor an appreciative glance. She just raised an eyebrow. Sweat was trickling down the small of her back. She needed in that basement.

The cat was staring at her. She bent down, scratched it on the ears, and it started purring and turning in circles. A boy, she saw, and lonely. She wondered how long he'd been here alone. Maybe she hadn't chased the guy off.

"McKenzie, check and see if the cat has food."

"Why?" he asked.

She just looked at him. He nodded then went into the kitchen. He was back in a moment.

"There are three big full bowls of dry, and a massive bowl of water. Enough to last him at least a week, I'd say."

Damn, and damn again. They'd missed him.

Taylor sighed. "So do you think Mr. Adler took a trip, or did he abandon his pet?"

"I don't know. But come here, Taylor. Look at this."

McKenzie walked down the hallway and pointed into the living room. Taylor joined him. On the wall facing them was a poster from the Museum of Modern Art. *Desmoiselles D'Avignon.*

"Okay, that's just creepy. There's our link to Bangor. I bet Adler's on the guest list for the party."

Armstrong came back in. "Let's see what he keeps locked in the basement."

They went back to the basement door. "Careful," Taylor said. "Glove up. We don't want to lose any possible prints off that sucker."

"I know," he said. He slipped on his gloves, muscled the bolt cutters onto the hasp of the lock, then snapped it in two. It fell with a clatter. McKenzie retrieved it and handed it to Tim, who put it in an evidence bag.

She led the way. The stairs led straight into darkness, no landing, just a deep blackness at the bottom. There was a light switch on her left, she flipped the lights on. They were low wattage, so now the room glowed softly. She was reminded of her last trip into a basement, one that seemed innocuous but led to an amateur pornography studio. She could do without that again.

She took the last step, stuck her head around the corner looking for surprises, but saw no one.

She stepped fully into the gloom and saw the clear plastic box. A Plexiglas coffin. There was a woman lying inside it.

Kendra Kelley. And she wasn't moving.

There were two locks on the coffin, one at each end, holding the lid in place. A divider ran the length, cutting the coffin into two halves, each just big enough for a petite woman. Kendra was in the right slot. Taylor could see the bottom slab was open, with holes. The pattern on the bodies of Allegra Johnson and Leslie Horne came immediately to mind. The polka dots. They were, without a doubt, in the right place.

"Jesus, get me some more light. Armstrong, bring the bolt cutters."

"Is she alive?" McKenzie asked, his voice a strangled whisper.

"I don't know."

She could hear Armstrong running back up the stairs. She took in the rest of the room—it was segmented. There was a computer on the desk, open, but the screen was blank. A potbellied stove in the far corner, a small table with two chairs, an empty bottle of wine and melted candles. A mussed mattress with pillows in front of the stove—oh, she didn't even want to think about that. Not yet.

Armstrong was back, snapping off the locks. They opened the lid. The girl looked gray; her eyes hadn't opened. Taylor felt her carotid for a pulse, not expecting to feel anything. But there was a tiny flutter, like a bird's heart.

"She's still alive! Call rescue, now." Taylor bent over the girl, leaning in the coffin, checked her breathing. Faint, the rise and fall of her breasts barely discernible in the gentle light. She reconsidered.

"Armstrong, I don't know if we can wait for an ambulance. It will take them twenty minutes to get out here. Can you transport her?"

"Sure. Baptist?"

"Lights and sirens. She doesn't have much left in her, you need to hurry."

As Armstrong and Taylor lifted Kendra out of the coffin, her eyes fluttered open. They were full of panic, like a horse shying away from a snake, the pupils dilated.

Taylor murmured to her, trying to calm her. "It's okay, Kendra. We've got you. We're Metro Police. He's gone. You're safe now. You're going to be just fine."

A single meager tear slid down the girl's cheek, and she whispered a word in Taylor's ear. "Dolls," she said. Then her eyes closed. She was too weak to cry anymore.

Taylor looked around, saw an empty syringe on the floor beneath the coffin. Shit.

"Hurry, Armstrong. She looks drugged. He must have given her something to speed things up. She needs a hospital, fast."

They rushed up the stairs, got Kendra situated in the

back of the squad car, saw Armstrong off. Then Taylor called Rowena Wright.

"I found her, Rowena. She's on her way to Baptist right now."

The rest of Tim's crime-scene team arrived and spread throughout the house, collecting every bit of evidence that they could. Paula and Max had been called to another case. Tim Davis was printing the coffin while Keri Mc-Gee filmed everyone's actions for posterity. McKenzie had gone upstairs to get the warrant amended to include everything in the house. Julia Page was standing by the Plexiglas coffin, pale as a ghost, documenting their actions in a small Moleskine notebook.

Taylor was searching Gavin Adler's computer. The gray cat had settled onto her lap, purring its fool head off.

"Have you ever seen anything like this, Taylor?" Tim asked. She was surprised, he never used her first name.

"No," she answered. "I've seen a lot, but this takes the cake."

She looked around the room, now brightly lit with Tim's scene lights. She imagined the darkness, the fire in the stove casting shadows on the wall, the sounds of the girls' muffled screams as they lay dying in the Plexiglas coffin.

The computer was booted up. The screen asked for a password. Shit. Where was Lincoln when she needed him?

She made a few desultory tries, Gavin, Adler, GAdler. All failed. She had a birth date from the ticket Armstrong gave the man; she tried that, forward, backward. Nothing. Then she remembered the word Kendra had whispered. Dolls. It was such an innocuous word. Why not give that a try?

She typed in the word. Nothing. She tried it in all lowercase. Nope. She typed in DOLLS and the computer ran for a fraction of a second. She leaned closer. The desktop screen filled the monitor. Now that was just dumb luck.

"Open sesame," she whispered.

She saw an icon blinking—iChat. She clicked on it. She was vaguely familiar with instant messaging; it wasn't something she had a lot of time for nor an inclination to play with, but she knew enough. There was an ongoing chat, and Adler hadn't erased the history.

As she read, faster and faster, scanning the page, she felt the dread build in the pit of her stomach. They'd missed him. But that wasn't all.

"Oh, Jesus," she said. She pulled out her cell phone, called Dispatch. "We need to amend the BOLO on the Prius. Please include the state of Georgia."

She hung up, then speed-dialed Baldwin. He answered on the first ring.

She could hear the tremor in her voice. "I'm in Gavin Adler's basement. We were wrong. Oh, my God, we were so wrong. Gavin Adler isn't Il Macellaio."

"What are you talking about?"

"Baldwin, there's two of them."

"What do you mean, there's two of them?"

"Are you still in Quantico?" Taylor asked.

"Yes, I am. I was going to catch a plane in about an hour."

"Maybe you should sit tight. I'll come to you. We can catch a flight to Florence out of D.C. a helluva lot easier than from Nashville."

"Whoa. You need to back up, and tell me everything."

The words spilled out in a torrent. "All our leads ended up here, pointing to Gavin Adler. I'm at his house now, out in western Davidson County. We just recovered a victim, a young woman named Kendra Kelley, who was being held in a Plexiglas coffin. This is his house, Baldwin, this is the house of the man who killed Allegra

Johnson and Leslie Horne. But it's not Il Macellaio. We were completely wrong. Il Macellaio is still overseas. He's in Italy, in Florence. We have to go after them. This guy, Gavin Adler, is Il Macellaio's brother."

"His brother? Are you speaking figuratively, or do you mean a flesh-and-blood brother?"

"A real brother. And they've been working together. I've only gotten a glimpse into their world, and I'm telling you, it's horrific. By the way, I have a name for you to start working on for Il Macellaio. Tommaso. That's all I've got. I'm waiting for a specialist to come and go through the computer system."

"Christ. There's two of them. Okay, okay, give me a second."

She could hear him rustling papers, could imagine that he was running his hands through his hair, trying to get his mind to work harder.

"Is the computer a desktop?" he asked finally.

"No, it's a laptop."

"Okay. Take it. Get to the airport, get up here. I'll clear it with your bosses. We'll analyze the system, glean as much information as possible. Did Adler flee to Italy?"

"Yes. It's all right here. Tommaso tells Gavin to come to him. To drop everything, dispose of the 'doll,' as he calls the victim we found here, Kendra Kelley, and come to him. He sent instructions for him to drive to Hartsfield International in Atlanta, I guess to throw us off the trail if we thought he might have tried to flee, to pick up a ticket at Alitalia and fly to Rome. And he calls him brother."

"So he may not be physically related?"

"Baldwin, think about it. The DNA from Chattanooga matches the DNA from London and from Florence. The DNA *matches*."

"Holy shit," he murmured. "Of course. I was so blind. There's only one way the DNA could match two people."

"Exactly. They aren't just brothers. They're identical twins."

Thirty-Three

Taylor hung up the phone with Baldwin. She closed the laptop, looked for a case. She didn't find one, but did find a power cord. She bundled that together. Tim was wrapping things up with the coffin; the basement had been combed over. Samples of DNA had been taken, fingerprints, everything they'd need to nail Adler to the wall. If they could catch him.

Keri McGee was watching all this with a trained eye, waited until Julia Page had gone upstairs for some air before approaching Taylor.

"Is this something I need to erase from the tapes?"

Taylor gave the girl a smile. "No. This is an instance of me taking the initiative. If I get busted, so be it. But Quantico is better equipped to handle this than we are. I just have to go downtown and plead my case to whoever I can find who'll let me go. Baldwin said he'd fix it, but I can't exactly run up there with evidence without authorization."

"Okay. I heard what you said. Identical-twin killers, huh?"

"It looks that way."

Keri brushed her bangs out of her eyes. "You know, I

had a Cajun granddaddy, his name was Welton Keif. I
remember one time we'd gone out to the bayou to visit
him, in this flat-bottomed skiff, water moccasins slipping
through the murk, mosquitoes as big as your hand flitting
around. We'd been visiting with a cousin of mine who'd
had identical twins, and we brought pictures so he could
see. We showed him the babies, told him they were identicals. He looked at us funny, said, 'What the hell is an
identical twin?' We were taken aback, surely everyone
knew what that was. But my mom explained anyway, that
they were two little boys who were exactly alike who'd
been born at the same time. He got this look of recognition on his face. Said, 'Oh. Them's born partners, that's
what they are. Born partners.' Sounds like that's what you
have here, Detective Jackson. Born partners who are
driven to kill. I wonder what made them that way?"

"Born partners, huh? Well, they're certainly partners
in murder. I wonder what made them this way, too, Keri.
If I can find out more about them, I might be able to
answer that. Thanks for the input. Sounds like your granddaddy was a perceptive man."

"That he was, Detective. Too perceptive. He also said
I'd come across another pair, far away from him. Looks
like that was rather prophetic, don't you think?"

The hair rose on Taylor's arms. "Yes, Keri, that's a
little strange."

"I'll just get back to work now, Detective. You travel
safe. Good luck catching these guys."

McKenzie met her at the top of the stairs. He had the
gray cat in his arms, and the cat was snuggled into his
shoulder, purring loudly. He looked settled in and happy.

"His name is Art," McKenzie said. "It's on his tag."

"Art the cat. Well, that fits. These killers are imitating
famous paintings, why not have a cat named Art? Hey,

kiddo." She scratched the gray behind his ears again, and she swore he smiled.

"He's really friendly. He seemed lonely, so I thought I'd give him a little love. Now I'm afraid to put him down."

"McKenzie, we've got work to do. Have you found any pictures of this guy, anything that might help us identify him? We only have the photograph from his license to go on, and it was issued in 1998. You know how deceiving those pictures can be. He could have changed his look four times since then."

"No. This place is clean. Except for all those CDs and the basement, this place is sadly devoid of personality, actually. Um, Jackson? I kind of promised Art I'd take care of him."

Taylor ran her hand across her forehead. "Well, we need to call animal services and let them come take him."

"No. They'll, they'll—" He looked at her frantically, mouthed the words *put him down*.

"Not necessarily. What do you propose?"

"Can I keep him?"

McKenzie sounded so much like an eight-year-old who'd found a stray that Taylor had to laugh.

"McKenzie, this is going to be our little secret. You may foster the cat until we figure out what needs to happen with him. Is that fair?"

He just nodded, a wide grin plastered across his face.

"Okay then. That's settled. I need to go back to the CJC and secure permission to go to Quantico. Though I have no idea who I'm going to do that with. Can you stay here, continue running the scene? Tim has oodles of evidence that needs to be logged, and I want your eyes on it. Then I want you to take the license photo of Adler, put it in a six-pack, and see if Hugh Bangor can identify him. What's the word on Kendra Kelley?"

"She's being pumped full of Narcan and she's responded well. Looks like she'll be okay."

"That's great news," Taylor said. "Is she awake enough to talk?"

"Not yet. Why are you going to Quantico?"

"The Macellaio task force is all there already. They need this piece of the puzzle." She tapped the laptop. "Baldwin's working it with our superiors. I'll fight for you to come, too, you've been instrumental in this case from day one."

"Well, don't worry if they say no. I've got enough here to keep me busy."

Gracious of him. He walked into the kitchen, singing softly under his breath to the cat. Sheesh. Big man gone soft over a fuzzball. Though she had to admit, Art was kind of cute.

She had bigger problems to worry about than one of her detectives fostering a criminal's pet.

She caught herself. McKenzie wasn't one of her detectives, he was her partner. She didn't have her command back. Yet.

Taylor stopped at home to pack a bag and grab her passport, just in case. By the time she made it to the CJC, the orders had been secured for her trip to Quantico. A commander she'd worked with in the past, Joan Huston, was in the Homicide offices when she arrived.

"Commander," Taylor said.

Huston patted her sun-streaked brown hair and smiled, then handed her a file folder. "Detective. I'm overseeing Homicide until we get things straightened out with Lieutenant Elm. I've got your clearance for Quantico. I appreciate the request to take Detective McKenzie, but we've decided that he doesn't need to travel at this time. He can be your conduit to the investigation in Nashville.

You've been authorized on a TPSPA both for Quantico and for any overseas travel that may be necessary. A temporary special assignment to the FBI's behavioral unit was the best we could do on this short notice. It's on the FBI's dime, which made it easier for the chief to swallow. You need to hurry, you don't want to miss your flight. I do hope you'll keep me informed of your progress."

Wow. That was easy. Baldwin must have made some interesting phone calls. "I will. Thanks so much for helping."

"You got it. Do us proud. We'll have all this—" she waved her hand around in a circle, meaning Homicide "—figured out upon your return."

She smiled again and shook Taylor's hand. She'd always gotten along with Huston. It was nice to have someone of rank actually smile at her again. Maybe things were getting ready to turn around.

It was early enough that the drive to the airport wasn't too bad. She dumped the car at Executive Travel and had them shuttle her over to the terminal. Her flight to D.C. was in forty minutes, and she still needed to get her weapon checked and registered. Flying armed wasn't an easy proposition, but once she got to the airport, all the provisions she needed had been arranged for. With her weapon surrendered and secured, she was escorted through security, her bag x-rayed, and fifteen minutes later she was on the plane.

That had to be a record run through an airport. She liked working with the FBI. They knew how to make things happen.

The flight was going to take two hours. She did the only rational thing. She put her head against the window, and fell asleep.

Thirty-Four

Taylor woke when the plane began its skidding run down the Potomac. She reset her watch for Eastern time, brushed her hair, and swiped on some ChapStick. Baldwin was meeting her at the gate. Another perk for the FBI.

She deplaned, was met in the jetway by an airline official who handed her both her overnight bag and her gun case. She'd carried on the killer's laptop, in her own case, so she attached that to her bag and strolled up the jetway. As she exited, she saw Baldwin waiting. He had on a white Brooks Brothers button-down and chinos, looked endearingly preppy and handsome, his green eyes flashing in welcome. And weary. Too many long nights, too many murders. It was starting to take a toll. But his face lit up when he saw her, and he enveloped her in a hug that took her breath away.

God, just being near him made her feel more settled.

Reagan National Airport had changed since she was last here. Of course, that was ages ago, everything in this town but the monuments would have changed, and they'd added a few new ones to the city, too. D.C. could never be accused of being a static entity.

They chatted about nothing until they exited the terminal, the humidity smacking her in the face like a wet washcloth. Funny, she knew Nashville was just as humid, but it felt wetter here.

Dodging a multitude of people going in every direction but theirs, they reached the curb, where a driver sat with a big black sedan that fairly screamed government. Baldwin held the door for her. The air was on full blast and gave her a chill. Baldwin slid in beside her, and the driver wormed his way through the mass of taxis and cars to the exit. Within ten minutes, they were heading south, toward Quantico, on I-95.

"Ready?" Baldwin asked.

"As I'll ever be. Tell me what you know."

"We're heading to Italy in the morning. The carabinieri are looking for Adler. He landed in Rome early this afternoon, made it through customs before the alert went out. Well, I shouldn't say that. The alert had gone out, but they didn't pay it enough attention. He was smart, drove to Atlanta, took the first flight out. Georgia Bureau of Investigation has already impounded the Prius. Oh, and we have his passport photo." He handed her a black-and-white glossy eight-by-ten photograph.

It was a much more recent shot than Adler's driver's license. The man who looked back at her didn't send waves of fear crashing through her system. He was…boring. Nondescript. Not terribly handsome, not ugly. Where so many mixed-race children took on the most glorious aspects of their parents' blood, nothing elegant leapt out about Gavin Adler. He had curly black hair and a round face, with skin so light that if his full lips didn't have a slightly ethnic bent to them, she would have assumed he was white. Wide brown eyes. His nose wasn't big, nor was it small, but a bit thick through the nostrils. He looked…more scared than scary. How had this benign little man killed four women? How had he had sex with their corpses? How did he manage to have an elaborate chamber in his basement solely for the purpose of hastening his victims' deaths?

Taylor was used to evil, saw it every day. But she had a hard time seeing much of anything in Gavin Adler's face.

"This is him? This is the man who's created such havoc?"

"Half of him, anyway. We have the Italians, the Brits and Interpol using facial recognition software to look for another man like this in their passport rolls, people who've traveled in and out of the country. But we don't know what country issued Il Macellaio's passport, or what name he's traveling under, so that makes it difficult. We don't know travel dates. We have very little to go on over there. Tommaso isn't exactly an uncommon name over there. It's like us pulling all the records of people named Tom."

Taylor tapped her laptop bag.

"Hopefully, this will change everything. I assume you'll be able to trace the IP address he was using and narrow a location down pretty damn quick. I doubt Tommaso is his real name."

"Maybe, maybe not. We have been trying to track it down, and we do have a possible on the Tommaso front. There's a famous art photographer named Tommaso. It's a long shot, but it just might be him."

"An art photographer?"

"Yeah. And catch this. He takes photographs of paintings for the art catalogs for the museums."

"Well, that fits. How'd you find him?"

"One of my profilers, Charlaine Shultz, is a big art fan. When we said the name she mentioned this guy. We searched on Google for him and he showed up everywhere. We even know where he lives." He paused for a moment. "Care to guess?"

Taylor raised an eyebrow. "Florence?"

"Exactly. He warranted checking out, under the circumstances. He's well-known. Sought after. He goes simply by Tommaso, if that tells you anything."

"That's as good a start as any I've heard. Man, your team has been busy."

"Do you know what Tommaso means in Italian?"

Taylor shook her head. "No, what?"

"Twin. Tommaso means twin."

She spit out a laugh. "That's precious."

"You better believe it. Taylor, I don't want to lose these guys. I want to nail them, and then I want to study them. Identical-twin serial killers. Identical twin necrosadists. Can you imagine?"

Baldwin's voice had taken on that dreamy quality it always did when he was confronted by true evil. It was his calling, his purpose, to find out what made these men and women tick.

"No, I can't. What in the world would drive this type of pathology?"

"That's the fascinating thing about this. With identical twins, it's like they are the same person, just in two bodies. It makes sense that if one has the pathological desire to commune with the dead, the other would as well. Of course, that drives a massive stake in the nature versus nurture theory."

Taylor looked at him. "Are you assuming they were brought up in some sort of environment that made them this way?"

"I can't assume anything, not until we find out who they really are. The background on Gavin Adler shows he was adopted. We're trying to track down by whom.

Hopefully, that will give us the name of the other brother. It's going to be fascinating to see what their young lives were like. I'm telling you, Taylor, no matter what kind of environment a child is brought up in, there is a reasonable expectation that they'll understand what's right and what's wrong, that they will receive the tools to form a positive moral compass. Serial killers aren't made. They choose to be killers, they choose to take lives. A hidden desire for necrophilia is something that's probably not learned. Of course, that's another completely misunderstood pathology. Did you know that necrophilia is really just the desire to have sex with an unresisting partner, and the vast majority of necrophiliacs are stunted in the fantasy stage? Very few actually act on their desires, and when they do, they seek out role-playing partners who are willing to pretend with them. They're looking for compliant sex, completely submissive. Some of the more disturbed ones will drug their prey—like roofies. Classic necro behavior."

"You're saying that men who give roofies to women and rape them are actually necrophiliacs?"

"That's exactly what I'm saying. They want power and control, and they don't want to be told no. You should see the Web sites out there dedicated to this. They have what they call 'Sleepy Sex,' arranged for partners who are willing to be photographed during the role play, then share them."

"That's…disturbing. The thought of an undercurrent of men and women who are into this…well, everyone has their kink. From the instant messages it seems Adler didn't know Tommaso was his brother until yesterday. Do you think Tommaso and Gavin met through one of these sites?"

"I don't know. Here's the problem, though. Our boys

have moved on to something much more sinister. They are actually killing to have sex with the dead bodies. They are a highly evolved version of the classic necrophiliac. I wouldn't be surprised to see a background that includes working at or near a morgue, or in the funeral business. As it is, they're well beyond anything I've seen before. And the art, the painting? Leaving the postcards at the scenes? Think about it."

She did. "Oh… Static women, posed and at the ready."

"Exactly."

He settled back in the seat, took her hand. "I'll tell you one thing, Adler is panicked. You know when a suspect goes off his beaten path, does something that isn't in his normal routine, he messes up. Our boy has messed up, royally. We're going to catch him now, and we're going to catch his brother, too. There are a lot of people in Italy who will sleep easier once we have Il Macellaio off the streets."

"Should we be calling them I Macellai now, instead?" she asked.

"The Butchers. Plural. Yes, I guess we should."

"He left his cat behind."

"Adler?"

"Yes. McKenzie is going to foster it. I didn't have the heart to tell him no, animal control might have destroyed the poor thing. But guess what the cat's name is."

"What?"

"Art."

Baldwin just shook his head. "That's just too much. Adler's an artist of sorts. He's listed as the designer on the Picasso monograph. We're looking into anything that's got a copyright with his name near it. Any idea where he worked?"

"No. McKenzie is handling that part back in Nashville. But now that I know all of this, I can have McKenzie look deeper. It didn't seem like he worked out of the house. Granted, once we get into his computer all the way, we can find out all of this."

"It's like Son of Sam."

"Huh?"

"Remember, he got caught because of a parking ticket. Adler got caught because one of your patrol officers was sharp enough to spot that he was acting weird."

"He wasn't wearing his safety belt. Such a stupid little mistake. But we'd have found him anyway. I think that's what made him run, getting pulled over. I think he would have stuck it out with Kendra Kelley otherwise, and we might have actually gotten our hands on him in the act."

"How is the Kelley girl?"

"She'll live. She'd been drugged, they had to pump her full of Narcan to stop the overdose. I don't know what kind of emotional scars she might have. He glued the eyes of his last victim open. Imagine, being locked in a Plexiglas box, able to see your killer, feeling your life draining away inch by inch. You can imagine where he may go next. We saved her from a nasty fate."

"We're here," Baldwin said.

Taylor looked out the window. They were parked in front of a restaurant called the Globe and Laurel. It was nearly 10:00 p.m. Taylor was starving, her mouth watering at the mere thought of sustenance. Baldwin heard her stomach growl, looked sheepishly at her. "Everyone's already here. Thought we might eat before we worked."

"That, my dear, sounds wonderful."

Thirty-Five

The table ordered a round, and Wills Appleby suggested Memphis try the lager. Memphis had drunk beer at university, one of those things you do to fit in with the boys, but he'd never truly enjoyed it. He didn't have the heart to mention he'd much rather have a nice glass of cabernet.

The waitress brought their drinks and he took a sip of the lager. There was a surprise. He had to admit, it wasn't too bad. His cell rang, and he saw it was Pen calling. He put the phone to his ear, had just greeted her when Taylor Jackson walked into the room. His breath caught in his throat.

She was smiling, shaking hands, her full lips moving as she moved about the table greeting the team. She shook his in acknowledgment, and then she was gone, being introduced to that infernally tall Kevin Salt, who Memphis liked despite the fact that he had to look up at him. He had to look up to Baldwin, as well. But he and Taylor were exactly eye to eye. He couldn't help but think what that would mean if they were horizontal.

"Memphis? Memphis!"

"Oh, Pen, sorry. Sorry. Got distracted for a moment."

"A bit of skirt wandered by, no doubt."

"You could say that. So, where were we?"

Pen had been feverishly tracing down the latest London movements of the man called Tommaso. He listened to her rant with half an ear—so far no one could recall renting to the artist; they were combing the hotels for his name. There were inquiries being made at the British Museum, the National Portrait Gallery, the Saatchi, the Tate Modern, the Tate Britain, anywhere the man might have been working. The witness had fallen through. It would take a little bit of time, she was saying. Just a bit more time.

"Okay then, Pen. Call me when you have something."

He hung up, turned back to his lager and his soup. To the woman who took his breath away.

The females on the team were greeting the Nashville interloper with good grace. The power had shifted in the room—the boss's woman was there, and she was a force to be reckoned with. Both Charlaine Shultz and Pietra Dunmore were being deferential. Wills Appleby greeted her like an old friend, kisses on both cheeks—of course they'd know one another. Memphis had picked up on the closeness between Baldwin and Wills; they were two peas in a pod. Great minds, drawn together, with a long history. He had chums like that. Too bad they weren't here, maybe he wouldn't feel so fucking out of place.

He scooped a chunk of cheese from his soup. Everyone settled back into their seats, and the conversation became hushed. Now, if he could just turn off his senses, they'd all be better off.

Taylor ordered a Leatherhead Lager and a well-done filet. Memphis was stealing glances at her, as if determining if he'd stepped over the line in Nashville.

She shook it off. Stare away, poncy boy. If she didn't

reciprocate, he'd get bored by her soon enough. Though the thought of him flirting with someone else made a bloom of heat tear through her chest. She took in the restaurant's decor to distract herself. The floor was covered in a tartan plaid carpet, the rooms stocked to the gills with every imaginable piece of Marine and law enforcement memorabilia. The walls were covered in military items, the ceiling a swath of donated shoulder patches from every conceivable police agency. The restaurant was named the Globe and Laurel instead of the Marine traditional Globe and Anchor to symbolize the inclusion of the entire international brotherhood of Marines. She liked that. She also realized that the only women in the whole restaurant, outside of a waitress, were at her table. Interesting.

Baldwin pushed his salad plate away. "Taylor, when we're done here, Kevin's going to take the laptop, see what he can find."

"I'll take it now, if that's okay," Salt said.

"Of course." She handed it to him. "Password is DOLLS, all uppercase."

He went to work immediately, balancing the laptop on his knees, tapping the keyboard at a frenetic pace.

"Taylor, why don't you run through what you found for the rest of the team?" Baldwin was smiling at her. Encouraging.

"Of course." She wasn't prepared, didn't have any kind of presentation to give. She just laid out her actions, covering everything from the initial murder at Hugh Bangor's house to the victims from Radnor Lake, Manchester and Chattanooga, then went on to Gavin Adler's home in Nashville. How they put together clue after clue to find their killer. They listened, rapt, until she finished.

"Word is Kendra Kelley will live. That's the last that I know."

Charlaine shook her head. "Wow. That's a hell of an investigation in such a short period of time. Kudos, Detective."

Taylor nodded her thanks. "We don't have them yet."

"I've got something, though," Kevin interjected. "The message board was accessed through a number of different servers. It's going to take me some more time to back trace exactly where—this guy isn't stupid. He's covering his tracks, sending packets through multiple servers. But they all originated in central Italy. There's also another member of the private message board, call sign Necro. I've tracked him to someplace in the Caribbean. He doesn't talk to IlMorte69, who is Tommaso, only to Gavin Adler. His screen name is hot4cold, by the way. Classy guy. Any idea who Necro might be?"

Taylor met Baldwin's eyes. "It couldn't be."

"I wouldn't put it past him."

Memphis sat forward in his chair. "Do you mind sharing with the rest of the class?"

Baldwin nodded imperceptibly. Taylor said, "Last month, we had a run-in with a copycat killer in Nashville. He calls himself the Pretender, and he got away. One of my detectives, Peter Fitzgerald, phoned me from Barbados, said he thought he'd seen him down there. If he's been communicating with Gavin Adler, it's entirely possible that he's Necro."

"Which means we have more murders to look for, if he's really copycatting Adler," Baldwin added.

"Do you have any idea where they might have met?" Memphis asked.

She shook her head. "Seriously, I've had this information for a few hours at best. We don't know if it's him. It's all speculation at this point."

Pietra chimed in. "Detective, the DNA samples you sent up all match. I assume there will be more coming from today's scene, and I'm still waiting for the sequencing to finish on the samples from Leslie Horne. But it all looks good so far."

Salt unfolded himself, holding the laptop to his chest as if it was gold. "Okay. I'll keep working on it. See if I can't track the IP address closer to its origins. Will you excuse me? Charlaine, I need your help, too. We'll grab our meals to go." He loped away from the table. Charlaine excused herself and followed.

The rest of the meal arrived, the steak perfectly done, and they ate with gusto. But there was a sense of urgency not caused by hunger—they were all ready to get back to work.

"Okay," Baldwin said. "Wills, now that we know Tommaso and Gavin are working together, what do you think our next moves should be?"

Memphis jumped in. "We need to find out why the Adler boy was adopted, see what his real name is. Look for the parents. If we can find that, we might have a shot at the real name of our Tommaso."

"That's a good plan," Wills said.

"But adoption records…that will take weeks to sort through." Taylor was getting jumpy. "I think we need to get ourselves over there and track them down on foot."

Baldwin nodded. "I don't disagree. The carabinieri's on that, right now. But Memphis is right, our first step needs to be finding the adoption records. We need real names."

Memphis finished his steak and went to work on his beer, watching Taylor openly. He set down his empty pint glass and flicked a lazy hand through his hair. "Then let's go back to your offices. I think I know just the place to start."

Thirty-Six

Thomas Fielding, also known as Tommaso, also known as IlMorte69, licked his lips.

This moment had been in the works for years. As he bustled around his flat, dusting his paintings, picking up items he'd collected over time, examining them, putting them down, his heart was racing. His brother. His baby brother. Granted, only by two minutes. But his baby brother was going to be here at any moment. Tommaso couldn't wait.

He'd lived in Italy nearly all his life. His parents, his adoptive parents, were both in the military. His dad was an airplane mechanic, his mother a medic. They were wonderful parents. When his father had been transferred to Aviano Air Base in western Italy, above Venice, his mother had been very excited. They brought Thomas to Italy, enrolled him in a local school so he could learn the language, and embraced the Italian version of his name, Tommaso. Dad was a brilliant part of the 31st Fighter Wing, keeping the planes in repair, and Mom spent her days in the hospital. Which meant that after school, Tommaso would be dropped off at the E.R. entrance and would wend his way through the hospital corridors to find his mother.

He didn't see his first dead body in the hospital morgue. It was his second. His first dead body was his biological mother.

But he didn't want to think about that now.

He and his brother's paths were destined to cross. This was sooner than he anticipated, but that was fine. *Va bene.*

Gavin was going to be here any minute. Gavino. His little brother. In Italian, he was the White Hawk. Tommaso couldn't wait. Couldn't *wait* to see him.

Thirty-Seven

The four of them rode back to Quantico in silence. After about ten minutes, the driver stopped at a guard station. The car was checked, their credentials verified, then they were cleared. The parade grounds looked vaguely familiar, though Taylor knew she was probably ascribing a mental picture from a variety of movies and pictures and Baldwin's many descriptions.

The car stopped in front of a low office building, about four stories high.

"I thought you labored underground," she said.

"You watch too much TV. We haven't been underground for several years. They've uncaged us."

Wills and Memphis walked ahead, giving Baldwin a moment to squeeze her hand. He leaned in close. "We're gonna get them. I am so impressed with all you've done. We wouldn't be half as close to catching them without all your work," he whispered.

"Thank you. I'm just ready to catch them."

Within five minutes they were settled back in the conference room. Taylor didn't have time to assimilate much, but that didn't matter. Baldwin could give her the tour once they had the case solved.

"So, Memphis. Where do we start?" Baldwin asked.

The Brit slid back in his chair, crossed his arms across his chest. "I studied anthropology at Oxford. We did all sorts of analysis about identical twins. I'll wager that if one was adopted, the other was as well. And I recall an article in one of my courses about an adoption agency that was being shut down for unscrupulous practices. One here in America, in New York. They were separating identical twins. Highly unethical."

Baldwin felt a jolt of recognition. He remembered that; he'd had a case study in law school about the ethics of the situation.

"I know what you're talking about. I just can't remember—"

"Oh, I can. Louise Wise. My mother's name is Louisa, so it rather stuck with me."

"Louise Wise Services. That's exactly it. Nicely done."

Baldwin looked at the man in appreciation. That was the best suggestion he'd heard all day.

Wills said, "We have a birthday for one of them, Gavin Adler. September 14, 1980. If that's accurate, it could be the date to start looking at the New York adoption records. But this is such a long shot. Who knows if they were even born in New York? Who knows if that date is even right?"

"It's a shot, though," Memphis said.

Baldwin stared the younger man in the eye. "Okay," Baldwin said finally. "Let's go find them."

They were set up, assembly line, she and Baldwin and Memphis and Wills. She was searching the live births, handing them off to Memphis, who cross-referenced the adoption records with the hospital records. Baldwin was

making calls to every name he could find in association
with the now-defunct Louise Wise Services, and handing
off possibles to Wills.

She'd been combing through online records for an
hour, searching for births in New York between 1979
and 1981 with more than one living child. It was laborious, painstaking work. She had to do a new query for
every set of male twins she came across. Every time
she hit a multiple birth, she noted the record and gave
it to Memphis.

Having to use the computer was a blessing and a curse.
They could cross-reference more quickly, but Taylor's
wrist was getting sore. Kevin Salt had set them up with
access into the New York files. She didn't want to ask how.

It was hard to know if they were missing anything,
either. Reading on the screen wasn't her forte. Give her
hard copies any day.

It was close to 3:00 a.m. and they were making little
progress. Baldwin stepped out to make some more coffee,
Wills excused himself, as well.

The second the door closed behind them, Memphis
said, "I think I may have something here." Taylor could
hear the excitement in his voice.

"What is it?" she asked.

Memphis leaned back in his chair, stretching. His shirt
clung to his chest. Taylor forced herself to look away. She
wondered about the timing—Baldwin walks out,
Memphis finds something.

"Seriously, Memphis, what did you find? Time is
crucial. Tick-tock."

Memphis gave her a look. "You know, Jackson, you're
like an Amazon."

She eyed him suspiciously. If she had a dollar for every
man who'd used that come-on line… "Yeah, well, I don't

think I'm gonna be cutting off my right breast so I can draw my gun faster, but thanks for the thought."

He got up and crossed to her side of the conference table. She sat up straighter, involuntarily. He took the seat next to her, scooted the chair close. He nestled up to her, reached out to touch a strand of her hair. "I can see it perfectly. You'd carry a sword, a broadsword, and slay all the men in your path. Would you slay me, do you think?"

"Are you actually flirting with me?" she asked, half laughing, half…something. She pulled away from him. He was dangerous. Cute, funny, lovely accent, great ass, but none of that mattered to her. Memphis Highsmythe was a player, no question about it. And she'd gotten into serious trouble the last time she fell for a man who was looking for sex.

"What did you find?" she asked, trying to steer them back on course.

"I've found you." He started to move closer, but she stood up, knocking the chair back in her hurry. She got three feet away and turned back to him. He looked confused. She shook her finger at him, feeling foolishly like a school marm.

"Stop that. Right now. I am not free. Nor do I want to be. I'm engaged to the man you've asked for help, for Christ's sake. We have work to do. I refuse to sit here and have you…whatever it is you think you're doing. Knock it off. *Capiche?*"

He had the good sense not to come closer. He eyed her warily, as if she might explode at any moment.

"You think I'm just after a quick bunk-up, don't you?"

"Bunk-up…oh, I see." Damn British euphemisms. He was constantly renaming things in that superior, upper-crust accent. It made her want to scream. "Isn't it? Trust me, pal, I'm not the woman you want. There's plenty of bait for you elsewhere. I'm sure you have a few eager Sloane Rangers waiting for you at home. But I'm off-limits. Don't forget it." She was breathing heavily, infuriated for no good reason. *Jesus, Taylor. What's got you in such a fuss? All he did was hit on you. No harm, no foul. Right?*

Memphis started to laugh. She was half tempted to join him, but his smug smile made her want to hit him. Or kiss him. *Whoa, there, chickie. What in the hell are you thinking?* She closed her eyes for a fraction of a second, then stood straight as an arrow.

"How does a homicide detective from Nashville know what a Sloane Ranger is?" Memphis asked.

She eyed him suspiciously. "I went to a private school in Nashville. We had a transplant from London. She talked about them."

"You know, you never answered my question. What, aside from big-bad-daddy issues, drives a graduate of a Nashville finishing school to the life of a detective? Like the power of carrying a gun, do you?"

"What's a viscount doing in the Met?" she shot back.

"Oh, touché. We have more in common than you think. Both born with the proverbial silver spoon in our mouths."

"That is entirely beside the point." She softened for a moment. "You don't know me, Memphis. You don't know the first thing about me. I prefer to keep it that way. I have things to do. I'll talk to you later." She left him in the conference room, went to the Ladies' room on the opposite side of the building from Baldwin's office. Lord knows she didn't want to run into *him* right now.

She locked the door behind her and went to the sink. She splashed some cold water on her face, then stood gripping the porcelain. She looked at herself in the mirror. Her cheeks were flushed, her pupils dilated. Roused. And for what? For whom? Some guy she didn't know, didn't want to know. He looked at her like she was a steak. Damn anemic asshole.

So why did she respond to him? She'd felt it, that stirring, and she knew he'd picked up on it. Almost as if he could smell her attraction to him.

"Bah!" she yelled at the mirror. She was letting him get under her skin. Again. And it needed to stop.

When she got back to the conference room, all three men were leaning over the table looking at something. Baldwin turned to her when she entered. His face was a mask, but she could see the excitement in his eyes.

"Oh, good, you're here. Memphis may have found them."

Memphis was looking at her. She risked a glance, saw nothing threatening. He wasn't stupid. Baldwin was around, so he'd gone back to neutral. She needed to keep him there. Good. Maybe now they could get some work done.

"Tell me," she said.

Memphis straightened. "Assuming we're correct in our assumptions that we're dealing with Louise Wise Services, there's a record of twin boys being born to a Lucinda Sheppard, 14 June, 1980, in Manhattan. She was married to a chap named Michael Rickards. She was Caucasian, he was of Afro-Carribean descent."

"Well, that fits. Is there a reason why they put twin boys up for adoption?"

"The parents didn't, actually. The boys were orphaned. Lucinda Sheppard killed her husband, then killed herself. She was a paranoid schizophrenic, had a psychotic breakdown."

"Wills found the story in the papers. It was all over the news. The boys were alone in the apartment with the bodies for over twenty-four hours, lying in their crib in full view of the carnage."

Taylor felt the roaring sense of recognition she often got when a killer's motivation became clear.

"Those poor children," she said, thinking those poor babies grew up to be lethal, deadly killers. All the sympathy she felt for them fled.

Wills rustled through some papers he'd printed out. "Okay, here's the Louise Wise records on them. According to this report, no immediate family would take them because of the interracial relationship—in addition to their racial divide, Sheppard was Jewish. The boys went into the foster system, then were quickly picked up by Louise Wise. They had been placed by the time they were four months old."

Baldwin was reading the page over Wills's shoulder. "They were placed in separate homes. They were split up. Louise Wise was the preeminent Jewish adoption agency. They were doing groundbreaking adoptions in the seventies, placing not only Jewish kids, but American Indian and African-American children—Afro-Caribbean to you, Memphis—plus doing studies on the children of people with mental illnesses. The boys were separated, which was something only Louise Wise was doing at the time. The head psychiatrist at Louise Wise insisted asking a family to adopt twins was too much to ask. Nowadays, they'd be drawn and quartered for trying to separate twins, much less identicals, but back then, it was considered a great social experiment. I read about it in med school. It's actually horrifying, what they did. But it fits with the profile."

"So we know Gavin Adler is one of them. Who's the other?" Taylor asked.

Memphis took the page from Wills. "Thomas Fielding.

Here's the fascinating part. The boys are half black and half white, right? Gavin was placed with a black family who moved to Tennessee. Thomas was placed with a white family, and within a year of his adoption, they were transferred to Italy. His father was a mechanic at Aviano airbase, his mother was a doctor."

"A doctor, huh? That's interesting. So that's how Thomas got to Italy. How do we know he stayed there?"

Wills was shaking his head. "If he's still there, Kevin will find him. I'll go let him know."

Baldwin was clapping Memphis on the shoulder. "Great job. All of you. It's time for some sleep. We leave in three hours for Italy."

Sunday

Thirty-Eight

Gavin was lost. The maze of streets was overwhelming, the flocks of people pushing their way in every direction, the sneaker-clad tourists frantically following tour guides who held identifying flowers or flags over their heads so their temporary wards could follow along and not get lost in the crowd. He heard snatches of many languages: Italian, English, German, French, Spanish, Russian. Tommaso hadn't prepared him for the shuffle, the mess. He never envisioned Florence this way. Gavin felt a little panicky. He hated crowds.

The taxi had dropped him at the Duomo, per Tommaso's instructions. Up to this point, the directions had been easy to follow. Land in Rome, take the Pendolino train to Florence, the Santa Maria Novella station. Tommaso had been very clear on that point. "Not Rifredi, Gavin. The ticket will be reserved for you. S.M.N. is a ten-minute walk from the Duomo, but it will be easier for you to take a taxi."

He had followed the instructions to the letter, and everything was going smoothly until now. From the Duomo—the overwhelmingly large and beautiful neo-gothic façade with its white, pink and green marble panels stood gloriously in front of him. Gavin couldn't help but stop and crane his neck to look at it all, he'd never seen anything so stunning.

He was supposed to walk south, through the Piazza della Repubblica, then take his first right. Tommaso lived on a tiny side street just off the piazza, Via Montebello. It sounded so easy on the phone, but now Gavin wondered why he couldn't have taken a taxi directly to Tommaso's house. It would have been less confusing.

This is why he didn't travel—armchaired his desires and dreams. Gavin had gotten off-kilter, turned the wrong way somehow, and was surrounded by statues. He stopped, awestruck, by Michelangelo's *David*. It was so huge. He knew it wasn't the original, just a reproduction, but my God. All of the statues, the bronze sculptures, the fountain, were heartbreakingly beautiful. It was all just so Italian.

He found a shadowed corner of the piazza, fumbled in his pocket for the map he'd picked up as he exited the train station. A few minutes of searching and he found where he was, Piazza della Signoria. He regrouped. He needed to go back west, then turn south.

He started on his way. As he crossed the Via Porto Rosso, a man grabbed his arm.

"Tommaso, *bastardi! Che cosa è accaduto ai vostri capelli? Mi dovete i soldi! Dove sono i miei soldi?*" He smiled broadly, clapping Gavin on the back and speaking in rapid-fire Italian. Gavin could tell it was good-natured teasing, but he didn't understand a word the man was saying. He could only focus on one thing. This stranger had called him Tommaso.

The man continued to prattle on, oblivious to the fact Gavin wasn't answering. He walked him along, hand on his arm, and finally left him with a brisk slap on the back. *"Ciao, ciao. A demani, ciao!"*

Gavin was standing alone in an alleyway. He didn't have any idea where he was, what was going to happen to him. He'd just worked himself into a state when he noticed the address he was standing in front of.

Tommaso's house.

The man thought he was Tommaso. He obviously knew Tommaso, knew him well enough to know where he lived. He was beside himself. He didn't know whether to knock, or ring the bell.

In the end, he didn't have to. Tommaso must have been watching for him, because within moments of his advantageous arrival on his brother's doorstep, Tommaso opened the wooden door.

The dislocation he felt was immediate and overwhelming. It was like looking in a mirror. Tommaso was struck as well; Gavin saw his jaw drop slightly. Then he was enveloped in a bear hug that took his breath away, pulled inside a fragrant hallway. The door shut behind him, casting shadows in the foyer. He smelled rosemary, and wood and the harsh scent of Clorox.

The scents were familiar and alien. He shook his head, trying to assimilate. That's when he caught the fragrant undertone. His heart scudded a happy beat.

Tommaso grasped his hand, looked into their replica eyes.

"I've been waiting for this moment for so long. Come in, little brother."

Thirty-Nine

Taylor managed to rest on the Alitalia flight. Memphis was a few rows back, had walked past as she got settled with one of those cocksure grins on his face. At least they weren't seated together.

She couldn't remember the last time she'd been this exhausted. Baldwin had curled next to her right after takeoff and lost himself in sleep. She followed soon after, woke just as they began the descent into Florence.

The airport was terribly crowded; this was high tourist season for Italy. Florence, *Firenze,* was always a stop on every traveler's list. One of the big three—Rome, Venice and Florence, the city was the gateway to Tuscany, to the very representation of Italy that had entranced travelers for centuries.

They left the gate and were met by a striking man with deep brown eyes and gray hair combed back from a distinct widow's peak on his forehead. He was thick through the shoulders, about five foot eight, wearing a black silk suit. He spoke impeccable but heavily accented English. He zeroed in on them immediately. Taylor assumed they weren't exactly inconspicuous, even in this sea of foreigners.

"*Buona sera.* Supervisory Special Agent Baldwin, Detective Jackson. I am Chief Inspector Luigi Folarni, head of the Macellaio task force. I will see you to your hotel. Is Detective Inspector Highsmythe with you?"

"Here I am," Memphis said. He raised an eyebrow at Taylor. "Trying to ditch me?"

"No," she said. "We would have waited. For a minute."

"Sorry, but I needed to buzz the office. We've got confirmation on where our boy was staying. Looks like he sublet a flat in Battersea. Inspector Folarni, hello."

"*Buona sera,* Detective. If you'll follow me, I will get you collected and to your hotel. I am sure you will want to rest after your long flight."

Baldwin said, "Actually, we'd like to get started."

"Ah, but that is not possible. Everyone you will need to work with has gone home for the evening." He trotted along so quickly that Taylor had to stretch her stride to keep up. It looked like Folarni wanted to join his troops and head home. She was used to that—the Italians were wonderful workers, but when the day was over, it was time to decompress. It's what kept their stress levels so low. They could walk away, pick up an investigation the next day. Understandable. They'd been living with the specter of Il Macellaio far longer than she had.

Still, it drove her crazy. She wanted to get on their trail immediately. Baldwin, thankfully, read her mind.

"Chief Inspector," Baldwin started, but Folarni interrupted.

"Ah, *per favore,* Folarni. All these titles get in the way, I think."

"Folarni. Can we at least get briefed on where the investigation stands right now?"

Folarni sighed deeply. "I can take you back to my office for a brief time. We have not made very much progress since we spoke last night. Il Macellaio has been preying on our streets for many years. Another evening will not make a difference. Wouldn't the lady like to freshen up?"

Taylor started to decline, but Baldwin squeezed her arm.

"Detective Jackson and Detective Highsmythe can see to our rooms. You can brief me. *Inoltre, parlo italiano. Andrà più velocemente questo senso.*"

"Show-off," Memphis muttered under his breath. Taylor shot him a look.

Baldwin speaking Italian was easier than Folarni speaking English, especially when it came down to the little details. A broad smile crossed Folarni's face. "Ah. *Si. Io capisco. Perfecto. Va bene.*" Taylor had enough Italian to understand Folarni; he was very pleased by Baldwin's fluency.

They exited the building, Folarni and Baldwin speaking in rapid-fire Italian, Taylor and Memphis following behind. Folarni led them to a black four-door Alfa Romeo.

"Nice wheels," Memphis said.

"Shh," Taylor reproached him. They climbed in the backseat; Baldwin took the front.

The Amerigo Vespucci Aeroporto was only a few miles north of the center of Florence. They drove down the Viale Guidoni at breakneck speed. One thing Taylor had never gotten used to was the pace on the streets of Italy. It was like New York, with smaller vehicles and more shouting and gesturing.

They were soon in the heart of downtown Florence, and Folarni stopped in front of the hotel that Baldwin had arranged. He bustled out of the car, got Taylor's door, kissed her hand and bid her farewell. Baldwin and

Memphis grabbed the bags and loaded them inside the door for the porter.

Baldwin got back in the Alfa. He and Folarni roared off into the streets.

"Whew. Glad that's over. He drives like a maniac," Memphis said. "Shall we check in? You can freshen up in my room instead of yours, if you'd like."

"God, Memphis, give it a rest." The man was incorrigible, but she smiled at him, shaking her head.

Leave it to Baldwin to secure the best accommodations. He'd gotten them rooms on the Via de Tornabuoni, just off the Ponte Santa Trinita, one bridge down from the Ponte Vecchio. This was the fashion district, the most elegant street of shopping in all of Florence. Legendary names paraded up and down the storefronts along the via—Gucci, Ferragamo, Cartier, Bulgari, Versace, Yves St. Laurent—to name a few. Their hotel was actually nestled into the side of the Strozzi Palace. They were centrally located, and an easy walk to the carabinieri station. Taylor was familiar with the area—she and Baldwin had been here for their pseudo-honeymoon a few months prior.

She ditched Memphis at the front desk. She was tired, and hungry and tingling with anticipation. She tipped the porter when he dropped their bags in their room, washed her face, was ready to get started. It was smart of Baldwin to force the carabinieri chief to talk tonight. At least they'd have a sense of where the investigation stood. Baldwin's fluency had a tendency to open doors; the inspector had obviously been charmed by the prospect as well. Baldwin could speak Italian like a native. One of his many little talents. Taylor had just learned that he was more than conversational in thirteen languages.

She reset her watch to local time—the Tag Heuer dive

watch Baldwin had given her for her birthday last month
had sophisticated time-zone features. She made the secondary time read Nashville so she wouldn't be rousing
people in the middle of the night. Then she powered up
her cell phone and checked in with McKenzie.

It was lunchtime in Nashville, but McKenzie answered
the phone immediately.

"Hey! You're in safe?"

"Yes. Here's the hotel information in case you need to
reach me." She read off the numbers. "Where do we stand?"

"The media has made the connection between the
Conductor and Il Macellaio, for starters."

"Damn it."

"Yeah. They're running with it everywhere. But we've
been making progress. The tapes from Radnor Lake show
Adler's Prius on the street alongside the west parking lot
at 3:00 in the morning. He drove right past the barricade,
and then is gone for about twenty minutes. He returns the
same way, drives out again at 3:20, and that's it. They
don't have any shots of the spot where Leslie Horne was
put in the creek."

"Still, the car is great evidence. Anything else?"

"I talked to the woman from the FBI, Pietra Dunmore?
The DNA came back from Manchester. It matches all the
rest that we've retrieved. Your idea about the carpet really
was a stroke of brilliance, you know that?"

"I think it was his first murder. Adler's, that is. Did you
show the six-pack to Hugh Bangor?"

"I did, and he picked Adler out immediately. He was the
designer contracted to do the Frist catalog for the Italian
Masters exhibit. You were right, he was involved in the
local arts scene. Bangor says Adler's head is shaved now."

"Did you confirm how he knows Adler?"

"Yeah, it was that big party Hugh had for everyone

involved in the exhibit a few weeks back, including the artists and designers setting up the show. Adler was part of the team for the exhibit, he got an invite and came. Considering the fact that Adler has a poster of the Picasso in his living room, I think he was probably inspired to leave Allegra at Bangor's house when he saw the painting. It's the only thing that makes sense. Hugh says they talked about the piece a bit, and hasn't had any other meaningful contact with him."

Ah. That did make sense. She made a note to tell Baldwin about Adler's shaved head; it must be why the customs agents in Rome missed him. He didn't look like his picture anymore.

"Fabulous work. Can you get the pictures sent to Sheriff Simmons, see if he can show his brother and Marie Bender the photos?"

"I've already done that. I actually have a lot of great information for you. Adler's adopted family is from Manchester. They're dead now, the parents, but he went to high school at Central. Plus, Mrs. Bender said Adler is the one she remembered LaTara being friends with. There was something hinky about his parents, too. They died while he was in high school, right before his eighteenth birthday. Simmons told me it was a fluke accident—a carbon monoxide leak."

"How convenient. Think he killed his parents?"

"It's a possibility. Regardless, there's the connection."

She realized she hadn't thought of McKenzie as Just Renn in nearly two days. That boded well.

"That is great work, McKenzie. Thank you for handling all of this."

"No problem. By the way, Tim also found a pair of Asics running shoes at Adler's house that match the plaster casts from Hugh's house. Mr. Bangor, I mean. And

I talked with the boy who used to live next door, Christopher Gallagher, the one Bangor's partner was convicted of raping? He was at a party in Houston the night we found Allegra Johnson's body. I talked with the restaurant owner who confirmed it. So he's clear. I talked to the head of Riverbend about Arnold Fay, and the consensus is he's on the straight and narrow, doing his time without complaint. I'm comfortable that that aspect of the case is just a coincidence. Bangor and I talked about it further, he said all three of them were completely devastated by the situation."

"Okay then. Good work. This is a wrapping up in a nice little bow. Now we just need to catch them."

It was almost 9:00 p.m., and Baldwin still hadn't called. Arranging for three additional law-enforcement agencies to be working on Italian soil wasn't going to be an easy task. Taylor was thankful he was dealing with it, and not her. But she was hungry, and restless.

All the restaurants had reopened after their afternoon respites; the cafés had refreshed their supplies of gelato and espresso. She could walk around, find something, or sit someplace. She knew a great little place close by where she could get an espresso and a bite, maybe a bit of wine.

She knew enough about Italy to know that the investigation would be shuttered until tomorrow, that no more work would be done on it after the meetings tonight. They would be able to eat dinner, get some rest, and start tracking the brothers in the morning.

She knocked on the door to Memphis's room. He answered, broke into a wide smile when he saw it was her.

"Signorina!"

"Buona sera, Memphis. I'm hungry. Do you want to get something to eat?"

"Yes. I'm famished. Airline food just isn't what it used to be. Shouldn't we wait for your chap?"

"He said he'd be in touch when he was finished. I don't know about you, but I can't wait. I need to eat something to hold me over. Besides, we'll just be around the corner. I know a place. Come on. It's not far."

They exited the hotel, Memphis tagging along at her side like a happy Labrador. Taylor realized the sun was setting, the shadows lengthening. The summer days seemed to last forever here. She was struck by a thought. She reversed course, grabbed Memphis by the arm to turn him around.

"What?" he asked, but she just smiled.

"Follow me," she said.

She led him down the block to the Ponte Santa Trinita. The bridge was guarded at all four corners by statues of the four seasons—Spring, Summer, Autumn and Winter. They didn't have to walk far. The sun was disappearing, flashing off the neighboring bridge, the world-famous Ponte Vecchio. The medieval bridge was one of Florence's easiest landmarks to navigate by, second only to the Duomo, and Taylor recalled its beauty at this particular time of night.

She wasn't disappointed. The view was postcard perfect—the sun's luminous glow turning to fire as it slid into the western horizon, the Arno sparkling and reflecting off the edifice of the Ponte Vecchio, the Vassari Corridor, which connected the Pitti Palace with the Palazzo Vecchio.

Memphis stood next to her and sighed. "Why, Miss Jackson. I'm touched. Our first shared sunset."

She immediately regretted the gesture. Of course he'd misinterpret her intentions.

Not speaking, she swung away and headed back onto

the Via Tornabuoni. Memphis followed her. They passed the hotel, then turned right and walked through the Strozzi Palace courtyard and into an understated piazza. The aptly named Piazza degli Strozzi was more functional than ornamental, one of many little piazzas tucked away neatly on Florence's side streets. They were usually the best spots for homemade gelato, family-owned stores off the beaten path held treasures for anyone willing to look for them. But Taylor wanted something solid, some crostini or the like, so they got a table on the patio of Colle Bereto.

It was one of her favorite Italian-watching spots—the college students started flowing in around ten in the evening, pre- or post-movies at the theater around the corner, drinking cosmopolitans and martinis. There were plenty of tables now. They got a plate, some nuts and olives to nibble on, and a bottle of a fine Nero D'Avola Taylor remembered. A group of girls settled three tables over, shooting giggling glances at Memphis. She had to admit, lounging back in the chair, his sleeves rolled up, the brown skin of his wrists showing, he did look terribly handsome.

Sipping the wine, she looked around the piazza. Tried to ignore the fact that Memphis was running his fingers up and down the stem of his wineglass. What was it about this man that got under her skin? She was strangely attracted to him, even though he wasn't remotely her type. It wasn't a sexual thing, she thought, more of an intellectual curiosity. Besides, she was very, very much taken.

"What's your favorite flower?" he asked suddenly.

"What?"

"Your favorite flower. Come on, we're stuck here while FBI super-agent Baldwin lays the groundwork. Who knows how long it will take. Let's get to know one another."

"Memphis, I don't think—"

"Come on. It will be fun. Favorite flower."

She shook her head, took another sip of wine. "Fine. Roses."

"I knew it." His grin lit up his whole face.

"What?"

"Never mind. What's your favorite food?"

She sighed. "Italian anything."

"What's your favorite color?"

"Gray."

"Hmm. That's interesting. Because of those incredibly lovely eyes of yours?"

"Memphis—"

"Okay, okay. What's your favorite film ever?"

"Oh, come on. Who cares about that?"

"I care. Favorite film."

She had a strange sense of déjà vu. Baldwin had asked these questions of her, a long time ago. The same setting too, over wine, a getting-to-know-you session. It felt vaguely wrong to be having the same kind of conversation with Memphis. She pushed the thought away. She'd been doing that a lot lately.

"I liked *Gladiator.* Satisfied?"

"Fits with the Italian theme nicely. Though I would have guessed something like *Breakfast at Tiffany's.*"

She shook her head. "No way. I was too pissed at Holly for abandoning Cat in the rain."

"She came back for the poor slob, though."

"Still, it was selfish. I don't like selfish. She just wanted attention."

"Interesting. Moving along. Who's your favorite band?"

"How much time do you have?"

"We can have all night." He smirked.

She rolled her eyes at him. "I don't have a favorite. I like a lot of different music."

"Like who?"

"The Police, Josh Joplin, Death Cab for Cutie, Portis-head, Duran Duran, Evanescence, U2, all the way back to hair metal. I prefer the Stones over the Beatles, like blues more than jazz, and I'm passionate about classical. Okay?"

"But you live in Nashville. No country and western?"

She smiled at him. "Country and western? How quaint. We dropped the western a long time ago. And no. It's just not my style. Though you can never go wrong with a Johnny Cash tune."

"Now you're mocking me."

She just sipped from her wine.

"One more. What's your favorite book ever?"

"Oh, good grief. Eat your olives."

"Come on, answer." He poured them some more wine. "Favorite book."

She thought for a moment. That was a hard one. "*Sense and Sensibility.* No, *Pride and Prejudice.*"

"You like Jane Austen?" He sounded completely shocked, to the point that she laughed out loud.

"Of course I like Austen. Who doesn't? I think I've become engaged to Mr. Darcy, anyway, just like every girl dreams."

"I can see that. Stubborn bastard, your chap, just like your hero Mr. Darcy. Jane Austen, eh? It seems like such a girly choice. Funny, Miss Jackson, I never pegged you for a romantic."

"Quit calling me that." She shook out her hair, put it back up in a ponytail, off her neck. "Of course I'm a romantic. I'm a cop. I'm an idealist. I think I can change the world. How could I be anything but? And I'd prefer you not talk like that about Baldwin. He's been very good to you, and you're constantly spitting in his face. You should knock that off."

Memphis shrugged off her suggestion. "Why do you

call him Baldwin, anyway? Why don't you call him by his first name? If you were chums from school, or a bloke, I could understand. But you're his fiancée. It seems you would be a bit more familiar."

She struggled to explain that one, then settled for, "Because he asked me to. A long time ago. And he never asked me to call him anything else."

"You love him." Memphis sounded bereft, lonely. She was tempted to take his hand to comfort him, pushed that thought away.

"Yes, I do. He's, well, it sounds silly, but he's the other half of me. Until I met him, I didn't feel…complete. He's more than a lover, or a partner. Can you understand that?"

His blue eyes darkened with remembered pain. "Yes. When I lost Evan, my wife, it seemed like such a senseless thing. A car accident. Totally random. I've felt like a piece of me was missing ever since. She was pregnant, you know."

She didn't know exactly what to say. That was more information than she wanted to know about Memphis right now. She didn't need to see his vulnerable side. It was bad enough that they *did* have so much in common— both from privileged upbringings, both choosing a field that couldn't please their parents. Both having to fight for the respect of their peers, having to work just that much harder to prove themselves. She imagined his being a viscount had created more antagonism at the Met than he would ever let on. She knew she'd faced it, and she was just a little debutante from Belle Meade. Hardly on par with the peerage.

A melancholy silence lingered around them for a moment, almost peaceful, then Memphis started the barrage again.

"Favorite animal?"

"Oh, come on. Enough about me. What about you?

What's the son of a peer doing working for the Met? It must be strange, being the son of an earl. I thought you landed gentry weren't supposed to work."

"Ooh, someone's been doing her homework. Couldn't resist, could you?"

"Hardly. You're a little high up in the peerage to be playing with the working class, aren't you?"

"Ouch." Memphis grimaced, then said softly, "Evan insisted I have a real job. Wouldn't marry me otherwise. Ever hear the term morganatic?"

"No."

"Some people call it a left-hand marriage. It's an old term, reserved for marriages of rank. It's when someone of breeding marries well beneath their station. Like your Mr. Darcy."

"Okay. What does that have to do with you?"

"Evan's father wasn't a peer. It bothered her tremendously that mine was."

He paused, his gaze searching, like he could look right into her very soul. She felt trapped under his gaze; she couldn't look away. She could tell he wanted to tell her something, felt instinctively that it was important to understanding who the man really was, and what he wanted with her. What the hell?

Then he looked away, and the moment was gone.

"You were saying?" Taylor said.

He looked at her, then waved his hand in the air in front of them. "I'm showing off. My title means nothing to me, though it was always important to my parents. Being a viscount isn't all it's cracked up to be. But thankfully, my father never pressured me to be like him. He's quite philanthropic, you know. I'm more like you, an idealist. He supported me joining the Met, helped me get a foot in the door as a matter of fact. My mother, well, she was rather peeved."

"I love it. Your parents really are an earl and a countess."

He flashed her that cocksure grin. "Well, there's the illusion for you. All we have is several thousand acres in the Scottish Highlands and a draughty castle nestled up to the moors. Cobwebby old thing, impossible to heat properly, the roof leaks constantly, the taxes are crippling, and if you can actually find a bit of ground flat enough to play a chukka of polo, the chances are it's a quagmire for eight months out of every twelve. The grouse and pheasant are plentiful, though, the sheep outnumber the people and the trees outnumber the sheep, so there you have it. But it all gets rather old once you've been doing it forever."

"How very Brontë of you," Taylor said.

Memphis barked a laugh, then let a sly smile linger on his lips. "Shall I call you Cathy, then?"

She laughed. "You most certainly shall not, braggart. Scotland, huh? Why is your accent so…well, you don't sound like any Scot I've met."

"I received a proper education."

She laughed again. "You're just a plain old snob. How'd you get saddled with a name like Memphis, anyway?"

"My dear mamma, and the chaps at school. Mamma was awfully keen on Elvis Presley. Actually took me to Graceland when I was about eight. I came back home, talked everyone's ear off about Memphis. Couple of the chaps started making fun. Suddenly I was that Memphis boy. By the time I was ten, everyone took to calling me that. It stuck."

"Wow. You realize as a native Nashvillian, I've been born and bred to loathe all things Memphis?"

"Good lord, Miss Jackson, are you teasing me?"

She waved him off. "I told you to stop calling me that. Call me Jackson, or Taylor, but knock off the Miss shit.

And of course I'm not kidding. I never kid about important stuff."

"So, Jackson. I've been dying to know. I'm betting you aren't a candlelight, keep it gentle, missionary kind of girl?" He smiled, raised his eyebrow suggestively.

Okay, that was enough. "Screw you, Memphis."

"You've got quite a mouth on you. Do a sailor proud." But he smiled, and she knew he was teasing her. For some reason, it didn't bother her as much. They laughed together, easy for the first time.

They sat in companionable silence for a few minutes, sipping the wine, looking at everything but each other. Finally, Memphis scooted his chair closer to her. He set his hand on the table, inches from hers, leaned close. He waited until she looked him in the eye, waited for those little zings of recognition and attraction that skittered between them. She could get lost in that aching ocean of blue if she weren't careful.

"I could wake you up inside, Taylor. Bring you to life. All you have to do is give me the chance."

He said it so quietly that at first she didn't think she'd heard the words aloud, only that they'd appeared in her consciousness.

"What?" she said, sharper than she intended.

He moved fractionally closer, his hand reaching out to play with a bit of hair that had come loose from her ponytail. She was mesmerized for a moment, watching the slow, stroking movement of his finger on her hair. Like a cobra, hypnotizing a mongoose.

It was inevitable, really. She was only slightly surprised when he settled his mouth on hers. The kiss was soft, and lingering. His tongue flicked at the edge of her lip, and she was shocked to feel her mouth open, the warmth of the tongues touching. One kiss. Who cared about one little kiss? It could go on, and on, if she'd let it. Instead, she got her mind back and pushed him away, flustered.

"What in the hell are you doing?" she demanded, a little unnerved at how breathless she sounded.

He looked both hurt and embarrassed. "Nothing. Never mind. I've misread the signals. I…I must go. I need to make a phone call. I'll be back at the hotel if you need me."

He stood abruptly and left without saying goodbye, just walked away into the Strozzi.

Leaving her sitting at the table wondering just exactly what had just happened. He could wake her up inside? Granted, she felt a tiny pull toward him, some base, chemical thing. The kiss—oh, she didn't want to think about that right now.

She couldn't help herself. She started analyzing. Wasn't that what life was about? Aren't we all supposed to feel those twinges toward the opposite sex, even when we're in a stable, loving, happy relationship? That's just biology, propagation of the species. Perfectly natural, healthy even. It's whether you acted on them that made you a good person, or a bad person. Moments like these defined you.

Taylor was quickly grasping that Memphis Highsmythe would be perfectly happy to compromise her morals, and her body and her life. All she had to do was give him the go sign, and he'd be on her like a wolf on a lamb.

He wouldn't be gentle. She could feel the flame inside him, the raging inferno that he kept bottled inside, hidden carefully behind the panther grace with which he moved. Just the brief moment of his lips on hers had made that clear. Something was driving his need, and she suspected it was despair over the broken pieces of his marriage, the loss of his wife and unborn child. She could understand that. She'd gotten involved with hurt men in the past, with men who needed. Need was akin to desperation, and while the sex was always fantastic, the emotional toll was too much for her to bear.

Baldwin didn't have that edge of desperation to him. He was solid inside, not pieces of flickering fire.

She shook her head. What in the name of hell are you thinking about, Taylor?

Baldwin. She needed Baldwin. One kiss and he would ground her, grind out all the memories of Memphis and his blue eyes. Of his stupid soft lips.

She paid the check and stormed out of the café, heading into the city. Damn you, Memphis.

Bring me to life. I'd like to see you try that.

Baldwin watched the scene play out. Memphis was making his move. To Taylor's credit, once the immediate shock of the pass was over, she pushed him away.

He'd been expecting this. He could read the desire coming off of Memphis like Morse code, knew he'd be making a play for Taylor's affections soon enough. He couldn't help feeling shocked, though. Blatant and utter disrespect for their relationship. Unless Taylor had been giving him the go-ahead…no, she wouldn't. She loved him, not some pretty, moneyed playboy.

Memphis stalked off. Taylor tossed some Euros on the table and was coming right at him. He ducked back around the side of the building, then started walking like he didn't know she was going to bump into him.

He took a breath, turned the corner. Grabbed her by the arms so she wouldn't be knocked backward. He just needed to feel her.

"Whoa! Hey, sweetie. That was good timing. I was just going to call you. How did the meeting go?"

No trace of guilt on her face, she lit up when she saw him like she always did. Good girl.

He kissed her, and she wrapped her arms around his neck. They were in Italy; lovers embracing on a street corner wasn't going to set off anyone's alarms. After a few moments, he broke away and murmured, "Do you want to get something to eat?"

"Yes. I'm still hungry. I had a few bites with Memphis. That man is driving me crazy. Can we go to dinner ourselves, let him fend for himself?"

"That would be rude, wouldn't it?"

"I don't care. He's…he's…just one of those infuriatingly annoying people. I'm tired of him."

"Then your wish is my command, milady. How about Mama Gina's? We can see if Antonio is working."

He took her hand, and together they made their way back to the Via Tornabuoni, across the bridge. It was a still evening, the river reflected the lights of the Ponte Vecchio. It was beautiful, and he pretended not to notice her stiffen as they halted on the bridge to look. He decided not to ask what was bothering her. Who knew what sort of trouble Memphis had been trying to get into.

After a few moments, with unspoken timing, they both started walking. At the bottom of the bridge they turned left into a little side street that housed some of the best restaurants in Florence.

As the scent of garlic and tomatoes flooded his senses, Baldwin tried to push the specter of disaster away from his mind.

Forty

Gavin and Tommaso drank espresso, shared a simple meal of spaghetti carbonara and spent the evening getting to know each other. They had thirty years' worth of catching up to do.

Gavin was overwhelmingly happy. This was the other half of himself, the missing piece. He'd never felt so complete. Not even the dolls could give him this kind of joy.

He was still struck by their physical similarities. There were only two real discernible differences: Tommaso's hair, and their slightly different accents. Gavin had started shaving his head several months earlier, liking the feel of the bare skin. It also left fewer identifying pieces behind. And he spoke with the soft, rounded edges of a Southern upbringing, while Tommaso had unaccented English.

After dinner, Tommaso had taken one more look at Gavin's head and disappeared into the bathroom. He emerged with his head shaved to match. Thankfully he worked indoors; there was no real demarcation between the freshly shaved skin and his face. Now no one would be able to tell them apart.

So far he'd discovered that they were both fanatical

fans of Manchester United, though for entirely different reasons. Gavin had been drawn to the team because they were named after his hometown, Tommaso because they were the favorite of his adopted father. They both stirred three spoons full of sugar into their espresso with the handle of the spoon, both flossed their teeth religiously twice a day, both had emergency hernia surgery when they were three and fainted at the sight of blood.

But it was their passionate devotion to the arts that Gavin found utterly irresistible.

"I still feel like I'm dreaming," Gavin said. "Here I sit, across the table from one of the world's most talented photographers, the man I've been a fan of for years, and you're my own flesh and blood. I still can't believe it. I really didn't know you were Morte."

"I didn't want you to know, Gavin. I needed to find out if you were like me, and the only way to do that was to create a world in which you could flourish. I wanted the best for you, wanted you to know you weren't alone."

They washed the dishes, then settled onto the buttery leather couch with grappa. Gavin was feeling drunk—the time change, the win and now the grappa was too much for his system.

Tommaso went to his stereo and selected a CD. The strains of Beethoven's *Piano Sonata no. 14* drifted from the speakers. Gavin had never felt so completely happy in his life.

"When did you know, Tommaso? When did you realize the first time?"

"The first time." Tommaso got a dreamy look on his face. "My mother worked in the airbase hospital in Aviano. She used to have me dropped there from school, and I'd have to walk down this long corridor to meet her. The morgue was right there, and one day I slipped in. It was intoxicating. The smell, the chill. There was a woman on a gurney just inside the door—they must have left her there for a reason, but I never knew why. I ran my hand under the sheet covering her. She was so cold, so stiff. I realized I had an erection and masturbated. I hid my underwear in a trash can so my mother wouldn't see the mess. After that, I couldn't seem to help myself. I spent time there, in the afternoons. They didn't have a guard, it was easy to get in and play. It was a beautiful time."

"That's so nice. My first was a friend. I'd always dreamt about being with her, but she was too animated, too loud. I preferred silence, the stillness. We had a fight one afternoon, and I hit her. She fell down so hard, was finally quiet. I didn't know what to do. I knew she was hurt badly, knew I was going to be in so much trouble. I put her in a bathtub and filled it with water, held her down until her heart stopped. But seeing her naked…I couldn't help myself. I took her back out. I had to feel inside her. After that, it was all I could do to contain myself."

"I never bothered with containment. I couldn't. The drive, the desire was too strong."

"That's why you started killing them quicker?"

"Yes. I couldn't wait anymore."

"I still like to wait. I like the anticipation. It's like a reward for good behavior. Why do you think we like it this way, Tommaso?"

"I don't know. I just don't know. We work inside the ecstasy of love, you and I. There's no good explanation."

"Do you know who Necro is, too?"

"No, Gavin, I don't. I found him when I was looking for you, thought you might be him for a while. He's not as evolved as we are."

"That's true."

They sat for a few minutes, then Gavin said, "Tommaso, once you knew, why didn't you just come to me directly? Why didn't you let me know you were my brother from the beginning? How long had you known?"

Tommaso shot back the grappa, refilled his glass. "Only a year. When my mother was dying, she took me into her confidence. I knew I was adopted, but that had never been an issue. My parents loved me as much as they would have a creature of their own flesh. But they'd never told me that I was a twin. My father passed away six years ago, so it was just my mother and me. When she went, I had no one. I think she knew how terribly lonely I would be, gave me the most important present of my life. With her death, you were born."

"So she had my name the whole time?"

"No, she didn't. She only knew that we were separated, that the adoption agency had split us up. She didn't know anything else, your name, who your parents were, where you'd gone. At first I was angry, but then I searched for you. There's a database you can apply to find your biological parents. I applied, and since they were deceased, I received the information quickly. From there, I just did my research. Our birth mother was crazy, you know. A schizophrenic. She lost it one night, stabbed our father, then stabbed herself. We were in the apartment for at least a day. The papers talked about it for weeks, the horror of the two infants alone with their dead parents. Then the foster agency gave us to Louise Wise, who separated us, and you know the rest of the story."

"My God. Do you have the reports? I'd like to read about it myself."

"Of course. But we have plenty of time for that."

"It must have been nice to have good parents. Mine weren't very pleasant."

"I applaud you killing them. You became a man that day."

Gavin squirmed uncomfortably. He didn't like to

remember that part of his past. Tommaso was right; he was reborn that day. Just as he'd been reborn yesterday, when Tommaso told him who he really was. He had so far to travel. Tommaso was so sophisticated, so much more of an artist than he was.

"I had no choice. It was them or me. I just couldn't take it any longer."

"I'm sorry you had such a hard time. Let's talk about something more engaging then, something to make you happy. Tell me about your latest—Ophelia in the babbling brook. Do you have the photographs? I saw the Millais when I was in London, it is magnificent."

Gavin went to his carry-on bag and took out the jump drive.

"Do you have something I can plug this into?"

"What's that? Where is your laptop?"

"I left it at my house. I was worried that they might make me open it at security, that someone might see the pictures. So I downloaded them to this drive."

Tommaso was staring at him with a look of abject horror on his face.

"If you had destroyed the originals like I told you, no one would have seen anything on your laptop." He was yelling now. "You left it at your house? Did you at least destroy the drive?"

"Well, no. I password-protected it."

Tommaso stood angrily. His face no longer looked familiar. For a brief moment, Gavin wondered if that's what he looked like when he was furious and a tiny frisson of fear coursed through him. Tommaso's fists were balled, his shoulders tense. Gavin instinctively ducked a bit, tried to pull away.

"Please tell me you killed the girl, Gavin. Tell me you didn't leave behind any more evidence."

Gavin realized he'd made a very big mistake. "I'm sorry. I gave her a massive injection of heroin. There's no way she could have survived. She should have died in the night. And I was thinking, after I went back home... And I must go back home, Tommaso. I have to take care of Art. I only left him enough food for a week. I can't let him starve."

Tommaso turned white. "Holy mother of Christ. You're worried about a fucking cat."

Gavin was crushed. How could he say that about Art?

Tommaso went to the kitchen, picked up the phone and made a call. Within seconds, he was speaking in rapid Italian.

He came back in the living room, fury etched across his face.

"I just spoke to a friend of mine who works for the carabinieri, a friend who I have shared many intimate moments with. He told me the FBI has arrived in Florence, and they have your computer. They suspect the art world's Tommaso of being Il Macellaio. We have to get out of here. They probably already know where we are. You've led them right to me. You idiot!"

The screaming shattered him, broke all the recently repaired shards of his soul. Tommaso calling him an idiot hurt worse than any of the beatings he'd taken at the hands of his adoptive parents. They'd taken turns with the belt, ripped the skin from his back, his legs. Broken his fingers. None of that felt nearly as horrible as this.

He tried to fight back. "I am not an idiot. No one can break that password, it's much too unique. There is no chance the laptop led them to you."

"Gavin, are you totally mental? The laptop has my IP address, which in turn can be traced directly to my apartment. Here. We need to go. We need to go right now."

Gavin stood. His mind was muddled from all the drink, from the fury emanating from what felt like himself. It was as if his personality had fractured in two, that he was suddenly seeing the voices he'd always heard in the back of his mind. His anger gave him courage. He wasn't an idiot.

"You aren't being fair. I deleted out all the history of the chats."

"It doesn't matter. My God, you work with computers. You know that nothing is ever truly gone unless you wipe the hard drive, and even then they can find things. The FBI is here, in Italy, on my soil. They are looking for us. Don't you understand? We could lose everything."

"I'm sorry," Gavin whispered.

Tommaso didn't acknowledge the apology. He was rushing around the living room and into the bedroom, gathering clothes and bags and everything he could get his hands on. He went into the kitchen and loaded up some food.

Gavin watched, incredulous. "I didn't mean to cause trouble. I was just so excited to meet you. I didn't think things through."

Tommaso came back to the couch, grabbed him roughly by the shoulders. He looked into Gavin's soul, then pulled him to his chest. "I know. I *know,* Gavin. I have a place we can go. But you have to promise that from now on, you will do *exactly* as I say. I am the only hope you have anymore."

Forty-One

The food had been spicy and delicious, the wine superb, and Taylor was feeling just a little tipsy as they headed back to their room. She and Baldwin stopped on the bridge again, and this time Baldwin showered her with kisses—her lips, her nose, the soft hollow at the base of her neck, the spot right below her scar that had become so exquisitely sensitive after the surgery. She knew empirically the tingling was nerve damage, but preferred the more romantic version of events.

When they came up for air, she realized her cell phone was vibrating in her pocket.

"Whoops. I better get this," she said. Still insinuated between Baldwin's legs, she fumbled the phone and nearly dropped it. She didn't recognize the number.

She answered it with a brisk, "Taylor Jackson."

There was no sound, just a deep emptiness. Dread immediately paraded into her system. There was only one person who was making calls to her without saying anything.

She started to hang the phone up, heard whispering. She put the phone back to her ear.

"Did you hear me? I'm coming for you, Taylor."

The Pretender. What in the name of hell was this guy up to?

She was feeling reckless. After everything that had happened today, she felt like she had nothing more to lose. Her temper flared.

"You want me? Well, come and get me, you son of a bitch." She slammed the phone closed. Every nerve was on fire; she felt more alive than she had in years. She refused to let this creep slink around in the back of her mind anymore. She'd opened the door. With any luck, she would push him through.

Baldwin knew immediately what had happened; she could read the anger on his face.

"Taylor, was that the wisest—"

She slapped her hand on the concrete, painfully scraping her palm. She jerked her hand back, inspected the cut. She sucked a tiny drop of blood off her wrist and got quiet.

"Baldwin, I can't stand it. He's out there, and he wants me for something. So let's push his buttons and see how he feels for a while. It's ridiculous that I have to look over my shoulder, waiting to see where and who he's going to kill next. No, damn it. I'm sick of being manipulated, of being on my guard against everything and everyone. I want this done. I'm going to let him have a taste of what it means to tangle with me."

"Do you think he's nearby?"

"No. He's not ready. I doubt he'll be giving me a heads-up."

She started to walk away. He caught her hand, turned her to face him roughly. "I won't lose you, Taylor."

She stood tall, looked him deep in his green eyes. "Trust me, Baldwin, you won't. But if I live my life a minute longer waiting to see what he's going to do, I'll drive myself mad. I'm not happy sitting back, waiting and seeing. That's not me. If I could be more proactive, actually hunt his ass down, trust me, I would do that. I'll do whatever it takes. You're just going to have to trust me."

"I've been a little short on trust lately. I know. I'm sorry."

"Are you talking about Memphis? Don't be a fool. He's nothing to me."

"But you're not nothing to him, Taylor. He's head over heels in love with you. In lust with you—my God, I can practically hear his hormones shift into overdrive when your name comes up."

She fingered her ring, stifling a smile. She loved it when he acted jealous.

"Oh, John. You are the one and only man for me. Don't you know that?"

She swore she saw something move in the depths of his eyes. His kiss took her breath away. When he broke free, his voice was hoarse.

"You've never called me John before."

She didn't say anything, just kissed him again. When they came up for air, she tangled her fingers in his hair.

"How's this for irony. I guess you have Memphis to thank for that. He asked me why I don't call you John. I didn't have a good answer for him. So I thought I'd try it out."

"Let's keep it for special occasions, then. I don't think I could ever get tired of hearing you say it." He was quiet for a moment. "As a matter of fact, I'll make you a deal. The next time you call me John, it will be in front of a priest."

She looked at him and he smiled.

"We need to talk about when we're going to get married."

She kissed him lightly on the lips. "Now's not the time. But soon. Soon, honey. I promise. We have more pressing matters at hand. Let's go catch the twins."

They left the bridge. The hotel was only a hundred yards up the street; they were inside in less than five minutes. They took the elevator to the third floor, collected their key. Their room was two floors up but they took the stairs.

She didn't want to admit that her skin crawled the entire time.

Monday

Forty-Two

Daybreak came much too early for Gavin. He and Tommaso has been on the run for three hours, first driving out of Florence under cover of darkness, then winding their way into the Florentine hills to a little stone cottage with no electricity or running water. Tommaso's discovery of Gavin's mistakes in Nashville had spurred their desperation—the desire to get as far away as possible was stymied by the fact that Tommaso knew that by now, they might have photographs of the brothers. They couldn't travel right away, but he said he had a room in London that they could escape to if they could find a way past the border. He didn't think it had been compromised.

Spewing invectives, Tommaso had driven his tiny ten-year-old Renault up the hill to the cottage. They dropped all their gear—food, blankets, candles—in the rustic hideout, then Tommaso and Gavin drove the car five miles away and dumped it down an embankment, covered it with broken branches and tall grass. Then they hiked back to the cottage, trying to obscure their footprints on the dusty road. They saw no one outside of a cow, and Tommaso assured Gavin they would be safe.

This was his safe house, his laboratory, his world. It had served him well for all the years he'd been killing, and would serve to shelter them now.

Gavin's exhaustion was dragging him under. Tommaso took pity on him, allowed him to curl next to the cold, damp fireplace—a fire wouldn't do, someone might notice the smoke rising—and let him sleep.

He woke when Tommaso shook his shoulder, knew he couldn't have been asleep for more than an hour or two. Little bits of sunlight streamed in onto the tiled floor. It was morning.

"I have a present for you," Tommaso said. His smile was luminous, the transgressions of the night before seemed to be forgiven.

Gavin stretched and yawned, covering his mouth. He tasted wrong, somehow, though it wasn't an external cause. He knew he needed to brush his teeth and eradicate the sense of failure he'd been exhaling for the past hours. He followed Tommaso out of the tiny bedroom and stopped, all worry forgotten.

She was lying on the rough-hewn slab of wood that passed for a kitchen table. Her body was small, almost birdlike, her fine bones fragile, the skin so pale that Gavin could see the tracing of her veins. Next to her, Tommaso glowed with an almost effervescent beauty, standing so still he looked like a marble Adonis of barely human proportions.

"Do you want her?" Tommaso asked.

"It's your doll. You sent me her picture. Oh, Tommaso, she's so beautiful."

"She's our doll now."

Gavin's need overwhelmed him. He'd never had one so clear, so pure. His usual type was dark-skinned; he'd never loved a white girl before. The girl's tiny buds of breasts were unmoving and shone pink against her alabaster skin. Her pubis was covered in a downy blondness, like the fuzz of a baby chick. Her emaciated frame seemed to cry for his embrace. The deep purple bruises on her neck were a necklace of need and love, of remorse and forgiveness. Tommaso had done this for *him*.

He touched his brother on the shoulder, then stood with him, side by side. They were both shivering. "I brought her for you, Gavin. I wanted to give you the best of me. I've always dreamt of us together, as one, sharing. I'm so sorry for the way I acted last night."

"What is her name?" Gavin gasped. He ran his fingers along the inside of the girl's arm, tracing where the blood no longer flowed.

"I don't know. It doesn't matter. She is yours. She is ours."

Forty-Three

Taylor and Baldwin walked into the carabinieri station to meet with Luigi Folarni at 8:00 a.m. local time. Memphis was with them, sulky and quiet. They'd shared breakfast at the hotel—salami and ham and crusty bread, cheeses and croissants with fresh jam, cappuccinos. Memphis had come to breakfast wearing his sunglasses; Taylor could smell the raw reek of day-old alcohol on his breath. She couldn't judge, she'd used drink to get herself to sleep before. As they left the hotel for the carabinieri station she surreptitiously handed him a stick of gum. He accepted it with a weak smile.

Folarni greeted them like old friends, had more cappuccino brought.

"I have very good news," he said, beaming. "We have made progress from last evening. We have an address to look at. The photographer's *residenza* matches the billing address for the computer's IP address. The photographs were on the news this morning. We had many, many phone calls about this case. The people of Florence want to help catch Il Macellaio! There was a *tassista,* ah, how do you say?" He looked at Baldwin.

"Taxi driver," Baldwin answered, leaning forward in his chair.

"*Sì.* A taxi driver who recalls driving a man yesterday who fits the description of Il Macellaio. And the computer address your people in Quantico sent to my experts is close to where the *tassista* dropped the man. We will go to the address, see if we can find them."

"The photos have been circulating on television?" Memphis asked.

"And in the newspaper. We are very serious about catching these men, especially now that we know there is a second killer. We must keep the Florentine people safe."

"They've probably made a run for it then. Bolted. If I saw my picture on the telly, that's what I'd do."

Luigi gave a thoroughly Italian shrug. "Perhaps. But it will do us no good to hide from these things. So, come. We will go to the address and see what we can see."

The Via Montebello was crawling with police. Folarni wasn't being subtle, he had broken out the carabinieri's showiest pieces to ensure the Italian news saw that they, not the Florence Polizia, were responsible for capturing Il Macellaio and his twin brother.

Stern-faced shop owners stood in the street, smoking, arms crossed, watching the show. Sirens spun and echoed down the narrow cobblestone alleys behind them to ensure no escape.

With weapons drawn, the plainclothes carabinieri rushed the front door, splintering the thick wood with several well-placed kicks. It was quickly apparent that no one was inside the house.

But they had been close.

They talked to as many neighbors as they could find. A woman across the via with a hooked nose and unkempt gray hair told Folarni that she saw the man who lived in the house leave in the middle of the night. But she was convinced it was a ghost, because there were two of them.

Upset to no end, Folarni sat heavily on the hood of his Alfa Romeo and lit a cigarette. Marlboro Red. It made Taylor wish she could join him.

The three of them conferred quietly, just out of Folarni's earshot.

"Do you think this is the right place?" Taylor asked.

"It matches the address from the IP on the computer. So yes, I think so. Neighbors have confirmed that a man who looks like this lives here. Memphis was right, they were tipped off somehow."

"Or Tommaso figured out that Gavin left too much evidence behind and was being proactive."

Baldwin nodded at Taylor. "Or that. Gavin was certainly still learning, still evolving. It's not that uncommon for new serial killers to make mistakes. Regardless, now we have to start from scratch. All the border crossings have been notified, and the airports and train stations. They won't be able to get out of Italy."

"Is this where Il Macellaio has been doing his killing?" Memphis asked.

"Let's go in and see."

Folarni was happy to let them go upstairs with his forensic team. A quick search revealed good fingerprints, hairs, everything they would need to make a match to their previous items. But there was nothing to indicate this was the charnel house. It looked like a regular guy lived there, someone who had a passion for art. His walls were a testament to that—photographs, paintings, lithographs hung in every available space. There were no quiet little tuckaways, and the neighbors were obviously vigilant. But anything was possible. He'd had enough time to set things right in anticipation of their arrival.

It was nearly 10:00 a.m., and the brothers had several hours' head start.

They reconvened in the kitchen. "So, what's next?" Taylor asked.

Baldwin ran his fingers through his hair. "We need to get into the property records. If he's not killing here, he's killing somewhere more private. He needs someplace where he wouldn't be interrupted, where he can keep the girls. We need to find his hole."

"Agreed," Memphis said.

They approached Folarni with their request. He decided without hesitation, got on his phone. In Italian so rapid Taylor couldn't follow, he made several requests. Baldwin translated for them.

"He's asking for the property rolls. They are looking for anything under the name Tommaso."

"Tell them to widen the search. Have them try the name Thomas Fielding," Taylor suggested.

Baldwin winked at her, spoke to Folarni. "Okay. They've plugged that name in, too."

Fifteen minutes later, they still had nothing. The only address listed to Thomas Fielding was the one they were standing in front of.

"Might want to try one more name," Memphis said.

"What?" Baldwin asked.

"Gary Fielding."

"Tommaso's father. Of course!"

And that insight was the key. Within five minutes they had an address in the hills of Florence, and were on their way.

Forty-Four

Tommaso had never been quite so happy. Sated. Watching Gavin with the girl, seeing all his little tricks, was overwhelmingly special.

They were lying together, the three of them, on the bundle of blankets, sharing sips of wine and talking. Sifting through all those crazy moments of common ground, pinpointing the formation of their desires. It was fascinating, everything Tommaso could have hoped for. He was the stronger twin, he knew that. He'd always known that. His studies about twinning talked about imprinting, a phenomenon where identical twins find a way to separate themselves into an alpha and beta, an aggressive and a passive. Tommaso was the firstborn; he was the alpha twin. He was their leader, Gavin was the follower. They'd only been together for twenty-four hours, but it felt like forever.

Tommaso knew he had to bring up an unpleasant subject. He ran his fingers lightly down the girl's back, preparing.

"Gavin. We need to talk," he said softly.

Gavin merely nodded. It seemed he knew where Tommaso was heading with his words before they left his mouth.

"If we're caught," Gavin said simply.

"That's right. This has been a safe place for me for many years. But after today, it might be on their radar. We need to move on. We can steal a car, get to the border. Pass across on foot in an area no one will be able to see. Or better yet, we can go to Lago Guarda, and pass on a boat into Switzerland. There's only one thing that is stopping us. The only thing that separates us now."

Gavin was looking at his hand. "Our fingerprints."

"Yes. We must eradicate them. It is imperative. If we are ever caught, this is the only thing that will tell us apart. We can modulate our voices to match one another, easily manipulate the police into an inability to tell one of us from the other."

"How are we going to do it?"

"We burn them off."

Gavin sat up, his face pale. "Won't that hurt?"

"Yes," Tommaso said. "But only for a moment. It's the only way. I've been thinking about this for weeks. I knew there would come a time when we were together. We have to, Gavin. It can save us. Now that I've found you, I don't ever want to be parted from you."

Gavin lay back down, staring at the timber roof. "When?" he asked.

"Now."

Taylor felt the anticipation build. They were scouting the cottage registered to Tommaso's father, a barely kept, crumbling stone house that on a normal afternoon hike would look deserted. But a thin smudge of smoke rose from the decrepit chimney, indicating that someone was home.

"The fire started about an hour ago," Folarni whispered to her. "The man who owns the land next door has positively identified the photograph of Tommaso as someone he's seen around the area. It is not much to go on, but it may be enough."

"Folarni, if we're right, I'm going to kiss you. I will be in your debt."

The little man blushed happily. "My wife may not like that, Detective."

She laughed softly with him. Baldwin crept up to their position, high-powered binoculars in hand.

"There's been little movement, though I thought I saw a shadow earlier. It might have been an animal, but I could have sworn I heard a muffled scream."

Folarni's radio crackled quietly against his leg. He picked it up, listened to the hushed report. He locked the radio back onto his hip and nodded.

"We are ready when you are, Baldwin. DI Highsmythe is behind the house with two of my men. He says he sees definite movement. It is time, I think."

"I agree. We'll go on three."

Baldwin counted down, then started toward the cottage. They kept low to the ground in case someone were to look out the window. Taylor watched the cordon tighten, their guns drawn, the hillside prickly with summer vetch and cops. Entry was entry no matter what language you spoke.

Forlarni took the honor of kicking down the front door, and they flooded into the little room.

"Arresto, arresto! Non si muova, Polizia!"

There was instant chaos. Taylor followed Folarni and Baldwin through the front. She caught a glimpse of the scene in front of her. There was a man down, on the ground—she didn't know if he'd been shot, she didn't remember hearing any shots fired. She smelled the searing scent of burned flesh, couldn't put a place to it. There was a bundle of rags by the hearth; Taylor could see one small pale foot sticking out. And there was a man, standing in front of the fire. Il Macellaio. Bald-headed, emanating fury. He was holding something in the flames. It looked like a skillet.

"Smetta di muoversi!" Folarni was yelling. Stop moving.

The man, Taylor didn't know if it was Gavin or Tommaso, turned slowly, miming putting his hands up. He still held the skillet. Taylor could see it was glowing red-hot, a formidable weapon should they try to get close without disabling him. With Folarni and the other cops shouting at him, he slowly turned from the fire, bent at the waist, then put the skillet facedown on the rough tile floor.

He looked at her then, right into her eyes, and kept eye contact as he slammed both his hands down onto the burning flat of the skillet. He screamed, bloodcurdling, but never looked away. She could tell he was going to faint, there was no way anyone could withstand that kind of pain. His face red and sweating, his eyes rolled back in his head and he collapsed. The skillet still smoked with burning flesh; when he landed he was very close to it and his shirt caught on fire.

"Aqua, aqua," Folarni was yelling, but Memphis had already grabbed an open bottle of wine and dumped it on the man's shirt. It splashed out the fire, spread across the white fabric like a bloodstain, growing until it dribbled off the edges.

"What in the hell are they doing?" Memphis asked.

Baldwin holstered his weapon, leaned back against the cracked plaster wall.

"Christ. They were burning off their fingerprints so we won't be able to tell them apart."

Forlarni was cursing, rummaging through the bundle of rags that held the dead girl. He opened the wrapping, whispered a prayer over her body and crossed himself.

The brothers had collapsed against the far wall, unconscious, though one of them was beginning to stir. Taylor resisted the urge to kick him in the groin. The smell in the room was terrible, the sour reek of fear coupled with urine and burnt meat, the underlying note of decomposition. The girl had been dead for some time, one of Folarni's men estimated that she was at least a few days gone. They were doing their best to find out who she was.

The brother who was stirring opened his eyes. It was the one who was already burned and unconscious when they arrived. He took in the scene, looking at them under hooded eyes.

His hands were mangled. Skin dangled from the edges like leaves falling from a winter dead tree. He was white-faced, obviously in great pain. He looked at Taylor, swiveled his head to the right and saw his brother passed out next to him, his shirt red from the wine.

He turned back to Taylor and stared at her.

Then he started to laugh.

The scene was starting to wrap up, the Italians efficient and capable. They'd transported the brothers, dealt with the dead body, and were conducting a thorough forensics search throughout the house and the surrounding grounds. Tommaso's car had been located; a veritable treasure trove of evidence. Taylor watched the carabinieri officers, wishing there was more that she could do to help, then contented herself with making some notes for her report. She couldn't help but smile to herself; they'd just scored a massive coup. Two serial killers, two continents, four jurisdictions, countless lives affected. If this didn't put her back into the good graces of her administration, she didn't know what would.

Memphis and Baldwin were off in a corner, talking

about something. Memphis glanced over at her. His blue eyes were dark and dangerous, and she felt that crazy pull in her gut. She wondered what they were talking about, but dismissed it. There were more important things to worry about, like getting this investigation closed. Capturing their suspects was going to be just the beginning.

Baldwin and Memphis finished their discussion. Baldwin shot a glance her way then went outside. Memphis casually walked over to her. She nodded at him, not wanting to encourage him too much. For once, Memphis had something else on his mind.

"Good job, Miss Jackson," he said softly. "We wouldn't have caught them without your insights."

She accepted the compliment gracefully. "It was a team effort. We all played a part."

"Well said. Unfortunately, it looks like our time here is drawing to a close. I've been called back to London. I'm supposed to leave late tonight, but I'm stalling for more time."

"Oh. Well, we can handle the rest of this, no problem. The investigation is just starting, really. There's so much to do, especially with the extradition. We're going to be up to our ears for a while."

"I am well aware of that," he said, eyes flashing in anger.

"Hey, don't get pissed at me. It's not my fault."

"I'm not *pissed* at you. I have several open cases that need attention. The powers that be want briefings." He touched her arm briefly, made her meet his eyes. "And I think it might be a good idea to go home."

She understood exactly what he was talking about.

"Yes. I think so, too." She cleared her throat. "We can funnel information to you as it comes. Don't worry."

"Thank you. I believe I'm in need of some fresh air,"

Memphis said. He left the cottage; the void was palpable and left her wondering what she really felt toward him.

She needed to get Memphis out of her head. She needed to focus on this case, on getting back home, getting her career back on track, on getting married. And the best way she knew to do that, was work.

Tuesday

Forty-Five

It seemed unreal that they'd been in Italy for just two days. Taylor felt like she'd been here for at least a month.

At least she had one worry out of her hair. With Memphis being called back to New Scotland Yard, the tension level would dip dramatically. The Macellaio case complete for the time being, his superiors weren't willing to continue footing the bill, not when he had other cases to wrap up. She didn't mind taking on the extra work. Distance from Highsmythe would be a blessed thing.

The brothers had been transported to the hospital of Santa Maria Nouva, were being treated for second-degree burns on their fingers and palms. It was a crude attempt to erase their identities, but not enough for a permanent solution. The burns were severe, but they would heal without grafts. A third-degree burn might have worked, but the only real way to completely abrade their fingertips would be concentrated acid or plastic surgery. And even then, the result would leave them with a unique impression that could be identified from here on out.

Taylor knew what they were trying to do. It made a sick kind of sense. The police couldn't tell the twins apart from their DNA, but they would have easily been able to discern who was who from their fingerprints. No fingerprints, no way to tell the two apart, and no way the governments of either country could separate them until they discovered who was who.

Thankfully, the police were smarter than the twins.

She and Baldwin were congregated in the hallway outside the brothers' room. The carabinieri had seen no reason why the brothers shouldn't be housed together; space was at a premium in this hospital, and they were handcuffed to the railings of their beds. Their doctor, an elegantly coiffed ebony-haired woman with a Sicilian accent, gave her assessment in crisp English.

"Their fingertips will heal eventually. The burning is severe, but only what we call second degree. There will be extensive scarring, but they have not permanently eradicated their fingerprints. Patient A is the worse of the two. It looks like his hands were held on the skillet for a longer period of time than Patient B. His burns are slightly more severe, and as such we've scheduled him for a debridement in the morning to remove the remainder of the dead flesh. Patient B does not require quite this level of treatment."

"How long will it be until they are healed enough for us to try?" Baldwin asked.

"I cannot judge how long, nor how well the healing will be. Their palms were abraded entirely, the burns are more severe in the center of the hands. *Dio mio,* to place one's hands on a burning fire, I cannot imagine who could want to tolerate such pain. They are sedated, but conscious, if you need to speak to them. They want to know about a cat."

"That must be Gavin," Taylor said. "Which one asked?"

"They both did. On an eye signal, they spoke in unison. They both simply said *cat.*"

Clever boys.

They thanked the doctor, who nodded, shook their hands and went on her rounds.

"You ready to rattle their cages?" Baldwin asked.

"You bet."

Taylor opened the door to the twins' room. They were lying quietly in their beds, side by side, each facing the other. They were staring at each other so intently, the longing so concentrated that Taylor felt like they were communicating telepathically.

The sameness of their faces was eerie. Taylor had known identical twins in the past—she'd worked a case that centered around identical twin girls just last year—but Tommaso and Gavin were different. More alike. She knew it was a psychological response, the concept of the two being raised apart and still finding themselves on a psychotic path was mind-boggling. Identical twin necrophiliacs. This was one for the medical journals.

Neither man acknowledged their entrance. She knew Baldwin was itching to interview them, so she stepped aside and let him talk first.

"My name is Dr. John Baldwin," he began. Neither twin turned to him, though Taylor could see that the one in the bed they'd labeled A flinched a bit. So they didn't like doctors. Add to that the current situation; their pain must be tremendous. Interesting.

Baldwin continued. "I'm with the FBI. This is my colleague, Detective Jackson, from the Metro Nashville Police."

She watched for a tell, but neither man gave any indication that they knew, or cared, about Tennessee.

"You've been placed under arrest by the Italian judiciary, who have named you both *indagato*. Essentially, you've been indicted on the charge of murder. You will stand trial, most certainly be convicted. Italy isn't fond of Il Macellaio. In addition, we will be separating you as soon as we finish this interview. And I'll let you know, on the record, that while Italy does not have the death penalty, the United States most surely does. One of you will be extradited, and under federal law the United States has the right to seek the death penalty against you."

Still nothing. No word, no movement from either bed.

Baldwin took a small plastic chair and set it between the beds, at their feet. He settled into the chair and smiled pleasantly. "You may think that you've tricked us by obscuring your fingerprints. You were wrong. We know who each of you are."

He turned to the man in bed A. "Gavin." He looked to his right, to bed B. "Tommaso."

"Ha," the twin in bed B said. "See, you are already making incorrect assumptions. You have no way of identifying either one of us."

"Oh, but you're wrong. You may have thought you were clever, but we've seen much better. Your dental records are being flown here as we speak. The dentists at the 31st Dental Squadron at Aviano have kept detailed records on all of their patients. One call to the archives and they were able to locate the records of Thomas Fielding."

Taylor spoke for the first time, addressing the man in bed A. "And Gavin, Dr. Simpson from Manchester was very disappointed to hear that we needed your radiographs. He also kept meticulous records. He already told us to look for very slight lower anterior crowding. Thomas had braces when he was a teenager. Your foster parents wouldn't spring for it, decided you were just fine as is."

At the mention of foster parents, the man in bed A squirmed. They already knew it was Gavin, knew he was the man passed out when they arrived at the cottage. That his brother had held his hands to the face of the skillet for a fraction longer than necessary, like a child maliciously pulling off the wings of a fly to see what would happen.

Baldwin finished their assessment. "And Thomas, we know about the amalgam fillings. The military was a bit behind the times when it came to dentistry, they weren't concerned with the aesthetic, cosmetic advances being made in private practice. While all the boys your age, including Gavin here, had their teeth filled with tooth-colored resin composite, you were still receiving the amalgams. Identical twins don't have identical dentition, and environmental factors further indicate differences. So you burned yourselves, put yourselves through all this pain, for nothing. Gavin, you'll be returning to the States with us. Thomas, the Italians have a cell with your name on it."

Baldwin stood. Taylor was impressed; she knew what restraint it took not to try to wrestle every ounce of information out of them at once.

The twin they knew was Gavin started to cry.

Taylor spent the next hour on the phone with Julia Page, going through every permutation for extraditing Gavin back to Nashville.

The judiciary in Italy wasn't keen on the death penalty, and as such wouldn't extradite either of the brothers to a country that would charge them with death. And they had themselves a lovely little conundrum, one they hadn't told the brothers about. There was a massive limitation to using the dental records. The radiographs could prove only one thing—the identity of each of the twins.

But there was no way to definitively tie Gavin to the Tennessee murders and Tommaso to the Italian and British murders without a bite-mark match. Neither man had bitten his victims, and as such, it was inside the realm of possibility that the twin they knew as Tommaso had actually been in Tennessee, and the twin they knew as Gavin could have been in Italy. At least enough to force reasonable doubt into the jury's minds.

Without knowing who was who, they couldn't charge either brother with the separate murders. They knew Tommaso was responsible for the Italian murders and the murders in London, and Gavin was responsible for all the stateside murders. But knowing and proving in a court of law were two entirely different beasts. A good defense lawyer would blow the case to pieces with this simple fact. It was going to take hours of investigation to link every piece of circumstantial evidence to each individual's crimes.

Once Taylor wrapped things up with Julia, she chewed on the end of a pencil and thought about the situation. She wondered just how much the twins knew about the various ways their identities could be revealed. The plan to eradicate their fingerprints was simple, but ingenious. Taylor wondered which one had thought it up. Probably Tommaso, he of the more sophisticated and pronounced killing methods.

There was going to be a delay while all the details were sorted out. Which meant they had some time to themselves while the Italians, the U.S. and British Embassies, the Met, the FBI and Metro Nashville sorted through the mess. This situation was above all of their pay grades.

She needed sustenance. She found Baldwin, who was on the phone to Pietra Dunmore, making sure she listed all the forensics they had so the cases could start moving forward. He hung up the phone, ran his hands through his hair.

"I'm whipped. Let's go grab a drink and head back to the hotel."

"Sounds good." He retrieved his jacket from the chair

back, shrugged into it. She ran her hand up the smooth linen. Too bad they couldn't stay here, run away from all their troubles.

The walk back took five minutes—the beauty of Florence was its intimate size, and they quickly passed through the Strozzi Palace courtyard to Colle Berreto.

Memphis sat at a table, an untouched glass of wine to hand.

Taylor had that instance of annoyance coupled with attraction. She tamped it down, looked at Baldwin. "Should we join him?"

"Of course. He must be killing time before he leaves for the airport."

They crossed the piazza and greeted Memphis.

"Have a seat," he said.

They did, ordered espressos and tiramisu.

Memphis had been on his very best behavior for the past several hours. Taylor kept waiting for that to end. She knew they had unfinished business, that she needed to talk to him about the kiss. But he was supposed to be going back to London, and she didn't see that she was going to have the opportunity. The crime scene in the Tuscan hills just hadn't felt like the right place. Too much obsession already in evidence there.

Baldwin's phone rang and he looked at the caller ID. He excused himself and answered. "Garrett, hey. How are things back in D.C.?"

Taylor watched him listen for a moment, brows furrowing briefly. He excused himself, and walked across the piazza.

"What's that about?" Memphis asked.

"I don't know."

"Oh. I bet I know."

She turned to him. "What?"

"Well, things have changed a bit. I'm not going back to London right away."

She felt the first edges of skepticism start to build. She should have known it was too good to be true, that she'd been granted a reprieve from Memphis's searing glances.

"What do you mean?"

"It had been in the works for some time, though I was planning on declining. I've been offered a position. At Quantico."

It took her a moment for that to register. "What?" she asked.

"I've been offered a position—"

"I heard you. What position?"

"The BAU terrorism team. Special Liaison to the Metropolitan Police at New Scotland Yard. I've taken quite a shine to the place, you see. Thought it might be fun, so I agreed to come on board. That's probably why your chap is pacing around over there. He doesn't like me much."

"Neither do I," she said.

He leaned forward conspiratorially. "Yes, you do. And this will mean I'm that much closer to you."

"Oh, don't even think about it. I have been exceptionally clear with you. I. Am. Not. Interested."

"Then why did you kiss me?"

"I didn't, you asshole. You kissed me."

"You kissed me back." He caught her eye. "And you enjoyed it."

Jesus, talking to him was like fighting with a five-year-old. *I know you are, but what am I? I know you are, but what am I? Infinity.*

"No, I didn't. And I would really appreciate you just letting the whole incident go. I'm willing to forget that it ever happened. Okay?"

"Absolutely, darling. For now." He reached across the table and touched her hand, gently. She jerked it away.

"Get home safe, Memphis. Please, do us both a favor and don't be in touch."

She ignored him when he said, "Taylor," and left him at the table. Let him get the damn bill this time. She didn't look back as she joined Baldwin, who was turning off his phone.

"What's up?" she asked.

"The usual. Garrett wanted a lowdown on the case. You're all flushed, what's wrong?"

She felt the burn of a blush on her cheeks. "Nothing. It's…nothing."

"Is it Memphis?"

"Really, it's nothing. He just spilled the beans that he's joining the BAU."

"Let's walk," he said.

As they moved together, her hand naturally found his. The lights of Florence surrounded them; the calls of the homeless beggars, the tourists, the crowds had dissipated. Nighttime in Florence was magical. The warmth of his strong fingers allayed all her fears. This was the one. Baldwin was the one. As they entered the Piazza della Signoria, he stopped and kissed her briefly.

"Hmm," she said. "Do that again."

He complied, then they started strolling again.

"Memphis won't be going to Quantico anytime soon," he said.

"What?"

"I requested to have him sent back to London."

She stopped, pulled him to face her. "You didn't."

"I most certainly did."

"That's not fair, Baldwin. He's a good cop. He's helped us break this case."

Defending Memphis was the wrong tact to take. She saw the fire start to burn in Baldwin's eyes. His voice grew tight.

"A good cop who was making a play for you. I figured you'd appreciate having him off your back."

"I can take care of myself, Baldwin."

"I know that, damn it. That's what I'm worried about." He ran his hands through his hair and took a deep breath, mastering his temper. She rarely saw him lose it, was surprised at the intensity of this particular conversation.

"I don't want to fight with you," she said.

"I don't want to fight with you either. We just need to watch our steps. Everything is changing. I can feel it coming. I'm not sure exactly how, but between this, the threats of the Pretender, Memphis, something bad is about to go down. I want to keep an eye on you. Maybe it's time to think about coming home for good."

She pulled away from him. "Don't do that. Deep down, that's not what you want. I know you. You don't want to be tied to a house, to a staid life in one city. You'd miss the chase, miss the chance to make a difference."

He looked at her queerly. "Do you actually believe that being with you full-time isn't my priority?"

She looked away, discomfited. "In your heart, yes. But in your head? No, honey. You need the BAU, just like I need Metro. It's a part of you."

"You're a part of me. The BAU is just a job."

"It's more than that. It's your whole life."

"No, Taylor. You're my whole life." He kissed her again, more deeply this time. "And don't you forget it. Come on now. Let's go back to the hotel and get some sleep. We have a long day tomorrow."

She let herself be towed away, knowing full well the conversation was far from over.

Forty-Six

Once in their room, she took advantage of the small distance between them and stole away to the bathroom, took a shower, taking her time. Too much had happened in the past few days. Too many emotions stirred up. Baldwin couldn't leave the BAU, especially for her. It wasn't right.

She toweled off, brushed her wet hair out. Now that it was over, she finally allowed herself to think about the horror of the brothers' actions. What the victims had gone through at their hands. How they'd slowly wasted away, their organs shutting down, the pain dulling with the blur of unconsciousness.

She brushed her teeth, spit, then opened her mouth wide, looking at the molars, the incisors, the way each tooth aligned perfectly with its neighbor. Precision. Teeth were as unique as fingerprints. What would it look like if all the flesh were gone? If she'd been locked in a Plexiglas cage, had slowly, inexorably starved to death, then rotted away? She tried to imagine her skull as an anthropologist from an archeological dig might. Would he look at the teeth, the brow ridge, the nasal cavity, and think wow, this woman must have been beautiful when she was alive? The teeth must have flashed bright and ready in happiness when this skull breathed. Many men must have found her attractive.

She wished she'd slapped Memphis when he kissed her. The bastard was right. She had kissed him back. And she would have to live with that knowledge. Baldwin could never know.

She pushed all thoughts of Memphis away. She needed to focus on the good here, the fact that she'd caught her killers, solved the case. She'd made all the right moves. She'd proven herself, and that would be nothing but good for her career. There would be plenty of time later to worry about where things would go from here. Baldwin moving back to Nashville full-time would be lovely, but he wouldn't be happy, even if he didn't know that now. She had her own demons to wrestle with, her own issues to resolve. It was all bad timing.

With a sigh, she snapped off the bathroom light and went into the bedroom. She'd find a way to fix things; she always did.

Baldwin was already in the bed, reading through the news clippings on the Macellaio case. A special evening edition of the *La Nazione* had been printed. The front-desk clerk, knowing they were working the case, had kindly held the paper for them, handed it over with a silent smile when they retrieved their key. The headline screamed *Il Macellaio Interferito*—The Butcher Caught. He had dark smudges under his eyes and she felt an un-bearable fondness wash over her. They needed a break, someplace with no killers, no specters.

Baldwin rustled the print, the covers tossed carelessly across his legs. At least, he was pretending to read. He was watching her. She could feel his eyes on her, felt the warmth and love in them. She crawled onto the bed, put her head on his chest.

"We need to sleep. At least for a little bit. Put those away."

"Does this mean I'm forgiven?" he said.

She gave him an embarrassed smile. "There's nothing to forgive. I didn't mean to be a brat. And I'm, well, that's neither here nor there."

"Still thinking about Memphis?"

She looked at him in surprise. How he read her mind sometimes was unnerving.

"Taylor, it's blatantly apparent to anyone within a fifty-mile radius. I've never seen a man fall so hard. He's going to keep pursuing you."

"Oh, don't be silly. He's just…just…a player. I would be a notch in his belt, that's all."

"Well, I'd certainly prefer you not becoming a notch in his belt."

She rolled her eyes. "You know what I mean. He holds no interest for me. I can handle him."

"I doubt he's going to limit his pursuit. I did some more digging into his background. He didn't have an easy time of it. Being a peer and working for the Met isn't a match made in heaven. He took a lot of heat at the beginning, didn't fit in. Then he lost his wife, you know, and a child. She was eight months pregnant when she was killed in a car accident. Her name was Evan, and she looked an awful lot like you. After Evan died, he threw himself into the Met, rose through the ranks. He's a damn good investigator, but he's haunted. You're bringing it all back to the forefront for him, and he's ready to snap."

"He's told me all about it."

"He's a fragile man, despite what he may have told

you. He's been in treatment, and is grasping at anything that might get him back on track."

"So you think I'm just a reminder of his dead wife? Thanks for that." Her temper flashed briefly; she tamped it down. "I'm just ready to get back to Nashville. At least there I have a handle on my enemies."

"Are you running from him, Taylor?" There was a strange tone in his voice, a lingering vulnerability that made her narrow her eyes.

"Baldwin, what is the deal? Are you honestly that jealous?"

He tossed his book to the side. He was angry; she could feel the control he was measuring out. "Damn straight I am. What, you think I'm going to sit back and watch some guy sweep you off your feet?"

She realized that he knew exactly what had been going through her head. All the little what-ifs that had been creeping around the edges of her mind. No wonder he was thinking about moving back to Nashville, where he could keep an eye on her. It was time to put those thoughts away, for good. She took his chin in her hand, made him look her straight in the eye.

"Yes, honey, Memphis is attractive. Yes, he's funny and urbane."

"And the son of a peer. Don't forget that part," Baldwin said.

"And the son of a peer. But sweetheart, you have to know that the thought never crossed my mind. Not the way you think it did."

"So you're admitting you thought about it?"

"Baldwin. Stop. I'm not thinking about anything. No one in the world matters more to me than you. Memphis is just a silly little boy. You're a man, and the only one I love. You're the only man for me. Don't ever think otherwise. You hear me?"

"I saw him kiss you," he said.

So that's what all this was about. She'd wondered, that night in the piazza when she turned the corner and he was there. It felt contrived, and she assumed Baldwin had witnessed the whole scenario.

She tipped his face toward hers. "That was unconscionable of him, and I've told him so. I have made it very, very clear that I am not interested. I was hoping with this case partially wrapped he'd go back to London and be gone. Now it looks like he's going to be around, at least around you. I will talk to him again, warn him off. If that doesn't work, you have my permission to beat him up."

She smiled, snuggled up next to him, rested her head on his shoulder. He put his arms around her and she was struck by how tightly he held her. As if he thought she might actually slip away. Surely he couldn't seriously think that she wanted out, wanted to go with the British playboy.

Of course he thought that, Taylor. He saw how Memphis was looking at you. He saw him kiss you, for Christ's sake. He must have seen you respond, even if it was brief. He's not an idiot. He's just human, a man like any other. In some ways.

"Baby." She kissed him on the neck, softly. "I'm sorry."

He accepted the invitation. He rolled over on her, grabbed her hair roughly in his right hand.

"You're mine, Taylor. Don't forget it." His lips crushed hers, and took her breath away with the intensity. He kept a hold of her hair, had his other hand between her legs, was kissing her as if it was the last kiss they'd ever share, and she had no idea how much time had passed, just knew that she was almost there, almost, when she heard the phone jangling two feet from her ear.

"Ignore it," she said, breathless, urging him on with her hips.

"It's yours." He stopped, inches from entering her, breath ragged with the effort.

Groaning, she wiggled out from under his hips far enough to grab her cell.

There was static, then emptiness. A void surrounded her.

That tinny, childlike voice, the one from her answering machine, from the earlier call, spoke. "I'll see you soon, Taylor."

The line went dead, and she started to shiver. It wasn't over. It would never be over.

Epilogue

Taylor had spent the overnight flight home from Italy thinking. Her life, her world with Baldwin, her father and the letter she'd been towing around for days. She'd made some decisions, small steps toward taking her life back. They landed right after the dawn, the warm sunlight of Nashville enveloping her in calm. She felt safest when she was home.

The house was still standing when the cab dropped them off, tired and a little giddy from lack of sleep. Sam had taken care of stopping their mail, arranging to have it held until they returned. Delivery would begin again today. The first thing Taylor did when they pulled in the drive was march to the mailbox with the letter to her father in hand. It was time for her to say goodbye.

She pulled open the door to the mailbox. It wasn't empty. Sitting quietly on a white note card was a bullet. Chills crept across her body, and she backed away like it was a poisonous snake.

"Baldwin?" she called.

He came to her immediately, sensing the strain in her voice.

"What is it? What's wrong?"

She pointed. "In the mailbox."

He wheeled around and looked, cursing under his breath when he saw the bullet.

"Camera and gloves," he said, voice low and controlled with fury.

She fumbled in her briefcase, pulled out a single latex glove and her camera. Baldwin took them from her grimly, started taking pictures.

"It's him, isn't it?" she asked. "He was here."

Baldwin didn't answer, just reached in the box and pulled out the bullet. A .40 caliber Winchester jacketed hollow point, the standard issue for her service weapon.

Holding it gingerly, he read the handwritten note, then extended it to her. She didn't touch it, just read the words, feeling the pressure start to build in her chest.

Dear Taylor,

May I be the first to congratulate you, Lieutenant? You'll be getting the call tomorrow that you're being reinstated, and may I just say how proud I am? You showed courage and ingenuity to solve the case of poor little Gavin and his big bad brother Tommaso. Of course, I knew you would. That's why I removed the copyright pages from the Picasso monographs. Gavin wouldn't think that far ahead, the silly child. But I knew you'd find that little clue, and it would lead you to them.

Bravo, my lady. Bravo.

Keep this little gift handy. You never know when you might need it.

Until we meet again…

Love and bloody kisses,

THE PRETENDER

* * * * *

Author's Note

When I began the voyage of writing this novel, I was captivated by the thought of two men, separated soon after birth, brought up in two vastly different households, yet both developing sociopathic tendencies, finding themselves compelled to kill. The trick, of course, was to have identical crimes on two continents, with the dates staggered so it appeared that the same person was committing the crimes. Evidence and forensics would also point to a single perpetrator.

The basic premise of the book is so fantastical, so horrific, that I was immediately forced to reconsider. Identical-twin serial killers, killing wholly independent of one another, with practically identical crime scenes? Couldn't happen.

Yet the further I delved into the research, the more I realized that not only *could* it happen, in this particular scenario, it could happen just as I've portrayed. Extensive nature-versus-nurture studies have been done on identical twins. Those studied show over and over again that twins raised separately show an incredible propensity to have very, very parallel lives. IQ tests administered show results that would mimic the same person taking the test twice. Career paths and job choices are eerily similar, as there seems to be an epigenetic predisposition toward skills and interests.

For instance, take the bizarre case of the "Jim Twins." Jim Lewis and Jim Springer had been separated at birth and raised in different families. They didn't meet until 1979, thirty-nine years after they were separated. Jim Lewis had been searching for his brother for many years, and when the two first met, Lewis described it as "like looking into a mirror." They were more than just identical in appearance; they had an astounding array of coincidental behaviors and life actions, what any novelist would be lambasted for using in a story.

They'd both had dogs growing up named Toy. They both married a woman named Linda, then divorced and married a woman named Betty. They named their firstborn sons James Allen and James Alan. They both bit their nails, suffered from insomnia and migraines. They vacationed at the same Florida beach, drove the same kind of car, drank the same beer, smoked the same brand of cigarettes, followed NASCAR but hated baseball, left love notes for their wives, made doll furniture in their basements. And in a coincidence too great to be anything but reality, they both died on the same day, of the same illness.

They had differences as well, in their speech patterns, how they wore their hair. But the major components of their lives were more than just similar; they were exactly the same.

This seems unreal, but it's true, documented and impossible to refute. There are many more examples in the Minnesota Twin Studies of identicals raised apart who have eerily parallel lives. The earlier the children are separated, the more alike they turn out to be.

The moment I read about the Jim Twins, I knew Gavin and Tommaso had come to life.

But the story turned darker when I realized their preferred method of killing.

Necrophilia is a taboo subject, one of the darkest, basest actions a man, or woman, can engage in. It disturbed me to no end, gave me nightmares and writer's block, and I often thought of abandoning the topic and staying with something less…disturbing.

But when I stumbled across a Web site that discussed the use of narcotics in rape and the subsequent diagnosis of necrophilia, I knew I needed to explore that territory. It was difficult, but with fascinating aspects. Anytime you have a killer who goes off the beaten path, who gets intimate with their victim either through sex or with a specific hand weapon, like a knife, the cases are going to be a bit more bizarre.

The extensive research led me to a few conclusions. Yes, it would be possible, perhaps even likely to have identical-twin serial killers, especially if those men were separated soon after birth. Yes, their pathological growth would parallel one another. In this case, I felt it too horrific to have two killers working independently of each other and chose to have the alpha twin guiding the beta. It's one of the things that allowed me to sleep at night.

Many of the Louise Wise Services' twin separation psychological studies won't be released to the public until 2066. There is something in those reports. Something that the myriad psychiatrists, psychologists, counselors and other doctors involved in the studies didn't want their subjects to know. Were they hiding their own guilt at separating children who should have been together? Did the testing go awry? Did they find the key to our evolution, or that nature trumps nurture? Vice versa? The questions abound.

Whether they prove or disprove nature versus nurture, for the purposes of this work of fiction, I've chosen to think like a mystery writer and assume they are hiding a bombshell in the reports, a secret so inflammatory that they don't want anyone to know.

Perhaps there is a real-life Tommaso and Gavin among their study subjects. Perhaps genetics are unreliable, and our environment plays the largest role in determining our outcomes. Or maybe, just maybe, there is a predisposition to kill. A killer gene.

With that in mind, I've done my best not to strain credulity too much. I hope you'll forgive a writer her overactive imagination.

Acknowledgments for THE COLD ROOM

It takes a village to write a book, and THE COLD ROOM was possibly the most difficult, research-intensive novel I've ever written. I owe a debt of thanks and gratitude to the following:

First, the Team:

Scott Miller—my wonderful agent, friend and partner, who never ceases to make me laugh.

Linda McFall—my editor, my friend, my sanity. Without you, these books would be mere shadows of the stories I want to tell.

Stephanie Sun and MacKenzie Fraser-Bub—assistants extraordinaire, whose energy and enthusiasm are always appreciated.

Adam Wilson—my right hand, and sometimes left hand, too. I couldn't do it without you.

Marianna Ricciuto—publicist to the stars and unflagging cheerleader.

Christine Lowman—for dealing with my finicky ways.

Kim Dettwiller—indie publicist and Nashville girl. You rock!

The rest of the Mira team: Donna Hayes, Alex Osusek, Loriana Sacilotto, Heather Foy, Don Lucey, Michelle Renaud, Adrienne Macintosh, Megan Lorius, Nick Ursino, Tracey Langmuire, Kathy Lodge, Emily Ohanjanians, Margaret Marbury, Diane Moggy and the artists Tara Kelly and Gigi Lau.

Second, the Research, the heart and soul of this novel:

Sean Chercover, for giving me the access point.

The Federal Bureau of Investigation, for being so incredibly open and generous with time and expertise, especially:

Angela Bell, Office of Public Affairs, Federal Bureau of Investigation
Special Agent Ann Todd, Office of Public Affairs, FBI Laboratory
Supervisory Special Agent Kenneth Gross, Chief Division Counsel, Critical Incident Response Group, FBI
Supervisory Special Agent Mark Hilts, Unit Chief, BAU, CIRG, FBI

Dr. Vince Tranchida, Deputy Chief Medical Examiner, Manhattan

Dr. Michael Tabor, Chief Forensic Odontologist for the State of Tennessee

Detective David Achord, Metro Nashville Police Department

Elizabeth Fox, Metro Nashville Police Department (Ret.)

Shirley Holley, Manchester Public Library, Manchester, Tennessee

Assistant Chief Bob Bellamy, Manchester Police

Captain Frank Watkins, Coffee County Sherriff's Office

James Tillman, for sharing his Uncle Welton Keif's term for identical twins, "Born Partners."

John Elliot, former Interpol Agent, who steered me in the right directions.

Sharon Owen, for the fishing expertise.

Christine Kling, for the boating expertise.

And the Personal:

Zoë Sharp, whose debt can never be fully repaid, for bringing Memphis to life, all the Britishisms (and an amusing and lengthy discourse on the correct term for erections).

The Bodacious Music City Wordsmiths—Del Tinsley, JB Thompson, Janet McKeown, Peggy Peden, Cecelia Tichi, RaiLynn Wood—for everything.

A special thanks to JB, who read, and read, and read this book for me, and my other mother, Del Tinsley, who always cheers me up and cheers me on.

Joan Huston, first reader and friend.

Tasha Alexander and Laura Benedict, for always knowing the right thing to say.

Murderati—you know why.

Rosemary Harris, for bidding on a character name at auction and presenting me with Patrol Officer Paula Simari, and her canine companion Max.

Charlaine Harris, for bidding on a name in another auction and appears here and forevermore as Special Agent Charlaine Shultz, FBI Profiler.

Elyse Schein and Paula Bernstein, for sharing their incredible journey in the book *Identical Strangers*.

Evanescence, whose songs more than inspired; they got me through this very difficult subject matter.

All the libraries and bookstores who have shown such unflagging support, especially Murder by the Book in Houston, Davis Kidd in Nashville, Sherlock's Books in Lebanon, Poisoned Pen Press in Phoenix, the Seattle Mystery Bookshop in…you guessed it, Seattle, and the great staffs at Borders and Barnes & Noble who hand-sell me all over the country.

My incredible parents and brothers and nephews and niece, for constantly believing in me. I love you all. More.

My rock, my love, my Randy, who just plain gets it. Without you, none of this would matter.

And to the people of Nashville. Thank you for allowing me the honor of writing about our great city, for opening the doors and for giving me such great background to work with. Your support honors me. I've taken some liberties in this novel for the purpose of poetic license. All mistakes, exaggerations, opinions and interpretations, especially about the inner workings of Metro Nashville, are mine, and mine alone.